Peter Pan

彼得潘

原著雙語彩圖本

作者——
詹姆斯・馬修・巴里
（J. M. Barrie）

譯者——
羅竹君

Contents Peter Pan

目錄 彼得潘

Peter Pan

Peter Breaks Through

Chapter 1

All children, except one, grow up. They soon know that they will grow up, and the way Wendy knew was this. One day when she was two years old she was playing in a garden, and she plucked another flower and ran with it to her mother. I suppose she must have looked rather delightful, for Mrs. Darling put her hand to her heart and cried, "Oh, why can't you remain like this for ever!" This was all that passed between them on the subject, but henceforth Wendy knew that she must grow up. You always know after you are two. Two is the beginning of the end.

Of course they lived at 14, and until Wendy came her mother was the chief one. She was a lovely lady, with a romantic mind and such a sweet mocking mouth. Her romantic mind was like the tiny boxes, one within the other, that come from the puzzling East, however many you discover there is always one more; and her sweet mocking mouth had one kiss on it that Wendy could never get, though there it was, perfectly conspicuous in the right-hand corner.

The way Mr. Darling won her was this: the many gentlemen who had been boys when she was a girl discovered simultaneously that they loved her, and they all ran to her house to propose to her except Mr. Darling, who took a cab and nipped in first, and so he got her. He got all of her, except the innermost box and the kiss. He never knew about the box, and in time he gave up trying for the kiss. Wendy thought Napoleon could have got it, but I can picture him trying, and then going off in a passion, slamming the door.

Mr. Darling used to boast to Wendy that her mother not only loved him but respected him. He was one of those deep ones who know about stocks and shares. Of course no one really knows, but he quite seemed to know, and he often said stocks were up and shares were down in a way that would have made any woman respect him.

Mrs. Darling was married in white, and at first she kept the books perfectly, almost gleefully, as if it were a game, not so much as a Brussels sprout was missing; but by and by whole cauliflowers dropped out, and instead of them there were pictures of babies without faces. She drew them when she should have been totting up. They were Mrs. Darling's guesses.

Wendy came first, then John, then Michael.

For a week or two after Wendy came it was doubtful whether they would be able to keep her, as she was another mouth to feed. Mr. Darling was frightfully proud of her, but he was very honourable, and he sat on the edge of Mrs. Darling's bed, holding her hand and calculating expenses, while she looked at him imploringly. She wanted to risk it, come what might, but that was not his way; his way was with a pencil and a piece of paper, and if she confused him with suggestions he had to begin at the beginning again.

"Now don't interrupt," he would beg of her. "I have one pound seventeen here, and two and six at the office; I can cut off my coffee at the office, say ten shillings, making two nine and six, with your eighteen and three makes three nine seven, with five naught naught in my cheque-book makes eight nine seven—who is that moving?—eight nine seven, dot and carry seven—don't speak, my own—and the pound you lent to that man who came to the door—quiet, child—dot and carry child—there, you've done it!—did I say nine nine seven? yes, I said nine nine seven; the question is, can we try it for a year on nine nine seven?"

"Of course we can, George," she cried. But she was prejudiced in Wendy's favour, and he was really the grander character of the two.

"Remember mumps," he warned her almost threateningly, and off he went again. "Mumps one pound, that is what I have put down, but I daresay it will be more like thirty shillings—don't speak—measles one five, German measles half a guinea, makes two fifteen six—don't waggle your finger—whooping-cough, say fifteen shillings"—and so on it went, and it added up differently each time; but at last Wendy just got through, with mumps reduced to twelve six, and the two kinds of measles treated as one.

There was the same excitement over John, and Michael had even a narrower squeak; but both were kept, and soon, you might have seen the three of them going in a row to Miss Fulsom's Kindergarten school, accompanied by their nurse.

Mrs. Darling loved to have everything just so, and Mr. Darling had a passion for being exactly like his neighbours; so, of course, they had a nurse. As they were poor, owing to the amount of milk the children drank, this nurse was a prim Newfoundland dog, called Nana, who had belonged to no one in particular until the Darlings engaged her. She had always thought children important, however, and the Darlings had become acquainted with her in Kensington Gardens, where she spent most of her spare time peeping into perambulators, and was much hated by careless nursemaids, whom she followed to their homes and complained of to their mistresses. She proved to be quite a treasure of a nurse. How thorough she was at bath-time, and up at any moment of the night if one of her charges made the slightest cry. Of course her kennel

was in the nursery. She had a genius for knowing when a cough is a thing to have no patience with and when it needs stocking around your throat. She believed to her last day in old-fashioned remedies like rhubarb leaf, and made sounds of contempt over all this new-fangled talk about germs, and so on. It was a lesson in propriety to see her escorting the children to school, walking sedately by their side when they were well behaved, and butting them back into line if they strayed. On John's footer days she never once forgot his sweater, and she usually carried an umbrella in her mouth in case of rain. There is a room in the basement of Miss Fulsom's school where the nurses wait. They sat on forms, while Nana lay on the floor, but that was the only difference. They affected to ignore her as of an inferior social status to themselves, and she despised their light talk. She resented visits to the nursery from Mrs. Darling's friends, but if they did come she first whipped off Michael's pinafore and put him into the one with blue braiding, and smoothed out Wendy and made a dash at John's hair.

No nursery could possibly have been conducted more correctly, and Mr. Darling knew it, yet he sometimes wondered uneasily whether the neighbours talked.

He had his position in the city to consider.

Nana also troubled him in another way. He had sometimes a feeling that she did not admire him. "I know she admires you tremendously, George," Mrs. Darling would assure him, and then she would sign to the children to be specially nice to father. Lovely dances followed, in which the only other servant, Liza, was sometimes allowed to join. Such a midget she looked in her long skirt and maid's cap, though she had sworn, when engaged, that she would never see ten again. The gaiety of those romps! And gayest of all was Mrs. Darling, who would pirouette so wildly that all you could see of her was the kiss, and then if you had dashed at her you might have got it. There never was a simpler happier family until the coming of Peter Pan.

Mrs. Darling first heard of Peter when she was tidying up her children's minds. It is the nightly custom of every good mother after her children are asleep to rummage in their minds and put things straight for next morning, repacking into their proper places the many articles that have wandered during the day. If you could keep awake (but of course you can't) you would see your own mother doing this, and you would find it very interesting to watch her. It is quite like tidying up drawers. You would see her on her knees, I expect, lingering humorously over some of your contents, wondering where on earth you had picked this thing up, making discoveries sweet and not so sweet, pressing this to her cheek as if it were as nice as a kitten, and hurriedly stowing that out of sight. When you wake in the morning, the naughtiness and evil passions with which you went to bed have been folded up small and placed at the bottom of your mind and on the top, beautifully aired, are spread out your prettier thoughts, ready for you to put on.

I don't know whether you have ever seen a map of a person's mind. Doctors sometimes draw maps of other parts of you, and your own map can become intensely interesting, but catch them trying to draw a map of a child's mind, which is not only confused, but keeps going round all the time. There are zigzag lines on it, just like your temperature on a card, and these are probably roads in the island, for the Neverland is always more or less an island, with astonishing splashes of colour here and there, and coral reefs and rakish-looking craft in the offing, and savages and lonely lairs, and gnomes who are mostly tailors, and caves through which a river runs, and princes with six elder brothers, and a hut fast going to decay, and one very small old lady with a hooked nose. It would be an easy map if that were all, but there is also first day at school, religion, fathers, the round pond, needle-work, murders, hangings, verbs that take the dative, chocolate pudding day, getting into

braces, say ninety-nine, three-pence for pulling out your tooth yourself, and so on, and either these are part of the island or they are another map showing through, and it is all rather confusing, especially as nothing will stand still.

Of course the Neverlands vary a good deal. John's, for instance, had a lagoon with flamingoes flying over it at which John was shooting, while Michael, who was very small, had a flamingo with lagoons flying over it. John lived in a boat turned upside down on the sands, Michael in a wigwam, Wendy in a house of leaves deftly sewn together. John had no friends, Michael had friends at night, Wendy had a pet wolf forsaken by its parents, but on the whole the Neverlands have a family resemblance, and if they stood still in a row you could say of them that they have each other's nose, and so forth. On these magic shores children at play are for ever beaching their coracles. We too have been there; we can still hear the sound of the surf, though we shall land no more.

Of all delectable islands the Neverland is the snuggest and most compact, not large and sprawly, you know, with tedious distances between one adventure and another, but nicely crammed. When you play at it by day with the chairs and table-cloth, it is not in the least alarming, but in the two minutes before you go to sleep it becomes very nearly real. That is why there are night-lights.

Occasionally in her travels through her children's minds Mrs. Darling found things she could not understand, and of these quite the most perplexing was the word Peter. She knew of no Peter, and yet he was here and there in John and Michael's minds, while Wendy's began to be scrawled all over with him. The name stood out in bolder letters than any of the other words, and as Mrs. Darling gazed she felt that it had an oddly cocky appearance.

"Yes, he is rather cocky," Wendy admitted with regret. Her mother had been questioning her.

"But who is he, my pet?"

"He is Peter Pan, you know, mother."

At first Mrs. Darling did not know, but after thinking back into her childhood she just remembered a Peter Pan who was said to live with the fairies. There were odd stories about him, as that when children died he went part of the way with them, so that they should not be frightened. She had believed in him at the time, but now that she was married and full of sense she quite doubted whether there was any such person.

"Besides," she said to Wendy, "he would be grown up by this time."

"Oh no, he isn't grown up," Wendy assured her confidently, "and he is just my size." She meant that he was her size in both mind and body; she didn't know how she knew, she just knew it.

Mrs. Darling consulted Mr. Darling, but he smiled pooh-pooh. "Mark my words," he said, "it is some nonsense Nana has been putting into their heads; just the sort of idea a dog would have. Leave it alone, and it will blow over."

But it would not blow over and soon the troublesome boy gave Mrs. Darling quite a shock.

Children have the strangest adventures without being

troubled by them. For instance, they may remember to mention, a week after the event happened, that when they were in the wood they had met their dead father and had a game with him. It was in this casual way that Wendy one morning made a disquieting revelation. Some leaves of a tree had been found on the nursery floor, which certainly were not there when the children went to bed, and Mrs. Darling was puzzling over them when Wendy said with a tolerant smile:

"I do believe it is that Peter again!"

"Whatever do you mean, Wendy?"

"It is so naughty of him not to wipe his feet," Wendy said, sighing. She was a tidy child.

She explained in quite a matter-of-fact way that she thought Peter sometimes came to the nursery in the night and sat on the foot of her bed and played on his pipes to her. Unfortunately she never woke, so she didn't know how she knew, she just knew.

"What nonsense you talk, precious. No one can get into the house without knocking."

"I think he comes in by the window," she said.

"My love, it is three floors up."

"Were not the leaves at the foot of the window, mother?"

It was quite true; the leaves had been found very near the window.

Mrs. Darling did not know what to think, for it all seemed so natural to Wendy that you could not dismiss it by saying she had been dreaming.

"My child," the mother cried, "why did you not tell me of this before?"

Gwynedd M.
Hudson.

"I forgot," said Wendy lightly. She was in a hurry to get her breakfast.

Oh, surely she must have been dreaming.

But, on the other hand, there were the leaves. Mrs. Darling examined them carefully; they were skeleton leaves, but she was sure they did not come from any tree that grew in England. She crawled about the floor, peering at it with a candle for marks of a strange foot. She rattled the poker up the chimney and tapped the walls. She let down a tape from the window to the pavement, and it was a sheer drop of thirty feet, without so much as a spout to climb up by.

Certainly Wendy had been dreaming.

But Wendy had not been dreaming, as the very next night showed, the night on which the extraordinary adventures of these children may be said to have begun.

On the night we speak of all the children were once more in bed. It happened to be Nana's evening off, and Mrs. Darling had bathed them and sung to them till one by one they had let go her hand and slid away into the land of sleep.

All were looking so safe and cosy that she smiled at her fears now and sat down tranquilly by the fire to sew.

It was something for Michael, who on his birthday was getting into shirts. The fire was warm, however, and the nursery dimly lit by three night-lights, and presently the sewing lay on Mrs. Darling's lap. Then her head nodded, oh, so gracefully. She was asleep. Look at the four of them, Wendy and Michael over there, John here, and Mrs. Darling by the fire. There should have been a fourth night-light.

While she slept she had a dream. She dreamt that the Neverland had come too near and that a strange boy had broken through from it. He did not alarm her, for she thought she had seen him before in the faces of many women who have no children. Perhaps he is to be found in the faces of some mothers also. But in her dream he had rent the film that obscures the Neverland, and she saw Wendy and John and Michael peeping through the gap.

The dream by itself would have been a trifle, but while she was dreaming the window of the nursery blew open, and a boy did drop on the floor. He was accompanied by a strange light, no bigger than your fist, which darted about the room like a living thing and I think it must have been this light that wakened Mrs. Darling.

She started up with a cry, and saw the boy, and somehow she knew at once that he was Peter Pan. If you or I or Wendy had been there we should have seen that he was very like Mrs. Darling's kiss. He was a lovely boy, clad in skeleton leaves and the juices that ooze out of trees but the most entrancing thing about him was that he had all his first teeth. When he saw she was a grown-up, he gnashed the little pearls at her.

The Shadow

Chapter 2

Mrs. Darling screamed, and, as if in answer to a bell, the door opened, and Nana entered, returned from her evening out. She growled and sprang at the boy, who leapt lightly through the window. Again Mrs. Darling screamed, this time in distress for him, for she thought he was killed, and she ran down into the street to look for his little body, but it was not there; and she looked up, and in the black night she could see nothing but what she thought was a shooting star.

She returned to the nursery, and found Nana with something in her mouth, which proved to be the boy's shadow. As he leapt at the window Nana had closed it quickly, too late to catch him, but his shadow had not had time to get out; slam went the window and snapped it off.

You may be sure Mrs. Darling examined the shadow carefully, but it was quite the ordinary kind.

Nana had no doubt of what was the best thing to do with this shadow. She hung it out at the window, meaning "He is sure to come back for it; let us put it where he can get it easily without disturbing the children."

But unfortunately Mrs. Darling could not leave it hanging out at the window, it looked so like the washing and lowered the whole tone of the house. She thought of showing it to Mr. Darling, but he was totting up winter great coats for John and Michael, with a wet towel around his head to keep his brain clear, and it seemed a shame to trouble him; besides, she knew exactly what he would say: "It all comes of having a dog for a nurse."

She decided to roll the shadow up and put it away carefully in a drawer, until a fitting opportunity came for telling her husband. Ah me!

The opportunity came a week later, on that never-to-be-forgotten Friday. Of course it was a Friday.

"I ought to have been specially careful on a Friday," she used to say afterwards to her husband, while perhaps Nana was on the other side of her, holding her hand.

"No, no," Mr. Darling always said, "I am responsible for it all. I, George Darling, did it. *Mea culpa, mea culpa.*" He had had a classical education.

They sat thus night after night recalling that fatal Friday, till every detail of it was stamped on their brains and came through on the other side like the faces on a bad coinage.

"If only I had not accepted that invitation to dine at 27," Mrs. Darling said.

"If only I had not poured my medicine into Nana's bowl," said Mr. Darling.

"If only I had pretended to like the medicine," was what Nana's wet eyes said.

"My liking for parties, George."

"My fatal gift of humour, dearest."

"My touchiness about trifles, dear master and mistress."

Then one or more of them would break down altogether; Nana at the thought, "It's true, it's true, they ought not to have had a dog for a nurse." Many a time it was Mr. Darling who put the handkerchief to Nana's eyes.

"That fiend!" Mr. Darling would cry, and Nana's bark was the echo of it, but Mrs. Darling never upbraided Peter; there was something in the right-hand corner of her mouth that wanted her not to call Peter names.

They would sit there in the empty nursery, recalling fondly every smallest detail of that dreadful evening. It had begun so uneventfully, so precisely like a hundred other evenings, with Nana putting on the water for Michael's bath and carrying him to it on her back.

"I won't go to bed," he had shouted, like one who still believed that he had the last word on the subject, "I won't, I won't. Nana, it isn't six o'clock yet. Oh dear, oh dear, I shan't love you any more, Nana. I tell you I won't be bathed, I won't, I won't!"

Then Mrs. Darling had come in, wearing her white evening-gown. She had dressed early because Wendy so loved to see her in her evening-gown, with the necklace

George had given her. She was wearing Wendy's bracelet on her arm; she had asked for the loan of it. Wendy loved to lend her bracelet to her mother.

She had found her two older children playing at being herself and father on the occasion of Wendy's birth, and John was saying:

"I am happy to inform you, Mrs. Darling, that you are now a mother," in just such a tone as Mr. Darling himself may have used on the real occasion.

Wendy had danced with joy, just as the real Mrs. Darling must have done.

Then John was born, with the extra pomp that he conceived due to the birth of a male, and Michael came from his bath to ask to be born also, but John said brutally that they did not want any more.

Michael had nearly cried. "Nobody wants me," he said, and of course the lady in the evening-dress could not stand that.

"I do," she said, "I so want a third child."

"Boy or girl?" asked Michael, not too hopefully.

"Boy."

Then he had leapt into her arms. Such a little thing for Mr. and Mrs. Darling and Nana to recall now, but not so little if that was to be Michael's last night in the nursery.

They go on with their recollections.

"It was then that I rushed in like a tornado, wasn't it?" Mr. Darling would say, scorning himself; and indeed he had been like a tornado.

Perhaps there was some excuse for him. He, too, had been dressing for the party, and all had gone well with him until he came to his tie. It is an astounding thing to have to tell, but this man, though he knew about stocks and shares, had no real mastery of his tie. Sometimes the thing yielded to him without a contest, but there were occasions when it would have been better for the house if he had swallowed his pride and used a made-up tie.

This was such an occasion. He came rushing into the nursery with the crumpled little brute of a tie in his hand.

"Why, what is the matter, father dear?"

"Matter!" he yelled; he really yelled. "This tie, it will not tie." He became dangerously sarcastic. "Not round my neck! Round the bed-post! Oh yes, twenty times have I made it up round the bed-post, but round my neck, no! Oh dear no! begs to be excused!"

He thought Mrs. Darling was not sufficiently impressed, and he went on sternly, "I warn you of this, mother, that unless this tie is round my neck we don't go out to dinner to-night, and if I don't go out to dinner to-night, I never go to the office again, and if I don't go to the office again, you and I starve, and our children will be flung into the streets."

Even then Mrs. Darling was placid. "Let me try, dear," she said, and indeed that was what he had come to ask her to do, and with her nice cool hands she tied his tie for him, while the children stood around to see their fate decided. Some men would have resented her being able to do it so easily, but Mr. Darling had far too fine a nature for that; he thanked her carelessly, at once forgot his rage, and in another moment was dancing round the room with Michael on his back.

"How wildly we romped!" says Mrs. Darling now, recalling it.

"Our last romp!" Mr. Darling groaned.

"O George, do you remember Michael suddenly said to me, 'How did you get to know me, mother?'"

"I remember!"

"They were rather sweet, don't you think, George?"

"And they were ours, ours! and now they are gone."

The romp had ended with the appearance of Nana, and most unluckily Mr. Darling collided against her, covering his trousers with hairs. They were not only new trousers, but they were the first he had ever had with braid on them, and he had had to bite his lip to prevent the tears coming. Of course Mrs. Darling brushed him, but he began to talk again about its being a mistake to have a dog for a nurse.

"George, Nana is a treasure."

"No doubt, but I have an uneasy feeling at times that she looks upon the children as puppies."

"Oh no, dear one, I feel sure she knows they have souls."

"I wonder," Mr. Darling said thoughtfully, "I wonder." It was an opportunity, his wife felt, for telling him about the boy. At first he pooh-poohed the story, but he became thoughtful when she showed him the shadow.

"It is nobody I know," he said, examining it carefully, "but it does look a scoundrel."

"We were still discussing it, you remember," says Mr. Darling, "when Nana came in with Michael's medicine. You will never carry the bottle in your mouth again, Nana, and it is all my fault."

Strong man though he was, there is no doubt that he had behaved rather foolishly over the medicine. If he had a weakness, it was for thinking that all his life he had taken medicine boldly, and so now, when Michael dodged the spoon in Nana's mouth, he had said reprovingly, "Be a man, Michael."

"Won't; won't!" Michael cried naughtily. Mrs. Darling left the room to get a chocolate for him, and Mr. Darling thought this showed want of firmness.

"Mother, don't pamper him," he called after her. "Michael, when I was your age I took medicine without a murmur. I said, 'Thank you, kind parents, for giving me bottles to make me well.'"

He really thought this was true, and Wendy, who was now in her night-gown, believed it also, and she said, to encourage Michael, "That medicine you sometimes take, father, is much nastier, isn't it?"

"Ever so much nastier," Mr. Darling said bravely, "and I would take it now as an example to you, Michael, if I hadn't lost the bottle."

He had not exactly lost it; he had climbed in the dead of night to the top of the wardrobe and hidden it there. What he did not know was that the faithful Liza had found it, and put it back on his wash-stand.

"I know where it is, father," Wendy cried, always glad to be of service. "I'll bring it," and she was off before he could stop her. Immediately his spirits sank in the strangest way.

"John," he said, shuddering, "it's most beastly stuff. It's that nasty, sticky, sweet kind."

"It will soon be over, father," John said cheerily, and

then in rushed Wendy with the medicine in a glass.

"I have been as quick as I could," she panted.

"You have been wonderfully quick," her father retorted, with a vindictive politeness that was quite thrown away upon her. "Michael first," he said doggedly.

"Father first," said Michael, who was of a suspicious nature.

"I shall be sick, you know," Mr. Darling said threateningly.

"Come on, father," said John.

"Hold your tongue, John," his father rapped out.

Wendy was quite puzzled. "I thought you took it quite easily, father."

"That is not the point," he retorted. "The point is, that there is more in my glass than in Michael's spoon." His proud heart was nearly bursting. "And it isn't fair: I would say it though it were with my last breath; it isn't fair."

"Father, I am waiting," said Michael coldly.

"It's all very well to say you are waiting; so am I waiting."

"Father's a cowardly custard."

"So are you a cowardly custard."

"I'm not frightened."

"Neither am I frightened."

"Well, then, take it."

"Well, then, you take it."

Wendy had a splendid idea. "Why not both take it at the same time?"

"Certainly," said Mr. Darling. "Are you ready, Michael?"

Wendy gave the words, one, two, three, and Michael

took his medicine, but Mr. Darling slipped his behind his back.

There was a yell of rage from Michael, and "O father!" Wendy exclaimed.

"What do you mean by 'O father'?" Mr. Darling demanded. "Stop that row, Michael. I meant to take mine, but I—I missed it."

It was dreadful the way all the three were looking at him, just as if they did not admire him. "Look here, all of you," he said entreatingly, as soon as Nana had gone into the bathroom. "I have just thought of a splendid joke. I shall pour my medicine into Nana's bowl, and she will drink it, thinking it is milk!"

It was the colour of milk; but the children did not have their father's sense of humour, and they looked at him reproachfully as he poured the medicine into Nana's bowl. "What fun!" he said doubtfully, and they

did not dare expose him when Mrs. Darling and Nana returned.

"Nana, good dog," he said, patting her, "I have put a little milk into your bowl, Nana."

Nana wagged her tail, ran to the medicine, and began lapping it. Then she gave Mr. Darling such a look, not an angry look: she showed him the great red tear that makes us so sorry for noble dogs, and crept into her kennel.

Mr. Darling was frightfully ashamed of himself, but he would not give in. In a horrid silence Mrs. Darling smelt the bowl. "O George," she said, "it's your medicine!"

"It was only a joke," he roared, while she comforted her boys, and Wendy hugged Nana. "Much good," he said bitterly, "my wearing myself to the bone trying to be funny in this house."

And still Wendy hugged Nana. "That's right," he shouted. "Coddle her! Nobody coddles me. Oh dear no! I am only the breadwinner, why should I be coddled— why, why, why!"

"George," Mrs. Darling entreated him, "not so loud; the servants will hear you." Somehow they had got into the way of calling Liza the servants.

"Let them!" he answered recklessly. "Bring in the whole world. But I refuse to allow that dog to lord it in my nursery for an hour longer."

The children wept, and Nana ran to him beseechingly, but he waved her back. He felt he was a strong man again. "In vain, in vain," he cried; "the proper place for you is the yard, and there you go to be tied up this instant."

"George, George," Mrs. Darling whispered, "remember what I told you about that boy."

Alas, he would not listen. He was determined to show who was master in that house, and when commands would not draw Nana from the kennel, he lured her out of it with honeyed words, and seizing her roughly, dragged her from the nursery. He was ashamed of himself, and yet he did it. It was all owing to his too affectionate nature, which craved for admiration. When he had tied her up in the back-yard, the wretched father went and sat in the passage, with his knuckles to his eyes.

In the meantime Mrs. Darling had put the children to bed in unwonted silence and lit their night-lights. They could hear Nana barking, and John whimpered, "It is because he is chaining her up in the yard," but Wendy was wiser.

"That is not Nana's unhappy bark," she said, little guessing what was about to happen; "that is her bark when she smells danger."

Danger!

"Are you sure, Wendy?"

"Oh, yes."

Mrs. Darling quivered and went to the window. It was securely fastened. She looked out, and the night was peppered with stars. They were crowding round the house, as if curious to see what was to take place there, but she did not notice this, nor that one or two of the smaller ones winked at her. Yet a nameless fear clutched at her heart and made her cry, "Oh, how I wish that I wasn't going to a party to-night!"

Even Michael, already half asleep, knew that she

was perturbed, and he asked, "Can anything harm us, mother, after the night-lights are lit?"

"Nothing, precious," she said; "they are the eyes a mother leaves behind her to guard her children."

She went from bed to bed singing enchantments over them, and little Michael flung his arms round her. "Mother," he cried, "I'm glad of you." They were the last words she was to hear from him for a long time.

No. 27 was only a few yards distant, but there had been a slight fall of snow, and Father and Mother Darling picked their way over it deftly not to soil their shoes. They were already the only persons in the street, and all the stars were watching them. Stars are beautiful, but they may not take an active part in anything, they must just look on for ever. It is a punishment put on them for something they did so long ago that no star now knows what it was. So the older ones have become glassy-eyed and seldom speak (winking is the star language), but the little ones still wonder. They are not really friendly to Peter, who had a mischievous way of stealing up behind them and trying to blow them out; but they are so fond of fun that they were on his side to-night, and anxious to get the grown-ups out of the way. So as soon as the door of 27 closed on Mr. and Mrs. Darling there was a commotion in the firmament, and the smallest of all the stars in the Milky Way screamed out:

"Now, Peter!"

Chapter 3

Come Away, Come Away!

For a moment after Mr. and Mrs. Darling left the house the night-lights by the beds of the three children continued to burn clearly. They were awfully nice little night-lights, and one cannot help wishing that they could have kept awake to see Peter; but Wendy's light blinked and gave such a yawn that the other two yawned also, and before they could close their mouths all the three went out.

There was another light in the room now, a thousand times brighter than the night-lights, and in the time we have taken to say this, it had been in all the drawers in the nursery, looking for Peter's shadow, rummaged the wardrobe and turned every pocket inside out. It was not really a light; it made this light by flashing about so quickly, but when it came to rest for a second you saw it was a fairy, no longer than your hand, but still growing. It was a girl called Tinker Bell exquisitely gowned in a skeleton leaf, cut low and square, through which her figure could be seen to the best advantage. She was slightly inclined to *embonpoint*.

A moment after the fairy's entrance the window was blown open by the breathing of the little stars, and Peter

dropped in. He had carried Tinker Bell part of the way, and his hand was still messy with the fairy dust.

"Tinker Bell," he called softly, after making sure that the children were asleep, "Tink, where are you?" She was in a jug for the moment, and liking it extremely; she had never been in a jug before.

"Oh, do come out of that jug, and tell me, do you know where they put my shadow?"

The loveliest tinkle as of golden bells answered him. It is the fairy language. You ordinary children can never hear it, but if you were to hear it you would know that you had heard it once before.

Tink said that the shadow was in the big box. She meant the chest of drawers, and Peter jumped at the drawers, scattering their contents to the floor with both hands, as kings toss ha'pence to the crowd. In a moment he had recovered his shadow, and in his delight he forgot that he had shut Tinker Bell up in the drawer.

If he thought at all, but I don't believe he ever thought, it was that he and his shadow, when brought near each other, would join like drops of water, and when they did not he was appalled. He tried to stick it on with soap from the bathroom, but that also failed. A shudder passed through Peter, and he sat on the floor and cried.

His sobs woke Wendy, and she sat up in bed. She was not alarmed to see a stranger crying on the nursery floor; she was only pleasantly interested.

"Boy," she said courteously, "why are you crying?"

Peter could be exceeding polite also, having learned the grand manner at fairy ceremonies, and he rose and bowed to her beautifully. She was much pleased, and bowed beautifully to him from the bed.

"What's your name?" he asked.

"Wendy Moira Angela Darling," she replied with some satisfaction. "What is your name?"

"Peter Pan."

She was already sure that he must be Peter, but it did seem a comparatively short name.

"Is that all?"

"Yes," he said rather sharply. He felt for the first time that it was a shortish name.

"I'm so sorry," said Wendy Moira Angela.

"It doesn't matter," Peter gulped.

She asked where he lived.

"Second to the right," said Peter, "and then straight on till morning."

"What a funny address!"

Peter had a sinking. For the first time he felt that perhaps it was a funny address.

"No, it isn't," he said.

"I mean," Wendy said nicely, remembering that she was hostess, "is that what they put on the letters?"

He wished she had not mentioned letters.

"Don't get any letters," he said contemptuously.

"But your mother gets letters?"

"Don't have a mother," he said. Not only had he no mother, but he had not the slightest desire to have one. He thought them very over-rated persons. Wendy, however, felt at once that she was in the presence of a tragedy.

"O Peter, no wonder you were crying," she said, and got out of bed and ran to him.

"I wasn't crying about mothers," he said rather

indignantly. "I was crying because I can't get my shadow to stick on. Besides, I wasn't crying."

"It has come off?"

"Yes."

Then Wendy saw the shadow on the floor, looking so draggled, and she was frightfully sorry for Peter. "How awful!" she said, but she could not help smiling when she saw that he had been trying to stick it on with soap. How exactly like a boy!

Fortunately she knew at once what to do. "It must be sewn on," she said, just a little patronisingly.

"What's sewn?" he asked.

"You're dreadfully ignorant."

"No, I'm not."

But she was exulting in his ignorance. "I shall sew it on for you, my little man," she said, though he was tall as herself, and she got out her housewife, and sewed the shadow on to Peter's foot.

"I daresay it will hurt a little," she warned him.

"Oh, I shan't cry," said Peter, who was already of the opinion that he had never cried in his life. And he clenched his teeth and did not cry, and soon his shadow was behaving properly, though still a little creased.

"Perhaps I should have ironed it," Wendy said thoughtfully, but Peter, boylike, was indifferent to appearances, and he was now jumping about in the wildest glee. Alas, he had already forgotten that he owed his bliss to Wendy. He thought he had attached the shadow himself. "How clever I am!" he crowed rapturously, "oh, the cleverness of me!"

It is humiliating to have to confess that this conceit of

Peter was one of his most fascinating qualities. To put it with brutal frankness, there never was a cockier boy.

But for the moment Wendy was shocked. "You conceit," she exclaimed, with frightful sarcasm; "of course I did nothing!"

"You did a little," Peter said carelessly, and continued to dance.

"A little!" she replied with hauteur; "if I am no use I can at least withdraw," and she sprang in the most dignified way into bed and covered her face with the blankets.

To induce her to look up he pretended to be going away, and when this failed he sat on the end of the bed and tapped her gently with his foot. "Wendy," he said, "don't withdraw. I can't help crowing, Wendy, when I'm pleased with myself." Still she would not look up, though she was listening eagerly. "Wendy," he continued, in a voice that no woman has ever yet been able to resist, "Wendy, one girl is more use than twenty boys."

Now Wendy was every inch a woman, though there were not very many inches, and she peeped out of the bed-clothes.

"Do you really think so, Peter?"

"Yes, I do."

"I think it's perfectly sweet of you," she declared, "and I'll get up again," and she sat with him on the side of the bed. She also said she would give him a kiss if he liked, but Peter did not know what she meant, and he held out his hand expectantly.

"Surely you know what a kiss is?" she asked, aghast.

"I shall know when you give it to me," he replied stiffly, and not to hurt his feeling she gave him a thimble.

"Now," said he, "shall I give you a kiss?" and she replied with a slight primness, "If you please." She made herself rather cheap by inclining her face toward him, but he merely dropped an acorn button into her hand, so she slowly returned her face to where it had been before, and said nicely that she would wear his kiss on the chain around her neck. It was lucky that she did put it on that chain, for it was afterwards to save her life.

When people in our set are introduced, it is customary for them to ask each other's age, and so Wendy, who always liked to do the correct thing, asked Peter how old he was. It was not really a happy question to ask him; it was like an examination paper that asks grammar, when what you want to be asked is Kings of England.

"I don't know," he replied uneasily, "but I am quite young." He really knew nothing about it, he had merely suspicions, but he said at a venture, "Wendy, I ran away the day I was born."

Wendy was quite surprised, but interested; and she indicated in the charming drawing-room manner, by a touch on her night-gown, that he could sit nearer her.

"It was because I heard father and mother," he explained in a low voice, "talking about what I was to be when I became a man." He was extraordinarily agitated now. "I don't want ever to be a man," he said with passion. "I want always to be a little boy and to have fun. So I ran away to Kensington Gardens and lived a long long time among the fairies."

She gave him a look of the most intense admiration, and he thought it was because he had run away, but it was really because he knew fairies. Wendy had lived such a home life that to know fairies struck her as quite delightful. She poured out questions about them, to his surprise, for they were rather a nuisance to him, getting in his way and so on, and indeed he sometimes had to give them a hiding. Still, he liked them on the whole, and he told her about the beginning of fairies.

"You see, Wendy, when the first baby laughed for the first time, its laugh broke into a thousand pieces, and they all went skipping about, and that was the beginning of fairies."

Tedious talk this, but being a stay-at-home she liked it.

"And so," he went on good-naturedly, "there ought to be one fairy for every boy and girl."

"Ought to be? Isn't there?"

"No. You see children know such a lot now, they soon don't believe in fairies, and every time a child says, 'I don't believe in fairies,' there is a fairy somewhere that falls down dead."

Really, he thought they had now talked enough about fairies, and it struck him that Tinker Bell was keeping very quiet. "I can't think where she has gone to," he said, rising, and he called Tink by name. Wendy's heart went flutter with a sudden thrill.

"Peter," she cried, clutching him, "you don't mean to tell me that there is a fairy in this room!"

"She was here just now," he said a little impatiently. "You don't hear her, do you?" and they both listened.

"The only sound I hear," said Wendy, "is like a tinkle of bells."

"Well, that's Tink, that's the fairy language. I think I hear her too."

The sound came from the chest of drawers, and Peter made a merry face. No one could ever look quite so merry as Peter, and the loveliest of gurgles was his laugh. He had his first laugh still.

"Wendy," he whispered gleefully, "I do believe I shut her up in the drawer!"

He let poor Tink out of the drawer, and she flew about the nursery screaming with fury. "You shouldn't say such things," Peter retorted. "Of course I'm very sorry, but how could I know you were in the drawer?"

Wendy was not listening to him. "O Peter," she cried, "if she would only stand still and let me see her!"

"They hardly ever stand still," he said, but for one

moment Wendy saw the romantic figure come to rest on the cuckoo clock. "O the lovely!" she cried, though Tink's face was still distorted with passion.

"Tink," said Peter amiably, "this lady says she wishes you were her fairy."

Tinker Bell answered insolently.

"What does she say, Peter?"

He had to translate. "She is not very polite. She says you are a great ugly girl, and that she is my fairy."

He tried to argue with Tink. "You know you can't be my fairy, Tink, because I am an gentleman and you are a lady."

To this Tink replied in these words, "You silly ass," and disappeared into the bathroom. "She is quite a common fairy," Peter explained apologetically, "she is called Tinker Bell because she mends the pots and kettles."

They were together in the armchair by this time, and Wendy plied him with more questions.

"If you don't live in Kensington Gardens now—"

"Sometimes I do still."

"But where do you live mostly now?"

"With the lost boys."

"Who are they?"

"They are the children who fall out of their perambulators when the nurse is looking the other way. If they are not claimed in seven days they are sent far away to the Neverland to defray expenses. I'm captain."

"What fun it must be!"

"Yes," said cunning Peter, "but we are rather lonely. You see we have no female companionship."

"Are none of the others girls?"

"Oh, no; girls, you know, are much too clever to fall out of their prams."

This flattered Wendy immensely. "I think," she said, "it is perfectly lovely the way you talk about girls; John there just despises us."

For reply Peter rose and kicked John out of bed, blankets and all; one kick. This seemed to Wendy rather forward for a first meeting, and she told him with spirit that he was not captain in her house. However, John continued to sleep so placidly on the floor that she allowed him to remain there. "And I know you meant to be kind," she said, relenting, "so you may give me a kiss."

For the moment she had forgotten his ignorance about kisses. "I thought you would want it back," he said a little bitterly, and offered to return her the thimble.

"Oh dear," said the nice Wendy, "I don't mean a kiss, I mean a thimble."

"What's that?"

"It's like this." She kissed him.

"Funny!" said Peter gravely. "Now shall I give you a thimble?"

"If you wish to," said Wendy, keeping her head erect this time.

Peter thimbled her, and almost immediately she screeched. "What is it, Wendy?"

"It was exactly as if someone were pulling my hair."

"That must have been Tink. I never knew her so naughty before."

And indeed Tink was darting about again, using offensive language.

"She says she will do that to you, Wendy, every time I

give you a thimble."

"But why?"

"Why, Tink?"

Again Tink replied, "You silly ass." Peter could not understand why, but Wendy understood, and she was just slightly disappointed when he admitted that he came to the nursery window not to see her but to listen to stories.

"You see, I don't know any stories. None of the lost boys knows any stories."

"How perfectly awful," Wendy said.

"Do you know," Peter asked "why swallows build in the eaves of houses? It is to listen to the stories. O Wendy, your mother was telling you such a lovely story."

"Which story was it?"

"About the prince who couldn't find the lady who wore the glass slipper."

"Peter," said Wendy excitedly, "that was Cinderella, and he found her, and they lived happily ever after."

Peter was so glad that he rose from the floor, where they had been sitting, and hurried to the window.

"Where are you going?" she cried with misgiving.

"To tell the other boys."

"Don't go Peter," she entreated, "I know such lots of stories."

Those were her precise words, so there can be no denying that it was she who first tempted him.

He came back, and there was a greedy look in his eyes now which ought to have alarmed her, but did not.

"Oh, the stories I could tell to the boys!" she cried, and then Peter gripped her and began to draw her toward the window.

"Let me go!" she ordered him.

"Wendy, do come with me and tell the other boys."

Of course she was very pleased to be asked, but she said, "Oh dear, I can't. Think of mummy! Besides, I can't fly."

"I'll teach you."

"Oh, how lovely to fly."

"I'll teach you how to jump on the wind's back, and then away we go."

"Oo!" she exclaimed rapturously.

"Wendy, Wendy, when you are sleeping in your silly bed you might be flying about with me saying funny things to the stars."

"Oo!"

"And, Wendy, there are mermaids."

"Mermaids! With tails?"

"Such long tails."

"Oh," cried Wendy, "to see a mermaid!"

He had become frightfully cunning. "Wendy," he said, "how we should all respect you."

She was wriggling her body in distress. It was quite as if she were trying to remain on the nursery floor.

But he had no pity for her.

"Wendy," he said, the sly one, "you could tuck us in at night."

"Oo!"

"None of us has ever been tucked in at night."

"Oo," and her arms went out to him.

"And you could darn our clothes, and make pockets for us. None of us has any pockets."

How could she resist. "Of course it's awfully fascinating!" she cried. "Peter, would you teach John and Michael to fly too?"

"If you like," he said indifferently, and she ran to John and Michael and shook them. "Wake up," she cried, "Peter Pan has come and he is to teach us to fly."

John rubbed his eyes. "Then I shall get up," he said. Of course he was on the floor already. "Hallo," he said, "I am up!"

Michael was up by this time also, looking as sharp as a knife with six blades and a saw, but Peter suddenly signed silence. Their faces assumed the awful craftiness of children listening for sounds from the grown-up world. All was as still as salt. Then everything was right. No, stop! Everything was wrong. Nana, who had been barking distressfully all the evening, was quiet now. It was her silence they had heard.

"Out with the light! Hide! Quick!" cried John, taking command for the only time throughout the whole adventure. And thus when Liza entered, holding Nana, the nursery seemed quite its old self, very dark, and you could have sworn you heard its three wicked inmates breathing angelically as they slept. They were really doing it artfully from behind the window curtains.

Liza was in a bad temper, for she was mixing the Christmas puddings in the kitchen, and had been drawn away from them, with a raisin still on her cheek, by Nana's absurd suspicions. She thought the best way of getting a little quiet was to take Nana to the nursery for a moment, but in custody of course.

"There, you suspicious brute," she said, not sorry that

Nana was in disgrace. "They are perfectly safe, aren't they? Every one of the little angels sound asleep in bed. Listen to their gentle breathing."

Here Michael, encouraged by his success, breathed so loudly that they were nearly detected. Nana knew that kind of breathing, and she tried to drag herself out of Liza's clutches.

But Liza was dense. "No more of it, Nana," she said sternly, pulling her out of the room. "I warn you if you bark again I shall go straight for master and missus and bring them home from the party, and then, oh, won't master whip you, just."

She tied the unhappy dog up again, but do you think Nana ceased to bark? Bring master and missus home from the party! Why, that was just what she wanted. Do you think she cared whether she was whipped so long as her charges were safe? Unfortunately Liza returned to her puddings, and Nana, seeing that no help would come from her, strained and strained at the chain until at last she broke it. In another moment she had burst into the dining-room of 27 and flung up her paws to heaven, her most expressive way of making a communication. Mr. and Mrs. Darling knew at once that something terrible was happening in their nursery, and without a good-bye to their hostess they rushed into the street.

But it was now ten minutes since three scoundrels had been breathing behind the curtains, and Peter Pan can do a great deal in ten minutes.

We now return to the nursery.

"It's all right," John announced, emerging from his hiding-place. "I say, Peter, can you really fly?"

Instead of troubling to answer him Peter flew around the room, taking the mantelpiece on the way.

"How topping!" said John and Michael.

"How sweet!" cried Wendy.

"Yes, I'm sweet, oh, I am sweet!" said Peter, forgetting his manners again.

It looked delightfully easy, and they tried it first from the floor and then from the beds, but they always went down instead of up.

"I say, how do you do it?" asked John, rubbing his knee. He was quite a practical boy.

"You just think lovely wonderful thoughts," Peter explained, "and they lift you up in the air."

He showed them again.

"You're so nippy at it," John said, "couldn't you do it very slowly once?"

Peter did it both slowly and quickly. "I've got it now, Wendy!" cried John, but soon he found he had not. Not one of them could fly an inch, though even Michael was in words of two syllables, and Peter did not know A from Z.

Of course Peter had been trifling with them, for no one can fly unless the fairy dust has been blown on him. Fortunately, as we have mentioned, one of his hands was messy with it, and he blew some on each of them, with the most superb results.

"Now just wiggle your shoulders this way," he said, "and let go."

They were all on their beds, and gallant Michael let go first. He did not quite mean to let go, but he did it, and immediately he was borne across the room.

"I flewed!" he screamed while still in mid-air.

John let go and met Wendy near the bathroom.

"Oh, lovely!"

"Oh, ripping!"

"Look at me!"

"Look at me!"

"Look at me!"

They were not nearly so elegant as Peter, they could not help kicking a little, but their heads were bobbing against the ceiling, and there is almost nothing so delicious as that. Peter gave Wendy a hand at first, but had to desist, Tink was so indignant.

Up and down they went, and round and round. Heavenly was Wendy's word.

"I say," cried John, "why shouldn't we all go out?"

Of course it was to this that Peter had been luring them.

Michael was ready: he wanted to see how long it took him to do a billion miles. But Wendy hesitated.

"Mermaids!" said Peter again.

"Oo!"

"And there are pirates."

"Pirates," cried John, seizing his Sunday hat, "let us go at once."

It was just at this moment that Mr. and Mrs. Darling hurried with Nana out of 27. They ran into the middle of the street to look up at the nursery window; and, yes, it was still shut, but the room was ablaze with light, and most heart-gripping sight of all, they could see in shadow on the curtain three little figures in night attire circling round and round, not on the floor but in the air.

Not three figures, four!

In a tremble they opened the street door. Mr. Darling would have rushed upstairs, but Mrs. Darling signed him to go softly. She even tried to make her heart go softly.

Will they reach the nursery in time? If so, how delightful for them, and we shall all breathe a sigh of relief, but there will be no story. On the other hand, if they are not in time, I solemnly promise that it will all come right in the end.

They would have reached the nursery in time had it not been that the little stars were watching them. Once again the stars blew the window open, and that smallest star of all called out:

"Cave, Peter!"

Then Peter knew that there was not a moment to lose. "Come," he cried imperiously, and soared out at once into the night, followed by John and Michael and Wendy.

Mr. and Mrs. Darling and Nana rushed into the nursery too late. The birds were flown.

The Flight

Chapter 4

ff Second to the right, and straight on till morning."

That, Peter had told Wendy, was the way to the Neverland; but even birds, carrying maps and consulting them at windy corners, could not have sighted it with these instructions. Peter, you see, just said anything that came into his head.

At first his companions trusted him implicitly, and so great were the delights of flying that they wasted time circling round church spires or any other tall objects on the way that took their fancy.

John and Michael raced, Michael getting a start.

They recalled with contempt that not so long ago they had thought themselves fine fellows for being able to fly round a room.

Not long ago. But how long ago? They were flying over the sea before this thought began to disturb Wendy seriously. John thought it was their second sea and their third night.

Sometimes it was dark and sometimes light, and now they were very cold and again too warm. Did they really feel hungry at times, or were they merely pretending, because Peter had such a jolly new way of feeding them?

Gwynedd M. Hudson.

His way was to pursue birds who had food in their mouths suitable for humans and snatch it from them; then the birds would follow and snatch it back; and they would all go chasing each other gaily for miles, parting at last with mutual expressions of good-will. But Wendy noticed with gentle concern that Peter did not seem to know that this was rather an odd way of getting your bread and butter, nor even that there are other ways.

Certainly they did not pretend to be sleepy, they were sleepy; and that was a danger, for the moment they popped off, down they fell. The awful thing was that Peter thought this funny.

"There he goes again!" he would cry gleefully, as Michael suddenly dropped like a stone.

"Save him, save him!" cried Wendy, looking with horror at the cruel sea far below. Eventually Peter would dive through the air, and catch Michael just before he could strike the sea, and it was lovely the way he did it; but he always waited till the last moment, and you felt it was his cleverness that interested him and not the saving of human life. Also he was fond of variety, and the sport that engrossed him one moment would suddenly cease to engage him, so there was always the possibility that the next time you fell he would let you go.

He could sleep in the air without falling, by merely lying on his back and floating, but this was, partly at least, because he was so light that if you got behind him and blew he went faster.

"Do be more polite to him," Wendy whispered to John, when they were playing "Follow my Leader."

"Then tell him to stop showing off," said John.

When playing Follow my Leader, Peter would fly close to the water and touch each shark's tail in passing, just as in the street you may run your finger along an iron railing. They could not follow him in this with much success, so perhaps it was rather like showing off, especially as he kept looking behind to see how many tails they missed.

"You must be nice to him," Wendy impressed on her brothers. "What could we do if he were to leave us!"

"We could go back," Michael said.

"How could we ever find our way back without him?"

"Well, then, we could go on," said John.

"That is the awful thing, John. We should have to go on, for we don't know how to stop."

This was true, Peter had forgotten to show them how to stop.

John said that if the worst came to the worst, all they had to do was to go straight on, for the world was round, and so in time they must come back to their own window.

"And who is to get food for us, John?"

"I nipped a bit out of that eagle's mouth pretty neatly, Wendy."

"After the twentieth try," Wendy reminded him. "And even though we became good at picking up food, see how we bump against clouds and things if he is not near to give us a hand."

Indeed they were constantly bumping. They could now fly strongly, though they still kicked far too much; but if they saw a cloud in front of them, the more they tried to avoid it, the more certainly did they bump into it. If Nana had been with them, she would have had a bandage round Michael's forehead by this time.

Peter was not with them for the moment, and they felt rather lonely up there by themselves. He could go so much faster than they that he would suddenly shoot out of sight, to have some adventure in which they had no share. He would come down laughing over something fearfully funny he had been saying to a star, but he had already forgotten what it was, or he would come up with mermaid scales still sticking to him, and yet not be able to say for certain what had been happening. It was really rather irritating to children who had never seen a mermaid.

"And if he forgets them so quickly," Wendy argued,

"how can we expect that he will go on remembering us?"

Indeed, sometimes when he returned he did not remember them, at least not well. Wendy was sure of it. She saw recognition come into his eyes as he was about to pass them the time of day and go on; once even she had to call him by name.

"I'm Wendy," she said agitatedly.

He was very sorry. "I say, Wendy," he whispered to her, "always if you see me forgetting you, just keep on saying 'I'm Wendy,' and then I'll remember."

Of course this was rather unsatisfactory. However, to make amends he showed them how to lie out flat on a strong wind that was going their way, and this was such a pleasant change that they tried it several times and found that they could sleep thus with security. Indeed they would have slept longer, but Peter tired quickly of sleeping, and soon he would cry in his captain voice, "We get off here." So with occasional tiffs, but on the whole rollicking, they drew near the Neverland; for after many moons they did reach it, and, what is more, they had been going pretty straight all the time, not perhaps so much owing to the guidance of Peter or Tink as because the island was looking for them. It is only thus that any one may sight those magic shores.

"There it is," said Peter calmly.

"Where, where?"

"Where all the arrows are pointing."

Indeed a million golden arrows were pointing it out to the children, all directed by their friend the sun, who wanted them to be sure of their way before leaving them for the night.

Gwynedd M. Hudson.

Wendy and John and Michael stood on tip-toe in the air to get their first sight of the island. Strange to say, they all recognized it at once, and until fear fell upon them they hailed it, not as something long dreamt of and seen at last, but as a familiar friend to whom they were returning home for the holidays.

"John, there's the lagoon."

"Wendy, look at the turtles burying their eggs in the sand."

"I say, John, I see your flamingo with the broken leg!"

"Look, Michael, there's your cave!"

"John, what's that in the brushwood?"

"It's a wolf with her whelps. Wendy, I do believe that's your little whelp!"

"There's my boat, John, with her sides stove in!"

"No, it isn't. Why, we burned your boat."

"That's her, at any rate. I say, John, I see the smoke of the redskin camp!"

"Where? Show me, and I'll tell you by the way smoke curls whether they are on the war-path."

"There, just across the Mysterious River."

"I see now. Yes, they are on the war-path right enough."

Peter was a little annoyed with them for knowing so much, but if he wanted to lord it over them his triumph was at hand, for have I not told you that anon fear fell upon them?

It came as the arrows went, leaving the island in gloom.

In the old days at home the Neverland had always begun to look a little dark and threatening by bedtime.

Then unexplored patches arose in it and spread, black shadows moved about in them, the roar of the beasts of prey was quite different now, and above all, you lost the certainty that you would win. You were quite glad that the night-lights were on. You even liked Nana to say that this was just the mantelpiece over here, and that the Neverland was all make-believe.

Of course the Neverland had been make-believe in those days, but it was real now, and there were no night-lights, and it was getting darker every moment, and where was Nana?

They had been flying apart, but they huddled close to Peter now. His careless manner had gone at last, his eyes were sparkling, and a tingle went through them every time they touched his body. They were now over the fearsome island, flying so low that sometimes a tree grazed their feet. Nothing horrid was visible in the air, yet their progress had become slow and laboured, exactly as if they were pushing their way through hostile forces. Sometimes they hung in the air until Peter had beaten on it with his fists.

"They don't want us to land," he explained.

"Who are they?" Wendy whispered, shuddering.

But he could not or would not say. Tinker Bell had been asleep on his shoulder, but now he wakened her and sent her on in front.

Sometimes he poised himself in the air, listening intently, with his hand to his ear, and again he would stare down with eyes so bright that they seemed to bore two holes to earth. Having done these things, he went on again.

His courage was almost appalling. "'Do you want an adventure now," he said casually to John, "or would you like to have your tea first?"

Wendy said "tea first" quickly, and Michael pressed her hand in gratitude, but the braver John hesitated.

"What kind of adventure?" he asked cautiously.

"There's a pirate asleep in the pampas just beneath us," Peter told him. "If you like, we'll go down and kill him."

"I don't see him," John said after a long pause.

"I do."

"Suppose," John said, a little huskily, "he were to wake up."

Peter spoke indignantly. "You don't think I would kill him while he was sleeping! I would wake him first, and then kill him. That's the way I always do."

"I say! Do you kill many?"

"Tons."

John said "how ripping," but decided to have tea first. He asked if there were many pirates on the island just now, and Peter said he had never known so many.

"Who is captain now?"

"Hook," answered Peter, and his face became very stern as he said that hated word.

"Jas. Hook?"

"Ay."

Then indeed Michael began to cry, and even John could speak in gulps only, for they knew Hook's reputation.

"He was Blackbeard's bo'sun," John whispered huskily. "He is the worst of them all. He is the only man of whom Barbecue was afraid."

"That's him," said Peter.

"What is he like? Is he big?"

"He is not so big as he was."

"How do you mean?"

"I cut off a bit of him."

"You!"

"Yes, me," said Peter sharply.

"I wasn't meaning to be disrespectful."

"Oh, all right."

"But, I say, what bit?"

"His right hand."

"Then he can't fight now?"

"Oh, can't he just!"

"Left-hander?"

"He has an iron hook instead of a right hand, and he claws with it."

"Claws!"

"I say, John," said Peter.

"Yes."

"Say, 'Ay, ay, sir.'"

"Ay, ay, sir."

"There is one thing," Peter continued, "that every boy who serves under me has to promise, and so must you."

John paled.

"It is this, if we meet Hook in open fight, you must leave him to me."

"I promise," John said loyally.

For the moment they were feeling less eerie, because

Tink was flying with them, and in her light they could distinguish each other. Unfortunately she could not fly so slowly as they, and so she had to go round and round them in a circle in which they moved as in a halo. Wendy quite liked it, until Peter pointed out the drawbacks.

"She tells me," he said, "that the pirates sighted us before the darkness came, and got Long Tom out."

"The big gun?"

"Yes. And of course they must see her light, and if they guess we are near it they are sure to let fly."

"Wendy!"

"John!"

"Michael!"

"Tell her to go away at once, Peter," the three cried simultaneously, but he refused.

"She thinks we have lost the way," he replied stiffly, "and she is rather frightened. You don't think I would send her away all by herself when she is frightened!"

For a moment the circle of light was broken, and something gave Peter a loving little pinch.

"Then tell her," Wendy begged, "to put out her light."

"She can't put it out. That is about the only thing fairies can't do. It just goes out of itself when she falls asleep, same as the stars."

"Then tell her to sleep at once," John almost ordered.

"She can't sleep except when she's sleepy. It is the only other thing fairies can't do."

"Seems to me," growled John, "these are the only two things worth doing."

Here he got a pinch, but not a loving one.

"If only one of us had a pocket," Peter said, "we could

carry her in it." However, they had set off in such a hurry that there was not a pocket between the four of them.

He had a happy idea. John's hat!

Tink agreed to travel by hat if it was carried in the hand. John carried it, though she had hoped to be carried by Peter. Presently Wendy took the hat, because John said it struck against his knee as he flew; and this, as we shall see, led to mischief, for Tinker Bell hated to be under an obligation to Wendy.

In the black topper the light was completely hidden, and they flew on in silence. It was the stillest silence they had ever known, broken once by a distant lapping, which Peter explained was the wild beasts drinking at the ford, and again by a rasping sound that might have been the branches of trees rubbing together, but he said it was the redskins sharpening their knives.

Even these noises ceased. To Michael the loneliness was dreadful. "If only something would make a sound!" he cried.

As if in answer to his request, the air was rent by the most tremendous crash he had ever heard. The pirates had fired Long Tom at them.

The roar of it echoed through the mountains, and the echoes seemed to cry savagely, "Where are they, where are they, where are they?"

Thus sharply did the terrified three learn the difference between an island of make-believe and the same island come true.

When at last the heavens were steady again, John and Michael found themselves alone in the darkness. John was treading the air mechanically, and Michael without

knowing how to float was floating.

"Are you shot?" John whispered tremulously.

"I haven't tried yet," Michael whispered back.

We know now that no one had been hit. Peter, however, had been carried by the wind of the shot far out to sea, while Wendy was blown upwards with no companion but Tinker Bell.

It would have been well for Wendy if at that moment she had dropped the hat.

I don't know whether the idea came suddenly to Tink, or whether she had planned it on the way, but she at once popped out of the hat and began to lure Wendy to her destruction.

Tink was not all bad; or, rather, she was all bad just now, but, on the other hand, sometimes she was all good. Fairies have to be one thing or the other, because being so small they unfortunately have room for one feeling only at a time. They are, however, allowed to change, only it must be a complete change. At present she was full of jealousy of Wendy. What she said in her lovely tinkle Wendy could not of course understand, and I believe some of it was bad words, but it sounded kind, and she flew back and forward, plainly meaning "Follow me, and all will be well."

What else could poor Wendy do? She called to Peter and John and Michael, and got only mocking echoes in reply. She did not yet know that Tink hated her with the fierce hatred of a very woman. And so, bewildered, and now staggering in her flight, she followed Tink to her doom.

Chapter 5

The Island Come True

Feeling that Peter was on his way back, the Neverland had again woke into life. We ought to use the pluperfect and say wakened, but woke is better and was always used by Peter.

In his absence things are usually quiet on the island. The fairies take an hour longer in the morning, the beasts attend to their young, the redskins feed heavily for six days and nights, and when pirates and lost boys meet they merely bite their thumbs at each other. But with the coming of Peter, who hates lethargy, they are under way again: if you put your ear to the ground now, you would hear the whole island seething with life.

On this evening the chief forces of the island were disposed as follows. The lost boys were out looking for Peter, the pirates were out looking for the lost boys, the redskins were out looking for the pirates, and the beasts were out looking for the redskins. They were going round and round the island, but they did not meet because all were going at the same rate.

All wanted blood except the boys, who liked it as a rule, but to-night were out to greet their captain. The boys on the island vary, of course, in numbers, according as they get killed and so on; and when they seem to be growing up, which is against the rules, Peter thins them out; but at this time there were six of them, counting the twins as two. Let us pretend to lie here among the sugar-cane and watch them as they steal by in single file, each with his hand on his dagger.

They are forbidden by Peter to look in the least like him, and they wear the skins of the bears slain by themselves, in which they are so round and furry that when they fall they roll. They have therefore become very sure-footed.

The first to pass is Tootles, not the least brave but the most unfortunate of all that gallant band. He had been in fewer adventures than any of them, because the big things constantly happened just when he had stepped round the corner; all would be quiet, he would take the opportunity of going off to gather a few sticks for firewood, and then when he returned the others would be sweeping up the blood. This ill-luck had given a gentle melancholy to his countenance, but instead of souring his nature had sweetened it, so that he was quite the humblest of the boys. Poor kind Tootles, there is danger in the air for you to-night. Take care lest an adventure is now offered you, which, if accepted, will plunge you in deepest woe. Tootles, the fairy Tink, who is bent on mischief this night is looking for a tool, and she thinks you are the most easily tricked of the boys. 'Ware Tinker Bell.

Would that he could hear us, but we are not really on the island, and he passes by, biting his knuckles.

Next comes Nibs, the gay and debonair, followed by Slightly, who cuts whistles out of the trees and dances

ecstatically to his own tunes. Slightly is the most conceited of the boys. He thinks he remembers the days before he was lost, with their manners and customs, and this has given his nose an offensive tilt. Curly is fourth; he is a pickle, and so often has he had to deliver up his person when Peter said sternly, "Stand forth the one who did this thing," that now at the command he stands forth automatically whether he has done it or not. Last come the Twins, who cannot be described because we should be sure to be describing the wrong one. Peter never quite knew what twins were, and his band were not allowed to know anything he did not know, so these two were always vague about themselves, and did their best to give satisfaction by keeping close together in an apologetic sort of way.

The boys vanish in the gloom, and after a pause, but not a long pause, for things go briskly on the island, come the pirates on their track. We hear them before they are seen, and it is always the same dreadful song:

"Avast belay, yo ho, heave to,
A-pirating we go,
And if we're parted by a shot
We're sure to meet below!"

A more villainous-looking lot never hung in a row on Execution dock. Here, a little in advance, ever and again with his head to the ground listening, his great arms bare, pieces of eight in his ears as ornaments, is the handsome Italian Cecco, who cut his name in letters of blood on the back of the governor of the prison at Gao.

That gigantic black behind him has had many names since he dropped the one with which dusky mothers still terrify their children on the banks of the Guadjo-mo. Here is Bill Jukes, every inch of him tattooed, the same Bill Jukes who got six dozen on the WALRUS from Flint before he would drop the bag of moidores; and Cookson, said to be Black Murphy's brother (but this was never proved), and Gentleman Starkey, once an usher in a public school and still dainty in his ways of killing; and Skylights (Morgan's Skylights); and the Irish bo'sun Smee, an oddly genial man who stabbed, so to speak, without offence, and was the only Non-conformist in Hook's crew; and Noodler, whose hands were fixed on backwards; and Robt. Mullins and Alf Mason and many another ruffian long known and feared on the Spanish Main.

In the midst of them, the blackest and largest in that dark setting, reclined James Hook, or as he wrote himself, Jas. Hook, of whom it is said he was the only man that the Sea-Cook feared. He lay at his ease in a rough chariot drawn and propelled by his men, and instead of a right hand he had the iron hook with which ever and anon he encouraged them to increase their pace. As dogs this terrible man treated and addressed them, and as dogs they obeyed him. In person he was cadaverous and blackavized, and his hair was dressed in long curls, which at a little distance looked like black candles, and gave a singularly threatening expression to his handsome countenance. His eyes were of the blue of the forget-me-not, and of a profound melancholy, save when he was plunging his hook into you, at which time two red spots appeared in them and lit them up horribly. In manner, something of the grand seigneur still clung to him, so that he even ripped you up with an air, and I have been told that he was a *raconteur* of repute. He was never more sinister than when he was most polite, which is probably the truest test of breeding; and the elegance of his diction, even when he was swearing, no less than the distinction of his demeanour, showed him one of a different cast from his crew. A man of indomitable courage, it was said that the only thing he shied at was the sight of his own blood, which was thick and of an unusual colour. In dress he somewhat aped the attire associated with the name of Charles II, having heard it said in some earlier period of his career that he bore a strange resemblance to the ill-fated Stuarts; and in his mouth he had a holder of his own contrivance which enabled him to smoke two cigars at once. But undoubtedly the grimmest part of him was his iron claw.

Let us now kill a pirate, to show Hook's method. Skylights will do. As they pass, Skylights lurches clumsily against him, ruffling his lace collar; the hook shoots forth, there is a tearing sound and one screech, then the body is kicked aside, and the pirates pass on. He has not even taken the cigars from his mouth.

Such is the terrible man against whom Peter Pan is pitted. Which will win?

On the trail of the pirates, stealing noiselessly down the war-path, which is not visible to inexperienced eyes, come the redskins, every one of them with his eyes peeled. They carry tomahawks and knives, and their naked bodies gleam with paint and oil. Strung around them are scalps, of boys as well as of pirates, for these are the Piccaninny tribe, and not to be confused with the softer-hearted Delawares or the Hurons. In the van, on all fours, is Great Big Little Panther, a brave of so many scalps that in his present position they somewhat impede his progress. Bringing up the rear, the place of greatest danger, comes Tiger Lily, proudly erect, a princess in her own right. She is the most beautiful of dusky Dianas and the belle of the Piccaninnies, coquettish, cold and amorous by turns; there is not a brave who would not have the wayward thing to wife, but she staves off the altar with a hatchet. Observe how they pass over fallen twigs without making the slightest noise. The only sound to be heard is their somewhat heavy breathing. The fact is that they are all a little fat just now after the heavy gorging, but in time they will work this off. For the moment, however, it constitutes their chief danger.

The redskins disappear as they have come like shadows, and soon their place is taken by the beasts, a great and motley procession: lions, tigers, bears, and the innumerable smaller savage things that flee from them, for every kind of beast, and, more particularly, all the man-eaters, live cheek by jowl on the favoured island. Their tongues are hanging out, they are hungry to-night.

When they have passed, comes the last figure of all, a gigantic crocodile. We shall see for whom she is looking presently.

The crocodile passes, but soon the boys appear again, for the procession must continue indefinitely until one of the parties stops or changes its pace. Then quickly they will be on top of each other.

All are keeping a sharp look-out in front, but none suspects that the danger may be creeping up from behind. This shows how real the island was.

The first to fall out of the moving circle was the boys. They flung themselves down on the sward, close to their underground home.

"I do wish Peter would come back," every one of them said nervously, though in height and still more in breadth they were all larger than their captain.

"I am the only one who is not afraid of the pirates," Slightly said, in the tone that prevented his being a general favourite; but perhaps some distant sound disturbed him, for he added hastily, "but I wish he would come back, and tell us whether he has heard anything more about Cinderella."

They talked of Cinderella, and Tootles was confident that his mother must have been very like her.

It was only in Peter's absence that they could speak of mothers, the subject being forbidden by him as silly.

"All I remember about my mother," Nibs told them, "is that she often said to my father, 'Oh, how I wish I had a cheque-book of my own!' I don't know what a cheque-book is, but I should just love to give my mother one."

While they talked they heard a distant sound. You or I, not being wild things of the woods, would have heard nothing, but they heard it, and it was the grim song:

"Yo ho, yo ho, the pirate life,
The flag o' skull and bones,
A merry hour, a hempen rope,
And hey for Davy Jones."

At once the lost boys—but where are they? They are no longer there. Rabbits could not have disappeared more quickly.

I will tell you where they are. With the exception of Nibs, who has darted away to reconnoitre, they are already in their home under the ground, a very delightful residence of which we shall see a good deal presently. But how have they reached it? for there is no entrance to be seen, not so much as a large stone, which if rolled away, would disclose the mouth of a cave. Look closely, however, and you may note that there are here seven large trees, each with a hole in its hollow trunk as large as a boy. These are the seven entrances to the home under the ground, for which Hook has been searching in vain these many moons. Will he find it tonight?

As the pirates advanced, the quick eye of Starkey sighted Nibs disappearing through the wood, and at once his pistol flashed out. But an iron claw gripped his shoulder.

"Captain, let go!" he cried, writhing.

Now for the first time we hear the voice of Hook. It was a black voice. "Put back that pistol first," it said threateningly.

"It was one of those boys you hate. I could have shot him dead."

"Ay, and the sound would have brought Tiger Lily's redskins upon us. Do you want to lose your scalp?"

"Shall I after him, Captain," asked pathetic Smee, "and tickle him with Johnny Corkscrew?" Smee had pleasant names for everything, and his cutlass was Johnny Corkscrew, because he wiggled it in the wound. One could mention many lovable traits in Smee. For instance, after killing, it was his spectacles he wiped instead of his weapon.

"Johnny's a silent fellow," he reminded Hook.

"Not now, Smee," Hook said darkly. "He is only one, and I want to mischief all the seven. Scatter and look for them."

The pirates disappeared among the trees, and in a moment their Captain and Smee were alone. Hook heaved a heavy sigh, and I know not why it was, perhaps it was because of the soft beauty of the evening, but there came over him a desire to confide to his faithful bo'sun the story of his life. He spoke long and earnestly, but what it was all about Smee, who was rather stupid, did not know in the least.

Anon he caught the word Peter.

"Most of all," Hook was saying passionately, "I want their captain, Peter Pan. 'Twas he cut off my arm." He brandished the hook threateningly. "I've waited long to shake his hand with this. Oh, I'll tear him!"

"And yet," said Smee, "I have often heard you say that hook was worth a score of hands, for combing the hair and other homely uses."

"Ay," the captain answered, "if I was a mother I would pray to have my children born with this instead of that," and he cast a look of pride upon his iron hand and one of scorn upon the other. Then again he frowned.

"Peter flung my arm," he said, wincing, "to a crocodile that happened to be passing by."

"I have often," said Smee, "noticed your strange dread of crocodiles."

"Not of crocodiles," Hook corrected him, "but of that one crocodile." He lowered his voice. "It liked my arm so much, Smee, that it has followed me ever since, from sea to sea and from land to land, licking its lips for the rest of me."

"In a way," said Smee, "it's sort of a compliment."

"I want no such compliments," Hook barked petulantly. "I want Peter Pan, who first gave the brute its taste for me."

He sat down on a large mushroom, and now there was a quiver in his voice. "Smee," he said huskily, "that crocodile would have had me before this, but by a lucky chance it swallowed a clock which goes tick tick inside it, and so before it can reach me I hear the tick and bolt." He laughed, but in a hollow way.

"Some day," said Smee, "the clock will run down, and then he'll get you."

Hook wetted his dry lips. "Ay," he said, "that's the fear that haunts me."

Since sitting down he had felt curiously warm. "Smee," he said, "this seat is hot." He jumped up. "Odds bobs, hammer and tongs I'm burning."

They examined the mushroom, which was of a size and solidity unknown on the mainland; they tried to pull it up, and it came away at once in their hands, for it had no root. Stranger still, smoke began at once to ascend. The pirates looked at each other. "A chimney!" they both exclaimed.

They had indeed discovered the chimney of the home under the ground. It was the custom of the boys to stop it with a mushroom when enemies were in the neighbourhood.

Not only smoke came out of it. There came also children's voices, for so safe did the boys feel in their hiding-place that they were gaily chattering. The pirates listened grimly, and then replaced the mushroom. They looked around them and noted the holes in the seven trees.

"Did you hear them say Peter Pan's from home?" Smee whispered, fidgeting with Johnny Corkscrew.

Hook nodded. He stood for a long time lost in thought, and at last a curdling smile lit up his swarthy face. Smee had been waiting for it. "Unrip your plan, captain," he cried eagerly.

"To return to the ship," Hook replied slowly through his teeth, "and cook a large rich cake of a jolly thickness with green sugar on it. There can be but one room below, for there is but one chimney. The silly moles had not the sense to see that they did not need a door apiece. That shows they have no mother. We will leave the cake on the shore of the Mermaids' Lagoon. These boys are always swimming about there, playing with the mermaids. They will find the cake and they will gobble it up, because, having no mother, they don't know how dangerous 'tis to eat rich damp cake." He burst into laughter, not hollow laughter now, but honest laughter. "Aha, they will die."

Smee had listened with growing admiration.

"It's the wickedest, prettiest policy ever I heard of!" he cried, and in their exultation they danced and sang:

"Avast, belay, when I appear,
By fear they're overtook;
Nought's left upon your bones when you
Have shaken claws with Hook."

They began the verse, but they never finished it, for another sound broke in and stilled them. There was at first such a tiny sound that a leaf might have fallen on it and smothered it, but as it came nearer it was more distinct.

Tick tick tick tick!

Hook stood shuddering, one foot in the air.

"The crocodile!" he gasped, and bounded away, followed by his bo'sun.

It was indeed the crocodile. It had passed the redskins, who were now on the trail of the other pirates. It oozed on after Hook.

Once more the boys emerged into the open; but the dangers of the night were not yet over, for presently Nibs rushed breathless into their midst, pursued by a pack of wolves. The tongues of the pursuers were hanging out; the baying of them was horrible.

"Save me, save me!" cried Nibs, falling on the ground.

"But what can we do, what can we do?"

It was a high compliment to Peter that at that dire moment their thoughts turned to him.

"What would Peter do?" they cried simultaneously.

Almost in the same breath they cried, "Peter would look at them through his legs."

And then, "Let us do what Peter would do."

It is quite the most successful way of defying wolves, and as one boy they bent and looked through their legs. The next moment is the long one, but victory came quickly, for as the boys advanced upon them in the terrible attitude, the wolves dropped their tails and fled.

Now Nibs rose from the ground, and the others thought that his staring eyes still saw the wolves. But it

was not wolves he saw.

"I have seen a wonderfuller thing," he cried, as they gathered round him eagerly. "A great white bird. It is flying this way."

"What kind of a bird, do you think?"

"I don't know," Nibs said, awestruck, "but it looks so weary, and as it flies it moans, 'Poor Wendy.'"

"Poor Wendy?"

"I remember," said Slightly instantly, "there are birds called Wendies."

"See, it comes!" cried Curly, pointing to Wendy in the heavens.

Wendy was now almost overhead, and they could hear her plaintive cry. But more distinct came the shrill voice of Tinker Bell. The jealous fairy had now cast off all disguise of friendship, and was darting at her victim from every direction, pinching savagely each time she touched.

"Hullo, Tink," cried the wondering boys.

Tink's reply rang out: "Peter wants you to shoot the Wendy."

It was not in their nature to question when Peter ordered. "Let us do what Peter wishes!" cried the simple boys. "Quick, bows and arrows!"

All but Tootles popped down their trees. He had a bow and arrow with him, and Tink noted it, and rubbed her little hands.

"Quick, Tootles, quick," she screamed. "Peter will be so pleased."

Tootles excitedly fitted the arrow to his bow. "Out of the way, Tink," he shouted, and then he fired, and Wendy fluttered to the ground with an arrow in her breast.

The Little House

Chapter 6

Foolish Tootles was standing like a conqueror over Wendy's body when the other boys sprang, armed, from their trees.

"You are too late," he cried proudly, "I have shot the Wendy. Peter will be so pleased with me."

Overhead Tinker Bell shouted "Silly ass!" and darted into hiding. The others did not hear her. They had crowded round Wendy, and as they looked a terrible silence fell upon the wood. If Wendy's heart had been beating they would all have heard it.

Slightly was the first to speak. "This is no bird," he said in a scared voice. "I think this must be a lady."

"A lady?" said Tootles, and fell a-trembling.

"And we have killed her," Nibs said hoarsely.

They all whipped off their caps.

"Now I see," Curly said: "Peter was bringing her to us." He threw himself sorrowfully on the ground.

"A lady to take care of us at last," said one of the twins, "and you have killed her!"

They were sorry for him, but sorrier for themselves, and when he took a step nearer them they turned from him.

Tootles' face was very white, but there was a dignity about him now that had never been there before.

"I did it," he said, reflecting. "When ladies used to come to me in dreams, I said, 'Pretty mother, pretty mother.' But when at last she really came, I shot her."

He moved slowly away.

"Don't go," they called in pity.

"I must," he answered, shaking; "I am so afraid of Peter."

It was at this tragic moment that they heard a sound which made the heart of every one of them rise to his mouth. They heard Peter crow.

"Peter!" they cried, for it was always thus that he signalled his return.

"Hide her," they whispered, and gathered hastily around Wendy. But Tootles stood aloof.

Again came that ringing crow, and Peter dropped in front of them. "Greetings, boys," he cried, and mechanically they saluted, and then again was silence.

He frowned.

"I am back," he said hotly, "why do you not cheer?"

They opened their mouths, but the cheers would not come. He overlooked it in his haste to tell the glorious tidings.

"Great news, boys," he cried, "I have brought at last a mother for you all."

Still no sound, except a little thud from Tootles as he dropped on his knees.

"Have you not seen her?" asked Peter, becoming troubled. "She flew this way."

"Ah me!" one voice said, and another said, "Oh,

mournful day."

Tootles rose. "Peter," he said quietly, "I will show her to you," and when the others would still have hidden her he said, "Back, twins, let Peter see."

So they all stood back, and let him see, and after he had looked for a little time he did not know what to do next.

"She is dead," he said uncomfortably. "Perhaps she is frightened at being dead."

He thought of hopping off in a comic sort of way till he was out of sight of her, and then never going near the spot any more. They would all have been glad to follow if he had done this.

But there was the arrow. He took it from her heart and faced his band.

"Whose arrow?" he demanded sternly.

"Mine, Peter," said Tootles on his knees.

"Oh, dastard hand," Peter said, and he raised the arrow to use it as a dagger.

Tootles did not flinch. He bared his breast. "Strike, Peter," he said firmly, "strike true."

Twice did Peter raise the arrow, and twice did his hand fall. "I cannot strike," he said with awe, "there is something stays my hand."

All looked at him in wonder, save Nibs, who fortunately looked at Wendy.

"It is she," he cried, "the Wendy lady, see, her arm!"

Wonderful to relate, Wendy had raised her arm. Nibs bent over her and listened reverently. "I think she said, 'Poor Tootles,'" he whispered.

"She lives," Peter said briefly.

Slightly cried instantly, "The Wendy lady lives."

Then Peter knelt beside her and found his button. You remember she had put it on a chain that she wore round her neck.

"See," he said, "the arrow struck against this. It is the kiss I gave her. It has saved her life."

"I remember kisses," Slightly interposed quickly, "let me see it. Ay, that's a kiss."

Peter did not hear him. He was begging Wendy to get better quickly, so that he could show her the mermaids. Of course she could not answer yet, being still in a frightful faint; but from overhead came a wailing note.

"Listen to Tink," said Curly, "she is crying because the Wendy lives."

Then they had to tell Peter of Tink's crime, and almost never had they seen him look so stern.

"Listen, Tinker Bell," he cried, "I am your friend no more. Begone from me for ever."

She flew on to his shoulder and pleaded, but he brushed her off. Not until Wendy again raised her arm did he relent sufficiently to say, "Well, not for ever, but for a whole week."

Do you think Tinker Bell was grateful to Wendy for raising her arm? Oh dear no, never wanted to pinch her so much. Fairies indeed are strange, and Peter, who understood them best, often cuffed them.

But what to do with Wendy in her present delicate state of health?

"Let us carry her down into the house," Curly suggested.

"Ay," said Slightly, "that is what one does with ladies."

"No, no," Peter said, "you must not touch her. It would not be sufficiently respectful."

"That," said Slightly, "is what I was thinking."

"But if she lies there," Tootles said, "she will die."

"Ay, she will die," Slightly admitted, "but there is no way out."

"Yes, there is," cried Peter. "Let us build a little house round her."

They were all delighted. "Quick," he ordered them, "bring me each of you the best of what we have. Gut our house. Be sharp."

In a moment they were as busy as tailors the night before a wedding. They skurried this way and that, down for bedding, up for firewood, and while they were at it, who should appear but John and Michael. As they dragged along the ground they fell asleep standing, stopped, woke up, moved another step and slept again.

"John, John," Michael would cry, "wake up! Where is Nana, John, and mother?"

And then John would rub his eyes and mutter, "It is true, we did fly."

You may be sure they were very relieved to find Peter.

"Hullo, Peter," they said.

"Hullo," replied Peter amicably, though he had quite forgotten them. He was very busy at the moment measuring Wendy with his feet to see how large a house she would need. Of course he meant to leave room for chairs and a table. John and Michael watched him.

"Is Wendy asleep?" they asked.

"Yes."

"John," Michael proposed, "let us wake her and get

her to make supper for us," but as he said it some of the other boys rushed on carrying branches for the building of the house. "Look at them!" he cried.

"Curly," said Peter in his most captainy voice, "see that these boys help in the building of the house."

"Ay, ay, sir."

"Build a house?" exclaimed John.

"For the Wendy," said Curly.

"For Wendy?" John said, aghast. "Why, she is only a girl!"

"That," explained Curly, "is why we are her servants."

"You? Wendy's servants!"

"Yes," said Peter, "and you also. Away with them."

The astounded brothers were dragged away to hack and hew and carry. "Chairs and a fender first," Peter ordered. "Then we shall build a house round them."

"Ay," said Slightly, "that is how a house is built; it all comes back to me."

Peter thought of everything. "Slightly," he cried, "fetch a doctor."

"Ay, ay," said Slightly at once, and disappeared, scratching his head. But he knew Peter must be obeyed, and he returned in a moment, wearing John's hat and looking solemn.

"Please, sir," said Peter, going to him, "are you a doctor?"

The difference between him and the other boys at such a time was that they knew it was make-believe, while to him make-believe and true were exactly the same thing. This sometimes troubled them, as when they had to make-believe that they had had their dinners.

If they broke down in their make-believe he rapped them on the knuckles.

"Yes, my little man," Slightly anxiously replied, who had chapped knuckles.

"Please, sir," Peter explained, "a lady lies very ill."

She was lying at their feet, but Slightly had the sense not to see her.

"Tut, tut, tut," he said, "where does she lie?"

"In yonder glade."

"I will put a glass thing in her mouth," said Slightly, and he made-believe to do it, while Peter waited. It was an anxious moment when the glass thing was withdrawn.

"How is she?" inquired Peter.

"Tut, tut, tut," said Slightly, "this has cured her."

"I am glad!" Peter cried.

"I will call again in the evening," Slightly said; "give her beef tea out of a cup with a spout to it;" but after he had returned the hat to John he blew big breaths, which was his habit on escaping from a difficulty.

In the meantime the wood had been alive with the sound of axes; almost everything needed for a cosy dwelling already lay at Wendy's feet.

"If only we knew," said one, "the kind of house she likes best."

"Peter," shouted another, "she is moving in her sleep."

"Her mouth opens," cried a third, looking respectfully into it. "Oh, lovely!"

"Perhaps she is going to sing in her sleep," said Peter. "Wendy, sing the kind of house you would like to have."

Immediately, without opening her eyes, Wendy began to sing:

"I wish I had a pretty house,
The littlest ever seen,
With funny little red walls
And roof of mossy green."

They gurgled with joy at this, for by the greatest good luck the branches they had brought were sticky with red sap, and all the ground was carpeted with moss. As they rattled up the little house they broke into song themselves:

"We've built the little walls and roof
And made a lovely door,
So tell us, mother Wendy,
What are you wanting more?"

To this she answered greedily:

"Oh, really next I think I'll have
Gay windows all about,
With roses peeping in, you know,
And babies peeping out."

With a blow of their fists they made windows, and large yellow leaves were the blinds. But roses—?

"Roses," cried Peter sternly.

Quickly they made-believe to grow the loveliest roses up the walls.

Babies?

To prevent Peter ordering babies they hurried into song again:

"We've made the roses peeping out,
The babes are at the door,
We cannot make ourselves, you know,
'cos we've been made before."

Peter, seeing this to be a good idea, at once pretended that it was his own. The house was quite beautiful, and no doubt Wendy was very cosy within, though, of course, they could no longer see her. Peter strode up and down, ordering finishing touches. Nothing escaped his eagle eyes. Just when it seemed absolutely finished:

"There's no knocker on the door," he said.

They were very ashamed, but Tootles gave the sole of his shoe, and it made an excellent knocker.

Absolutely finished now, they thought.

Not of bit of it. "There's no chimney," Peter said; "we must have a chimney."

"It certainly does need a chimney," said John importantly. This gave Peter an idea. He snatched the hat off John's head, knocked out the bottom, and put the hat on the roof. The little house was so pleased to have such a capital chimney that, as if to say thank you, smoke immediately began to come out of the hat.

Now really and truly it was finished. Nothing remained to do but to knock.

"All look your best," Peter warned them; "first impressions are awfully important."

He was glad no one asked him what first impressions

are; they were all too busy looking their best.

He knocked politely, and now the wood was as still as the children, not a sound to be heard except from Tinker Bell, who was watching from a branch and openly sneering.

What the boys were wondering was, would any one answer the knock? If a lady, what would she be like?

The door opened and a lady came out. It was Wendy. They all whipped off their hats.

She looked properly surprised, and this was just how they had hoped she would look.

"Where am I?" she said.

Of course Slightly was the first to get his word in. "Wendy lady," he said rapidly, "for you we built this house."

"Oh, say you're pleased," cried Nibs.

"Lovely, darling house," Wendy said, and they were the very words they had hoped she would say.

"And we are your children," cried the twins.

Then all went on their knees, and holding out their arms cried, "O Wendy lady, be our mother."

"Ought I?" Wendy said, all shining. "Of course it's frightfully fascinating, but you see I am only a little girl. I have no real experience."

"That doesn't matter," said Peter, as if he were the only person present who knew all about it, though he was really the one who knew least. "What we need is just a nice motherly person."

"Oh dear!" Wendy said, "you see, I feel that is exactly what I am."

"It is, it is," they all cried; "we saw it at once."

"Very well," she said, "I will do my best. Come inside at once, you naughty children; I am sure your feet are damp. And before I put you to bed I have just time to finish the story of Cinderella."

In they went; I don't know how there was room for them, but you can squeeze very tight in the Neverland. And that was the first of the many joyous evenings they had with Wendy. By and by she tucked them up in the great bed in the home under the trees, but she herself slept that night in the little house, and Peter kept watch outside with drawn sword, for the pirates could be heard carousing far away and the wolves were on the prowl. The little house looked so cosy and safe in the darkness, with a bright light showing through its blinds, and the chimney smoking beautifully, and Peter standing on guard. After a time he fell asleep, and some unsteady fairies had to climb over him on their way home from an orgy. Any of the other boys obstructing the fairy path at night they would have mischiefed, but they just tweaked Peter's nose and passed on.

The Home
Under the
Chapter 7
Ground

One of the first things Peter did next day was to measure Wendy and John and Michael for hollow trees. Hook, you remember, had sneered at the boys for thinking they needed a tree apiece, but this was ignorance, for unless your tree fitted you it was difficult to go up and down, and no two of the boys were quite the same size. Once you fitted, you drew in your breath at the top, and down you went at exactly the right speed, while to ascend you drew in and let out alternately, and so wriggled up. Of course, when you have mastered the action you are able to do these things without thinking of them, and nothing can be more graceful.

But you simply must fit, and Peter measures you for your tree as carefully as for a suit of clothes: the only difference being that the clothes are made to fit you, while you have to be made to fit the tree. Usually it is done quite easily, as by your wearing too many garments or too few, but if you are bumpy in awkward places or the only available tree is an odd shape, Peter does some things to you, and after that you fit. Once you fit, great care must be taken to go on fitting, and this, as Wendy was to discover to her delight, keeps a whole family in perfect condition.

Wendy and Michael fitted their trees at the first try, but John had to be altered a little.

After a few days' practice they could go up and down as gaily as buckets in a well. And how ardently they grew to love their home under the ground; especially Wendy. It consisted of one large room, as all houses should do, with a floor in which you could dig if you wanted to go fishing, and in this floor grew stout mushrooms of a charming colour, which were used as stools. A Never tree tried hard to grow in the centre of the room, but every morning they sawed the trunk through, level with the floor. By tea-time it was always about two feet high, and then they put a door on top of it, the whole thus becoming a table; as soon as they cleared away, they sawed off the trunk again, and thus there was more room to play. There was an enormous fireplace which was in almost any part of the room where you cared to light it, and across this Wendy stretched strings, made of fibre, from which she suspended her washing. The bed was tilted against the wall by day, and let down at 6:30, when it filled nearly half the room; and all the boys slept in it, except Michael, lying like sardines in a tin. There was a strict rule against turning round until one gave the signal, when all turned at once. Michael should have used it also, but Wendy would have a baby, and he was the littlest, and you know what women are, and the short and long of it is that he was hung up in a basket.

It was rough and simple, and not unlike what baby bears would have made of an underground house in the same circumstances. But there was one recess in the

wall, no larger than a bird-cage, which was the private apartment of Tinker Bell. It could be shut off from the rest of the house by a tiny curtain, which Tink, who was most fastidious, always kept drawn when dressing or undressing. No woman, however large, could have had a more exquisite boudoir and bed-chamber combined. The couch, as she always called it, was a genuine Queen Mab, with club legs; and she varied the bedspreads according to what fruit-blossom was in season. Her mirror was a Puss-in-Boots, of which there are now only three, unchipped, known to fairy dealers; the washstand was Pie-crust and reversible, the chest of drawers an authentic Charming the Sixth, and the carpet and rugs the best (the early) period of Margery and Robin. There was a chandelier from Tiddlywinks for the look of the thing, but of course she lit the residence herself. Tink was very contemptuous of the rest of the house, as indeed was perhaps inevitable, and her chamber, though beautiful, looked rather conceited, having the appearance of a nose permanently turned up.

I suppose it was all especially entrancing to Wendy, because those rampagious boys of hers gave her so much to do. Really there were whole weeks when, except perhaps with a stocking in the evening, she was never above ground. The cooking, I can tell you, kept her nose to the pot, and even if there was nothing in it, even if there was no pot, she had to keep watching that it came aboil just the same. You never exactly knew whether there would be a real meal or just a make-believe, it all depended upon Peter's whim: he could eat, really eat, if it was part of a game, but he could not stodge just to feel stodgy, which is what most children like better than anything else; the next best thing being to talk about it. Make-believe was so real to him that during a meal of it you could see him getting rounder. Of course it was trying, but you simply had to follow his lead, and if you could prove to him that you were getting loose for your tree he let you stodge.

Wendy's favourite time for sewing and darning was after they had all gone to bed. Then, as she expressed it, she had a breathing time for herself; and she occupied it in making new things for them, and putting double pieces on the knees, for they were all most frightfully hard on their knees.

When she sat down to a basketful of their stockings, every heel with a hole in it, she would fling up her arms and exclaim, "Oh dear, I am sure I sometimes think spinsters are to be envied!"

Her face beamed when she exclaimed this.

You remember about her pet wolf. Well, it very soon discovered that she had come to the island and it found her out, and they just ran into each other's arms. After that it followed her about everywhere.

As time wore on did she think much about the beloved parents she had left behind her? This is a difficult question, because it is quite impossible to say how time does wear on in the Neverland, where it is calculated by moons and suns, and there are ever so many more of them than on the mainland. But I am afraid that Wendy did not really worry about her father and mother; she was absolutely confident that they would always keep the window open for her to fly back by, and this gave her complete ease of mind. What did disturb her at times was that John remembered his parents vaguely only, as people he had once known, while Michael was quite willing to believe that she was really his mother. These things scared her a little, and nobly anxious to do her duty, she tried to fix the old life in their minds by setting them examination papers on it, as like as possible to the ones she used to do at school. The other boys thought this awfully interesting, and insisted on joining, and they made slates for themselves, and sat round the table, writing and thinking hard about the questions she had written on another slate and passed round. They were the most ordinary questions— "What was the colour of Mother's eyes? Which was taller, Father or Mother? Was Mother blonde or brunette? Answer all three questions if possible." "(A) Write an essay of not less than 40 words on How I spent my last Holidays, or The Characters of Father and Mother compared. Only one of these to be attempted." Or "(1) Describe Mother's laugh; (2) Describe Father's laugh; (3) Describe Mother's Party Dress; (4) Describe the Kennel and its Inmate."

They were just everyday questions like these, and when you could not answer them you were told to make a cross; and it was really dreadful what a number of crosses even John made. Of course the only boy who replied to every question was Slightly, and no one could have been more hopeful of coming out first, but his answers were perfectly ridiculous, and he really came out last: a melancholy thing.

Peter did not compete. For one thing he despised all

mothers except Wendy, and for another he was the only boy on the island who could neither write nor spell; not the smallest word. He was above all that sort of thing.

By the way, the questions were all written in the past tense. What was the colour of Mother's eyes, and so on. Wendy, you see, had been forgetting, too.

Adventures, of course, as we shall see, were of daily occurrence; but about this time Peter invented, with Wendy's help, a new game that fascinated him enormously, until he suddenly had no more interest in it, which, as you have been told, was what always happened with his games. It consisted in pretending not to have adventures, in doing the sort of thing John and Michael had been doing all their lives, sitting on stools flinging balls in the air, pushing each other, going out for walks and coming back without having killed so much as a grizzly. To see Peter doing nothing on a stool was a great sight; he could not help looking solemn at such times, to sit still seemed to him such a comic thing to do. He boasted that he had gone walking for the good of his health. For several suns these were the most novel of all adventures to him; and John and Michael had to pretend to be delighted also; otherwise he would have treated them severely.

He often went out alone, and when he came back you were never absolutely certain whether he had had an adventure or not. He might have forgotten it so completely that he said nothing about it; and then when you went out you found the body; and, on the other hand, he might say a great deal about it, and yet you could not find the body. Sometimes he came home with his head bandaged, and then Wendy cooed over him and bathed it in lukewarm water, while he told a dazzling tale. But she was never quite sure, you know. There were, however, many adventures which she knew to be true because she was in them herself, and there were still more that were at least partly true, for the other boys were in them and said they were wholly true. To describe them all would require a book as large as an English-Latin, Latin-English Dictionary, and the most we can do is to give one as a specimen of an average hour on the island. The difficulty is which one to choose. Should we take the brush with the redskins at Slightly Gulch? It was a sanguinary affair, and especially interesting as showing one of Peter's peculiarities, which was that in the middle of a fight he would suddenly change sides. At the Gulch, when victory was still in the balance, sometimes leaning this way and sometimes that, he called out, "I'm redskin to-day; what are you, Tootles?" And Tootles answered, "Redskin; what are you, Nibs?" and Nibs said, "Redskin; what are you Twin?" and so on; and they were all redskins; and of course this would have ended the fight had not the real redskins fascinated by Peter's methods, agreed to be lost boys for that once, and so at it they all went again, more fiercely than ever.

The extraordinary upshot of this adventure was—but we have not decided yet that this is the adventure we are to narrate. Perhaps a better one would be the night attack by the redskins on the house under the ground, when several of them stuck in the hollow trees and had to be pulled out like corks. Or we might tell how Peter saved Tiger Lily's life in the Mermaids' Lagoon, and so made her his ally.

Or we could tell of that cake the pirates cooked so that the boys might eat it and perish; and how they placed it in one cunning spot after another; but always Wendy snatched it from the hands of her children, so that in time it lost its succulence, and became as hard as a stone, and was used as a missile, and Hook fell over it in the dark.

Or suppose we tell of the birds that were Peter's friends, particularly of the Never bird that built in a tree overhanging the lagoon, and how the nest fell into the water, and still the bird sat on her eggs, and Peter gave orders that she was not to be disturbed. That is a pretty story, and the end shows how grateful a bird can be; but if we tell it we must also tell the whole adventure of the lagoon, which would of course be telling two adventures rather than just one. A shorter adventure, and quite as exciting, was Tinker Bell's attempt, with the help of some street fairies, to have the sleeping Wendy conveyed on a great floating leaf to the mainland. Fortunately the leaf gave way and Wendy woke, thinking it was bath-time, and swam back. Or again, we might choose Peter's defiance of the lions, when he drew a circle round him on the ground with an arrow and dared them to cross it; and though he waited for hours, with the other boys and Wendy looking on breathlessly from trees, not one of them dared to accept his challenge.

Which of these adventures shall we choose? The best way will be to toss for it.

I have tossed, and the lagoon has won. This almost makes one wish that the gulch or the cake or Tink's leaf had won. Of course I could do it again, and make it best out of three; however, perhaps fairest to stick to the lagoon.

The Mermaids' Lagoon

Chapter 8

If you shut your eyes and are a lucky one, you may see at times a shapeless pool of lovely pale colours suspended in the darkness; then if you squeeze your eyes tighter, the pool begins to take shape, and the colours become so vivid that with another squeeze they must go on fire. But just before they go on fire you see the lagoon. This is the nearest you ever get to it on the mainland, just one heavenly moment; if there could be two moments you might see the surf and hear the mermaids singing.

The children often spent long summer days on this lagoon, swimming or floating most of the time, playing the mermaid games in the water, and so forth. You must not think from this that the mermaids were on friendly terms with them: on the contrary, it was among Wendy's lasting regrets that all the time she was on the island she never had a civil word from one of them. When she stole softly to the edge of the lagoon she might see them by the score, especially on Marooners' Rock, where they loved to bask, combing out their hair in a lazy way that quite irritated her; or she might even swim, on tiptoe as it were, to within a yard of them, but then they saw her

and dived, probably splashing her with their tails, not by accident, but intentionally.

They treated all the boys in the same way, except of course Peter, who chatted with them on Marooners' Rock by the hour, and sat on their tails when they got cheeky. He gave Wendy one of their combs.

The most haunting time at which to see them is at the turn of the moon, when they utter strange wailing cries; but the lagoon is dangerous for mortals then, and until the evening of which we have now to tell, Wendy had never seen the lagoon by moonlight, less from fear, for of course Peter would have accompanied her, than because she had strict rules about every one being in bed by seven. She was often at the lagoon, however, on sunny days after rain, when the mermaids come up in extraordinary numbers to play with their bubbles. The bubbles of many colours made in rainbow water they treat as balls, hitting them gaily from one to another with their tails, and trying to keep them in the rainbow till they burst. The goals are at each end of the rainbow, and the keepers only are allowed to use their hands. Sometimes a dozen of these games will be going on in the lagoon at a time, and it is quite a pretty sight.

But the moment the children tried to join in they had to play by themselves, for the mermaids immediately disappeared. Nevertheless we have proof that they secretly watched the interlopers, and were not above taking an idea from them; for John introduced a new way of hitting the bubble, with the head instead of the hand, and the mermaids adopted it. This is the one mark that John has left on the Neverland.

It must also have been rather pretty to see the children resting on a rock for half an hour after their mid-day meal. Wendy insisted on their doing this, and it had to be a real rest even though the meal was make-believe. So they lay there in the sun, and their bodies glistened in it, while she sat beside them and looked important.

It was one such day, and they were all on Marooners' Rock. The rock was not much larger than their great bed, but of course they all knew how not to take up much room, and they were dozing, or at least lying with their eyes shut, and pinching occasionally when they thought Wendy was not looking. She was very busy, stitching.

While she stitched a change came to the lagoon. Little shivers ran over it, and the sun went away and shadows stole across the water, turning it cold. Wendy could no longer see to thread her needle, and when she looked up, the lagoon that had always hitherto been such a laughing place seemed formidable and unfriendly.

It was not, she knew, that night had come, but something as dark as night had come. No, worse than that. It had not come, but it had sent that shiver through the sea to say that it was coming. What was it?

There crowded upon her all the stories she had been told of Marooners' Rock, so called because evil captains put sailors on it and leave them there to drown. They drown when the tide rises, for then it is submerged.

Of course she should have roused the children at once; not merely because of the unknown that was stalking toward them, but because it was no longer good for them to sleep on a rock grown chilly. But she was a young mother and she did not know this; she thought you simply must stick to your rule about half an hour after the mid-day meal. So, though fear was upon her, and she longed to hear male voices, she would not waken them. Even when she heard the sound of muffled oars, though her heart was in her mouth, she did not waken them. She stood over them to let them have their sleep out. Was it not brave of Wendy?

It was well for those boys then that there was one among them who could sniff danger even in his sleep. Peter sprang erect, as wide awake at once as a dog, and with one warning cry he roused the others.

He stood motionless, one hand to his ear.

"Pirates!" he cried. The others came closer to him. A strange smile was playing about his face, and Wendy saw it and shuddered. While that smile was on his face no one dared address him; all they could do was to stand ready to obey. The order came sharp and incisive.

"Dive!"

There was a gleam of legs, and instantly the lagoon seemed deserted. Marooners' Rock stood alone in the forbidding waters as if it were itself marooned.

The boat drew nearer. It was the pirate dinghy, with three figures in her, Smee and Starkey, and the third a captive, no other than Tiger Lily. Her hands and ankles were tied, and she knew what was to be her fate. She was to be left on the rock to perish, an end to one of her race more terrible than death by fire or torture, for is it not written in the book of the tribe that there is no path through water to the happy hunting-ground? Yet her face was impassive; she was the daughter of a chief, she must die as a chief's daughter, it is enough.

They had caught her boarding the pirate ship with a knife in her mouth. No watch was kept on the ship, it being Hook's boast that the wind of his name guarded the ship for a mile around. Now her fate would help to guard it also. One more wail would go the round in that wind by night.

In the gloom that they brought with them the two pirates did not see the rock till they crashed into it.

"Luff, you lubber," cried an Irish voice that was Smee's; "here's the rock. Now, then, what we have to do is to hoist the redskin on to it and leave her here to drown."

It was the work of one brutal moment to land the beautiful girl on the rock; she was too proud to offer a vain resistance.

It was the pirate
dinghy o · o · o ·

Quite near the rock, but out of sight, two heads were bobbing up and down, Peter's and Wendy's. Wendy was crying, for it was the first tragedy she had seen. Peter had seen many tragedies, but he had forgotten them all. He was less sorry than Wendy for Tiger Lily: it was two against one that angered him, and he meant to save her. An easy way would have been to wait until the pirates had gone, but he was never one to choose the easy way.

There was almost nothing he could not do, and he now imitated the voice of Hook.

"Ahoy there, you lubbers!" he called. It was a marvellous imitation.

"The captain!" said the pirates, staring at each other in surprise.

"He must be swimming out to us," Starkey said, when they had looked for him in vain.

"We are putting the redskin on the rock," Smee called out.

"Set her free," came the astonishing answer.

"Free!"

"Yes, cut her bonds and let her go."

"But, captain—"

"At once, d'ye hear," cried Peter, "or I'll plunge my hook in you."

"This is queer!" Smee gasped.

"Better do what the captain orders," said Starkey nervously.

"Ay, ay," Smee said, and he cut Tiger Lily's cords. At once like an eel she slid between Starkey's legs into the water.

Of course Wendy was very elated over Peter's

cleverness; but she knew that he would be elated also and very likely crow and thus betray himself, so at once her hand went out to cover his mouth. But it was stayed even in the act, for "Boat ahoy!" rang over the lagoon in Hook's voice, and this time it was not Peter who had spoken.

Peter may have been about to crow, but his face puckered in a whistle of surprise instead.

"Boat ahoy!" again came the voice.

Now Wendy understood. The real Hook was also in the water.

He was swimming to the boat, and as his men showed a light to guide him he had soon reached them. In the light of the lantern Wendy saw his hook grip the boat's side; she saw his evil swarthy face as he rose dripping from the water, and, quaking, she would have liked to swim away, but Peter would not budge. He was tingling with life and also top-heavy with conceit. "Am I not a wonder, oh, I am a wonder!" he whispered to her, and though she thought so also, she was really glad for the sake of his reputation that no one heard him except herself.

He signed to her to listen.

The two pirates were very curious to know what had brought their captain to them, but he sat with his head on his hook in a position of profound melancholy.

"Captain, is all well?" they asked timidly, but he answered with a hollow moan.

"He sighs," said Smee.

"He sighs again," said Starkey.

"And yet a third time he sighs," said Smee.

"What's up, captain?"

Then at last he spoke passionately.

"The game's up," he cried, "those boys have found a mother."

Affrighted though she was, Wendy swelled with pride.

"O evil day!" cried Starkey.

"What's a mother?" asked the ignorant Smee.

Wendy was so shocked that she exclaimed. "He doesn't know!" and always after this she felt that if you could have a pet pirate Smee would be her one.

Peter pulled her beneath the water, for Hook had started up, crying, "What was that?"

"I heard nothing," said Starkey, raising the lantern over the waters, and as the pirates looked they saw a strange sight. It was the nest I have told you of, floating on the lagoon, and the Never bird was sitting on it.

"See," said Hook in answer to Smee's question, "that is a mother. What a lesson! The nest must have fallen into the water, but would the mother desert her eggs? No."

There was a break in his voice, as if for a moment he recalled innocent days when—but he brushed away this weakness with his hook.

Smee, much impressed, gazed at the bird as the nest was borne past, but the more suspicious Starkey said, "If she is a mother, perhaps she is hanging about here to help Peter."

Hook winced. "Ay," he said, "that is the fear that haunts me."

He was roused from this dejection by Smee's eager voice.

"Captain," said Smee, "could we not kidnap these boys' mother and make her our mother?"

"It is a princely scheme," cried Hook, and at once it

took practical shape in his great brain. "We will seize the children and carry them to the boat: the boys we will make walk the plank, and Wendy shall be our mother."

Again Wendy forgot herself.

"Never!" she cried, and bobbed.

"What was that?"

But they could see nothing. They thought it must have been a leaf in the wind. "Do you agree, my bullies?" asked Hook.

"There is my hand on it," they both said.

"And there is my hook. Swear."

They all swore. By this time they were on the rock, and suddenly Hook remembered Tiger Lily.

"Where is the redskin?" he demanded abruptly.

He had a playful humour at moments, and they thought this was one of the moments.

"That is all right, captain," Smee answered complacently; "we let her go."

"Let her go!" cried Hook.

"'Twas your own orders," the bo'sun faltered.

"You called over the water to us to let her go," said Starkey.

"Brimstone and gall," thundered Hook, "what cozening is going on here!" His face had gone black with rage, but he saw that they believed their words, and he was startled. "Lads," he said, shaking a little, "I gave no such order."

"It is passing queer," Smee said, and they all fidgeted uncomfortably. Hook raised his voice, but there was a quiver in it.

"Spirit that haunts this dark lagoon to-night," he

cried, "dost hear me?"

Of course Peter should have kept quiet, but of course he did not. He immediately answered in Hook's voice:

"Odds, bobs, hammer and tongs, I hear you."

In that supreme moment Hook did not blanch, even at the gills, but Smee and Starkey clung to each other in terror.

"Who are you, stranger? Speak!" Hook demanded.

"I am James Hook," replied the voice, "captain of the Jolly Roger."

"You are not; you are not," Hook cried hoarsely.

"Brimstone and gall," the voice retorted, "say that again, and I'll cast anchor in you."

Hook tried a more ingratiating manner. "If you are Hook," he said almost humbly, "come tell me, who am I?"

"A codfish," replied the voice, "only a codfish."

"A codfish!" Hook echoed blankly, and it was then, but not till then, that his proud spirit broke. He saw his men draw back from him.

"Have we been captained all this time by a codfish!" they muttered. "It is lowering to our pride."

They were his dogs snapping at him, but, tragic figure though he had become, he scarcely heeded them. Against such fearful evidence it was not their belief in him that he needed, it was his own. He felt his ego slipping from him. "Don't desert me, bully," he whispered hoarsely to it.

In his dark nature there was a touch of the feminine, as in all the great pirates, and it sometimes gave him intuitions. Suddenly he tried the guessing game.

"Hook," he called, "have you another voice?"

Now Peter could never resist a game, and he answered blithely in his own voice, "I have."

"And another name?"

"Ay, ay."

"Vegetable?" asked Hook.

"No."

"Mineral?"

"No."

"Animal?"

"Yes."

"Man?"

"No!" This answer rang out scornfully.

"Boy?"

"Yes."

"Ordinary boy?"

"No!"

"Wonderful boy?"

To Wendy's pain the answer that rang out this time was "Yes."

"Are you in England?"

"No."

"Are you here?"

"Yes."

Hook was completely puzzled. "You ask him some questions," he said to the others, wiping his damp brow.

Smee reflected. "I can't think of a thing," he said regretfully.

"Can't guess, can't guess!" crowed Peter. "Do you give it up?"

Of course in his pride he was carrying the game too far, and the miscreants saw their chance.

"Yes, yes," they answered eagerly.

"Well, then," he cried, "I am Peter Pan."

Pan!

In a moment Hook was himself again, and Smee and Starkey were his faithful henchmen.

"Now we have him," Hook shouted. "Into the water, Smee. Starkey, mind the boat. Take him dead or alive!"

He leaped as he spoke, and simultaneously came the gay voice of Peter.

"Are you ready, boys?"

"Ay, ay," from various parts of the lagoon.

"Then lam into the pirates."

The fight was short and sharp. First to draw blood was John, who gallantly climbed into the boat and held Starkey. There was a fierce struggle, in which the cutlass was torn from the pirate's grasp. He wriggled overboard and John leapt after him. The dinghy drifted away.

Here and there a head bobbed up in the water, and there was a flash of steel followed by a cry or a whoop. In the confusion some struck at their own side. The corkscrew of Smee got Tootles in the fourth rib, but he was himself pinked in turn by Curly. Farther from the rock Starkey was pressing Slightly and the twins hard.

Where all this time was Peter? He was seeking bigger game.

The others were all brave boys, and they must not be blamed for backing from the pirate captain. His iron claw made a circle of dead water round him, from which they fled like affrighted fishes.

But there was one who did not fear him: there was one prepared to enter that circle.

Strangely, it was not in the water that they met. Hook rose to the rock to breathe, and at the same moment Peter scaled it on the opposite side. The rock was slippery as a ball, and they had to crawl rather than climb. Neither knew that the other was coming. Each feeling for a grip met the other's arm: in surprise they raised their heads; their faces were almost touching; so they met.

Some of the greatest heroes have confessed that just before they fell to they had a sinking. Had it been so with Peter at that moment I would admit it. After all, he was the only man that the Sea-Cook had feared. But Peter had no sinking, he had one feeling only, gladness; and he gnashed his pretty teeth with joy. Quick as thought he snatched a knife from Hook's belt and was about to drive it home, when he saw that he was higher up the rock than his foe. It would not have been fighting fair. He gave the pirate a hand to help him up.

It was then that Hook bit him.

Not the pain of this but its unfairness was what dazed Peter. It made him quite helpless. He could only stare, horrified. Every child is affected thus the first time he is treated unfairly. All he thinks he has a right to when he comes to you to be yours is fairness. After you have been unfair to him he will love you again, but will never afterwards be quite the same boy. No one ever gets over the first unfairness; no one except Peter. He often met it, but he always forgot it. I suppose that was the real difference between him and all the rest.

So when he met it now it was like the first time; and he could just stare, helpless. Twice the iron hand clawed him.

A few moments afterwards the other boys saw Hook in the water striking wildly for the ship; no elation on the pestilent face now, only white fear, for the crocodile was in dogged pursuit of him. On ordinary occasions the boys would have swum alongside cheering; but now they were uneasy, for they had lost both Peter and Wendy, and were scouring the lagoon for them, calling them by name. They found the dinghy and went home in it, shouting "Peter, Wendy" as they went, but no answer came save mocking laughter from the mermaids. "They must be swimming back or flying," the boys concluded. They were not very anxious, because they had such faith in Peter. They chuckled, boylike, because they would be late for bed; and it was all mother Wendy's fault!

When their voices died away there came cold silence over the lagoon, and then a feeble cry.

"Help, help!"

Two small figures were beating against the rock; the girl had fainted and lay on the boy's arm. With a last effort Peter pulled her up the rock and then lay down beside her. Even as he also fainted he saw that the water was rising. He knew that they would soon be drowned, but he could do no more.

As they lay side by side a mermaid caught Wendy by the feet, and began pulling her softly into the water. Peter, feeling her slip from him, woke with a start, and was just in time to draw her back. But he had to tell her the truth.

"We are on the rock, Wendy," he said, "but it is growing smaller. Soon the water will be over it."

She did not understand even now.

"We must go," she said, almost brightly.

"Yes," he answered faintly.

"Shall we swim or fly, Peter?"

He had to tell her.

"Do you think you could swim or fly as far as the island, Wendy, without my help?"

She had to admit that she was too tired.

He moaned.

"What is it?" she asked, anxious about him at once.

"I can't help you, Wendy. Hook wounded me. I can neither fly nor swim."

"Do you mean we shall both be drowned?"

"Look how the water is rising."

They put their hands over their eyes to shut out the sight. They thought they would soon be no more. As they sat thus something brushed against Peter as light as a kiss, and stayed there, as if saying timidly, "Can I be of any use?"

It was the tail of a kite, which Michael had made some days before. It had torn itself out of his hand and floated away.

"Michael's kite," Peter said without interest, but next moment he had seized the tail, and was pulling the kite toward him.

"It lifted Michael off the ground," he cried; "why should it not carry you?"

"Both of us!"

"It can't lift two; Michael and Curly tried."

"Let us draw lots," Wendy said bravely.

"And you a lady; never." Already he had tied the tail round her. She clung to him; she refused to go without him; but with a "Good-bye, Wendy," he pushed her from the rock; and in a few minutes she was borne out of his sight. Peter was alone on the lagoon.

The rock was very small now; soon it would be submerged. Pale rays of light tiptoed across the waters; and by and by there was to be heard a sound at once the most musical and the most melancholy in the world: the mermaids calling to the moon.

Peter was not quite like other boys; but he was afraid at last. A tremour ran through him, like a shudder passing over the sea; but on the sea one shudder follows another till there are hundreds of them, and Peter felt just the one. Next moment he was standing erect on the rock again, with that smile on his face and a drum beating within him. It was saying, "To die will be an awfully big adventure."

The Never Bird

Chapter 9

The last sound Peter heard before he was quite alone were the mermaids retiring one by one to their bedchambers under the sea. He was too far away to hear their doors shut; but every door in the coral caves where they live rings a tiny bell when it opens or closes (as in all the nicest houses on the mainland), and he heard the bells.

Steadily the waters rose till they were nibbling at his feet; and to pass the time until they made their final gulp, he watched the only thing on the lagoon. He thought it was a piece of floating paper, perhaps part of the kite, and wondered idly how long it would take to drift ashore.

Presently he noticed as an odd thing that it was undoubtedly out upon the lagoon with some definite purpose, for it was fighting the tide, and sometimes winning; and when it won, Peter, always sympathetic to the weaker side, could not help clapping; it was such a gallant piece of paper.

It was not really a piece of paper; it was the Never bird, making desperate efforts to reach Peter on the nest. By working her wings, in a way she had learned since the nest fell into the water, she was able to some extent to guide her strange craft, but by the time Peter recognised her she was very exhausted. She had come to save him, to give him her nest, though there were eggs in it. I rather wonder at the bird, for though he had been nice to her, he had also sometimes tormented her. I can suppose only that, like Mrs. Darling and the rest of them, she was melted because he had all his first teeth.

She called out to him what she had come for, and he called out to her what she was doing there; but of course neither of them understood the other's language. In fanciful stories people can talk to the birds freely, and I wish for the moment I could pretend that this were such a story, and say that Peter replied intelligently to the Never bird; but truth is best, and I want to tell you only what really happened. Well, not only could they not understand each other, but they forgot their manners.

"I—want—you—to—get—into—the—nest," the bird called, speaking as slowly and distinctly as possible, "and—then—you—can—drift—ashore, but—I—am—too—tired—to—bring—it—any—nearer—so—you—must—try to—swim—to—it."

"What are you quacking about?" Peter answered. "Why don't you let the nest drift as usual?"

"I—want—you—" the bird said, and repeated it all over.

Then Peter tried slow and distinct.

"What—are—you—quacking—about?" and so on.

The Never bird became irritated; they have very short tempers.

"You dunderheaded little jay!" she screamed, "Why

don't you do as I tell you?"

Peter felt that she was calling him names, and at a venture he retorted hotly:

"So are you!"

Then rather curiously they both snapped out the same remark:

"Shut up!"

"Shut up!"

Nevertheless the bird was determined to save him if she could, and by one last mighty effort she propelled the nest against the rock. Then up she flew; deserting her eggs, so as to make her meaning clear.

Then at last he understood, and clutched the nest and waved his thanks to the bird as she fluttered overhead.

It was not to receive his thanks, however, that she hung there in the sky; it was not even to watch him get into the nest; it was to see what he did with her eggs.

There were two large white eggs, and Peter lifted them up and reflected. The bird covered her face with her wings, so as not to see the last of them; but she could not help peeping between the feathers.

I forget whether I have told you that there was a stave on the rock, driven into it by some buccaneers of long ago to mark the site of buried treasure. The children had discovered the glittering hoard, and when in a mischievous mood used to fling showers of moidores, diamonds, pearls and pieces of eight to the gulls, who pounced upon them for food, and then flew away, raging at the scurvy trick that had been played upon them. The stave was still there, and on it Starkey had hung his hat, a deep tarpaulin, watertight, with a broad brim. Peter put the eggs into this hat and set it on the lagoon. It floated beautifully.

The Never bird saw at once what he was up to, and screamed her admiration of him; and, alas, Peter crowed his agreement with her. Then he got into the nest, reared the stave in it as a mast, and hung up his shirt for a sail. At the same moment the bird fluttered down upon the hat and once more sat snugly on her eggs. She drifted in one direction, and he was borne off in another, both cheering.

Of course when Peter landed he beached his barque in a place where the bird would easily find it; but the hat was such a great success that she abandoned the nest. It drifted about till it went to pieces, and often Starkey

came to the shore of the lagoon, and with many bitter feelings watched the bird sitting on his hat. As we shall not see her again, it may be worth mentioning here that all Never birds now build in that shape of nest, with a broad brim on which the youngsters take an airing.

Great were the rejoicings when Peter reached the home under the ground almost as soon as Wendy, who had been carried hither and thither by the kite. Every boy had adventures to tell; but perhaps the biggest adventure of all was that they were several hours late for bed. This so inflated them that they did various dodgy things to get staying up still longer, such as demanding bandages; but Wendy, though glorying in having them all home again safe and sound, was scandalised by the lateness of the hour, and cried, "To bed, to bed," in a voice that had to be obeyed. Next day, however, she was awfully tender, and gave out bandages to every one, and they played till bed-time at limping about and carrying their arms in slings.

The Happy Home

Chapter 10

One important result of the brush on the lagoon was that it made the redskins their friends. Peter had saved Tiger Lily from a dreadful fate, and now there was nothing she and her braves would not do for him. All night they sat above, keeping watch over the home under the ground and awaiting the big attack by the pirates which obviously could not be much longer delayed. Even by day they hung about, smoking the pipe of peace, and looking almost as if they wanted tit-bits to eat.

They called Peter the Great White Father, prostrating themselves before him; and he liked this tremendously, so that it was not really good for him.

"The great white father," he would say to them in a very lordly manner, as they grovelled at his feet, "is glad to see the Piccaninny warriors protecting his wigwam from the pirates."

"Me Tiger Lily," that lovely creature would reply. "Peter Pan save me, me his velly nice friend. Me no let pirates hurt him."

She was far too pretty to cringe in this way, but Peter thought it his due, and he would answer condescendingly, "It is good. Peter Pan has spoken."

Always when he said, "Peter Pan has spoken," it meant that they must now shut up, and they accepted it humbly in that spirit; but they were by no means so respectful to the other boys, whom they looked upon as just ordinary braves. They said "How-do?" to them, and things like that; and what annoyed the boys was that Peter seemed to think this all right.

Secretly Wendy sympathised with them a little, but she was far too loyal a housewife to listen to any complaints against father. "Father knows best," she always said, whatever her private opinion must be. Her private opinion was that the redskins should not call her a squaw.

We have now reached the evening that was to be known among them as the Night of Nights, because of its adventures and their upshot. The day, as if quietly gathering its forces, had been almost uneventful, and now the redskins in their blankets were at their posts above, while, below, the children were having their evening meal; all except Peter, who had gone out to get the time. The way you got the time on the island was to find the crocodile, and then stay near him till the clock struck.

The meal happened to be a make-believe tea, and they sat around the board, guzzling in their greed; and really, what with their chatter and recriminations, the noise, as Wendy said, was positively deafening. To be sure, she did not mind noise, but she simply would not have them grabbing things, and then excusing themselves by saying that Tootles had pushed their elbow. There was a fixed rule that they must never hit back at meals, but should refer the matter of dispute to Wendy by raising the right

arm politely and saying, "I complain of so-and-so;" but what usually happened was that they forgot to do this or did it too much.

"Silence," cried Wendy when for the twentieth time she had told them that they were not all to speak at once. "Is your mug empty, Slightly darling?"

"Not quite empty, mummy," Slightly said, after looking into an imaginary mug.

"He hasn't even begun to drink his milk," Nibs interposed.

This was telling, and Slightly seized his chance.

"I complain of Nibs," he cried promptly.

John, however, had held up his hand first.

"Well, John?"

"May I sit in Peter's chair, as he is not here?"

"Sit in father's chair, John!" Wendy was scandalised. "Certainly not."

"He is not really our father," John answered. "He didn't even know how a father does till I showed him."

This was grumbling. "We complain of John," cried the twins.

Tootles held up his hand. He was so much the humblest of them, indeed he was the only humble one, that Wendy was specially gentle with him.

"I don't suppose," Tootles said diffidently, "that I could be father."

"No, Tootles."

Once Tootles began, which was not very often, he had a silly way of going on.

"As I can't be father," he said heavily, "I don't suppose, Michael, you would let me be baby?"

"No, I won't," Michael rapped out. He was already in his basket.

"As I can't be baby," Tootles said, getting heavier and heavier and heavier, "do you think I could be a twin?"

"No, indeed," replied the twins; "it's awfully difficult to be a twin."

"As I can't be anything important," said Tootles, "would any of you like to see me do a trick?"

"No," they all replied.

Then at last he stopped. "I hadn't really any hope," he said.

The hateful telling broke out again.

"Slightly is coughing on the table."

"The twins began with mammee-apples."

"Curly is taking both tappa rolls and yams."

"Nibs is speaking with his mouth full."

"I complain of the twins."

"I complain of Curly."

"I complain of Nibs."

"Oh dear, oh dear," cried Wendy, "I'm sure I sometimes think that children are more trouble than they are worth."

She told them to clear away, and sat down to her work-basket, a heavy load of stockings and every knee with a hole in it as usual.

"Wendy," remonstrated Michael, "I'm too big for a cradle."

"I must have somebody in a cradle," she said almost tartly, "and you are the littlest. A cradle is such a nice homely thing to have about a house."

While she sewed they played around her; such a

group of happy faces and dancing limbs lit up by that romantic fire. It had become a very familiar scene, this, in the home under the ground, but we are looking on it for the last time.

There was a step above, and Wendy, you may be sure, was the first to recognize it.

"Children, I hear your father's step. He likes you to meet him at the door."

Above, the redskins crouched before Peter.

"Watch well, braves. I have spoken."

And then, as so often before, the gay children dragged him from his tree. As so often before, but never again.

He had brought nuts for the boys as well as the correct time for Wendy.

"Peter, you just spoil them, you know," Wendy simpered.

"Ah, old lady," said Peter, hanging up his gun.

"It was me told him mothers are called old lady," Michael whispered to Curly.

"I complain of Michael," said Curly instantly.

The first twin came to Peter. "Father, we want to dance."

"Dance away, my little man," said Peter, who was in high good humour.

"But we want you to dance."

Peter was really the best dancer among them, but he pretended to be scandalised.

"Me! My old bones would rattle!"

"And mummy too."

"What," cried Wendy, "the mother of such an armful, dance!"

"But on a Saturday night," Slightly insinuated.

It was not really Saturday night, at least it may have been, for they had long lost count of the days; but always if they wanted to do anything special they said this was Saturday night, and then they did it.

"Of course it is Saturday night, Peter," Wendy said, relenting.

"People of our figure, Wendy!"

"But it is only among our own progeny."

"True, true."

So they were told they could dance, but they must put on their nighties first.

"Ah, old lady," Peter said aside to Wendy, warming himself by the fire and looking down at her as she sat turning a heel, "there is nothing more pleasant of an evening for you and me when the day's toil is over than to rest by the fire with the little ones near by."

"It is sweet, Peter, isn't it?" Wendy said, frightfully gratified. "Peter, I think Curly has your nose."

"Michael takes after you."

She went to him and put her hand on his shoulder.

"Dear Peter," she said, "with such a large family, of course, I have now passed my best, but you don't want to change me, do you?"

"No, Wendy."

Certainly he did not want a change, but he looked at her uncomfortably, blinking, you know, like one not sure whether he was awake or asleep.

"Peter, what is it?"

"I was just thinking," he said, a little scared. "It is only make-believe, isn't it, that I am their father?"

"Oh yes," Wendy said primly.

"You see," he continued apologetically, "it would make me seem so old to be their real father."

"But they are ours, Peter, yours and mine."

"But not really, Wendy?" he asked anxiously.

"Not if you don't wish it," she replied; and she distinctly heard his sigh of relief. "Peter," she asked, trying to speak firmly, "what are your exact feelings to me?"

"Those of a devoted son, Wendy."

"I thought so," she said, and went and sat by herself at the extreme end of the room.

"You are so queer," he said, frankly puzzled, "and Tiger Lily is just the same. There is something she wants to be to me, but she says it is not my mother."

"No, indeed, it is not," Wendy replied with frightful emphasis. Now we know why she was prejudiced against the redskins.

"Then what is it?"

"It isn't for a lady to tell."

"Oh, very well," Peter said, a little nettled. "Perhaps Tinker Bell will tell me."

"Oh yes, Tinker Bell will tell you," Wendy retorted scornfully. "She is an abandoned little creature."

Here Tink, who was in her boudoir, eavesdropping, squeaked out something impudent.

"She says she glories in being abandoned," Peter interpreted.

He had a sudden idea. "Perhaps Tink wants to be my mother?"

"You silly ass!" cried Tinker Bell in a passion.

She had said it so often that Wendy needed no

translation.

"I almost agree with her," Wendy snapped. Fancy Wendy snapping! But she had been much tried, and she little knew what was to happen before the night was out. If she had known she would not have snapped.

None of them knew. Perhaps it was best not to know. Their ignorance gave them one more glad hour; and as it was to be their last hour on the island, let us rejoice that there were sixty glad minutes in it. They sang and danced in their night-gowns. Such a deliciously creepy song it was, in which they pretended to be frightened at their own shadows, little witting that so soon shadows would close in upon them, from whom they would shrink in real fear. So uproariously gay was the dance, and how they buffeted each other on the bed and out of it! It was a pillow fight rather than a dance, and when it was finished, the pillows insisted on one bout more, like partners who know that they may never meet again. The stories they told, before it was time for Wendy's good-night story! Even Slightly tried to tell a story that night, but the beginning was so fearfully dull that it appalled not only the others but himself, and he said gloomily:

"Yes, it is a dull beginning. I say, let us pretend that it is the end."

And then at last they all got into bed for Wendy's story, the story they loved best, the story Peter hated. Usually when she began to tell this story he left the room or put his hands over his ears; and possibly if he had done either of those things this time they might all still be on the island. But to-night he remained on his stool; and we shall see what happened.

Wendy's Story

Chapter 11

"Listen, then," said Wendy, settling down to her story, with Michael at her feet and seven boys in the bed. "There was once a gentleman—"

"I had rather he had been a lady," Curly said.

"I wish he had been a white rat," said Nibs.

"Quiet," their mother admonished them. "There was a lady also, and—"

"Oh, mummy," cried the first twin, "you mean that there is a lady also, don't you? She is not dead, is she?"

"Oh, no."

"I am awfully glad she isn't dead," said Tootles. "Are you glad, John?"

"Of course I am."

"Are you glad, Nibs?"

"Rather."

"Are you glad, Twins?"

"We are glad."

"Oh dear," sighed Wendy.

"Little less noise there," Peter called out, determined that she should have fair play, however beastly a story it might be in his opinion.

"The gentleman's name," Wendy continued, "was Mr.

Darling, and her name was Mrs. Darling."

"I knew them," John said, to annoy the others.

"I think I knew them," said Michael rather doubtfully.

"They were married, you know," explained Wendy, "and what do you think they had?"

"White rats," cried Nibs, inspired.

"No."

"It's awfully puzzling," said Tootles, who knew the story by heart.

"Quiet, Tootles. They had three descendants."

"What is descendants?"

"Well, you are one, Twin."

"Did you hear that, John? I am a descendant."

"Descendants are only children," said John.

"Oh dear, oh dear," sighed Wendy. "Now these three children had a faithful nurse called Nana; but Mr. Darling was angry with her and chained her up in the yard, and so all the children flew away."

"It's an awfully good story," said Nibs.

"They flew away," Wendy continued, "to the Neverland, where the lost children are."

"I just thought they did," Curly broke in excitedly. "I don't know how it is, but I just thought they did!"

"O Wendy," cried Tootles, "was one of the lost children called Tootles?"

"Yes, he was."

"I am in a story. Hurrah, I am in a story, Nibs."

"Hush. Now I want you to consider the feelings of the unhappy parents with all their children flown away."

"Oo!" they all moaned, though they were not really considering the feelings of the unhappy parents one jot.

"Think of the empty beds!"

"Oo!"

"It's awfully sad," the first twin said cheerfully.

"I don't see how it can have a happy ending," said the second twin. "Do you, Nibs?"

"I'm frightfully anxious."

"If you knew how great is a mother's love," Wendy told them triumphantly, "you would have no fear." She had now come to the part that Peter hated.

"I do like a mother's love," said Tootles, hitting Nibs with a pillow. "Do you like a mother's love, Nibs?"

"I do just," said Nibs, hitting back.

"You see," Wendy said complacently, "our heroine knew that the mother would always leave the window open for her children to fly back by; so they stayed away for years and had a lovely time."

"Did they ever go back?"

"Let us now," said Wendy, bracing herself up for her finest effort, "take a peep into the future;" and they all gave themselves the twist that makes peeps into the future easier. "Years have rolled by, and who is this elegant lady of uncertain age alighting at London Station?"

"O Wendy, who is she?" cried Nibs, every bit as excited as if he didn't know.

"Can it be—yes—no—it is—the fair Wendy!"

"Oh!"

"And who are the two noble portly figures accompanying her, now grown to man's estate? Can they be John and Michael? They are!"

"Oh!"

"'See, dear brothers,' says Wendy pointing upwards, 'there is the window still standing open. Ah, now we are rewarded for our sublime faith in a mother's love.' So up they flew to their mummy and daddy, and pen cannot describe the happy scene, over which we draw a veil."

That was the story, and they were as pleased with it as the fair narrator herself. Everything just as it should be, you see. Off we skip like the most heartless things in the world, which is what children are, but so attractive; and we have an entirely selfish time, and then when we have need of special attention we nobly return for it, confident that we shall be rewarded instead of smacked.

So great indeed was their faith in a mother's love that they felt they could afford to be callous for a bit longer.

But there was one there who knew better, and when Wendy finished he uttered a hollow groan.

"What is it, Peter?" she cried, running to him, thinking he was ill. She felt him solicitously, lower down than his chest. "Where is it, Peter?"

"It isn't that kind of pain," Peter replied darkly.

"Then what kind is it?"

"Wendy, you are wrong about mothers."

They all gathered round him in affright, so alarming was his agitation; and with a fine candour he told them what he had hitherto concealed.

"Long ago," he said, "I thought like you that my mother would always keep the window open for me, so I stayed away for moons and moons and moons, and then flew back; but the window was barred, for mother had forgotten all about me, and there was another little boy sleeping in my bed."

I am not sure that this was true, but Peter thought it was true; and it scared them.

"Are you sure mothers are like that?"

"Yes."

So this was the truth about mothers. The toads!

Still it is best to be careful; and no one knows so quickly as a child when he should give in. "Wendy, let us go home," cried John and Michael together.

"Yes," she said, clutching them.

"Not to-night?" asked the lost boys bewildered. They knew in what they called their hearts that one can get on quite well without a mother, and that it is only the mothers who think you can't.

"At once," Wendy replied resolutely, for the horrible thought had come to her: "Perhaps mother is in half mourning by this time."

This dread made her forgetful of what must be Peter's feelings, and she said to him rather sharply, "Peter, will you make the necessary arrangements?"

"If you wish it," he replied, as coolly as if she had asked him to pass the nuts.

Not so much as a sorry-to-lose-you between them! If she did not mind the parting, he was going to show her, was Peter, that neither did he.

But of course he cared very much; and he was so full of wrath against grown-ups, who, as usual, were spoiling everything, that as soon as he got inside his tree he breathed intentionally quick short breaths at the rate of about five to a second. He did this because there is a saying in the Neverland that, every time you breathe, a grown-up dies; and Peter was killing them off vindictively as fast as possible.

Then having given the necessary instructions to the redskins he returned to the home, where an unworthy scene had been enacted in his absence. Panic-stricken at the thought of losing Wendy the lost boys had advanced upon her threateningly.

"It will be worse than before she came," they cried.

"We shan't let her go."

"Let's keep her prisoner."

"Ay, chain her up."

In her extremity an instinct told her to which of them to turn.

"Tootles," she cried, "I appeal to you."

Was it not strange? She appealed to Tootles, quite the silliest one.

Grandly, however, did Tootles respond. For that one moment he dropped his silliness and spoke with dignity.

"I am just Tootles," he said, "and nobody minds me. But the first who does not behave to Wendy like an English gentleman I will blood him severely."

He drew back his hanger; and for that instant his sun was at noon. The others held back uneasily. Then Peter returned, and they saw at once that they would get no support from him. He would keep no girl in the Neverland against her will.

"Wendy," he said, striding up and down, "I have asked the redskins to guide you through the wood, as flying tires you so."

"Thank you, Peter."

"Then," he continued, in the short sharp voice of one accustomed to be obeyed, "Tinker Bell will take you across the sea. Wake her, Nibs."

Nibs had to knock twice before he got an answer, though Tink had really been sitting up in bed listening for some time.

"Who are you? How dare you? Go away," she cried.

"You are to get up, Tink," Nibs called, "and take Wendy on a journey."

Of course Tink had been delighted to hear that Wendy was going; but she was jolly well determined not to be her courier, and she said so in still more offensive language. Then she pretended to be asleep again.

"She says she won't!" Nibs exclaimed, aghast at such insubordination, whereupon Peter went sternly toward the young lady's chamber.

"Tink," he rapped out, "if you don't get up and dress at once I will open the curtains, and then we shall all see you in your negligee."

This made her leap to the floor. "Who said I wasn't getting up?" she cried.

In the meantime the boys were gazing very forlornly at Wendy, now equipped with John and Michael for the journey. By this time they were dejected, not merely because they were about to lose her, but also because they felt that she was going off to something nice to which they had not been invited. Novelty was beckoning to them as usual.

Crediting them with a nobler feeling Wendy melted.

"Dear ones," she said, "if you will all come with me I feel almost sure I can get my father and mother to adopt you."

The invitation was meant specially for Peter, but each

of the boys was thinking exclusively of himself, and at once they jumped with joy.

"But won't they think us rather a handful?" Nibs asked in the middle of his jump.

"Oh no," said Wendy, rapidly thinking it out, "it will only mean having a few beds in the drawing-room; they can be hidden behind the screens on first Thursdays."

"Peter, can we go?" they all cried imploringly. They took it for granted that if they went he would go also, but really they scarcely cared. Thus children are ever ready, when novelty knocks, to desert their dearest ones.

"All right," Peter replied with a bitter smile, and immediately they rushed to get their things.

"And now, Peter," Wendy said, thinking she had put everything right, "I am going to give you your medicine before you go." She loved to give them medicine, and undoubtedly gave them too much. Of course it was only water, but it was out of a bottle, and she always shook the bottle and counted the drops, which gave it a certain medicinal quality. On this occasion, however, she did not give Peter his draught, for just as she had prepared it, she saw a look on his face that made her heart sink.

"Get your things, Peter," she cried, shaking.

"No," he answered, pretending indifference, "I am not going with you, Wendy."

"Yes, Peter."

"No."

To show that her departure would leave him unmoved, he skipped up and down the room, playing gaily on his heartless pipes. She had to run about after him, though it was rather undignified.

"To find your mother," she coaxed.

Now, if Peter had ever quite had a mother, he no longer missed her. He could do very well without one. He had thought them out, and remembered only their bad points.

"No, no," he told Wendy decisively; "perhaps she would say I was old, and I just want always to be a little boy and to have fun."

"But, Peter—"

"No."

And so the others had to be told.

"Peter isn't coming."

Peter not coming! They gazed blankly at him, their sticks over their backs, and on each stick a bundle. Their first thought was that if Peter was not going he had probably changed his mind about letting them go.

But he was far too proud for that. "If you find your mothers," he said darkly, "I hope you will like them."

The awful cynicism of this made an uncomfortable impression, and most of them began to look rather doubtful. After all, their faces said, were they not noodles to want to go?

"Now then," cried Peter, "no fuss, no blubbering; good-bye, Wendy;" and he held out his hand cheerily, quite as if they must really go now, for he had something important to do.

She had to take his hand, and there was no indication that he would prefer a thimble.

"You will remember about changing your flannels, Peter?" she said, lingering over him. She was always so

particular about their flannels.

"Yes."

"And you will take your medicine?"

"Yes."

That seemed to be everything, and an awkward pause followed. Peter, however, was not the kind that breaks down before people. "Are you ready, Tinker Bell?" he called out.

"Ay, ay."

"Then lead the way."

Tink darted up the nearest tree; but no one followed her, for it was at this moment that the pirates made their dreadful attack upon the redskins. Above, where all had been so still, the air was rent with shrieks and the clash of steel. Below, there was dead silence. Mouths opened and remained open. Wendy fell on her knees, but her arms were extended toward Peter. All arms were extended to him, as if suddenly blown in his direction; they were beseeching him mutely not to desert them. As for Peter, he seized his sword, the same he thought he had slain Barbecue with, and the lust of battle was in his eye.

Chapter 12

The Children
Are Carried Off

The pirate attack had been a complete surprise: a sure proof that the unscrupulous Hook had conducted it improperly, for to surprise redskins fairly is beyond the wit of the white man.

By all the unwritten laws of savage warfare it is always the redskin who attacks, and with the wiliness of his race he does it just before the dawn, at which time he knows the courage of the whites to be at its lowest ebb. The white men have in the meantime made a rude stockade on the summit of yonder undulating ground, at the foot of which a stream runs, for it is destruction to be too far from water. There they await the onslaught, the inexperienced ones clutching their revolvers and treading on twigs, but the old hands sleeping tranquilly until just before the dawn.

Through the long black night the savage scouts wriggle, snake-like, among the grass without stirring a blade. The brushwood closes behind them, as silently as sand into which a mole has dived. Not a sound is to be heard, save when they give vent to a wonderful imitation of the lonely call of the coyote. The cry is answered by other braves; and some of them do it even better than the coyotes, who are not very good at it. So the chill hours wear on, and the long suspense is horribly trying to the paleface who has to live through it for the first time; but to the trained hand those ghastly calls and still ghastlier silences are but an intimation of how the night is marching.

That this was the usual procedure was so well known to Hook that in disregarding it he cannot be excused on the plea of ignorance.

The Piccaninnies, on their part, trusted implicitly to his honour, and their whole action of the night stands out in marked contrast to his. They left nothing undone that was consistent with the reputation of their tribe. With that alertness of the senses which is at once the marvel and despair of civilised peoples, they knew that the pirates were on the island from the moment one of them trod on a dry stick; and in an incredibly short space of time the coyote cries began.

Every foot of ground between the spot where Hook had landed his forces and the home under the trees was stealthily examined by braves wearing their mocassins with the heels in front. They found only one hillock with a stream at its base, so that Hook had no choice; here he must establish himself and wait for just before the dawn. Everything being thus mapped out with almost diabolical cunning, the main body of the redskins folded their blankets around them, and in the phlegmatic manner that is to them, the pearl of manhood squatted above the children's home, awaiting the cold moment when they should deal pale death.

Here dreaming, though wide-awake, of the exquisite

tortures to which they were to put him at break of day, those confiding savages were found by the treacherous Hook. From the accounts afterwards supplied by such of the scouts as escaped the carnage, he does not seem even to have paused at the rising ground, though it is certain that in that grey light he must have seen it: no thought of waiting to be attacked appears from first to last to have visited his subtle mind; he would not even hold off till the night was nearly spent; on he pounded with no policy but to fall to. What could the bewildered scouts do, masters as they were of every war-like artifice save this one, but trot helplessly after him, exposing themselves fatally to view, while they gave pathetic utterance to the coyote cry.

Around the brave Tiger Lily were a dozen of her stoutest warriors, and they suddenly saw the perfidious pirates bearing down upon them. Fell from their eyes then the film through which they had looked at victory. No more would they torture at the stake. For them the happy hunting-grounds was now. They knew it; but as their father's sons they acquitted themselves. Even then they had time to gather in a phalanx that would have been hard to break had they risen quickly, but this they were forbidden to do by the traditions of their race. It is written that the noble savage must never express surprise in the presence of the white. Thus terrible as the sudden appearance of the pirates must have been to them, they remained stationary for a moment, not a muscle moving; as if the foe had come by invitation. Then, indeed, the tradition gallantly upheld, they seized their weapons, and the air was torn with the war-cry; but it was now too late.

It is no part of ours to describe what was a massacre rather than a fight. Thus perished many of the flower of the Piccaninny tribe. Not all unavenged did they die, for with Lean Wolf fell Alf Mason, to disturb the Spanish Main no more, and among others who bit the dust were Geo. Scourie, Chas. Turley, and the Alsatian Foggerty. Turley fell to the tomahawk of the terrible Panther, who ultimately cut a way through the pirates with Tiger Lily and a small remnant of the tribe.

To what extent Hook is to blame for his tactics on this occasion is for the historian to decide. Had he waited on the rising ground till the proper hour he and his men would probably have been butchered; and in judging him it is only fair to take this into account. What he should perhaps have done was to acquaint his opponents that he proposed to follow a new method. On the other hand, this, as destroying the element of surprise, would have made his strategy of no avail, so that the whole question is beset with difficulties. One cannot at least withhold a reluctant admiration for the wit that had conceived so bold a scheme, and the fell genius with which it was carried out.

What were his own feelings about himself at that triumphant moment? Fain would his dogs have known, as breathing heavily and wiping their cutlasses, they gathered at a discreet distance from his hook, and squinted through their ferret eyes at this extraordinary man. Elation must have been in his heart, but his face did not reflect it: ever a dark and solitary enigma, he stood aloof from his followers in spirit as in substance.

The night's work was not yet over, for it was not the redskins he had come out to destroy; they were but the bees to be smoked, so that he should get at the honey. It was Pan he wanted, Pan and Wendy and their band, but chiefly Pan.

Peter was such a small boy that one tends to wonder at the man's hatred of him. True he had flung Hook's arm to the crocodile, but even this and the increased insecurity of life to which it led, owing to the crocodile's pertinacity, hardly account for a vindictiveness so relentless and malignant. The truth is that there was a something about Peter which goaded the pirate captain to frenzy. It was not his courage, it was not his engaging appearance, it was not—. There is no beating about the bush, for we know quite well what it was, and have got to tell. It was Peter's cockiness.

This had got on Hook's nerves; it made his iron claw twitch, and at night it disturbed him like an insect. While Peter lived, the tortured man felt that he was a lion in a cage into which a sparrow had come.

The question now was how to get down the trees, or how to get his dogs down? He ran his greedy eyes over them, searching for the thinnest ones. They wriggled uncomfortably, for they knew he would not scruple to ram them down with poles.

In the meantime, what of the boys? We have seen them at the first clang of the weapons, turned as it were into stone figures, open-mouthed, all appealing with outstretched arms to Peter; and we return to them as their mouths close, and their arms fall to their sides. The pandemonium above has ceased almost as suddenly as it arose, passed like a fierce gust of wind; but they know that in the passing it has determined their fate.

Which side had won?

The pirates, listening avidly at the mouths of the trees, heard the question put by every boy, and alas, they also heard Peter's answer.

"If the redskins have won," he said, "they will beat the tom-tom; it is always their sign of victory."

Now Smee had found the tom-tom, and was at that moment sitting on it. "You will never hear the tom-tom again," he muttered, but inaudibly of course, for strict silence had been enjoined. To his amazement Hook signed him to beat the tom-tom, and slowly there came to Smee an understanding of the dreadful wickedness of the order. Never, probably, had this simple man admired Hook so much.

Twice Smee beat upon the instrument, and then stopped to listen gleefully.

"The tom-tom," the miscreants heard Peter cry; "an Indian victory!"

The doomed children answered with a cheer that was music to the black hearts above, and almost immediately they repeated their good-byes to Peter. This puzzled the pirates, but all their other feelings were swallowed by a base delight that the enemy were about to come up the trees. They smirked at each other and rubbed their hands. Rapidly and silently Hook gave his orders: one man to each tree, and the others to arrange themselves in a line two yards apart.

Do You Believe in Fairies?

Chapter 13

The more quickly this horror is disposed of the better. The first to emerge from his tree was Curly. He rose out of it into the arms of Cecco, who flung him to Smee, who flung him to Starkey, who flung him to Bill Jukes, who flung him to Noodler, and so he was tossed from one to another till he fell at the feet of the black pirate. All the boys were plucked from their trees in this ruthless manner; and several of them were in the air at a time, like bales of goods flung from hand to hand.

A different treatment was accorded to Wendy, who came last. With ironical politeness Hook raised his hat to her, and, offering her his arm, escorted her to the spot where the others were being gagged. He did it with such an air, he was so frightfully *distingue*, that she was too fascinated to cry out. She was only a little girl.

Perhaps it is tell-tale to divulge that for a moment Hook entranced her, and we tell on her only because her slip led to strange results. Had she haughtily unhanded him (and we should have loved to write it of her), she would have been hurled through the air like the others, and then Hook would probably not have been present at the tying of the children; and had he not been at the

tying he would not have discovered Slightly's secret, and without the secret he could not presently have made his foul attempt on Peter's life.

They were tied to prevent their flying away, doubled up with their knees close to their ears; and for the trussing of them the black pirate had cut a rope into nine equal pieces. All went well until Slightly's turn came, when he was found to be like those irritating parcels that use up all the string in going round and leave no tags with which to tie a knot. The pirates kicked him in their rage, just as you kick the parcel (though in fairness you should kick the string); and strange to say it was Hook who told them to belay their violence. His lip was curled with malicious triumph.

While his dogs were merely sweating because every time they tried to pack the unhappy lad tight in one part he bulged out in another, Hook's master mind had gone far beneath Slightly's surface, probing not for effects but for causes; and his exultation showed that he had found them. Slightly, white to the gills, knew that Hook had surprised his secret, which was this, that no boy so blown out could use a tree wherein an average man need stick. Poor Slightly, most wretched of all the children now, for he was in a panic about Peter, bitterly regretted what he had done. Madly addicted to the drinking of water when he was hot, he had swelled in consequence to his present girth, and instead of reducing himself to fit his tree he had, unknown to the others, whittled his tree to make it fit him.

Sufficient of this Hook guessed to persuade him that Peter at last lay at his mercy, but no word of the dark design that now formed in the subterranean caverns of his mind crossed his lips; he merely signed that the captives were to be conveyed to the ship, and that he would be alone.

How to convey them? Hunched up in their ropes they might indeed be rolled down hill like barrels, but most of the way lay through a morass. Again Hook's genius surmounted difficulties. He indicated that the little house must be used as a conveyance. The children were flung into it, four stout pirates raised it on their shoulders, the others fell in behind, and singing the hateful pirate chorus the strange procession set off through the wood. I don't know whether any of the children were crying; if so, the singing drowned the sound; but as the little house disappeared in the forest, a brave though tiny jet of smoke issued from its chimney as if defying Hook.

Hook saw it, and it did Peter a bad service. It dried up any trickle of pity for him that may have remained in the pirate's infuriated breast.

The first thing he did on finding himself alone in the fast falling night was to tiptoe to Slightly's tree, and make sure that it provided him with a passage. Then for long he remained brooding; his hat of ill omen on the sward, so that any gentle breeze which had arisen might play refreshingly through his hair. Dark as were his thoughts his blue eyes were as soft as the periwinkle. Intently he listened for any sound from the nether world, but all was as silent below as above; the house under the ground seemed to be but one more empty tenement in the void. Was that boy asleep, or did

he stand waiting at the foot of Slightly's tree, with his dagger in his hand?

There was no way of knowing, save by going down. Hook let his cloak slip softly to the ground, and then biting his lips till a lewd blood stood on them, he stepped into the tree. He was a brave man, but for a moment he had to stop there and wipe his brow, which was dripping like a candle. Then, silently, he let himself go into the unknown.

He arrived unmolested at the foot of the shaft, and stood still again, biting at his breath, which had almost left him. As his eyes became accustomed to the dim light various objects in the home under the trees took shape; but the only one on which his greedy gaze rested, long sought for and found at last, was the great bed. On the bed lay Peter fast asleep.

Unaware of the tragedy being enacted above, Peter had continued, for a little time after the children left, to play gaily on his pipes: no doubt rather a forlorn attempt to prove to himself that he did not care. Then he decided not to take his medicine, so as to grieve Wendy. Then he lay down on the bed outside the coverlet, to vex her still more; for she had always tucked them inside it, because you never know that you may not grow chilly at the turn of the night. Then he nearly cried; but it struck him how indignant she would be if he laughed instead; so he laughed a haughty laugh and fell asleep in the middle of it.

Sometimes, though not often, he had dreams, and they were more painful than the dreams of other boys. For hours he could not be separated from these dreams, though he wailed piteously in them. They had to do, I think, with the riddle of his existence. At such times it had been Wendy's custom to take him out of bed and sit with him on her lap, soothing him in dear ways of her own invention, and when he grew calmer to put him back to bed before he quite woke up, so that he should not know of the indignity to which she had subjected him. But on this occasion he had fallen at once into a dreamless sleep. One arm dropped over the edge of the bed, one leg was arched, and the unfinished part of his laugh was stranded on his mouth, which was open, showing the little pearls.

Thus defenceless Hook found him. He stood silent at the foot of the tree looking across the chamber at his enemy. Did no feeling of compassion disturb his sombre breast? The man was not wholly evil; he loved flowers (I have been told) and sweet music (he was himself no mean performer on the harpsichord); and, let it be frankly admitted, the idyllic nature of the scene stirred him profoundly. Mastered by his better self he would have returned reluctantly up the tree, but for one thing.

What stayed him was Peter's impertinent appearance as he slept. The open mouth, the drooping arm, the arched knee: they were such a personification of cockiness as, taken together, will never again, one may hope, be presented to eyes so sensitive to their offensiveness. They steeled Hook's heart. If his rage had broken him into a hundred pieces every one of them would have disregarded the incident, and leapt at the sleeper.

Though a light from the one lamp shone dimly on the

bed, Hook stood in darkness himself, and at the first stealthy step forward he discovered an obstacle, the door of Slightly's tree. It did not entirely fill the aperture, and he had been looking over it. Feeling for the catch, he found to his fury that it was low down, beyond his reach. To his disordered brain it seemed then that the irritating quality in Peter's face and figure visibly increased, and he rattled the door and flung himself against it. Was his enemy to escape him after all?

But what was that? The red in his eye had caught sight of Peter's medicine standing on a ledge within easy reach. He fathomed what it was straightaway, and immediately knew that the sleeper was in his power.

Lest he should be taken alive, Hook always carried about his person a dreadful drug, blended by himself of all the death-dealing rings that had come into his possession. These he had boiled down into a yellow liquid quite unknown to science, which was probably the most virulent poison in existence.

Five drops of this he now added to Peter's cup. His hand shook, but it was in exultation rather than in shame. As he did it he avoided glancing at the sleeper, but not lest pity should unnerve him; merely to avoid spilling. Then one long gloating look he cast upon his victim, and turning, wormed his way with difficulty up the tree. As he emerged at the top he looked the very spirit of evil breaking from its hole. Donning his hat at its most rakish angle, he wound his cloak around him, holding one end in front as if to conceal his person from the night, of which it was the blackest part, and muttering strangely to himself, stole away through the trees.

Peter slept on. The light guttered and went out, leaving the tenement in darkness; but still he slept. It must have been not less than ten o'clock by the crocodile, when he suddenly sat up in his bed, wakened by he knew not what. It was a soft cautious tapping on the door of his tree.

Soft and cautious, but in that stillness it was sinister. Peter felt for his dagger till his hand gripped it. Then he spoke.

"Who is that?"

For long there was no answer: then again the knock.

"Who are you?"

No answer.

He was thrilled, and he loved being thrilled. In two strides he reached the door. Unlike Slightly's door, it filled the aperture, so that he could not see beyond it, nor could the one knocking see him.

"I won't open unless you speak," Peter cried.

Then at last the visitor spoke, in a lovely bell-like voice.

"Let me in, Peter."

It was Tink, and quickly he unbarred to her. She flew in excitedly, her face flushed and her dress stained with mud.

"What is it?"

"Oh, you could never guess!" she cried, and offered him three guesses. "Out with it!" he shouted, and in one ungrammatical sentence, as long as the ribbons that conjurers pull from their mouths, she told of the capture of Wendy and the boys.

Peter's heart bobbed up and down as he listened.

Wendy bound, and on the pirate ship; she who loved everything to be just so!

"I'll rescue her!" he cried, leaping at his weapons. As he leapt he thought of something he could do to please her. He could take his medicine.

His hand closed on the fatal draught.

"No!" shrieked Tinker Bell, who had heard Hook mutter about his deed as he sped through the forest.

"Why not?"

"It is poisoned."

"Poisoned? Who could have poisoned it?"

"Hook."

"Don't be silly. How could Hook have got down here?"

Alas, Tinker Bell could not explain this, for even she did not know the dark secret of Slightly's tree. Nevertheless Hook's words had left no room for doubt. The cup was poisoned.

"Besides," said Peter, quite believing himself, "I never fell asleep."

He raised the cup. No time for words now; time for deeds; and with one of her lightning movements Tink got between his lips and the draught, and drained it to the dregs.

"Why, Tink, how dare you drink my medicine?"

But she did not answer. Already she was reeling in the air.

"What is the matter with you?" cried Peter, suddenly afraid.

"It was poisoned, Peter," she told him softly; "and now I am going to be dead."

"O Tink, did you drink it to save me?"

"Yes."

"But why, Tink?"

Her wings would scarcely carry her now, but in reply she alighted on his shoulder and gave his chin a loving bite. She whispered in his ear "You silly ass," and then, tottering to her chamber, lay down on the bed.

His head almost filled the fourth wall of her little room as he knelt near her in distress. Every moment her light was growing fainter; and he knew that if it went out she would be no more. She liked his tears so much that she put out her beautiful finger and let them run over it.

Her voice was so low that at first he could not make out what she said. Then he made it out. She was saying that she thought she could get well again if children believed in fairies.

Peter flung out his arms. There were no children there, and it was night time; but he addressed all who might be dreaming of the Neverland, and who were therefore nearer to him than you think: boys and girls in their nighties, and naked papooses in their baskets hung from trees.

"Do you believe?" he cried.

Tink sat up in bed almost briskly to listen to her fate.

She fancied she heard answers in the affirmative, and then again she wasn't sure.

"What do you think?" she asked Peter.

"If you believe," he shouted to them, "clap your hands; don't let Tink die."

Many clapped.

Some didn't.

A few beasts hissed.

The clapping stopped suddenly; as if countless mothers had rushed to their nurseries to see what on earth was happening; but already Tink was saved. First her voice grew strong, then she popped out of bed, then she was flashing through the room more merry and impudent than ever. She never thought of thanking those who believed, but she would have liked to get at the ones who had hissed.

"And now to rescue Wendy!"

The moon was riding in a cloudy heaven when Peter rose from his tree, begirt with weapons and wearing little else, to set out upon his perilous quest. It was not such a night as he would have chosen. He had hoped to fly, keeping not far from the ground so that nothing unwonted should escape his eyes; but in that fitful light to have flown low would have meant trailing his shadow through the trees, thus disturbing birds and acquainting a watchful foe that he was astir.

He regretted now that he had given the birds of the island such strange names that they are very wild and difficult of approach.

There was no other course but to press forward in redskin fashion, at which happily he was an adept. But in what direction, for he could not be sure that the children had been taken to the ship? A light fall of snow had obliterated all footmarks; and a deathly silence pervaded the island, as if for a space Nature stood still in horror of the recent carnage. He had taught the children something of the forest lore that he had himself learned from Tiger Lily and Tinker Bell, and knew that in their dire hour they were not likely to forget it. Slightly, if he had an opportunity, would blaze the trees, for instance, Curly would drop seeds, and Wendy would leave her handkerchief at some important place. The morning was needed to search for such guidance, and he could not wait. The upper world had called him, but would give no help.

The crocodile passed him, but not another living thing, not a sound, not a movement; and yet he knew well that sudden death might be at the next tree, or stalking him from behind.

He swore this terrible oath: "Hook or me this time."

Now he crawled forward like a snake, and again erect, he darted across a space on which the moonlight played, one finger on his lip and his dagger at the ready. He was frightfully happy.

The Pirate Ship

Chapter 14

One green light squinting over Kidd's Creek, which is near the mouth of the pirate river, marked where the brig, the *Jolly Roger*, lay, low in the water; a rakish-looking craft foul to the hull, every beam in her detestable, like ground strewn with mangled feathers. She was the cannibal of the seas, and scarce needed that watchful eye, for she floated immune in the horror of her name.

She was wrapped in the blanket of night, through which no sound from her could have reached the shore. There was little sound, and none agreeable save the whir of the ship's sewing machine at which Smee sat, ever industrious and obliging, the essence of the commonplace, pathetic Smee. I know not why he was so infinitely pathetic, unless it were because he was so pathetically unaware of it; but even strong men had to turn hastily from looking at him, and more than once on summer evenings he had touched the fount of Hook's tears and made it flow. Of this, as of almost everything else, Smee was quite unconscious.

A few of the pirates leant over the bulwarks, drinking in the miasma of the night; others sprawled by barrels

over games of dice and cards; and the exhausted four who had carried the little house lay prone on the deck, where even in their sleep they rolled skillfully to this side or that out of Hook's reach, lest he should claw them mechanically in passing.

Hook trod the deck in thought. O man unfathomable. It was his hour of triumph. Peter had been removed for ever from his path, and all the other boys were in the brig, about to walk the plank. It was his grimmest deed since the days when he had brought Barbecue to heel; and knowing as we do how vain a tabernacle is man, could we be surprised had he now paced the deck unsteadily, bellied out by the winds of his success?

But there was no elation in his gait, which kept pace with the action of his sombre mind. Hook was profoundly dejected.

He was often thus when communing with himself on board ship in the quietude of the night. It was because he was so terribly alone. This inscrutable man never felt more alone than when surrounded by his dogs. They were socially inferior to him.

Hook was not his true name. To reveal who he really was would even at this date set the country in a blaze; but as those who read between the lines must already have guessed, he had been at a famous public school; and its traditions still clung to him like garments, with which indeed they are largely concerned. Thus it was offensive to him even now to board a ship in the same dress in which he grappled her, and he still adhered in his walk to the school's distinguished slouch. But above all he retained the passion for good form.

Good form! However much he may have degenerated, he still knew that this is all that really matters.

From far within him he heard a creaking as of rusty portals, and through them came a stern tap-tap-tap, like hammering in the night when one cannot sleep. "Have you been good form to-day?" was their eternal question.

"Fame, fame, that glittering bauble, it is mine," he cried.

"Is it quite good form to be distinguished at anything?" the tap-tap from his school replied.

"I am the only man whom Barbecue feared," he urged, "and Flint feared Barbecue."

"Barbecue, Flint—what house?" came the cutting retort.

Most disquieting reflection of all, was it not bad form to think about good form?

His vitals were tortured by this problem. It was a claw within him sharper than the iron one; and as it tore him, the perspiration dripped down his tallow countenance and streaked his doublet. Ofttimes he drew his sleeve across his face, but there was no damming that trickle.

Ah, envy not Hook.

There came to him a presentiment of his early dissolution. It was as if Peter's terrible oath had boarded the ship. Hook felt a gloomy desire to make his dying speech, lest presently there should be no time for it.

"Better for Hook," he cried, "if he had had less ambition!" It was in his darkest hours only that he referred to himself in the third person.

"No little children to love me!"

Strange that he should think of this, which had

never troubled him before; perhaps the sewing machine brought it to his mind. For long he muttered to himself, staring at Smee, who was hemming placidly, under the conviction that all children feared him.

Feared him! Feared Smee! There was not a child on board the brig that night who did not already love him. He had said horrid things to them and hit them with the palm of his hand, because he could not hit with his fist, but they had only clung to him the more. Michael had tried on his spectacles.

To tell poor Smee that they thought him lovable! Hook itched to do it, but it seemed too brutal. Instead, he revolved this mystery in his mind: why do they find Smee lovable? He pursued the problem like the sleuth-hound that he was. If Smee was lovable, what was it that made him so? A terrible answer suddenly presented itself—"Good form?"

Had the bo'sun good form without knowing it, which is the best form of all?

He remembered that you have to prove you don't know you have it before you are eligible for Pop.

With a cry of rage he raised his iron hand over Smee's head; but he did not tear. What arrested him was this reflection:

"To claw a man because he is good form, what would that be?"

"Bad form!"

The unhappy Hook was as impotent as he was damp, and he fell forward like a cut flower.

His dogs thinking him out of the way for a time, discipline instantly relaxed; and they broke into a

bacchanalian dance, which brought him to his feet at once, all traces of human weakness gone, as if a bucket of water had passed over him.

"Quiet, you scugs," he cried, "or I'll cast anchor in you;" and at once the din was hushed. "Are all the children chained, so that they cannot fly away?"

"Ay, ay."

"Then hoist them up."

The wretched prisoners were dragged from the hold, all except Wendy, and ranged in line in front of him. For a time he seemed unconscious of their presence. He lolled at his ease, humming, not unmelodiously, snatches of a rude song, and fingering a pack of cards. Ever and anon the light from his cigar gave a touch of colour to his face.

"Now then, bullies," he said briskly, "six of you walk the plank to-night, but I have room for two cabin boys. Which of you is it to be?"

"Don't irritate him unnecessarily," had been Wendy's instructions in the hold; so Tootles stepped forward politely. Tootles hated the idea of signing under such a man, but an instinct told him that it would be prudent to lay the responsibility on an absent person; and though a somewhat silly boy, he knew that mothers alone are always willing to be the buffer. All children know this about mothers, and despise them for it, but make constant use of it.

So Tootles explained prudently, "You see, sir, I don't think my mother would like me to be a pirate. Would your mother like you to be a pirate, Slightly?"

He winked at Slightly, who said mournfully, "I don't

think so," as if he wished things had been otherwise. "Would your mother like you to be a pirate, Twin?"

"I don't think so," said the first twin, as clever as the others. "Nibs, would—"

"Stow this gab," roared Hook, and the spokesmen were dragged back. "You, boy," he said, addressing John, "you look as if you had a little pluck in you. Didst never want to be a pirate, my hearty?"

Now John had sometimes experienced this hankering at maths. prep.; and he was struck by Hook's picking him out.

"I once thought of calling myself Red-handed Jack," he said diffidently.

"And a good name too. We'll call you that here, bully, if you join."

"What do you think, Michael?" asked John.

"What would you call me if I join?" Michael demanded.

"Blackbeard Joe."

Michael was naturally impressed. "What do you think, John?" He wanted John to decide, and John wanted him to decide.

"Shall we still be respectful subjects of the King?" John inquired.

Through Hook's teeth came the answer: "You would have to swear, 'Down with the King.'"

Perhaps John had not behaved very well so far, but he shone out now.

"Then I refuse," he cried, banging the barrel in front of Hook.

"And I refuse," cried Michael.

"Rule Britannia!" squeaked Curly.

The infuriated pirates buffeted them in the mouth; and Hook roared out, "That seals your doom. Bring up their mother. Get the plank ready."

They were only boys, and they went white as they saw Jukes and Cecco preparing the fatal plank. But they tried to look brave when Wendy was brought up.

No words of mine can tell you how Wendy despised those pirates. To the boys there was at least some glamour in the pirate calling; but all that she saw was that the ship had not been scrubbed for years. There was not a porthole on the grimy glass of which you might not have written with your finger "Dirty pig"; and she had already written it on several. But as the boys gathered round her she had no thought, of course, save for them.

"So, my beauty," said Hook, as if he spoke in syrup, "you are to see your children walk the plank."

Fine gentlemen though he was, the intensity of his communings had soiled his ruff, and suddenly he knew that she was gazing at it. With a hasty gesture he tried to hide it, but he was too late.

"Are they to die?" asked Wendy, with a look of such frightful contempt that he nearly fainted.

"They are," he snarled. "Silence all," he called gloatingly, "for a mother's last words to her children."

At this moment Wendy was grand. "These are my last words, dear boys," she said firmly. "I feel that I have a message to you from your real mothers, and it is this: 'We hope our sons will die like English gentlemen.'"

Even the pirates were awed, and Tootles cried out hysterically, "I am going to do what my mother hopes.

What are you to do, Nibs?"

"What my mother hopes. What are you to do, Twin?"

"What my mother hopes. John, what are—"

But Hook had found his voice again.

"Tie her up!" he shouted.

It was Smee who tied her to the mast. "See here, honey," he whispered, "I'll save you if you promise to be my mother."

But not even for Smee would she make such a promise. "I would almost rather have no children at all," she said disdainfully.

It is sad to know that not a boy was looking at her as Smee tied her to the mast; the eyes of all were on the plank: that last little walk they were about to take. They were no longer able to hope that they would walk it manfully, for the capacity to think had gone from them; they could stare and shiver only.

Hook smiled on them with his teeth closed, and took a step toward Wendy. His intention was to turn her face so that she should see the boys walking the plank one by one. But he never reached her, he never heard the cry of anguish he hoped to wring from her. He heard something else instead.

It was the terrible tick-tick of the crocodile.

They all heard it—pirates, boys, Wendy; and immediately every head was blown in one direction; not to the water whence the sound proceeded, but toward Hook. All knew that what was about to happen concerned him alone, and that from being actors they were suddenly become spectators.

Very frightful was it to see the change that came over

him. It was as if he had been clipped at every joint. He fell in a little heap.

The sound came steadily nearer; and in advance of it came this ghastly thought, "The crocodile is about to board the ship!"

Even the iron claw hung inactive; as if knowing that it was no intrinsic part of what the attacking force wanted. Left so fearfully alone, any other man would have lain with his eyes shut where he fell: but the gigantic brain of Hook was still working, and under its guidance he crawled on the knees along the deck as far from the sound as he could go. The pirates respectfully cleared a passage for him, and it was only when he brought up against the bulwarks that he spoke.

"Hide me!" he cried hoarsely.

They gathered round him, all eyes averted from the thing that was coming aboard. They had no thought of fighting it. It was Fate.

Only when Hook was hidden from them did curiosity loosen the limbs of the boys so that they could rush to the ship's side to see the crocodile climbing it. Then they got the strangest surprise of the Night of Nights; for it was no crocodile that was coming to their aid. It was Peter.

He signed to them not to give vent to any cry of admiration that might rouse suspicion. Then he went on ticking.

Chapter 15

"Hook or Me This Time"

Odd things happen to all of us on our way through life without our noticing for a time that they have happened. Thus, to take an instance, we suddenly discover that we have been deaf in one ear for we don't know how long, but, say, half an hour. Now such an experience had come that night to Peter. When last we saw him he was stealing across the island with one finger to his lips and his dagger at the ready. He had seen the crocodile pass by without noticing anything peculiar about it, but by and by he remembered that it had not been ticking. At first he thought this eerie, but soon concluded rightly that the clock had run down.

Without giving a thought to what might be the feelings of a fellow-creature thus abruptly deprived of its closest companion, Peter at once consider how he could turn the catastrophe to his own use; and he decided to tick, so that wild beasts should believe he was the crocodile and let him pass unmolested. He ticked superbly, but with one unforeseen result. The crocodile was among those who heard the sound, and it followed him, though whether with the purpose of regaining what it had lost, or merely as a friend under the belief that it was again ticking itself, will never be certainly known, for, like slaves to a fixed idea, it was a stupid beast.

Peter reached the shore without mishap, and went straight on, his legs encountering the water as if quite unaware that they had entered a new element. Thus many animals pass from land to water, but no other human of whom I know. As he swam he had but one thought: "Hook or me this time." He had ticked so long that he now went on ticking without knowing that he was doing it. Had he known he would have stopped, for to board the brig by help of the tick, though an ingenious idea, had not occurred to him.

On the contrary, he thought he had scaled her side as noiseless as a mouse; and he was amazed to see the pirates cowering from him, with Hook in their midst as abject as if he had heard the crocodile.

The crocodile! No sooner did Peter remember it than he heard the ticking. At first he thought the sound did come from the crocodile, and he looked behind him swiftly. Then he realised that he was doing it himself, and in a flash he understood the situation. "How clever of me!" he thought at once, and signed to the boys not to burst into applause.

It was at this moment that Ed Teynte the quarter-master emerged from the forecastle and came along the deck. Now, reader, time what happened by your watch. Peter struck true and deep. John clapped his hands on the ill-fated pirate's mouth to stifle the dying groan. He fell forward. Four boys caught him to prevent the thud. Peter gave the signal, and the carrion was cast overboard. There was a splash, and then silence. How long has it taken?

"One!" (Slightly had begun to count.)

None too soon, Peter, every inch of him on tiptoe, vanished into the cabin; for more than one pirate was screwing up his courage to look round. They could hear each other's distressed breathing now, which showed them that the more terrible sound had passed.

"It's gone, captain," Smee said, wiping off his spectacles. "All's still again."

Slowly Hook let his head emerge from his ruff, and listened so intently that he could have caught the echo of the tick. There was not a sound, and he drew himself up firmly to his full height.

"Then here's to Johnny Plank!" he cried brazenly, hating the boys more than ever because they had seen him unbend. He broke into the villainous ditty:

"Yo ho, yo ho, the frisky plank,
You walks along it so,
Till it goes down and you goes down
To Davy Jones below!"

To terrorize the prisoners the more, though with a certain loss of dignity, he danced along an imaginary plank, grimacing at them as he sang; and when he finished he cried, "Do you want a touch of the cat before you walk the plank?"

At that they fell on their knees. "No, no!" they cried so piteously that every pirate smiled.

"Fetch the cat, Jukes," said Hook; "it's in the cabin."

The cabin! Peter was in the cabin! The children gazed at each other.

"Ay, ay," said Jukes blithely, and he strode into the cabin. They followed him with their eyes; they scarce knew that Hook had resumed his song, his dogs joining in with him:

> *"Yo ho, yo ho, the scratching cat,*
> *Its tails are nine, you know,*
> *And when they're writ upon your back—"*

What was the last line will never be known, for of a sudden the song was stayed by a dreadful screech from the cabin. It wailed through the ship, and died away. Then was heard a crowing sound which was well understood by the boys, but to the pirates was almost more eerie than the screech.

"What was that?" cried Hook.

"Two," said Slightly solemnly.

The Italian Cecco hesitated for a moment and then swung into the cabin. He tottered out, haggard.

"What's the matter with Bill Jukes, you dog?" hissed Hook, towering over him.

"The matter wi' him is he's dead, stabbed," replied Cecco in a hollow voice.

"Bill Jukes dead!" cried the startled pirates.

"The cabin's as black as a pit," Cecco said, almost gibbering, "but there is something terrible in there: the thing you heard crowing."

The exultation of the boys, the lowering looks of the pirates, both were seen by Hook.

"Cecco," he said in his most steely voice, "go back and fetch me out that doodle-doo."

Cecco, bravest of the brave, cowered before his captain, crying "No, no"; but Hook was purring to his claw.

"Did you say you would go, Cecco?" he said musingly.

Cecco went, first flinging his arms despairingly. There was no more singing, all listened now; and again came a death-screech and again a crow.

No one spoke except Slightly. "Three," he said.

Hook rallied his dogs with a gesture. "'S'death and odds fish," he thundered, "who is to bring me that doodle-doo?"

"Wait till Cecco comes out," growled Starkey, and the others took up the cry.

"I think I heard you volunteer, Starkey," said Hook, purring again.

"No, by thunder!" Starkey cried.

"My hook thinks you did," said Hook, crossing to him. "I wonder if it would not be advisable, Starkey, to humour the hook?"

"I'll swing before I go in there," replied Starkey doggedly, and again he had the support of the crew.

"Is this mutiny?" asked Hook more pleasantly than ever. "Starkey's ringleader!"

"Captain, mercy!" Starkey whimpered, all of a tremble now.

"Shake hands, Starkey," said Hook, proffering his claw.

Starkey looked round for help, but all deserted him. As he backed up Hook advanced, and now the red spark was in his eye. With a despairing scream the pirate leapt upon Long Tom and precipitated himself into the sea.

"Four," said Slightly.

"And now," Hook said courteously, "did any other gentlemen say mutiny?" Seizing a lantern and raising his claw with a menacing gesture, "I'll bring out that doodle-doo myself," he said, and sped into the cabin.

"Five." How Slightly longed to say it. He wetted his lips to be ready, but Hook came staggering out, without his lantern.

"Something blew out the light," he said a little unsteadily.

"Something!" echoed Mullins.

"What of Cecco?" demanded Noodler.

"He's as dead as Jukes," said Hook shortly.

His reluctance to return to the cabin impressed them all unfavourably, and the mutinous sounds again broke forth. All pirates are superstitious, and Cookson cried, "They do say the surest sign a ship's accurst is when there's one on board more than can be accounted for."

"I've heard," muttered Mullins, "he always boards the pirate craft last. Had he a tail, captain?"

"They say," said another, looking viciously at Hook, "that when he comes it's in the likeness of the wickedest man aboard."

"Had he a hook, captain?" asked Cookson insolently; and one after another took up the cry, "The ship's doomed!" At this the children could not resist raising a cheer. Hook had well-nigh forgotten his prisoners, but as he swung round on them now his face lit up again.

"Lads," he cried to his crew, "now here's a notion.

Open the cabin door and drive them in. Let them fight the doodle-doo for their lives. If they kill him, we're so much the better; if he kills them, we're none the worse."

For the last time his dogs admired Hook, and devotedly they did his bidding. The boys, pretending to struggle, were pushed into the cabin and the door was closed on them.

"Now, listen!" cried Hook, and all listened. But not one dared to face the door. Yes, one, Wendy, who all this time had been bound to the mast. It was for neither a scream nor a crow that she was watching, it was for the reappearance of Peter.

She had not long to wait. In the cabin he had found the thing for which he had gone in search: the key that would free the children of their manacles, and now they all stole forth, armed with such weapons as they could find. First signing them to hide, Peter cut Wendy's bonds, and then nothing could have been easier than for them all to fly off together; but one thing barred the way, an oath, "Hook or me this time." So when he had freed Wendy, he whispered for her to conceal herself with the others, and himself took her place by the mast, her cloak around him so that he should pass for her. Then he took a great breath and crowed.

To the pirates it was a voice crying that all the boys lay slain in the cabin; and they were panic-stricken. Hook tried to hearten them; but like the dogs he had made them they showed him their fangs, and he knew that if he took his eyes off them now they would leap at him.

"Lads," he said, ready to cajole or strike as need be, but never quailing for an instant, "I've thought it out.

There's a Jonah aboard."

"Ay," they snarled, "a man wi' a hook."

"No, lads, no, it's the girl. Never was luck on a pirate ship wi' a woman on board. We'll right the ship when she's gone."

Some of them remembered that this had been a saying of Flint's. "It's worth trying," they said doubtfully.

"Fling the girl overboard," cried Hook; and they made a rush at the figure in the cloak.

"There's none can save you now, missy," Mullins hissed jeeringly.

"There's one," replied the figure.

"Who's that?"

"Peter Pan the avenger!" came the terrible answer; and as he spoke Peter flung off his cloak. Then they all knew who 'twas that had been undoing them in the cabin, and twice Hook essayed to speak and twice he failed. In that frightful moment I think his fierce heart broke.

At last he cried, "Cleave him to the brisket!" but without conviction.

"Down, boys, and at them!" Peter's voice rang out; and in another moment the clash of arms was resounding through the ship. Had the pirates kept together it is certain that they would have won; but the onset came when they were all unstrung, and they ran hither and thither, striking wildly, each thinking himself the last survivor of the crew. Man to man they were the stronger; but they fought on the defensive only, which enabled the boys to hunt in pairs and choose their quarry. Some of the miscreants leapt into the sea; others hid in dark recesses, where they were found by Slightly, who did not fight, but ran about with a lantern which he flashed in their faces, so that they were half blinded and fell as an easy prey to the reeking swords of the other boys. There was little sound to be heard but the clang of weapons, an occasional screech or splash, and Slightly monotonously counting—five—six—seven eight—nine—ten—eleven.

I think all were gone when a group of savage boys surrounded Hook, who seemed to have a charmed life, as he kept them at bay in that circle of fire. They had done for his dogs, but this man alone seemed to be a match for them all. Again and again they closed upon him, and again and again he hewed a clear space. He had lifted up one boy with his hook, and was using him as a buckler, when another, who had just passed his sword through Mullins, sprang into the fray.

"Put up your swords, boys," cried the newcomer, "this man is mine."

Thus suddenly Hook found himself face to face with Peter. The others drew back and formed a ring around them.

For long the two enemies looked at one another, Hook shuddering slightly, and Peter with the strange smile upon his face.

"So, Pan," said Hook at last, "this is all your doing."

"Ay, James Hook," came the stern answer, "it is all my doing."

"Proud and insolent youth," said Hook, "prepare to meet thy doom."

"Dark and sinister man," Peter answered, "have at thee."

Without more words they fell to, and for a space there was no advantage to either blade. Peter was a superb swordsman, and parried with dazzling rapidity; ever and anon he followed up a feint with a lunge that got past his foe's defence, but his shorter reach stood him in ill stead, and he could not drive the steel home. Hook, scarcely his inferior in brilliancy, but not quite so nimble in wrist play, forced him back by the weight of his onset, hoping suddenly to end all with a favourite thrust, taught him long ago by Barbecue at Rio; but to his astonishment he found this thrust turned aside again and again. Then he sought to close and give the quietus with his iron hook, which all this time had been

pawing the air; but Peter doubled under it and, lunging fiercely, pierced him in the ribs. At the sight of his own blood, whose peculiar colour, you remember, was offensive to him, the sword fell from Hook's hand, and he was at Peter's mercy.

"Now!" cried all the boys, but with a magnificent gesture Peter invited his opponent to pick up his sword. Hook did so instantly, but with a tragic feeling that Peter was showing good form.

Hitherto he had thought it was some fiend fighting him, but darker suspicions assailed him now.

"Pan, who and what art thou?" he cried huskily.

"I'm youth, I'm joy," Peter answered at a venture, "I'm a little bird that has broken out of the egg."

This, of course, was nonsense; but it was proof to the unhappy Hook that Peter did not know in the least who or what he was, which is the very pinnacle of good form.

"To't again," he cried despairingly.

He fought now like a human flail, and every sweep of that terrible sword would have severed in twain any man or boy who obstructed it; but Peter fluttered round him as if the very wind it made blew him out of the danger zone. And again and again he darted in and pricked.

Hook was fighting now without hope. That passionate breast no longer asked for life; but for one boon it craved: to see Peter show bad form before it was cold forever.

Abandoning the fight he rushed into the powder magazine and fired it.

"In two minutes," he cried, "the ship will be blown to pieces."

Now, now, he thought, true form will show.

But Peter issued from the powder magazine with the shell in his hands, and calmly flung it overboard.

What sort of form was Hook himself showing? Misguided man though he was, we may be glad, without sympathising with him, that in the end he was true to the traditions of his race. The other boys were flying around him now, flouting, scornful; and he staggered about the deck striking up at them impotently, his mind was no longer with them; it was slouching in the playing fields of long ago, or being sent up for good, or watching the wall-game from a famous wall. And his shoes were right, and his waistcoat was right, and his tie was right, and his socks were right.

James Hook, thou not wholly unheroic figure, farewell.

For we have come to his last moment.

Seeing Peter slowly advancing upon him through the air with dagger poised, he sprang upon the bulwarks to cast himself into the sea. He did not know that the crocodile was waiting for him; for we purposely stopped the clock that this knowledge might be spared him: a little mark of respect from us at the end.

He had one last triumph, which I think we need not grudge him. As he stood on the bulwark looking over his shoulder at Peter gliding through the air, he invited him with a gesture to use his foot. It made Peter kick instead of stab.

At last Hook had got the boon for which he craved.

"Bad form," he cried jeeringly, and went content to the crocodile.

Thus perished James Hook.

"Seventeen," Slightly sang out; but he was not quite correct in his figures. Fifteen paid the penalty for their crimes that night; but two reached the shore: Starkey to be captured by the redskins, who made him nurse for all their papooses, a melancholy come-down for a pirate; and Smee, who henceforth wandered about the world in his spectacles, making a precarious living by saying he was the only man that Jas. Hook had feared.

Wendy, of course, had stood by taking no part in the fight, though watching Peter with glistening eyes; but now that all was over she became prominent again. She praised them equally, and shuddered delightfully when Michael showed her the place where he had killed one; and then she took them into Hook's cabin and pointed to his watch which was hanging on a nail. It said "half-past one!"

The lateness of the hour was almost the biggest thing of all. She got them to bed in the pirates' bunks pretty quickly, you may be sure; all but Peter, who strutted up and down on the deck, until at last he fell asleep by the side of Long Tom. He had one of his dreams that night, and cried in his sleep for a long time, and Wendy held him tight.

The Return Home

Chapter 16

By three bells that morning they were all stirring their stumps; for there was a big sea running; and Tootles, the bo'sun, was among them, with a rope's end in his hand and chewing tobacco. They all donned pirate clothes cut off at the knee, shaved smartly, and tumbled up, with the true nautical roll and hitching their trousers.

It need not be said who was the captain. Nibs and John were first and second mate. There was a woman aboard. The rest were tars before the mast, and lived in the fo'c'sle. Peter had already lashed himself to the wheel; but he piped all hands and delivered a short address to them; said he hoped they would do their duty like gallant hearties, but that he knew they were the scum of Rio and the Gold Coast, and if they snapped at him he would tear them. The bluff strident words struck the note sailors understood, and they cheered him lustily. Then a few sharp orders were given, and they turned the ship round, and nosed her for the mainland.

Captain Pan calculated, after consulting the ship's chart, that if this weather lasted they should strike the Azores about the 21st of June, after which it would save

time to fly.

Some of them wanted it to be an honest ship and others were in favour of keeping it a pirate; but the captain treated them as dogs, and they dared not express their wishes to him even in a round robin. Instant obedience was the only safe thing. Slightly got a dozen for looking perplexed when told to take soundings. The general feeling was that Peter was honest just now to lull Wendy's suspicions, but that there might be a change when the new suit was ready, which, against her will, she was making for him out of some of Hook's wickedest garments. It was afterwards whispered among them that on the first night he wore this suit he sat long in the cabin with Hook's cigar-holder in his mouth and one hand clenched, all but for the forefinger, which he bent and held threateningly aloft like a hook.

Instead of watching the ship, however, we must now return to that desolate home from which three of our characters had taken heartless flight so long ago. It seems a shame to have neglected No. 14 all this time; and yet we may be sure that Mrs. Darling does not blame us. If we had returned sooner to look with sorrowful sympathy at her, she would probably have cried, "Don't be silly; what do I matter? Do go back and keep an eye on the children." So long as mothers are like this their children will take advantage of them; and they may lay to that.

Even now we venture into that familiar nursery only because its lawful occupants are on their way home; we are merely hurrying on in advance of them to see that their beds are properly aired and that Mr. and

Mrs. Darling do not go out for the evening. We are no more than servants. Why on earth should their beds be properly aired, seeing that they left them in such a thankless hurry? Would it not serve them jolly well right if they came back and found that their parents were spending the week-end in the country? It would be the moral lesson they have been in need of ever since we met them; but if we contrived things in this way Mrs. Darling would never forgive us.

One thing I should like to do immensely, and that is to tell her, in the way authors have, that the children are coming back, that indeed they will be here on Thursday week. This would spoil so completely the surprise to which Wendy and John and Michael are looking forward. They have been planning it out on the ship: mother's rapture, father's shout of joy, Nana's leap through the air to embrace them first, when what they ought to be prepared for is a good hiding. How delicious to spoil it all by breaking the news in advance; so that when they enter grandly Mrs. Darling may not even offer Wendy her mouth, and Mr. Darling may exclaim pettishly, "Dash it all, here are those boys again." However, we should get no thanks even for this. We are beginning to know Mrs. Darling by this time, and may be sure that she would upbraid us for depriving the children of their little pleasure.

"But, my dear madam, it is ten days till Thursday week; so that by telling you what's what, we can save you ten days of unhappiness."

"Yes, but at what a cost! By depriving the children of ten minutes of delight."

"Oh, if you look at it in that way!"

"What other way is there in which to look at it?"

You see, the woman had no proper spirit. I had meant to say extraordinarily nice things about her; but I despise her, and not one of them will I say now. She does not really need to be told to have things ready, for they are ready. All the beds are aired, and she never leaves the house, and observe, the window is open. For all the use we are to her, we might well go back to the ship. However, as we are here we may as well stay and look on. That is all we are, lookers-on. Nobody really wants us. So let us watch and say jaggy things, in the hope that some of them will hurt.

The only change to be seen in the night-nursery is that between nine and six the kennel is no longer there. When the children flew away, Mr. Darling felt in his bones that all the blame was his for having chained Nana up, and that from first to last she had been wiser than he. Of course, as we have seen, he was quite a simple man; indeed he might have passed for a boy again if he had been able to take his baldness off; but he had also a noble sense of justice and a lion's courage to do what seemed right to him; and having thought the matter out with anxious care after the flight of the children, he went down on all fours and crawled into the kennel. To all Mrs. Darling's dear invitations to him to come out he replied sadly but firmly:

"No, my own one, this is the place for me."

In the bitterness of his remorse he swore that he would never leave the kennel until his children came back. Of course this was a pity; but whatever Mr. Darling did he had to do in excess, otherwise he soon gave up doing it. And there never was a more humble man than the once proud George Darling, as he sat in the kennel of an evening talking with his wife of their children and all their pretty ways.

Very touching was his deference to Nana. He would not let her come into the kennel, but on all other matters he followed her wishes implicitly.

Every morning the kennel was carried with Mr. Darling in it to a cab, which conveyed him to his office, and he returned home in the same way at six. Something of the strength of character of the man will be seen if we remember how sensitive he was to the opinion of neighbours: this man whose every movement now attracted surprised attention. Inwardly he must have suffered torture; but he preserved a calm exterior even when the young criticised his little home, and he always lifted his hat courteously to any lady who looked inside.

It may have been Quixotic, but it was magnificent. Soon the inward meaning of it leaked out, and the great heart of the public was touched. Crowds followed the cab, cheering it lustily; charming girls scaled it to get his autograph; interviews appeared in the better class of papers, and society invited him to dinner and added, "Do come in the kennel."

On that eventful Thursday week, Mrs. Darling was in the night-nursery awaiting George's return home; a very sad-eyed woman. Now that we look at her closely and remember the gaiety of her in the old days, all gone now just because she has lost her babes, I find I won't be able to say nasty things about her after all. If she was too fond of her rubbishy children, she couldn't help it. Look at her in her chair, where she has fallen asleep. The corner of her mouth, where one looks first, is almost withered up. Her hand moves restlessly on her breast as if she had a pain there. Some like Peter best, and some like Wendy best, but I like her best. Suppose, to make her happy, we whisper to her in her sleep that the brats are coming back. They are really within two miles of the window now, and flying strong, but all we need whisper is that they are on the way. Let's.

It is a pity we did it, for she has started up, calling their names; and there is no one in the room but Nana.

"O Nana, I dreamt my dear ones had come back."

Nana had filmy eyes, but all she could do was put her paw gently on her mistress's lap; and they were sitting together thus when the kennel was brought back. As Mr. Darling puts his head out to kiss his wife, we see that his face is more worn than of yore, but has a softer expression.

He gave his hat to Liza, who took it scornfully; for she had no imagination, and was quite incapable of understanding the motives of such a man. Outside, the crowd who had accompanied the cab home were still cheering, and he was naturally not unmoved.

"Listen to them," he said; "it is very gratifying."

"Lots of little boys," sneered Liza.

"There were several adults to-day," he assured her with a faint flush; but when she tossed her head he had not a word of reproof for her. Social success had not spoilt him; it had made him sweeter. For some time he sat with his head out of the kennel, talking with

Mrs. Darling of this success, and pressing her hand reassuringly when she said she hoped his head would not be turned by it.

"But if I had been a weak man," he said. "Good heavens, if I had been a weak man!"

"And, George," she said timidly, "you are as full of remorse as ever, aren't you?"

"Full of remorse as ever, dearest! See my punishment: living in a kennel."

"But it is punishment, isn't it, George? You are sure you are not enjoying it?"

"My love!"

You may be sure she begged his pardon; and then, feeling drowsy, he curled round in the kennel.

"Won't you play me to sleep," he asked, "on the nursery piano?" and as she was crossing to the day-nursery he added thoughtlessly, "And shut that window. I feel a draught."

"O George, never ask me to do that. The window must always be left open for them, always, always."

Now it was his turn to beg her pardon; and she went into the day-nursery and played, and soon he was asleep; and while he slept, Wendy and John and Michael flew into the room.

Oh no. We have written it so, because that was the charming arrangement planned by them before we left the ship; but something must have happened since then, for it is not they who have flown in, it is Peter and Tinker Bell.

Peter's first words tell all.

"Quick Tink," he whispered, "close the window; bar it!

That's right. Now you and I must get away by the door; and when Wendy comes she will think her mother has barred her out; and she will have to go back with me."

Now I understand what had hitherto puzzled me, why when Peter had exterminated the pirates he did not return to the island and leave Tink to escort the children to the mainland. This trick had been in his head all the time.

Instead of feeling that he was behaving badly he danced with glee; then he peeped into the day-nursery to see who was playing. He whispered to Tink, "It's Wendy's mother! She is a pretty lady, but not so pretty as my mother. Her mouth is full of thimbles, but not so full as my mother's was."

Of course he knew nothing whatever about his mother; but he sometimes bragged about her.

He did not know the tune, which was "Home, Sweet Home," but he knew it was saying, "Come back, Wendy, Wendy, Wendy"; and he cried exultantly, "You will never see Wendy again, lady, for the window is barred!"

He peeped in again to see why the music had stopped, and now he saw that Mrs. Darling had laid her head on the box, and that two tears were sitting on her eyes.

"She wants me to unbar the window," thought Peter, "but I won't, not I!"

He peeped again, and the tears were still there, or another two had taken their place.

"She's awfully fond of Wendy," he said to himself. He was angry with her now for not seeing why she could not have Wendy.

The reason was so simple: "I'm fond of her too. We

can't both have her, lady."

But the lady would not make the best of it, and he was unhappy. He ceased to look at her, but even then she would not let go of him. He skipped about and made funny faces, but when he stopped it was just as if she were inside him, knocking.

"Oh, all right," he said at last, and gulped. Then he unbarred the window. "Come on, Tink," he cried, with a frightful sneer at the laws of nature; "we don't want any silly mothers;" and he flew away.

Thus Wendy and John and Michael found the window open for them after all, which of course was more than they deserved. They alighted on the floor, quite unashamed of themselves, and the youngest one had already forgotten his home.

"John," he said, looking around him doubtfully, "I think I have been here before."

"Of course you have, you silly. There is your old bed."

"So it is," Michael said, but not with much conviction.

"I say," cried John, "the kennel!" and he dashed across to look into it.

"Perhaps Nana is inside it," Wendy said.

But John whistled. "Hullo," he said, "there's a man inside it."

"It's father!" exclaimed Wendy.

"Let me see father," Michael begged eagerly, and he took a good look. "He is not so big as the pirate I killed," he said with such frank disappointment that I am glad Mr. Darling was asleep; it would have been sad if those had been the first words he heard his little Michael say.

Wendy and John had been taken aback somewhat at finding their father in the kennel.

"Surely," said John, like one who had lost faith in his memory, "he used not to sleep in the kennel?"

"John," Wendy said falteringly, "perhaps we don't remember the old life as well as we thought we did."

A chill fell upon them; and serve them right.

"It is very careless of mother," said that young scoundrel John, "not to be here when we come back."

It was then that Mrs. Darling began playing again.

"It's mother!" cried Wendy, peeping.

"So it is!" said John.

"Then are you not really our mother, Wendy?" asked Michael, who was surely sleepy.

"Oh dear!" exclaimed Wendy, with her first real twinge of remorse, "it was quite time we came back."

"Let us creep in," John suggested, "and put our hands over her eyes."

But Wendy, who saw that they must break the joyous news more gently, had a better plan.

"Let us all slip into our beds, and be there when she comes in, just as if we had never been away."

And so when Mrs. Darling went back to the night-nursery to see if her husband was asleep, all the beds were occupied. The children waited for her cry of joy, but it did not come. She saw them, but she did not believe they were there. You see, she saw them in their beds so often in her dreams that she thought this was just the dream hanging around her still.

She sat down in the chair by the fire, where in the old days she had nursed them.

They could not understand this, and a cold fear fell upon all the three of them.

"Mother!" Wendy cried.

"That's Wendy," she said, but still she was sure it was the dream.

"Mother!"

"That's John," she said.

"Mother!" cried Michael. He knew her now.

"That's Michael," she said, and she stretched out her arms for the three little selfish children they would never envelop again. Yes, they did, they went round Wendy and John and Michael, who had slipped out of bed and run to her.

"George, George!" she cried when she could speak; and Mr. Darling woke to share her bliss, and Nana came rushing in. There could not have been a lovelier sight; but there was none to see it except a little boy who was staring in at the window. He had had ecstasies innumerable that other children can never know; but he was looking through the window at the one joy from which he must be for ever barred.

When Wendy Grew Up

Chapter 17

I hope you want to know what became of the other boys. They were waiting below to give Wendy time to explain about them; and when they had counted five hundred they went up. They went up by the stair, because they thought this would make a better impression. They stood in a row in front of Mrs. Darling, with their hats off, and wishing they were not wearing their pirate clothes. They said nothing, but their eyes asked her to have them. They ought to have looked at Mr. Darling also, but they forgot about him.

Of course Mrs. Darling said at once that she would have them; but Mr. Darling was curiously depressed, and they saw that he considered six a rather large number.

"I must say," he said to Wendy, "that you don't do things by halves," a grudging remark which the twins thought was pointed at them.

The first twin was the proud one, and he asked, flushing, "Do you think we should be too much of a handful, sir? Because, if so, we can go away."

"Father!" Wendy cried, shocked; but still the cloud was on him. He knew he was behaving unworthily, but he could not help it.

"We could lie doubled up," said Nibs.

"I always cut their hair myself," said Wendy.

"George!" Mrs. Darling exclaimed, pained to see her dear one showing himself in such an unfavourable light.

Then he burst into tears, and the truth came out. He was as glad to have them as she was, he said, but he thought they should have asked his consent as well as hers, instead of treating him as a cypher in his own house.

"I don't think he is a cypher," Tootles cried instantly. "Do you think he is a cypher, Curly?"

"No, I don't. Do you think he is a cypher, Slightly?"

"Rather not. Twin, what do you think?"

It turned out that not one of them thought him a cypher; and he was absurdly gratified, and said he would find space for them all in the drawing-room if they fitted in.

"We'll fit in, sir," they assured him.

"Then follow the leader," he cried gaily. "Mind you, I am not sure that we have a drawing-room, but we pretend we have, and it's all the same. Hoop la!"

He went off dancing through the house, and they all cried "Hoop la!" and danced after him, searching for the drawing-room; and I forget whether they found it, but at any rate they found corners, and they all fitted in.

As for Peter, he saw Wendy once again before he flew away. He did not exactly come to the window, but he brushed against it in passing so that she could open it if she liked and call to him. That is what she did.

"Hullo, Wendy, good-bye," he said.

"Oh dear, are you going away?"

"Yes."

"You don't feel, Peter," she said falteringly, "that you would like to say anything to my parents about a very sweet subject?"

"No."

"About me, Peter?"

"No."

Mrs. Darling came to the window, for at present she was keeping a sharp eye on Wendy. She told Peter that she had adopted all the other boys, and would like to adopt him also.

"Would you send me to school?" he inquired craftily.

"Yes."

"And then to an office?"

"I suppose so."

"Soon I would be a man?"

"Very soon."

"I don't want to go to school and learn solemn things," he told her passionately. "I don't want to be a man. O Wendy's mother, if I was to wake up and feel there was a beard!"

"Peter," said Wendy the comforter, "I should love you in a beard;" and Mrs. Darling stretched out her arms to him, but he repulsed her.

"Keep back, lady, no one is going to catch me and make me a man."

"But where are you going to live?"

"With Tink in the house we built for Wendy. The fairies are to put it high up among the tree tops where they sleep at nights."

"How lovely," cried Wendy so longingly that Mrs.

Darling tightened her grip.

"I thought all the fairies were dead," Mrs. Darling said.

"There are always a lot of young ones," explained Wendy, who was now quite an authority, "because you see when a new baby laughs for the first time a new fairy is born, and as there are always new babies there are always new fairies. They live in nests on the tops of trees; and the mauve ones are boys and the white ones are girls, and the blue ones are just little sillies who are not sure what they are."

"I shall have such fun," said Peter, with eye on Wendy.

"It will be rather lonely in the evening," she said, "sitting by the fire."

"I shall have Tink."

"Tink can't go a twentieth part of the way round," she reminded him a little tartly.

"Sneaky tell-tale!" Tink called out from somewhere round the corner.

"It doesn't matter," Peter said.

"O Peter, you know it matters."

"Well, then, come with me to the little house."

"May I, mummy?"

"Certainly not. I have got you home again, and I mean to keep you."

"But he does so need a mother."

"So do you, my love."

"Oh, all right," Peter said, as if he had asked her from politeness merely; but Mrs. Darling saw his mouth twitch, and she made this handsome offer: to let Wendy go to him for a week every year to do his

spring cleaning. Wendy would have preferred a more permanent arrangement; and it seemed to her that spring would be long in coming; but this promise sent Peter away quite gay again. He had no sense of time, and was so full of adventures that all I have told you about him is only a halfpenny-worth of them. I suppose it was because Wendy knew this that her last words to him were these rather plaintive ones:

"You won't forget me, Peter, will you, before spring cleaning time comes?"

Of course Peter promised; and then he flew away. He took Mrs. Darling's kiss with him. The kiss that had been for no one else, Peter took quite easily. Funny. But she seemed satisfied.

Of course all the boys went to school; and most of them got into Class III, but Slightly was put first into Class IV and then into Class V. Class I is the top class. Before they had attended school a week they saw what goats they had been not to remain on the island; but it was too late now, and soon they settled down to being as ordinary as you or me or Jenkins minor. It is sad to have to say that the power to fly gradually left them. At first Nana tied their feet to the bed-posts so that they should not fly away in the night; and one of their diversions by day was to pretend to fall off buses; but by and by they ceased to tug at their bonds in bed, and found that they hurt themselves when they let go of the bus. In time they could not even fly after their hats. Want of practice, they called it; but what it really meant was that they no longer believed.

Michael believed longer than the other boys, though

they jeered at him; so he was with Wendy when Peter came for her at the end of the first year. She flew away with Peter in the frock she had woven from leaves and berries in the Neverland, and her one fear was that he might notice how short it had become; but he never noticed, he had so much to say about himself.

She had looked forward to thrilling talks with him about old times, but new adventures had crowded the old ones from his mind.

"Who is Captain Hook?" he asked with interest when she spoke of the arch enemy.

"Don't you remember," she asked, amazed, "how you killed him and saved all our lives?"

"I forget them after I kill them," he replied carelessly.

When she expressed a doubtful hope that Tinker Bell would be glad to see her he said, "Who is Tinker Bell?"

"O Peter," she said, shocked; but even when she explained he could not remember.

"There are such a lot of them," he said. "I expect she is no more."

I expect he was right, for fairies don't live long, but they are so little that a short time seems a good while to them.

Wendy was pained too to find that the past year was but as yesterday to Peter; it had seemed such a long year of waiting to her. But he was exactly as fascinating as ever, and they had a lovely spring cleaning in the little house on the tree tops.

Next year he did not come for her. She waited in a new frock because the old one simply would not meet; but he never came.

"Perhaps he is ill," Michael said.

"You know he is never ill."

Michael came close to her and whispered, with a shiver, "Perhaps there is no such person, Wendy!" and then Wendy would have cried if Michael had not been crying.

Peter came next spring cleaning; and the strange thing was that he never knew he had missed a year.

That was the last time the girl Wendy ever saw him. For a little longer she tried for his sake not to have growing pains; and she felt she was untrue to him when she got a prize for general knowledge. But the years came and went without bringing the careless boy; and when they met again Wendy was a married woman, and Peter was no more to her than a little dust in the box in which she had kept her toys. Wendy was grown up. You need not be sorry for her. She was one of the kind that likes to grow up. In the end she grew up of her own free will a day quicker than other girls.

All the boys were grown up and done for by this time; so it is scarcely worth while saying anything more about them. You may see the twins and Nibs and Curly any day going to an office, each carrying a little bag and an umbrella. Michael is an engine-driver. Slightly married a lady of title, and so he became a lord. You see that judge in a wig coming out at the iron door? That used to be Tootles. The bearded man who doesn't know any story to tell his children was once John.

Wendy was married in white with a pink sash. It is strange to think that Peter did not alight in the church and forbid the banns.

Years rolled on again, and Wendy had a daughter. This ought not to be written in ink but in a golden splash.

She was called Jane, and always had an odd inquiring look, as if from the moment she arrived on the mainland she wanted to ask questions. When she was old enough to ask them they were mostly about Peter Pan. She loved to hear of Peter, and Wendy told her all she could remember in the very nursery from which the famous flight had taken place. It was Jane's nursery now, for her father had bought it at the three per cents from Wendy's father, who was no longer fond of stairs. Mrs. Darling was now dead and forgotten.

There were only two beds in the nursery now, Jane's and her nurse's; and there was no kennel, for Nana also had passed away. She died of old age, and at the end she had been rather difficult to get on with; being very firmly convinced that no one knew how to look after children except herself.

Once a week Jane's nurse had her evening off; and then it was Wendy's part to put Jane to bed. That was the time for stories. It was Jane's invention to raise the sheet over her mother's head and her own, thus making a tent, and in the awful darkness to whisper:

"What do we see now?"

"I don't think I see anything to-night," says Wendy, with a feeling that if Nana were here she would object to further conversation.

"Yes, you do," says Jane, "you see when you were a little girl."

"That is a long time ago, sweetheart," says Wendy. "Ah

me, how time flies!"

"Does it fly," asks the artful child, "the way you flew when you were a little girl?"

"The way I flew? Do you know, Jane, I sometimes wonder whether I ever did really fly."

"Yes, you did."

"The dear old days when I could fly!"

"Why can't you fly now, mother?"

"Because I am grown up, dearest. When people grow up they forget the way."

"Why do they forget the way?"

"Because they are no longer gay and innocent and heartless. It is only the gay and innocent and heartless who can fly."

"What is gay and innocent and heartless? I do wish I were gay and innocent and heartless."

Or perhaps Wendy admits she does see something.

"I do believe," she says, "that it is this nursery."

"I do believe it is," says Jane. "Go on."

They are now embarked on the great adventure of the night when Peter flew in looking for his shadow.

"The foolish fellow," says Wendy, "tried to stick it on with soap, and when he could not he cried, and that woke me, and I sewed it on for him."

"You have missed a bit," interrupts Jane, who now knows the story better than her mother. "When you saw him sitting on the floor crying, what did you say?"

"I sat up in bed and I said, 'Boy, why are you crying?'"

"Yes, that was it," says Jane, with a big breath.

"And then he flew us all away to the Neverland and the fairies and the pirates and the redskins and the mermaids' lagoon, and the home under the ground, and the little house."

"Yes! which did you like best of all?"

"I think I liked the home under the ground best of all."

"Yes, so do I. What was the last thing Peter ever said to you?"

"The last thing he ever said to me was, 'Just always be waiting for me, and then some night you will hear me crowing.'"

"Yes."

"But, alas, he forgot all about me," Wendy said it with a smile. She was as grown up as that.

"What did his crow sound like?" Jane asked one evening.

"It was like this," Wendy said, trying to imitate Peter's crow.

"No, it wasn't," Jane said gravely, "it was like this;" and she did it ever so much better than her mother.

Wendy was a little startled. "My darling, how can you know?"

"I often hear it when I am sleeping," Jane said.

"Ah yes, many girls hear it when they are sleeping, but I was the only one who heard it awake."

"Lucky you," said Jane.

And then one night came the tragedy. It was the spring of the year, and the story had been told for the night, and Jane was now asleep in her bed. Wendy was sitting on the floor, very close to the fire, so as to see to darn, for there was no other light in the nursery; and while she sat darning she heard a crow. Then the window blew open as of old, and Peter dropped in on the floor.

He was exactly the same as ever, and Wendy saw at once that he still had all his first teeth.

He was a little boy, and she was grown up. She huddled by the fire not daring to move, helpless and guilty, a big woman.

"Hullo, Wendy," he said, not noticing any difference, for he was thinking chiefly of himself; and in the dim light her white dress might have been the nightgown in which he had seen her first.

"Hullo, Peter," she replied faintly, squeezing herself as small as possible. Something inside her was crying "Woman, Woman, let go of me."

"Hullo, where is John?" he asked, suddenly missing the third bed.

"John is not here now," she gasped.

"Is Michael asleep?" he asked, with a careless glance at Jane.

"Yes," she answered; and now she felt that she was untrue to Jane as well as to Peter.

"That is not Michael," she said quickly, lest a judgment should fall on her.

Peter looked. "Hullo, is it a new one?"

"Yes."

"Boy or girl?"

"Girl."

Now surely he would understand; but not a bit of it.

"Peter," she said, faltering, "are you expecting me to fly away with you?"

"Of course; that is why I have come." He added a little

sternly, "Have you forgotten that this is spring cleaning time?"

She knew it was useless to say that he had let many spring cleaning times pass.

"I can't come," she said apologetically, "I have forgotten how to fly."

"I'll soon teach you again."

"O Peter, don't waste the fairy dust on me."

She had risen; and now at last a fear assailed him. "What is it?" he cried, shrinking.

"I will turn up the light," she said, "and then you can see for yourself."

For almost the only time in his life that I know of, Peter was afraid. "Don't turn up the light," he cried.

She let her hands play in the hair of the tragic boy. She was not a little girl heart-broken about him; she was a grown woman smiling at it all, but they were wet-eyed smiles.

Then she turned up the light, and Peter saw. He gave a cry of pain; and when the tall beautiful creature stooped to lift him in her arms he drew back sharply.

"What is it?" he cried again.

She had to tell him.

"I am old, Peter. I am ever so much more than twenty. I grew up long ago."

"You promised not to!"

"I couldn't help it. I am a married woman, Peter."

"No, you're not."

"Yes, and the little girl in the bed is my baby."

"No, she's not."

But he supposed she was; and he took a step towards

the sleeping child with his dagger upraised. Of course he did not strike. He sat down on the floor instead and sobbed; and Wendy did not know how to comfort him, though she could have done it so easily once. She was only a woman now, and she ran out of the room to try to think.

Peter continued to cry, and soon his sobs woke Jane. She sat up in bed, and was interested at once.

"Boy," she said, "why are you crying?"

Peter rose and bowed to her, and she bowed to him from the bed.

"Hullo," he said.

"Hullo," said Jane.

"My name is Peter Pan," he told her.

"Yes, I know."

"I came back for my mother," he explained, "to take her to the Neverland."

"Yes, I know," Jane said, "I have been waiting for you."

When Wendy returned diffidently she found Peter sitting on the bed-post crowing gloriously, while Jane in her nighty was flying round the room in solemn ecstasy.

"She is my mother," Peter explained; and Jane descended and stood by his side, with the look in her face that he liked to see on ladies when they gazed at him.

"He does so need a mother," Jane said.

"Yes, I know," Wendy admitted rather forlornly; "no one knows it so well as I."

"Good-bye," said Peter to Wendy; and he rose in the air, and the shameless Jane rose with him; it was already her easiest way of moving about.

Wendy rushed to the window.

"No, no," she cried.

"It is just for spring cleaning time," Jane said, "he wants me always to do his spring cleaning."

"If only I could go with you," Wendy sighed.

"You see you can't fly," said Jane.

Of course in the end Wendy let them fly away together. Our last glimpse of her shows her at the window, watching them receding into the sky until they were as small as stars.

As you look at Wendy, you may see her hair becoming white, and her figure little again, for all this happened long ago. Jane is now a common grown-up, with a daughter called Margaret; and every spring cleaning time, except when he forgets, Peter comes for Margaret and takes her to the Neverland, where she tells him stories about himself, to which he listens eagerly. When Margaret grows up she will have a daughter, who is to be Peter's mother in turn; and thus it will go on, so long as children are gay and innocent and heartless.

彼得潘

彼得・潘登場

Chapter 1

每個孩子都要長大，只有一個例外。他們很快就會知道自己即將長大成人，而溫蒂知道的過程是這樣的：在兩歲時的某一天，她在花園裡玩，摘了一朵花，握在手裡向媽媽跑去。我想她當時的模樣一定非常可愛，因為達林太太手按著胸口，說道：「要是妳永遠長不大該多好啊！」這就是事情的經過，自此以後，溫蒂就明白她總有一天會長大，每個人一到兩歲就知道了，兩歲，是終點也是起點。

是的，他們一家住在十四號，在溫蒂來到世上以前，媽媽是家裡的靈魂人物。過去，她是位美麗動人的小姐，腦子裡裝著不切實際的幻想，還有一張甜甜的、喜歡逗弄人的嘴。她那愛做夢的腦袋，就像那些來自神祕東方的盒子，一個套著一個，無論你打開多少，裡面總還藏有另一個，而她那張甜甜的、逗弄人的嘴，有著溫蒂一直得不到的吻，即使它就掛在右邊的嘴角上。

達林先生當初是這樣贏得她芳心的：許多與她年紀相當的男生，長大以後，同時發現自己愛上了她，想要用跑的到她家去向她求婚。但達林先生用的方法不同，他搭著馬車搶先來到她家，贏得了她的芳心。他擁有了全部的她，除了她心底深處的神祕盒子和親吻。他從不知道有盒子存在，而她的吻，他後來也就索性不想了。溫蒂想過，要是拿破崙或許還能得到那個吻，但是我能想像他費盡心思，最後卻怒氣沖沖地甩門而去的模樣。

達林先生過去常對溫蒂誇口，說她媽媽不但愛他，更是敬重他。他是屬於有深度的那種人，懂得股票、債券這些東西。這些事沒人真正了解，不過達林先生看似挺在行的。他常說哪支股票會上漲，哪支會下跌，那種講話的神情，好像哪個女人都會拜倒似的。

達林太太穿著一襲白禮服嫁了出去。新婚時，她會仔細地記帳，也做得很開心，就像玩遊戲一樣，連一根甘藍菜芽都不漏記。但漸漸地，她連一整顆花椰菜都漏掉了，反而在該記帳的地方，畫了一些沒有臉孔的娃娃，算計著這些嬰兒就快來報到了。

第一個出生的是溫蒂，接著是約翰，再來是麥可。

溫蒂出生後的一兩個星期，父母親不知道能不能養活她，因為又多了張嘴等著吃飯。達林先生頗為自豪有了溫蒂這個女兒，但他是個務實的人，他坐在達林太太的床沿，握著她的手，計算起開支。達林太太神情哀求地望著他，她無論如何都想放手一搏。但這不是達林先生的作風，他的做法是拿出一支筆和一張紙在那邊打算盤，只要達林太太一提出意見打亂他，他就又得從頭算起。

「好了，別打斷我。」他央求她。「我這裡有一鎊十七先令，公司還有兩先令六便士。公司的咖啡也就不要喝了，當十先令來算，就有兩鎊九先令六便士，加上你的十八先令三便士，合計三鎊九先令七便士，我的存摺上還有五鎊，總共八鎊九先令七便士……是誰在那兒動？八……九……七，小數點進位七……先別說話，我的錢，加上你借出去的一磅……安靜點，孩子……小數點進位，瞧，你又把我搞亂了……我剛才是說九磅九先令七便士嗎？沒錯，就是這樣，問題是，我們靠這點錢能不能撐個一年？」

「沒問題的啦，喬治。」達林太太嚷道，她當然是偏袒溫蒂的，但達林先生比她更有能耐。

「別忘了還有腮腺炎。」達林先生語帶威脅，接著算下去，「腮腺炎算一鎊，不過我敢說，可能要花三十先令才夠呢……先別說話……麻疹會花個一鎊五先令，德國麻疹半個基尼，加起來是兩鎊十五先令六便士……妳手指頭不要動來動去的……百日咳，算十五先令。」他就這樣不停地盤算，每回算出來的結果都不一樣。不過最後溫蒂也總算熬了過來，腮腺炎只花了十二先令六便士，再把兩種麻疹一次處理掉。

約翰出生時也遇到同樣的風波，麥可的情況更為驚險，不過他們兩個到底還是活了下來。沒多久，就看見三姐弟排成一列，在褓母陪伴下，到福桑小姐的幼稚園上學去了。

達林太太很滿足於現在的生活，不過達林先生喜歡事事向鄰居看齊，所以理所當然也要請一位褓母。由於達林家並不富有，孩子們喝牛奶的量又大，就雇了一隻個性拘謹、名字叫娜娜的紐芬蘭大狗來當褓母。在達林夫婦雇用娜娜以前，娜娜沒有主人，不過她一直把孩子看得很重要。達林一家是在肯辛頓公園裡遇見她的，她過去老愛在那兒消磨時光，盯著嬰兒車瞧，惹得那些粗心大意的褓母們十分厭惡，因為她老是跟著她們回家，向她們的主人告起狀來。事實證明，她的確是不可多得的好幫手，在幫孩子洗澡時，她絕不遺漏任何細節；而無論多晚，即使孩子發出最細微的哭聲，她都會一躍而起。她當然就住在育兒室裡。

她有種獨特的天分，知道哪種咳嗽是要立刻處理，哪種只需要用長襪圍著脖子保暖。她只相信傳統的藥物治療，像是大黃葉子之類的，聽到類似細菌的新名詞，便不屑地哼了一聲。她護送孩子們去上學時，看起來就像在上禮儀課：孩子們規規矩矩走路，她靜靜跟在一旁。要是他們閒晃脫離隊伍，她就把他們推進行列。約翰踢足球的那幾天，她從沒忘記帶上他的毛衣，嘴裡叼著一把傘，好未雨綢繆。福桑幼稚園的地下室，是褓母等候孩子們的地方。別的褓母們會坐在長凳上，而娜娜則趴在地板上，這是她和其他人唯一不同之處。不過其他褓母會刻意忽略娜娜，認為她的地位卑賤，但娜娜也瞧不起她們有的沒的閒聊。她痛恨達林太太的朋友來育兒室探訪，不過如果他們真的來了，她會脫下麥可的圍兜，換上有藍色緞帶的那一件，再弄平溫蒂的衣服，並迅速梳理約翰的頭髮。

沒有誰在育兒室會做得比她更有條理了，這一點達林先生也不是不知道，不過他有時仍會不安地擔心鄰居會不會在背後竊竊私語。

　　他得顧及他在城裡的地位。

　　娜娜還在其他方面對他造成困擾，有時候他感覺娜娜不怎麼尊敬他。達林太太向他擔保：「我知道她可是對你敬佩得很呢，喬治。」她暗示孩子們要對父親好一點，說完就輕盈地跳起舞來。他們唯一的另一位女僕莉莎，有時也獲准加入舞蹈。她穿著長裙，戴著女僕帽，顯得異常矮小，儘管她在受聘時發誓自己絕對超過十歲。大夥兒興高采烈，好不快樂呀！最愉快的要算是達林太太了，她恣意地旋轉著，而你眼裡只有她那個吻，似乎只要此刻你飛奔過去，定能得到那一吻。再也沒有人比他們家更單純、快樂的了，直到彼得‧潘的出現。

　　達林太太頭次聽到彼得這個名字，是她為孩子們整理思緒時。要當好媽媽，就該在孩子睡著後仔細檢查他們腦中的思緒，看看有什麼東西在白天被擺錯了位置，再將它們回歸原位，為第二天做準備。倘若你可以保持清醒的話（當然這你是做不到啦），就會看見你媽媽在做這事，而且你會發現看她做事好有趣哦，就像在整理抽屜一樣。我猜，你會瞧見她跪在那兒，饒富興味地檢視每樣東西，納悶你是在哪兒找到的，瞧出哪些是有趣的，哪些又不是那麼有趣的，把它們像溫馴的小貓咪般地靠在臉頰上，然後草草收起來不讓人看見。你一早醒來，臨睡前那些頑皮的心思和壞念頭都被折疊成小小的，放在思緒的最底層。而在最上頭則整整齊齊地放著你那些美好的念頭，等著你去使用。

　　不曉得你是否見過人的心智地圖？醫生有時會畫你身體其他部分的地圖，而你自己的地圖總是看起來格外有趣的。不過，要是你碰巧瞧見他們畫起小孩的心智地圖，你會發現，那不只是雜亂無章，還一直在繞圈圈呢。這無數曲曲折折像體溫表的線條，就該是夢幻島上的道路了。因為夢幻島多少可說是個海島，海上有珊瑚礁，漂著一葉葉輕舟。島上處處撒著奇異的色彩，住著野蠻人；有荒涼的洞穴；有多半是裁縫師的矮人；也有河流穿過的洞穴；有一位王子和他的六個哥哥；有一間幾近坍塌的小屋，還有一位有著鷹鉤鼻的小老太太。若僅止於這些，夢幻島的地圖倒也不難畫，但還有呢，第一天上學啊，宗教啊，祖先

啊，圓池塘啊，針線活啊，謀殺啊，絞刑啊，格動詞啊，吃巧克力布丁的日子啊，穿吊帶褲啊，數到九十九啊，自己拔牙賺到三便士啊等等的。這些要嘛不是島上的一部分，就是另一張地圖上的畫了，總之啊，都是亂七八糟的，況且還沒有一樣東西是靜止不動的。

　　當然啦，每個人心中的夢幻島都大不相同。拿約翰來說好了，他的夢幻島上有一個潟湖，湖上飛著火鶴，約翰會拿箭射牠們；而麥可呢，他還小，他的湖泊會在火鶴上面飛。約翰住在整艘翻倒在沙灘上的船裡，麥可住簡陋小屋，而溫蒂則住在一間以樹葉精巧編製的房子裡。約翰沒有朋友，麥可的朋友只在夜晚出現，溫蒂則有一隻被父母遺棄的寵物狼。整體來看，他們心中各自的夢幻島同中有異，異中有同，要是把它們排成一列，你會發現它們不只鼻子長得像，其他地方也都很神似。在這神奇海岸上，嬉戲的孩子們會將小舟拖上岸，那是一處你我也曾經到過的地方，我們雖已不再上岸，卻仍能聽見那浪花的拍打聲。

　　在所有帶給人們快樂的島中，夢幻島算是最舒適、最適中的了，不會太大，也不會太散。你知道的，從一個冒險到另一個冒險，距離不會太遠，緊湊適宜。白天時，你用椅子和桌布玩島上的遊戲，絕無任何危險，等到你入睡前的兩分鐘，它會變得幾可亂真，而這就是晚上得點夜燈的原因了。

　　偶爾達林太太漫游在孩子的心思裡時，會發現讓她有些困惑的東西，而最令人費解的，就是彼得這個名字了。她不知道有誰叫彼得，但在約翰和麥可的心思中，它不停出現，而溫蒂的心裡更是填滿了這個名字。「彼德」比其他字來得更大，達林太太仔細地打量著，覺得它帶有異常

的傲氣與自信。

媽媽問溫蒂，溫蒂遺憾地承認：「沒錯，他是滿傲氣的。」

「可是他到底是誰呢，小乖？」

「他就是彼得·潘呀！媽媽。」

起初達林太太真的不認得他，不過後來她回憶童年時，想起的確有個彼得·潘，傳說他和小仙女們住在一起。他呀，他的故事可怪著呢，比如有小孩死掉時，他會陪他們走上一段路，不讓他們受怕。達林太太小時候是相信的，只不過現在她結了婚，長了見識，便十分懷疑是否真有這麼一個人。

她對溫蒂說：「但是，現在他應該已經長大了吧。」

「哦，他才沒有長大呢，」溫蒂很確信地告訴媽媽，「他就跟我一樣大呀。」溫蒂說的一樣大，包括身材和心智。她也不知道自己怎麼會知道，反正她就是知道。

達林太太去詢問先生的意見，達林先生只是輕描淡寫地帶過：「相信我，這一定是娜娜對他們胡說八道的，這是狗才會有的想法吧。別去管它，一會兒就沒事了。」

但並非是沒事的，很快地，這個專門製造麻煩的小男孩就讓達林太太嚇了一大跳。

小孩子常會經歷一些稀奇古怪的冒險，卻不會覺得驚嚇。例如，他們會突然想起一個星期前在樹林中遇到去世的爸爸，還一起玩遊戲。溫蒂就是這樣，一天早上，她不經意說出了一件讓人憂心的事。達林太太在育兒室的地板上發現了幾片樹葉，她正覺得納悶，前一晚孩子們上床睡覺時明明沒有樹葉的呀，這時溫蒂卻毫不在意地笑著說：

「一定又是彼得做的好事啦！」

「你這是什麼意思呀，溫蒂？」

「他真淘氣，玩完了也不掃地。」溫蒂嘆了口氣，她是個愛整潔的孩子。

她說得彷彿真有那麼一回事兒，她認為彼得有時會在夜裡來到育兒室，坐在床角吹笛子給她聽。可惜她沒醒來過，不清楚自己是怎麼知道的，可是她就是知道。

「你在亂說些什麼呀，寶貝！沒有人可以不敲門就進來屋裡的。」

「他是從窗戶進來的吧。」她說。

「親愛的，這裡是三樓耶！」

「樹葉不就落在窗角邊的嗎，媽媽？」

這倒是真的，樹葉就是在窗戶邊被發現的。

達林太太不知道該怎麼想才是，因為一切在溫蒂看來是那麼自然，又不能唬她說她在做夢就算了事。

「孩子啊，為什麼不早點跟我說呢？」媽媽喊道。

「我忘了。」溫蒂不在意地說道，她趕著要去吃早餐。

啊！她一定是做夢。

不過話又說回來，樹葉明明就在那裡啊！達林太太仔細觀察了一會兒，那都是些枯葉，不過她敢斷定那絕非英國的樹葉。她趴在地板上，用蠟燭照著查看有沒有陌生人的腳印，又把撥火棒探進煙囪，敲打牆壁，還把捲尺從窗口放到地面上，量到垂直的高度高達三十英尺，而牆上連個供人攀爬的出水口都沒有。

溫蒂一定是在做夢。

但她並不是在做夢，隔天晚上發生的事證明了這一點。那晚，可說是孩子們偉大冒險的開端。

我們說的那晚，孩子們又都上床睡覺了。那晚，娜娜

Gwynedd M. Hudson.

正好放假，達林太太剛幫孩子洗過澡，唱歌哄他們，直到他們一一鬆開她的手，溜進了夢鄉。

一切都顯得那麼平靜安詳，達林太太不禁對自己的擔憂笑了笑，靜靜坐在爐火旁，縫起衣服來。

這是要給麥可在生日那天穿的襯衫，爐火暖烘烘的，育兒室裡閃著微弱的三盞夜燈。不一會兒，針線掉到了達林太太的腿上。她不住地打起瞌睡，一切是那麼平靜美好。她睡著了。看看這一家四口，溫蒂和麥可睡在那兒，約翰睡這裡，達林太太在爐火旁，真該點上第四盞夜燈的！

達林太太睡著後做了一個夢，她夢見夢幻島越來越近，一位陌生小男孩從那裡闖了過來。男孩並沒有嚇到她，因為她覺得她曾在那些還沒生過孩子的女人眼中見過他，不過或許在一些母親的臉上也還找得到吧。然而在她這個夢裡，他把遮蓋著夢幻島的那一層薄幕撥開，此時她看到溫蒂、約翰和麥可，正從那道縫中向夢幻島裡窺探。

這夢本來只是件小事，但就在她做夢的當兒，育兒室的窗戶被風吹開了，竟然真有個小男孩跳到了地板上！還有一團光芒伴隨他來，那團光芒比拳頭還小，在屋裡四處亂飛，彷彿是有生命的東西。我想，一定是那團光芒把達林太太給驚醒了。

她大叫了起來。一見到那男孩，不知為何，她立刻明白他就是彼得・潘。若是你我或溫蒂當時在現場看到，一定會覺得他就像是達林太太嘴角上的吻。他是一個很可愛的男孩，穿著用樹葉和樹漿製成的衣服，而他身上最迷人的地方，是他仍保有一口乳牙。他一見達林太太是大人，就露出珍珠般的小牙，齜牙咧嘴地對著她。

影子

Chapter 2

達林太太大聲尖叫,接著,房門就像回應門一樣打開,晚上出門才剛回來的娜娜衝進來,吼叫著撲向男孩。男孩輕巧地從窗口地跳了出去,達林太太又尖叫一聲,不過這次是為了那男孩,以為他會摔死。她連忙跑下樓,到路上找他小小的身軀,卻沒找著。她抬頭張望,夜裡黑漆漆的什麼也看不見,就只看到了一顆流星。

達林太太回到育兒室,看見娜娜嘴裡銜著一樣東西,一看竟是男孩的影子。原來當男孩跳出窗戶的時候,娜娜立刻把窗戶一關,人雖然是沒捉住,但他的影子來不及逃出去,窗子啪地一聲關上,便把影子給扯了下來。

想當然爾,達林太太仔細檢查了影子一番,但它不就是個普通的影子罷了。

很顯然娜娜知道該怎麼處理這個影子,她把它掛在窗外,意思是「那男孩一定會回來拿，就把它放在容易拿到的地方，才不會吵到孩子們。」

但達林太太不能讓影子就這麼掛在窗外，看起來就像曬了一件衣服在那兒，有損整棟房子的格調。她也想過把影子拿給達林先生看，但達林先生正在算為約翰與麥可買冬季大衣的開銷，為了保持清醒，他還拿了一條濕毛巾圍在頭上，這時候去打擾他似乎不太恰當。況且，她算準了他一定會說：「這都怪我們找了一隻狗來當褓母。」

達林太太決定把影子捲起來，放在抽屜裡，等適當時機再告訴她先生。

一個星期之後，機會來了，那是一個永難忘記的星期五，絕對是星期五沒錯。

「星期五我應該要特別小心才對。」她在事發後常對丈夫說這些話，這時娜娜會在她身邊，握住她的手安慰她。

「不，不！」達林先生則會說：「我才應該負責呢，這是我喬治・達林的錯。吾之過也，吾之過也！」他是接受過古典教育的。

他們就這樣每晚坐著，回憶著那個無可挽回的星期五，直到所有記憶點點滴滴印穿腦袋，再從另一邊浮現出來，就像劣質硬幣上的人頭肖像一樣。

「要是我那天沒去參加二十七號的晚宴就好了。」達林太太說。

「要是我那天沒把藥倒進娜娜的碗裡就好了。」達林先生說。

「要是我假裝喜歡喝那碗藥就好了。」娜娜濕潤的眼眶透露出這樣的訊息。

「只怪我太愛參加宴會了，喬治。」

「都怪我該死的幽默感，我親愛的。」

「該怪我對瑣事太敏感了，親愛的主人們。」

接著他們其中一兩個就這麼放聲痛哭，娜娜想著：「的確是，的確是，他們不該雇一隻狗來當褓母的。」好幾次都是達林先生拿出手帕來為娜娜擦眼淚。

「那個小惡魔！」達林先生吼罵，娜娜也吠叫著呼應，不過達林太太從沒責罵過彼得，她右嘴角上的某樣東西讓她不想說出彼得的名字。

他們會坐在空蕩的育兒室裡，回想那個可怕夜晚所發生的每個細節，一開始太平無事，一如其他無數個夜晚一樣，娜娜為麥可放好洗澡水，把他背到浴室。

「我不要上床睡覺！」麥可喊道，以為這件事他能自己做得了主，「我不要，我不要，娜娜，現在還不到六點耶，我再也不喜歡妳了。娜娜，跟妳說我不要洗澡，我不洗，我不洗！」

達林太太走了進來，她穿著白色的晚禮服，老早就穿著打扮好了，因為溫蒂喜歡看她穿晚禮服，頸上繫著喬治送她的項鍊，手上還戴著她向溫蒂借的手鐲。溫蒂很喜歡把手鐲借給媽媽戴。

達林太太看到溫蒂和約翰正在玩扮家家酒，裝成她和達林先生，演著溫蒂出生那天的情景。約翰說：「恭喜妳，達林太太，你已經成為母親了。」說得好像達林先生當時真那麼說過似的。

溫蒂歡欣地跳起舞，彷彿達林太太當時也真是這麼跳著舞。

然後約翰出生了，因為是個男孩，他的神情顯得更為得意。這時麥可洗完澡出來，也想被生出來，不過約翰狠

心地說，他們不要再生了。

　　麥可幾乎要哭出來，「沒有人要我。」這下子穿禮服的那位女士可不忍心了。

　　「我要！」她說：「我很想要第三個孩子呢。」
　　「妳要男孩還是女孩？」麥可不太抱希望地問。
　　「男孩。」

　　他跳進她懷裡。如今達林夫婦和娜娜回想起來，這在當時不過是一件小事，但要是早知道那是麥可在育兒室待的最後一夜，可就不是小事了。

　　他們繼續回憶著。

　　「就是那時候，我像龍捲風一樣衝了進來，是吧？」達林先生說道，嘲笑當時的自己，他確實像是陣龍捲風。

　　或許這也不該怪他，當時他也為赴宴穿戴打扮，本來一切順利，直到要打領帶……說來也頗令人驚訝，雖然他懂得股票債券這些東西，卻無法應付領帶。有時領帶會對他屈服，但有些時候，如果他能吞下傲氣，戴上現成的領結，對全家人都是好事。

　　這一次正好就是這樣的日子，他衝進育兒室，手裡握著一小坨皺成一團的領帶。

　　「怎麼？發生什麼事啦，孩子的爸？」

　　「什麼事！」他大吼，的確是用吼地說道：「領帶就是打不起來！」接著酸溜溜地說：「可以打在床柱上，就是在脖子上打不起來！是不是？我在床柱上打了二十次都可以，一打在我脖子上就不行！好啊，看我怎麼收拾它！」

　　他覺得達林太太對他的話不太在意，就更加嚴厲地說道：「我告訴你，孩子的媽，除非我脖子能打上領帶，不然我今晚就不赴宴。如果我今晚去不成宴會，我就再也不去辦公室。如果我不去上班，那我們就等著捱餓，孩子們就準備流落街頭吧！」

即使如此，達林太太還是很沉著，「讓我來試試，親愛的。」她說。她知道達林先生就是來找她來打領帶的，她用靈巧冷靜的雙手幫他繫上領帶，孩子們就站在旁邊，等著看他們未來的命運。她三兩下就打好領帶，這可能會讓一些男士吃味，但達林先生不是這樣的人，他隨口道了聲謝謝，立刻就忘了自己剛才的怒氣，下一刻，就背著麥可在房裡跳起舞來。

「那一次我們玩得多瘋狂啊！」達林太太回憶著說。

「我們的最後一次玩耍！」達林先生感嘆。

「喔，喬治！記不記得麥可那時突然對我說：『你是怎麼認識我的，媽媽？』」

「我記得！」

「他們實在太美好了，你說是不是？」

「他們曾經屬於我們，是我們的，現在他們卻走了。」

一直到娜娜進來，當天那場打鬧才停止。達林先生不幸和娜娜撞個正著，褲子沾滿了狗毛，這可不只是一條新褲子，還是達林先生第一次穿上的鑲邊褲子。他緊咬下唇，強忍住眼淚。當然啦，達林太太有為他拂去狗毛，但他又開始抱怨請一隻狗來當褓母根本就是個錯誤。

「喬治，娜娜是我們最珍貴的寶藏。」

「的確是，但是我有種不舒服的感覺，總覺得她把孩子們當小狗狗看待。」

「不，親愛的，我確定她知道孩子們擁有自己的靈魂。」

「我很懷疑。」達林先生沉思地說：「我很懷疑。」

達林太太想，這是個好時機，可以把那男孩的事告訴他。起初達林先生對這件事嗤之以鼻，直到達林太太把影子拿來給他看，他才認真地推敲起來。

「這人我不認識。」他邊說，邊仔細端詳，「但他看起來的確不像善類。」

「那時我們還在討論，記得嗎？」達林先生繼續回憶著，「娜娜帶著麥可的藥進來。娜娜，妳以後再也不能把藥瓶銜在嘴裡了。這全都是我的錯。」

雖然他是個剛強的男人，不過一提到吃藥，他的反應可就有點蠢了。要說他這人有什麼弱點的話，那就是他一直以為自己吃藥很勇敢，因此，當麥可閃避娜娜銜在嘴裡的那一湯匙藥時，他訓道：「麥可，要像個男子漢。」

「不要，不要。」麥可賴皮地回嘴。達林太太走出房間去幫麥可拿巧克力，達林先生覺得這是不夠堅強的表現。

「孩子的媽，不要把他給慣壞了。」他在達林太太後面喊著：「麥可，我和你一樣大的時候，一聲不吭就把藥吃下去了。我會說：『親愛的父母，謝謝你們給我吃藥，讓我的病能早點痊癒。』」

他的確相信自己曾經說過這種話，這時已經換上睡衣的溫蒂也深信不疑，為了激勵麥可，她說：「爸爸，你吃的藥比這個藥還難吃，對不對？」

「難吃多了！」達林先生勇敢地說：「麥可，要是我沒把藥丟掉的話，我現在就可以吃給你看。」

其實藥並沒有被丟掉，達林先生在半夜爬到衣櫃上把它藏了起來，但他不知道的是，他忠心的女僕莉莎找到了那瓶藥，又把它放回盥洗台了。

「我知道藥在哪裡，爸爸。」溫蒂喊道，十分樂意幫

忙，「我去幫你拿。」達林先生還來不及阻止，她就跑掉了，他的心立刻一沉。

「約翰，」達林先生發著抖說：「那玩意兒難吃死了，又噁又黏又太甜。」

「一下子就好了，爸爸。」約翰幫他打氣。這時溫蒂急忙跑了進來，手裡拿著用玻璃杯裝的藥。

「我已經用最快的速度趕來了。」她氣喘吁吁地說。

「妳還真是快啊！」她爸爸帶著報復意味地譏諷道：「麥可先吃。」他很堅持地說。

「爸爸先。」麥可說，他語帶懷疑。

「我會吐，你知道的。」達林先生威脅。

「快點啊，爸爸。」約翰說。

「你閉嘴，約翰。」爸爸厲聲說道。

溫蒂很不解：「我以為你吃藥很容易，爸爸。」

「這不是重點。」達林先生反駁道：「重點是，我杯子裡的藥比麥可湯匙裡的藥多。」他高傲的心幾乎要氣炸。「這不公平，就算剩下最後一口氣，我也要說，這不公平。」

「爸爸，我在等你吃。」麥可冷冷地說。

「你倒說得輕鬆，我也等著你吃呢。」

「爸爸是軟趴趴的懦夫。」

「那你也是。」

「我才不怕呢。」

「我也不怕。」

「那好，你就吃啊。」

「好啊，你吃啊。」

溫蒂靈光一閃：「為什麼不兩個一起吃？」

「當然！」達林先生說：「你準備好了嗎，麥可？」

溫蒂開始數，一、二、三，麥可把藥吃了，但達林先生卻把藥藏到背後。

　　麥可發出憤怒的吼叫。「天啊，爸爸！」溫蒂驚呼。

　　「『天啊，爸爸！』是什麼意思？」達林先生質問，「先別叫，麥可，我本來是要吃的，不過……我錯過了，沒吃著。」

　　三個孩子盯著達林先生的那種眼神令人生畏，一副很不服他的樣子。「你們三個，都過來看看。」就在娜娜走進浴室時，達林先生說：「我剛想到一個很棒的玩笑：把我的藥倒進娜娜碗裡，她就會把它喝下去的，因為她會以為那是牛奶！」

　　藥的顏色的確很像牛奶，不過孩子們沒有爸爸的幽默感，在他把藥倒進娜娜碗裡的時候，他們神情責備地看著他。「很好玩吧。」達林先生有點兒遲疑地說。孩子們在達林太太和娜娜回到房間之後，沒敢去揭穿這件事。

　　「娜娜，乖狗狗。」達林先生拍拍她，「我在妳的碗裡倒了一些牛奶。」

　　娜娜對他搖搖尾巴，跑過去舔了幾下。接著，她看了達林先生一眼，那不是憤怒的眼神，而是濕紅的眼眶，那眼淚會讓我們為一隻品德高尚的狗感到難過。之後，她兀自爬進了狗屋。

　　達林先生為自己所作所為感到慚愧，卻仍不肯讓步。在駭人的沉寂中，達林太太去聞了娜娜的碗。「噢，喬治！」她說：「這是你的藥！」

　　「開個玩笑而已！」他吼著。達林太太安撫兩個男孩，溫蒂則過去摟住娜娜。「很好，」達林先生不悅地說：「我這麼做，還不是為了讓全家開心啊。」

　　溫蒂仍摟著娜娜。「很好！」他嚷道：「只理她，沒

人理我，沒有！反正我就只會賺錢養家嘛，為什麼要理我呢！為什麼，為什麼，為什麼！」

達林太太請求他，「喬治，別那麼大聲，僕人們會聽到的。」不知從何時開始，他們習慣了叫莉沙為「僕人們」。

「就讓他們聽啊！」他不在乎地說：「就讓全世界的人都聽到，我不允許那隻狗在我的育兒室裡當老大，一刻也不行。」

孩子們哭了起來，娜娜想跑來跟他求情，但他揮手叫她走開。這讓他覺得自己又是個堅強的男人了。「沒用的，沒用的！」他叫道：「最適合你的地方就是後院，現在就去院子裡用繩子拴起來。」

「喬治，喬治！」達林太太低聲說：「別忘了我跟你說的那個男孩。」

可是哎呀，達林先生就是不聽。他決心要讓大家知道誰才是當家的。當他的命令無法把娜娜從狗屋裡叫出來，他就用好話將她騙出來，然後粗魯地抓住她，把她拖出育兒室。他對自己的行為感到慚愧，但他還是做了。這實在是因為他生性感情豐富，太渴望得到孩子們的敬重。把娜娜拴在後院之後，這位可憐的父親便到走廊坐下，用雙手掩住眼睛。

這同時，在少見的寂靜中，達林太太帶孩子們上床睡覺，並點上夜燈。他們可以聽見娜娜吠叫，約翰嗚咽地說：「都是因為他要把娜娜栓在院子裡。」但溫蒂比他敏銳。

「娜娜不是因為生氣在叫的。」她雖然不知道會發生什麼事，但說道：「這是她嗅到危險的叫聲。」

危險！

「你確定嗎，溫蒂？」

「哦，當然。」

達林太太打起冷顫，她走到窗前，窗戶緊閉著。她朝窗外望去，夜空裡滿天星斗。星星圍繞在房子周圍，一副等著看好戲的樣子。可她沒察覺這一點，也沒注意到有一兩顆星星正對著她眨眼。但一股莫名的恐懼攫住了她的心，讓她忍不住叫道：「啊，真希望我今晚沒去參加宴會！」

麥可已經快睡著了，他知道媽媽心緒不安，便問道：「媽媽，我們已經點了夜燈，沒有什麼能傷害我們吧？」

「沒有，寶貝。」達林太太說：「它們是媽媽的眼睛，留下來保護孩子的。」

她在每張床之間走來走去，唱歌給他們聽，小麥可伸出雙臂抱住她。「媽媽，」他叫道：「我好喜歡你。」這是很長一段時間裡，她聽到他說的最後一句話。

二十七號離他們家只有幾碼遠，不過因為下過一點雪，所以達林夫婦得小心地挑著路走，以免弄髒了鞋子。街上只有他們兩個人，滿天的星星都盯著他們瞧。星星是很美，但什麼事都不能參與，永遠只能做個旁觀者。這是對他們的懲罰，因為他們在很久以前犯了錯，至於是什麼錯呢？由於年代太久遠，現在已經沒有星星知道了。年長的星星眼睛失去光采，很少說話（眨眼就是星星的語言），小星星們則仍深感疑惑。他們並不真喜歡彼得，因為彼得常搗蛋，溜到他們身後，想把他們吹熄。不過，他們很喜歡找樂子，所以今晚都站在彼得這一邊，巴不得大人都離開。當達林夫婦走進二十七號，門一被關上時，天空就起了一陣騷動。銀河中最小的一顆星星喊了出來：

「彼得，就是現在！」

走吧！走吧！

Chapter 3

達林夫婦離開後好一會兒，孩子床邊的三盞夜燈依然明亮。那是三盞很好的小夜燈，希望它們都能醒著看到彼得，但是溫蒂的燈眨了一下眼睛，打了個大呵欠，另外兩盞燈也跟著打起呵欠來，它們的嘴還沒來得及閉上，三盞燈都熄滅了。

　　這時房裡又出現另一道光，比那三盞夜燈亮上千倍，就在我們說話的當下，照亮了育兒室每一個抽屜，尋找著彼得的影子。它跑到衣櫃裡東翻西找，翻出每個衣袋。不過啊，那其實不是光，而是飛行而生的亮光。只要它停下片刻，你會發現那其實是個小仙子。她比你的手掌還小，不過她還在長大。她是個仙女，名叫亭可·貝爾，身上穿著一片精緻的樹葉，方形領口的裁剪頗低，展現出身材的優點，體態略顯豐滿。

　　小仙女進來不久，窗戶就被那些小星星給吹開了。彼得跳進來，他帶著小仙女亭可飛了一小段路程，手上還沾了一些仙塵。

　　他確定孩子都睡著了才低聲叫道：「亭可，亭可，妳在哪兒呀？」她在一個水壺裡，她太愛那裡了，她以前都沒待過水壺裡呢。

「喂，出來吧，快告訴我，妳知不知道他們把我的影子放在哪兒呀？」

一陣像金鈴般最美的鈴噹聲回應了他，那是小仙女的語言，你們這些平凡小孩是聽不到的，不過要是你聽到，你會發現你以前早聽過了。

亭可說影子就在大盒子裡，她指的其實是櫃子的抽屜。彼得跳到抽屜前，把裡面的東西全倒在地板上，那動作就像國王將硬幣拋向人群一般。不一會兒工夫，他就找到了他的影子。他興奮不已，完全忘了自己把亭可關在抽屜裡。

如果他會思考的話，但我相信他從不用大腦思考，那他應該會認為，等他和他的影子一靠近，就會像水滴一樣接合在一起，但結果卻連不起來，他可嚇壞了。他想用浴室的肥皂把影子黏起來，可是又失敗了。他身體一抖，就坐在地板上哭了起來。

他的哭聲吵醒了溫蒂。溫蒂坐在床上，看到房間裡有個陌生人在哭，也不怕，也不慌，只覺得有趣。

「小男孩啊，」她有禮貌地問：「你在哭什麼呀？」

彼得也表現得十分有禮，他跟仙子學了一些禮儀。他起身，優雅地向溫蒂欠了個身。溫蒂十分滿意，也在床上對他鞠躬回禮。

「妳叫什麼名字？」彼得問。

「溫蒂·莫伊拉·安琪拉·達林。」她得意地回道：「那你叫什麼名字？」

「彼得·潘。」

溫蒂早就認定他就是彼得，只是這名字真是有點短。

「就這樣啊？」

「是啊。」彼得厲聲回答，他第一次有點覺得自己的

名字太短。

「不好意思。」溫蒂・莫伊拉・安琪拉說道。

「沒關係。」彼得忍住這口氣。

溫蒂問他住在哪裡。

「右手邊的第二條街，接著向前直走，一直走到早晨。」彼得說。

「這地址真怪！」

彼得的心沉了下來，他頭一回覺得這地址好像真有點兒怪。

「不，才不會呢！」他說。

「我的意思是，」溫蒂想起了她現在是女主人，便客氣地說：「這是你們寫在信封上的地址嗎？」

他真希望她沒提到信的事。

「我從不收信的。」他不屑地說。

「可是你媽媽總會收信吧？」

「我沒有媽媽。」彼得說。他沒有媽媽，也從沒想過要有個媽媽，他認為人們把母親看得太重了。不過溫蒂直覺他的母親遭遇了不幸。

「喔，彼得，怪不得你剛才在哭。」她說著下床跑到他面前。

「我又不是因為沒有媽媽才哭的。」彼得憤慨地說：「是因為我沒辦法把影子黏回去啦，再說，才沒有哭呢。」

「它掉下來了嗎？」

「是啊。」

溫蒂瞧見地板上的影子被拖得髒兮兮的，忍不住為彼得難過。她說：「真糟糕！」然而她一看到彼得竟拿肥皂來黏影子，又忍俊不禁。這真像男生會做的事呀！

幸好她立刻就知道該怎麼做。「應該把它縫上去才對。」她帶著自信的口吻說。

　　「什麼是縫？」彼得問。

　　「你實在太無知了！」

　　「我才不無知呢！」

　　不過她倒很喜歡他的無知。她說：「我的小朋友，我會幫你縫上的。」雖然他和她長得一般高。她拿出針線盒，想把影子縫到彼得的腳上。

　　「這應該會有點痛哦。」她先警告他。

　　「我不會哭。」彼得說。他自認為自己都沒哭過。他咬著唇，沒有哭，沒多久影子便縫好，可以正常活動，只是有點皺。

「我應該用熨斗把它燙平的。」溫蒂邊想邊說。可彼得就和所有男孩一樣，一點也不在乎外表。他興高采烈地蹦蹦跳跳，哎呀，他根本忘記這全是溫蒂的功勞，還以為影子是自己接上去的。「我真是太聰明了！」他開心地歡呼：「啊，我太聰明啦！」

說來有點不好意思，但不得不承認，彼得的自負正是他吸引人的地方。說白話一點，就是從來沒有一個男孩比彼得更有自信的了。

不過當時溫蒂可嚇了一跳。「你這個自大狂！」她嘲諷地表示：「當然嘛，我什麼也沒做！」

「妳是做了一點。」彼得漫不經心地說，繼續跳著。

「一點？」她傲慢地回答：「如果我沒什麼用的話，至少我可以走吧。」她一副嚴肅的模樣跳回床上，用被子把臉蒙住。

彼得假裝要離開，想騙溫蒂抬起頭來，但不管用。他坐在床尾，用腳輕輕拍她。「溫蒂！」他說：「不要走啦，溫蒂，我一高興就會忍不住大叫。」溫蒂還是不肯抬頭，但倒很專注地聽，「溫蒂！」彼得用女生無法抗拒的聲調說：「溫蒂，一個女生可比二十個男生還要有用喔。」

這會兒溫蒂可從頭到腳每一吋都是個女生了，雖然她的身高根本沒幾吋。她從被子裡探出頭。

「你真的這麼認為嗎，彼得？」

「是啊，我是這麼認為。」

她說：「你這麼說，真貼心。我要起來了。」她和彼得一起坐在床邊，她又說如果他願意，她可以給他一個吻。彼得不明白什麼是吻，便有所期待地把手伸了出來。

「你該知道吻是什麼吧？」她有些吃驚地問。

「妳給我，我就知道了嘛。」他倔強地回答。為了不傷彼得的心，溫蒂給了他一個頂針。

他說：「那我也要給妳一個吻嗎？」溫蒂一本正經地答道：「如果你肯的話。」她把臉頰挪向彼得，他卻把一顆橡實放在她手中。溫蒂只好慢慢把臉移回去，親切地說，她會把他的吻繫上項鍊戴在脖子上。幸好，她真戴上了那條項鍊，因為後來它救了她一命。

人們在寒暄認識後，習慣問問對方的年齡，而凡事照規距來的溫蒂，便問起彼得的年齡。這對彼得而言可不是個好問題，因為這就好比考卷上明明問的是文法，你卻希望它問的是英國國王是誰一樣。

「我不知道，」他不安地回答：「但是我還很年輕。」他真的一點也不知道，只能稍作猜想。他唐突地說道：「溫蒂，我生下來的那一天就逃跑了。」

溫蒂很吃驚，也很感興趣。她用優雅的待客禮儀，碰了一下自己的睡衣，示意彼得可以再坐近一些。

「那是因為我聽到父母在談論，」彼得低聲解釋：「談到我長大成人以後會變得如何如何的。」他突然激動起來：「我永遠不想變成大人！」他激烈地說：「我想要永遠當小男生，一直玩。所以我就逃到肯辛頓公園，和小仙子們住在一起，住了很久了。」

溫蒂露出羨慕的神情，彼得以為是羨慕他逃家，不過她其實是羨慕他認識小仙子們。溫蒂過著平淡的家庭生活，所以她想，要是能結識仙子的話，該多有趣啊。她問了一連串關於仙女的問題，彼得很驚訝，在他看來，仙子們都是問題人物，專門給他添麻煩，有時他還要躲著她們呢。不過他大體上還是滿喜歡她們的啦。然後他告訴了溫蒂仙子的由來。

「溫蒂，妳看，當第一個出生的小嬰兒第一次笑時，笑聲會碎成一千片，碎片到處跳來跳去，就變成仙子了。」

這故事很乏味，溫蒂很少出門，才會喜歡這個故事。

「所以呢，」彼得和氣地說下去：「每個男孩和女孩都應該有一個仙子囉。」

「應該？現在難道沒有嗎？」

「沒有。你看現在的小孩都懂很多，他們很快就不會相信有仙子了。只要有小孩說『我不相信有仙子』時，就會有仙子從那裡墜落下來死掉。」

說實在的，他覺得仙子的話題談得夠多了，他想起來亭可怎麼那麼安靜。「我想不起來她會去哪裡。」他一面說，一面站起身，叫亭可的名字。溫蒂一陣興奮，心怦怦地跳著。

「彼得，」她嚷道，緊緊抓住他，「你該不會說這房裡有仙子吧？」

「她剛才還在這兒的。」彼得不耐煩地說：「妳也沒聽到她的聲音吧？」他們倆仔細聽著。

「我只聽到一個聲音，像是鈴噹叮叮響的聲音。」溫蒂說。

「沒錯，那就是亭可！那是小仙女的語言，我好像也聽到她了。」

聲音是從抽屜裡傳出來的，彼得露出了快活的神情。沒人像彼得看起來那麼開心，他咯咯的笑聲真是世界上最討人愛的笑聲了。他還保有著初生的第一個笑。

彼得快樂地低語：「溫蒂，我好像把她關在抽屜裡了！」

他將亭可從抽屜裡放出來，亭可就在屋子裡飛來飛去，氣呼呼地尖叫著。「妳真不該這樣說的。」彼得反駁說：「我是真的很抱歉啦，可是我怎麼會知道妳在抽屜裡呢？」

溫蒂沒去理會他的話，喊道：「啊，彼得！要是她能停一下，讓我看看她就好了。」

「她們是很難得靜下來的。」彼得說。但有一瞬間，溫蒂瞧見神奇的小仙女停在布穀時鐘上。她喊道：「哦，好可愛呀！」雖然亭可的臉還氣得扭曲著。

「亭可，」彼得親切地說，「這位小姐希望妳能當她的仙子。」

亭可無禮地回了一句。

「她說什麼，彼得？」

他只得幫她翻譯：「她不太有禮貌，她說妳是個醜陋的大女生，況且她還是我的仙子。」

他向亭可解釋說：「亭可，妳知道妳不能做我的仙子，因為我是紳士，而妳是淑女。」

亭可回應：「你這大笨蛋！」說罷便飛進浴室裡了。

「她只是個很普通的仙子。她的名字叫亭可·貝爾，因為她的工作是修補鍋碗瓢盆的。」彼得帶著歉意解釋。

這會兒他們倆一塊坐在扶手椅上，溫蒂又問了彼得一連串問題。

「你現在不住肯辛頓公園了嗎？」

「有時候還是會住啊。」

「那你現在大部分時間都住在哪裡呀？」

「和走失的男生們住一起。」

「他們是誰啊？」

「他們是在褓母不注意時從嬰兒車掉下來的小孩，只要七天內沒有人認領，就被送到遙遠的夢幻島，好省下開

支，而我是他們的隊長。」

「那一定很好玩耶！」

「對啊，」狡猾的彼得說：「不過我們也滿寂寞的，妳看我們都沒有女生作伴。」

「一個女生都沒有嗎？」

「沒有。女生嘛，妳知道的，都鬼靈精怪得很呢，哪會掉下嬰兒車啊！」

這番奉承話很討溫蒂歡心。她說：「我覺得，你這麼說女生真是很棒，睡在那裡的約翰就瞧不起我們女生呢。」

為此，彼得站了起來，大腳一踢，就把約翰連同毯子那些都踢下了床。他們才剛認識，溫蒂覺得他這樣做太魯莽了，就生氣地對他說，在這房間裡他可不是什麼隊長。不過約翰倒是還安穩地睡在地板上，溫蒂也就沒去管他。「我知道你這麼做是為了我，」溫蒂緩了緩口氣說道：「所以呢，你可以給我一個吻。」

溫蒂一時忘了彼得根本不懂吻是什麼。「我剛才就想妳會想把它要回去的。」彼得有點悻悻然地說道，並把頂針交還給她。

「哎呀，我指的不是吻，是頂針啦。」好心的溫蒂說。

「那是什麼？」

「就像這樣子。」溫蒂親了他一下。

「真有趣！」彼得嚴肅地表示，「那我現在也要給你一個頂針嗎？」

「如果你想的話。」溫蒂說著頭抬得高高的。

彼得也給了她一個頂針，她卻立刻叫了起來。

「怎麼了啊，溫蒂？」

「好像有人在扯我的頭髮。」

「一定是亭可，我還不知道她這麼淘氣呢。」

果然，亭可又四處飛來飛去，口中還罵罵有詞。

「溫蒂，她說只要我給妳頂針，她就要扯妳的頭髮。」

「為什麼呢？」

「為什麼呀，亭可？」

亭可答道：「你這大笨蛋！」彼得還很納悶，但溫蒂懂了。彼得坦承自己來育兒室窗邊，是想聽故事，不是來看她的，溫蒂聽了有點失望。

「妳知道，我沒聽過什麼故事，那些走失的小孩也都不會說故事。」

「那真是太慘了。」溫蒂說。

「妳可知道為什麼燕子要在屋簷下築巢嗎？」彼得說：「就是為了要聽故事啊。溫蒂啊，妳媽媽那天說了一個好好聽的故事哦。」

「什麼故事？」

「就是講有個王子找不到穿玻璃鞋的姑娘啊。」

「彼得，那是灰姑娘，王子後來有找到她喔，然後兩個人就過著幸福快樂的日子了。」溫蒂興奮地說。

彼得聽了興奮得急忙從地上站起來，匆匆走到窗口。

「你要去哪裡啊？」溫蒂不安地叫道。

「去跟那些男生說啊。」

「不要走嘛，彼得！」溫蒂懇求道：「我還知道很多故事喔。」

千真萬確，溫蒂就是這麼說的，所以啊，沒有人可以否認是她先誘惑彼得的。

彼得回過頭，他那貪婪的眼神，原該要嚇住溫蒂的，可是溫蒂沒被嚇到。

「我有好多故事可以說給那些小孩子聽喔！」她喊道。於是彼得抓住她，想把她拉向窗戶。

「放開我！」溫蒂用命令的語氣說。

「溫蒂，跟我一起走，去講故事給那些孩子聽。」

溫蒂當然開心有人這樣央求她，不過她說：「唉呀，我不能去啊！媽媽怎麼辦呢？何況我也不會飛呀。」

「我教妳。」

「哇，會飛一定很棒。」

「我會教妳怎麼跳到風的背上，我們就可以出發了。」

「哇！」溫蒂興奮地大叫。

「溫蒂呀溫蒂，妳不要傻乎乎躺在床上睡覺，妳可以和我一起飛翔，和星星說說有趣的事。」

「哇！」

「溫蒂，還有美人魚喔。」

「美人魚？有尾巴的？」

「尾巴很長喔。」

「哇！」溫蒂大喊：「可以看美人魚耶！」

彼得更狡猾了，他說：「溫蒂，我們都會很尊敬妳喔。」

溫蒂不安地扭動身體，一副好像努力要讓自己乖乖待在育兒室裡的樣子。

彼得可一點也不同情她。

「溫蒂，」這奸詐的傢伙說：「晚上妳可以幫我們蓋被子喔。」

「啊！」

「晚上都沒人幫我們蓋被子。」

「真可憐。」溫蒂對他伸出雙臂。

「妳還可以幫我們補衣服、做口袋，我們都沒有口袋。」

　　這叫溫蒂怎麼拒絕得了呢？「這實在太好玩了！」她喊道：「彼得，你也會教約翰和麥可怎麼飛嗎？」

　　「隨你啊！」彼得無所謂地說。於是溫蒂跑到約翰和麥可的床前搖搖他們。她叫著：「醒醒啊！彼得‧潘來了，他要教我們飛喔。」

　　約翰揉揉眼睛地說：「那我要起來。」其實他已經站在地上了。他說：「哈囉！我起來了！」

　　這時麥可也起床了，他精神奕奕得像把瑞士刀。不過彼得立刻示意大伙安靜，他們就露出機伶的表情，一副留神聆聽大人說話的樣子。一切悄然無聲，安全了嗎？不，等一下！出狀況了，猛叫了一整晚的娜娜此刻卻安靜下來了。他們聽到她無聲無息。

　　「熄燈，躲起來！快！」約翰喊著。在這場冒險中，這是約翰唯一一次發號施令。莉莎牽著娜娜進房，育兒室恢復了安靜與漆黑。你敢擔保聽見了三個小惡魔天使般的鼾聲，而其實這是他們躲在窗簾後巧裝的。

　　莉莎一肚子火，她本來在廚房做聖誕節布丁的，臉頰上還粘著一粒葡萄乾。就只因娜娜不合理的懷疑，讓她丟下了正事，她想，要是想要安靜些，最好就帶娜娜去巡巡育兒室，當然她得看管著娜娜。

　　「看吧，你這疑神疑鬼的畜生。」她一點情面也不給娜娜，說道：「他們都安全得很吧？每個小天使都睡得那麼香甜，聽聽他們平靜的呼吸吧！」

　　麥可看到自己假裝得很成功，一來勁，呼吸聲一大，差點兒被發現。娜娜聽出異樣，想要掙脫莉莎。

　　莉莎卻鈍得很。「不要這樣啦，娜娜！」她將娜娜拖出房間，嚴厲地說：「我警告妳喔，妳要是再叫一聲，我

就直接去找先生和太太，把他們從舞會上請回來，到時呢，哼，妳不捱鞭子才怪！」

　　她把這隻憂悶的狗又給拴了起來，但是你以為娜娜就停止吠叫？把先生和太太從舞會帶回來？那才正中下懷呢，只要她照顧的孩子們沒事，她才不怕被鞭打呢！不過只可惜，莉莎又回去做她的布丁了。娜娜眼看沒人幫她忙，便不斷使勁要掙脫狗鍊。最後，終於讓她給掙開了。下一秒鐘，她已衝進了二十七號公寓的飯廳。她腳掌往上一舉起，這是她與人溝通最有效的方法。達林夫婦立刻明白育兒室裡有事發生了，來不及向女主人道別，就急忙衝出了門。

　　不過此時此刻離三個小淘氣躲在窗簾後面裝出鼾聲，已經有十分鐘了。十分鐘的時間，彼得·能做的事可多了。

　　現在，讓我們再回到育兒室。

　　「沒事了！」約翰從躲藏處現身，宣布：「我說啊，彼得，你真的會飛嗎？」

　　彼得懶得回答，就逕自在房間裡飛來飛去，還順手拿起了壁爐架。

　　「太棒了！」約翰和麥可說。

　　「太妙了！」溫蒂喊道。

　　「對呀，我真是太妙了，喔，我真是太妙了！」彼得說著說著又得意忘形了。

　　飛行看起來易如反掌。他們先在地上練習，又跑到床鋪上練習，可是只會掉下來，而不會往上飛。

　　「我說啊，你到底是怎麼做到的？」約翰揉著膝蓋問。他是個講究實際的男生。

　　彼得解釋道：「只要想一些美好的事情，它們會把你舉到半空中。」

彼得又示範了一次。

「你太快了，你不能慢慢地做一次嗎？」約翰說。

彼得慢的、快的又都示範了一次。「我會了，溫蒂！」約翰喊道。不過啊，他馬上又發現到並非如此。他們三個連一吋高都飛不上去，雖說談到學問，麥可認得兩個音節的字，而彼得連一個字母都不認識。

其實呢，彼得根本是在逗著他們玩，因為啊，除非身上沾了仙塵，不然根本飛不起來。還好，剛才我們說過，彼得的一隻手上沾了仙塵，他往他們每個人身上吹了一些，結果全都奏效了。

他說：「現在，你們就像這樣擺動肩膀，然後飛吧！」

他們站在床上，勇敢的麥可第一個起飛，可是他還沒準備好，竟然就飛了起來，一下子就飛到了房間的另一頭。

「我飛起來了！」他在半空中尖叫起來。

約翰也飛了起來了，還和溫蒂在浴室旁碰上了。

「啊，太妙了！」

「哇，太棒啦！」

「看我！」

「看看我！」

「你看我！」

他們飛得一點也不像彼得那樣優雅，他們老是忍不住踢一踢腳，頭還往天花板東碰西頂的。再沒比這更有趣的事了。一開始，彼得還會伸手幫溫蒂一把，不過看到亭可一張臭臉，他就忍住了。

他們飛上飛下，繞了一圈又一圈。溫蒂說，這就好像在天堂一樣。

「我說啊，」約翰嚷道：「我們大家飛出去吧？」

這正是彼得想引誘他們做的事啊。

麥可準備好了，他想看看飛一萬億英里要花多久時間，不過溫蒂有些猶豫。

「記得美人魚吧！」彼得又說。

「啊！」

「還有海盜呢。」

約翰大喊：「海盜！」一把抓起他禮拜天戴的帽子說：「我們馬上走吧！」

此時，達林夫婦帶著娜娜衝出二十七號公寓的大門，他們走到街上，抬頭望著育兒室的窗戶。還好，窗子還關著，但房間卻閃著亮光，最駭人的是，可以看到窗簾上映出三個穿睡衣的小身影，不斷地繞著圈圈，不是在地上，而是在半空中！

不是三個身影，是四個！

他們身子發抖地推開大門，達林先生想衝到樓上，但達林太太示意要他放慢腳步。她還想盡量緩下自己的心跳。

他們來得及趕到育兒室嗎？如果答案是肯定的，他們可就開心了，而我們也會鬆一口氣，只不過啊，那樣就沒有故事可以聽了。不過要是相反地來不及的話，我鄭重向大家保證，最後一定會以圓滿的結局收場的。

要不是星星一直監視著一切，他們就可以及時趕到育兒室了。然而，星星再一次吹開了窗戶，最小的一顆星星大喊著：「走吧，彼得！」

彼得知道不能再耽誤下去了。「快來！」他專橫地叫著，隨後飛進了夜空中，後面跟著約翰、麥可和溫蒂。

當達林夫婦和娜娜衝進育兒室時，已經為時已晚。

小鳥兒已經飛了。

飛行

Chapter 4

「右手邊第二條街，向前直走，一直走到早晨。」這就是彼得告訴過溫蒂往夢幻島的方向，但即使是鳥兒帶著地圖，在每一道風的角落在地圖上找路，依照這樣的指路法，也找不到夢幻島的。彼得這個人啊，你也知道，就是腦中想到什麼就隨口說出來罷了。

一開始，同伴們很信任他，況且飛行實在太愉快了。在冒險途中，他們浪費不少時間，繞著教堂尖塔或什麼好玩的高聳建築物飛行。

約翰和麥可比賽誰飛得快，結果麥可拔得頭籌。

他們回想起，不久前還覺得能在房間飛著繞圈就了不得了，現在呢，倒頗為瞧不起當時的自己。

不久前？但到底是多久啊？他們飛越了大片海洋，這問題就擾得溫蒂心神不寧了。約翰想，這是他們飛越的第二片大海，飛了三個夜晚了。

有時天黑，有時天亮；這一刻大伙還覺得冷，下一刻又熱死人了。有時，他們也不知是真餓還假餓，只知彼得幫他們覓食的方法實在太好玩了。他的方法呢，就是追逐嘴裡叼著人類食物的鳥兒，把牠們嘴裡的食物搶過來。接著，鳥兒們就會跟在他們後面，把食物搶回去。他們就這

Gwynedd M. Hudson.

樣彼此追逐，一連好幾英里，最後大家互表善意，分道揚鑣。可溫蒂發現，彼得似乎一點也不覺得這種覓食方式很怪，他甚至不懂還有其他覓食方式。

當然囉，他們也會想睡覺，這可不是裝出來的。這啊可危險了，只要一打瞌睡，就往下墜。更可怕的是，彼得竟然還覺得這樣好玩極了。

「他又掉下去了！」麥可突然像石頭往下掉時，彼得興奮地大喊。

「快救他！快救他！」溫蒂叫道，驚慌地望著下方遙遠凶險的大海。終於，彼得從空中向下俯衝，在麥可差點掉入海裡的前一刻抓起他。彼得的姿態很優美，但他喜歡等到最後一刻才出手，真讓人覺得他要賣弄本領，而非真心要救人。而他又愛喜新厭舊，現在愛玩這種遊戲，下一刻又興趣缺缺，因此要是你下次再往下墜，他很有可能會讓你就這樣掉下去了。

彼得能在空中睡覺卻不往下掉，因為他很輕，能在空中仰躺漂浮，你要是在他身後吹氣，他會飛得更快呢。

「我們最好對他客氣一點兒。」溫蒂在大家玩「請你跟我這樣做」的時候，悄悄對約翰說。

「那就叫他少愛現！」約翰回答。

他們玩著這遊戲，彼得會飛近水面，用手摸每條鯊魚的尾巴，就像你在街上沿路摸鐵欄杆一樣。這個動作他們做得不如他，顯得彼得是在炫耀，尤其是他老愛回頭看他們漏摸了幾隻尾巴。

「你們要對他好一點兒，」溫蒂告訴老弟們說：「要是他扔下我們不管怎麼辦？」

「我們就往回走啊。」麥可說。

「他不在，我們怎麼認得回去的路？」

「那我們可以繼續往前呀。」約翰說。

「那就更可怕了，約翰。那我們就要這樣一直往前飛了，因為我們根本不知道要怎麼停下來。」

這倒是真的，彼得忘了教他們怎麼停下來。

約翰說，要是倒楣到頭了，就只管繼續往前飛就是了，反正地球是圓的，最後一定能飛回家裡的窗戶的。

「可是誰要找東西給我們吃呢，約翰？」

「我可以小心搶一些老鷹嘴裡的東西吃啊，溫蒂。」

「你試了二十次才成功耶，」溫蒂提醒他，「就算我們越來越會搶食物好了，可是你想想看，彼得不在身邊時，我們是怎麼撞上那些雲朵什麼的。」

的確，他們常常撞到東西。現在他們飛得很不錯了，

只是偶爾腿還會踢得太用力。不過呢，要是看到前方有一團雲，越想躲開，反而越容易撞上。娜娜若跟在身邊啊，這時候一定會在麥可的額頭上綁上繃帶。

這時，彼得沒和他們一起飛翔，他們感覺有點落寞。彼得飛得比他們快多了，他可以一溜煙就失去了蹤影，飛到他們到不了的地方去冒險。有時，彼得笑著從上方飛下來，笑話他剛剛和星星說的趣事，卻忘了是什麼趣事。有時，他又會從下面飛上來，身上粘著美人魚的鱗片，卻說不上來到底發生了什麼事。對沒見過美人魚的小孩來說，這實在是讓人很火大。

「要是他這麼快就忘了這些事，」溫蒂表示，「那怎麼期待他會記得我們呢？」

確實，有時彼得回來後，就認不得他們是誰，起碼是記不清楚了，這點溫蒂非常確定。有一天，彼得飛過他們身邊，差點就飛走了，溫蒂看見他露出認出了他們的眼神。還有一次，她甚至還得把名字再告訴他。

「我是溫蒂啊。」她激動地說。

彼得感到很抱歉。「我說溫蒂啊，」他低聲說：「要是以後我把妳忘記了，妳只要一直對我說『我是溫蒂』，我就會想起來了。」

這說法當然不怎麼讓人滿意。不過為了拉攏他們，彼得教他們如何平躺在順向的勁風上。他們可樂死了，他們試幾次，終於能安安穩穩地睡上一覺了。他們本想多睡一會兒，彼得卻沒多久就睡膩了，很快便用命令的口吻說道：「我們動身吧。」雖然一路上偶有些小爭執，但這段旅程還算愉快，而夢幻島也越來越近了。日夜趕路之後，他們最後抵達了夢幻島。而且，這路上他們都是直線飛行的，與其說是由彼得和亭可來帶路，倒不如說是因為夢幻島一直盼著他們的到來。也唯有如此，人們才能看得見這神奇的海岸。

「就是那裡。」彼得平靜地說。

「哪裡？在哪裡？」

「就在所有箭頭指向的地方。」

沒錯，有百萬支金箭為孩子們指引著島的方向，這些金箭都是他的朋友——太陽——所射出來的，要趁黑夜降臨前，為他們指引明路。

溫蒂、約翰和麥可在空中踮起腳尖，想看看他們這頭一回見到的島。說來也奇怪，他們一眼就認出了它，心裡沒想到害怕，就先歡呼了起來。他們感覺，夢幻島並非長久的夢境成真，反倒像渡假回家遇見的老友。

「約翰，那就是瀉湖。」

「溫蒂，看那些烏龜，把蛋埋到沙堆裡了。」

「約翰啊，我看到你那隻斷了腿的紅鶴了。」

「快看，麥可，那是你的洞穴！」

「約翰，小樹叢裡面是什麼東西啊？」

「是一隻狼和狼寶寶，溫蒂，那是妳的寵物狼吧。」

「那邊那個是我的船，約翰，船的兩邊還破了洞呢。」

「不是，那才不是呢，我們已經把你的船給燒掉了。」

「反正那就是我的船，約翰，我看到印第安人的帳棚在冒煙呢！」

「在哪裡？指給我看！只要看到煙上升的彎曲度，我就能告訴你他們是不是要打仗喔。」

「那裡啊，就在神祕河的對面嘛。」

「我看到了，沒錯，他們要打仗了。」

Gwynedd M. Hudson.

他們知道這麼多事，讓彼得有點氣惱，不過要是他想重拾指揮權，那機會就在手邊了，因為我不是說過，他們的恐懼很快就會降臨了嘛？

　　金箭一消逝，整座島陷入了黑暗之中。

　　以前在家裡時，每到睡前，夢幻島就會變得陰森恐怖，島上會出現一些野蠻之地，越來越大，那裡黑影幢幢，獵食的野獸吼聲也變得不同了，尤其是這會讓你失去贏得勝利的信心。這時你會為點燃了夜燈而高興，甚至希望聽娜娜說，那不過是壁爐而已啦，夢幻島只是個虛構的地方。

　　在家時，夢幻島當然只是個假想國，現在它可是真真實實的存在。這兒沒有夜燈，天色也越來越暗，而娜娜又在哪兒呢？

　　本來他們是分開飛翔的，現在全擠到彼得身邊，而彼得也終於收起漫不經心的神情，眼神閃爍發光。他們一碰到他，就感到身體微微一震。他們正飛越這令人生畏的島，飛得很低，有時腳還會被樹給擦破皮。在空中，沒遇見什麼恐怖的東西，速度卻越飛越慢，越飛越吃力，像要推開某種阻力似的。有時他們得在空中盤旋，等彼得在空中揮拳擊退那股阻力，才能繼續前進。

　　「他們不想讓我們著陸。」他解釋。

　　「他們是誰？」溫蒂小聲問道，打了個寒顫。

　　彼得沒說，還是不想說。亭可‧貝爾原本睡在彼得肩上，現在他叫醒她，讓她飛在前頭。

　　有時，他會漂浮在半空中，兩手放在耳邊仔細聆聽，明亮的雙眼直盯著下面，彷彿要把地面射出兩個洞。過一會兒，他又繼續往前飛。

　　彼得的勇氣可真叫人佩服。他對約翰說：「你現在想

冒險呢，還是想先喝杯茶？」

溫蒂立刻回說：「先喝茶。」麥可感激地捏了捏她的手，但膽子較大的約翰有點遲疑。

「什麼樣的冒險啊？」他小心地問。

「就在我們下方的草原上，有個海盜睡得正熟呢。」彼得告訴他：「你想的話，我們就飛下去殺死他。」

「我沒看到他呀。」約翰停頓了好一會兒說。

「我看到了。」

「萬一，他要是醒了怎麼辦？」約翰沙啞著嗓子說道。

彼得激動地說：「你以為我要趁他睡著殺他？我會先叫醒他，再殺掉他的。這才是我一貫的作風。」

「你殺過很多海盜嗎？」

「一堆呢。」

約翰說：「真了不起。」但他還是決定先喝茶，他問現在島上是不是還有很多海盜。彼得回答盛況空前。

「現在誰是船長？」

彼得答：「虎克。」說到這讓人厭惡的名字，他的臉色嚴肅了起來。

「詹姆斯‧虎克？」

「嗯。」

麥可一聽，竟真哭了起來，連約翰講話也喘不過氣來了，他們早聽過惡名昭彰的虎克啦。

「他就是黑鬍子船長，」約翰壓著嗓子小聲說：「他是最兇狠的海盜了，巴比克就怕他一個。」

「就是他沒錯。」彼得說。

「他長得什麼樣子？個頭大嗎？」

「他不像以前那麼高大了。」

「什麼意思？」

「我把他削掉了一塊。」

「你！」

「沒錯，就是我！」彼得厲聲地說。

「我沒有要冒犯你啦。」

「喔，好吧。」

「那……你把他哪裡削掉了？」

「右手。」

「所以他現在不能幹架了喔？」

「喔，他還不照幹嘛！」

「他是左撇子？」

「他用鐵鉤代替右手抓東西。」

「抓？」

「我說，約翰！」彼得說。

「是！」

「要說『是的，是的，先生』。」

「是的，是的，先生。」

「只要是聽我命令做事的男生，」彼得接著說：「都要答應我一件事，你當然也不例外。」

約翰的臉一陣蒼白。

「那就是，要是我們和虎克火拼了起來，你要把他留給我對付。」

「我答應。」約翰忠心耿耿地說。

這時，亭可和他們一起飛翔，大伙就感覺沒那麼害怕了，在她的亮光照耀下，他們可以分辨出彼此的身影。只不過，她無法飛得像他們那麼慢，只好一圈一圈地繞著飛，一群人看起來就像在光環中前進。溫蒂還滿喜歡這樣的，彼得卻點出這樣飛是有危險的。

「亭可告訴我，」彼得說：「海盜天黑前就看到我們了，還把『長湯姆』推了出來。」

「那個大炮？」

「沒錯，而且他們想必看得見亭可的亮光，如果他們猜到我們就在附近，一定會開火打我們的。」

「溫蒂！」

「約翰！」

「麥可！」

「叫亭可馬上離開，彼得。」他們三人同時喊起來。但彼得拒絕了。

「她認為我們是迷路了，」彼得執拗地回答：「她也怕得要死呢，你們不會以為我會在她那麼害怕的時候，還丟下她一個吧！」

這時那圈亮光滅了一下，有什麼親暱地捏了彼得一下。

「那就告訴她，」溫蒂拜託他說：「把亮光熄滅吧。」

「她熄滅不了，那是仙女唯一做不到的事。等她睡著，亮光就會自然熄滅了，就像星星一樣。」

「那就叫她馬上去睡覺。」約翰幾乎是用命令的口氣說道。

「她要是不睏，就沒辦法睡著，這是另一件仙子做不到的事了。」

「我看，」約翰咆哮道：「這兩件事才是該做的！」

約翰也被捏了一下，但動作可一點也不親暱。

「我們要是有口袋就好了。」彼得說：「那就可以把她放到口袋裡了。」只可惜，他們倉促出發，四個人都沒有口袋。

彼得倒有了個絕妙的想法：用約翰的帽子！

亭可同意，只要帽子是用拿的，那她就藏在帽子裡面前進。儘管亭可希望彼得幫她拿帽子，不過還是由約翰來拿。不久，約翰說他飛翔時帽子會打到膝蓋，溫蒂便把帽子接了過去。但這樣一來，就惹出了我們接下來會看到的大麻煩，因為亭可不想欠溫蒂的人情。

在帽子的遮蓋下，亮光完全被掩住了。大伙靜悄悄地繼續往前飛，這種寂靜前所未有，只聽到遠處傳來舔東西的聲響。彼得說，那是野獸在河邊喝水的聲音。有時，又聽到像是樹枝在摩擦的刺耳沙沙聲，但彼得說那是印第安人磨刀的聲音。

這時聲音停了，麥可反而覺得靜得可怕。「有點聲音還比較好！」他喊道。

就像回應他的請求似的，一聲從未聽過的可怕巨響劃破了天際。海盜用「長湯姆」對著他們開炮了。

巨響在山間迴盪著，那些回聲似乎嘶吼著：「他們在哪兒？他們在哪兒？他們在哪兒？」

三個嚇壞的孩子這才猛然驚覺，想像中的島和真實的島簡直天壤之別啊。

　　天空終於歸於平靜，約翰和麥可發現黑夜中只剩他們倆。約翰機械式地在空中踏步，而原本不會漂浮的麥可，這時浮在了空中。

　　「你被打中了嗎？」約翰顫抖著低聲問。

　　「還沒嚐到呢。」麥可也低聲回答。

　　現在我們知道沒有人被打中，但彼得被大砲轟起的風吹到遙遠的海上，而溫蒂被吹到上面去了，身邊沒有別人，只有亭可。

　　要是溫蒂的帽子此時掉了下去，那就太好了。

　　我不知道亭可是突發奇想，還是一路上就在盤算著，總之她立刻從帽子裡跳出來，帶領溫蒂走向死路。

　　亭可也並不是那麼壞啦，或者，說得更明一點兒，她也只有這時才那麼壞，她有些時候還是很好的啦。仙子的想法不是這樣就是那樣，她們身體太小，一次只能容下一種感情。不過她們也是會變的，只是一變就是全盤改變。現在呢，她滿心嫉妒著溫蒂。她那甜美說話的叮叮聲，溫蒂當然是聽不懂，我相信裡頭一定藏有什麼壞心眼的話，只是聽來很和善。她前後來回地飛，彷彿告訴溫蒂說：「跟我來，就什麼事都沒了。」

　　可憐的溫蒂還能怎麼辦呢？她呼喚著彼得、約翰和麥可，回應她的卻只有嘲弄的回音。她不知道亭可討厭她，帶著一種女性強烈的妒恨之心。於是，她東搖西晃茫然地飛著，跟隨著亭可走向自己的厄運。

夢幻島夢境成真

夢幻島覺察到彼得正飛回來，就甦醒過來，恢復了生氣。更正確的字眼應該是說它「被叫醒了」，不過說它「醒過來了」更好，彼得也都是這麼說的。

彼得不在，島上冷冷清清的。小仙女們早上多睡了一個時辰；野獸們照顧著自己的小孩；印第安人大吃大喝了六天六夜，而海盜撞見那些走失的男孩，也只能咬著大拇指互相對視。等到最討厭這樣死氣沉沉的彼得一回來，大夥全都又活躍起來。要是你把耳朵貼在地面上，就會聽見整座島生氣盎然的囉。

這天晚上，島上主要在進行以下的布署：走失的男孩們出來找彼得；海盜出來找走失的男孩；印第安人出門找海盜的蹤跡；野獸則跑出來找印第安人。他們全都繞著島行進，彼此卻碰不到頭，因為啊，大家前進速度全都一樣。

除了小男孩，其他人都殺氣騰騰，巴不得來個一番廝殺。男孩們平時雖熱衷此道，不過今晚是出來迎接隊長的。島上男孩人數不定，因為他們可能會被幹掉了等等，況且依照規定，他們是不該長大的，一旦快要長大，彼得就會讓他們挨餓，以削減數量。目前，要把那對雙胞胎當兩個人算的話，一共有六個男孩。現在，讓我們假想自己正伏在甘蔗林

298

裡，看著大伙兒人人手握短劍，排成一列偷偷摸摸地前進。

　　彼得不許他們看起來有一丁點像他。他們穿著自己獵來的熊皮，全身圓滾滾、毛茸茸的，一摔跤就在地上打滾，所以他們走路都格外小心。

　　第一個走過去的是圖圖。在這支英勇隊伍裡，他不算是最不勇敢，但運氣卻是最背的人。眾人之中他的冒險次數最少，因為只要他一拐過彎，不一會兒就會發生大事。等事情平靜下來，他趁機出外撿生火的柴枝，回來時卻看到其他人已在清洗血跡了。運氣不佳讓他看起來悶悶不樂，不過他的個性非但沒有變得酸溜溜的，反而變得更討人喜歡，也成為幾個孩子裡最謙虛的一個。可憐又體貼的圖圖，今晚危機正等著你呢，要小心啊！一場冒險在等著你了，要是你去了，就會陷入悲慘的境地。圖圖啊，小仙女亭可今晚一心想搞蛋，正想找個人來辦事呢，她覺得你是最容易受騙的一個孩子。要提防亭可啊！

　　要是他能聽到我們的話就好了，可惜我們不是真的在島上，而他就從我們眼前咬著手指頭走過去了。

　　下一個經過的是尼布斯。他是個快樂和氣的孩子，後面跟著史萊特利。尼布斯把樹枝削成哨子，和著自己的曲調手舞足蹈。史萊特利是最自負的一個，自認還記得自己走丟以前的事，還記得那些禮儀習俗什麼的，他鼻子翹得可高了，真惹人厭。捲毛在隊伍中排第四，是個淘氣鬼。每當彼得扳起臉說「誰幹的誰站出來」時，第一個站出來的準是他。現在只要一聽到這句話，他就自動站出來，也不管到底是誰幹的。押尾的是那對雙胞胎，沒什麼字眼可以形容他們，因為只要一形容，一定會把他們兩個搞錯。彼得壓根不曉得什麼叫雙胞胎，而他不懂的事，其他隊員

也不准知道。因此，這兩兄弟自己也搞不清楚，只好一副愧疚，緊挨在一起，盡量取悅旁人。

　　孩子們的身影沒入黑暗之中，隨後不久，換海盜上場了。在島上，事情都發生得很快。未見海盜，先聞其聲，就是那首駭人的歌曲：

> 停船喝，綁繩喝！
> 咱們這就打劫去！
> 要是炮彈來打散，
> 咱們海底必相見！

　　像這幫如此凶惡的人，哪怕在絞刑架上也找不到。看，打前面的是義大利帥哥契科，他赤裸著魁梧的手臂，耳垂上裝飾著兩枚西班牙銀幣，頻頻把頭貼在地面仔細聆聽。他在加奧監獄時，曾用血把自己的名字刻到典獄長背上。跟在他後頭的黑人是個彪形大漢，很多加若木河沿岸的黑人媽媽，常用他的名字來嚇唬孩子，後來他改名換姓，用盡各種名號。接下來這一位呢，是全身布滿刺青的比爾‧鳩克斯，就是那個在海象號上被弗林特砍了七十二刀才扔下金幣袋子的人。還有庫克森，聽說他是布萊克‧默菲的兄弟（不過，從未經證實）。而紳士斯塔奇曾是一所公立學校的警衛，殺起人來仍維持他一貫的優雅。還有史凱萊，亦即摩根‧史凱萊。而愛爾蘭水手長史密，生性出奇和藹，即使他刺了別人一刀，也不會得罪對方，在虎克的船員中，他也是唯一不信英國國教的。還有老是把手放在背後的努得勒，以及羅伯特、穆林斯、阿爾夫‧梅森，和其他一些在西班牙無人不知、無人不怕的暴徒。

　　在這群匪徒中，最邪惡、權力最大的要屬詹姆斯‧虎克了。他把自己的名字寫成詹士‧虎克，據說他是海盜庫克唯一害怕的人。虎克安逸地躺在一輛製作粗糙的馬車上，由手下推著車。他沒有右手，用一支鐵鉤代替，還不時揮動著，催促底下的人加快腳步。這凶狠的傢伙，把他們當狗一般使喚，而他們也像狗一樣服從他。論外表，他的臉孔蒼白暗沉，頭髮長而鬈，遠望如一根根黑蠟燭，讓他英挺的五官更具威脅感。他的雙眼藍得像勿忘我花，透著一股深沉的憂鬱，要是他把鐵鉤對準了你，那兩眼就會燃燒起可怕的紅光。談到舉止，他身上仍保有古代貴族領主的氣概，那氣勢一出即能讓你心驚膽戰。聽說他以前還素以健談聞名呢。他最彬彬有禮時，也就是他最陰險時，這可能是他出身貴族最可信的證據了。即使在咒罵時，他的用詞仍和神態一樣優雅，這證明他和船員們來自於不同的階層。據說他天不怕，地不怕，只怕看到自己的血。他的血很濃稠，顏色也異於常人。在穿著方面，他有點在模仿查理二世，那是因為他早年聽說自己長得和那位倒楣的斯圖亞特王室君主很像。他嘴裡叼著自己設計的煙斗，可以同時吸上兩支雪茄不成問題。不過，他身上最恐怖之處，無疑就屬他的鐵鉤了。

　　現在我們就犧牲一名海盜，來看看虎克是如何殺人的。我們就找史凱萊好了。在眾人前進時，史凱萊笨手笨腳地湊到了虎克跟前，弄皺了他那鑲著花邊的衣領，結果虎克鐵鉤一伸，只聽見一聲撕裂聲，一聲慘叫，史凱萊的屍體已被踢到旁邊了。海盜們繼續前進，虎克嘴裡的雪茄都沒拿出來呢。

　　這可怕的男人，就是彼得‧潘要對抗的人。究竟鹿死誰手呢？

　　尾隨海盜後面、無聲無息潛行過來的是印第安人。他們

一個個瞪大眼睛，走的那條小路只有眼尖的人才看得到。他們手持戰斧和小刀，赤裸的身上塗著油亮亮的顏料，身上掛著一串串海盜啊、小男孩啊的頭皮。這群印第安人屬皮卡尼尼族，可別把他們和那些軟心腸的達拉威族和休倫族給搞混了喔。在前鋒匍匐前進的是身材魁武的黑豹，他是一名勇士，身上掛的頭皮多到簡直要絆住他了。走在隊伍最後方、也是最危險位置的是猛虎莉莉，她是個天生的公主，站得直挺挺的，自負得不得了。在膚色黝黑的女將中，她的臉蛋最標致，是皮卡尼尼族的大美人。她一下騷，一下冷，一下熱，眾勇士都恨不得能娶這個難以捉摸的女子為妻，但她用斧頭擊退了所有的求婚者。瞧瞧這群印第安人怎樣一聲不響地踩過地上的樹枝，唯一能聽見的只有粗重的呼吸聲，原來，他們在大吃大喝後都變肥了，只是過不了多久，他們就會消耗變瘦。然而在此刻，肥胖卻會帶來危機四伏。

之後，印第安人如影子般消失無蹤，不久，出現一大群隊伍，各類野獸混雜其中，有獅子、老虎、熊，還有在牠們眼前奔竄逃命、數不清的小野獸。在這個得天獨厚的島上，各種野獸，特別是所有吃人的野獸，皆要雜處並存。牠們垂著舌頭，今晚都餓扁了。

野獸群走過之後，最後一個角色登場了，那是隻龐大的鱷魚，而牠追逐的目標是誰，很快就會揭曉。

鱷魚走過沒多久，男孩們又現身。這一列隊伍持續前進著，要是有誰停止了，或改變了速度，大伙很快就會打成一團。

大家全都凝神仔細盯著前方瞧，沒有人想到危險會從背後襲來。看來，夢幻島是多麼地真實呀。

那群男孩首先脫離了這支循環不息的行進隊伍，他們往草地一撲，靠近地底的家。

「真希望彼得回來呀。」大伙焦急不安地說，儘管他們都長得比隊長高，比隊長壯。

史萊特利說道：「我可是唯一不怕海盜的哦。」那腔調真惹人嫌呀。或許是遠處什麼聲響驚動了他，他趕緊補充：「不過我還是希望他能回來，跟我們說他是不是又聽說了什麼灰姑娘的故事了。」

他們聊起了灰姑娘，圖圖相信，他媽媽一定長得很像灰姑娘。

只有彼得不在時，他們才能談到媽媽。彼得禁止大家談論這話題，他覺得這無聊透頂了。

「我只記得我媽媽一件事，」尼布斯告訴他們：「她老愛對我父親說：『啊，我真希望有自己的支票簿啊。』我是不知道什麼是支票簿啦，可是我真想送給她一本呢。」

就在說話當兒，眾人聽到遠處傳來聲響。你或我，不是森林走獸，當然是聽不到任何聲音啦，但他們聽到了，那是海盜唱的那首陰森恐怖的歌：

> 唷喝，唷喝，海盜生涯
> 骷髏白骨的旗幟，
> 歡樂時光，麻繩一根，
> 好啊，大衛·瓊斯。

轉眼間，走失的孩子們都上哪兒去啦？他們不在那兒，兔子也沒法溜那麼快呀。

我會告訴你他們在哪兒。除了尼布斯跑到別處偵察敵情，其他人全回到了地底家園。那是個美好之家，我們待會就能看到。他們是怎麼回去的呢？看不到任何入口，連塊大石頭也沒有，就是那種一挪開就會露出洞窟的石頭。不過呢，只要仔細瞧，就會發現這兒有七株大樹，樹幹全是空心的，和小男孩的身體一般大小，這就是通往地底家園的七個入口。虎克找了好長時間，卻老是找不著，今晚他會找到嗎？

海盜們趨近這裡時，斯塔奇眼尖，瞧見尼布斯穿過樹林跑掉，他立即亮出手槍，一支鐵鉤卻攫住了他的肩膀。

「船長，放開我！」他扭動著身體叫道。

「先把槍收起來！」他威脅道。這是我們頭一回聽到虎克的嗓音，低沉而陰鬱。

「那個也是你痛恨的男孩呀，我本來可以打死他的。」

「是啊，然後槍聲就把印第安人猛虎莉莉引來，你頭皮是不想要了嗎？」

「船長，那去追他吧？」史密可憐兮兮地問：「然後再用我的『強尼開瓶器』給他搔一搔癢？」史密愛幫每樣東西取個好聽的名字，他喜歡拿刀往傷口裡扭轉，所以管自己的短彎刀叫『強尼開瓶器』。史密可愛的特點可多了，像他殺人後不擦武器，卻去擦眼鏡呢。

「強尼可是個安靜的傢伙呢。」史密提醒虎克。

「不是現在，史密。」虎克陰沉地說：「這才一個，我的目標是把他們七個統統解決掉。分頭去找！」

海盜們紛紛走入樹林裡，不久只剩下船長和史密兩個人。虎克重重嘆了一口氣，我不知道他為何嘆氣，或許是夜色很柔美吧，他一時興起，想將自己這一生的故事講給他忠心的水手聽。他認真地講了很久，只不過，愚蠢的史密一點也聽不懂他在說什麼。

這時，史密忽然聽到彼得的名字。

「我最想抓到的，」虎克激動地說：「就是他們的隊長彼得‧潘，就是他砍掉我的手臂的。」他凶狠地揮動著鐵鉤，「我等了很久，就是要用這玩意兒和他握握手。噢，我要把他給撕碎！」

「可是，我常聽你說，那支鉤子比二十隻手還管用呢，能用來梳頭髮，還能做家事什麼的。」史密說。

船長回答：「是啊，我要是個媽媽，我會祈禱我的孩子生下來就有這玩意兒，不要有手那個東西。」他得意地瞄了一眼鐵鉤，又輕蔑地瞥了左手一眼，又皺起眉頭。

他有些畏縮地說：「彼得把我的胳臂，扔給了一隻正好路過的鱷魚。」

「我常發現，你對於鱷魚有種奇怪的恐懼。」史密說。

虎克糾正他：「我不是怕鱷魚，我只怕那一隻鱷魚。」他壓低嗓子說：「那隻鱷魚很喜歡我的手臂，史密。從那次以後，牠就一直跟著我，上山下海，口水直流，多想吃我身體的其他地方啊。」

「換個角度看，這也算是一種恭維吧。」史密說

「我才不要這種恭維呢！」虎克怒吼道：「我要的是彼得‧潘，那個最先讓鱷魚嚐到了我滋味的人！」

虎克坐在大蘑菇上，聲音顫抖，啞聲說道：「史密，那隻鱷魚本來該把我吞下肚的，幸好牠之前吞了一個鐘，鐘在肚子裡滴答滴答響個不停，只要牠想靠近我，我一聽到滴答聲，就一溜煙逃跑了。」他大笑著，卻是一陣乾笑。

「總有一天，時鐘會停掉，到時牠就逮著你了。」史密說。

虎克舔舔乾澀的唇，說：「唉！這就是我老擔心的事。」

他坐下後就一直感覺身上出奇地熱。「史密，這個位子是燙的耶。」說罷猛地跳了起來，「活見鬼，要命了，

我都快被燒焦了！」

　　他們仔細檢查蘑菇，蘑菇的大小和硬度都非本地所見。兩人本想把蘑菇拔下來，沒想到它卻立刻掉下來，原來這蘑菇沒長根呀。更怪的是，一陣煙立刻冒了上來。兩個海盜面面相覷，「煙囪！」他們同時驚呼。

　　他們發現的果真是地底家園的煙囪。這是孩子們的習慣，當敵人來到附近時，就用蘑菇把煙囪蓋上。

　　不只有煙冒了上來，也傳出來了孩子們的聲音，他們覺得躲在這藏身之處十分安全，便快快活活地閒聊起來。兩名海盜狡詐地聽了一會，又把蘑菇放回原處。他們環視周圍，發現了七棵樹裡的洞。

　　「你有沒有聽到他們說彼得‧潘不在家？」史密小聲說著，一面把玩著強尼開瓶器。

　　虎克點點頭。他站著沉思了好一陣子，黑黝黝的臉上露出一道凝結的笑。史密就等這個，「說出你的計畫吧，船長。」史密急切地喊。

　　虎克緩緩從牙縫中擠出話來：「回船上去，烤個又香又濃的大蛋糕，再灑上綠色糖粉。這下面只見到一個煙囪，想必只有一間房子。這群地鼠笨得很，不知道不需要每人一個單獨的出口，可見他們都沒有媽媽。我們把蛋糕放在美人魚的礁湖邊，這夥小子們常到那兒游泳，和美人魚玩耍。當他們看到了蛋糕，就會狼吞虎嚥。他們沒有媽媽，不會知道吃香濃潮濕的大蛋糕會有多危險。」他放聲大笑，這回可不是乾笑，而是開懷大笑，「哈哈，他們死定了！」

　　史密越聽越佩服。

　　他喊：「這真是我聽過最邪惡、最妙的計謀啦！」他們得意地邊跳邊唱：

上纜繩唷，我一來，

他們就害怕；

只要你和虎克的鐵鉤握手，

你就只剩下一身骨頭。

　　他們唱起了這首歌，還不等唱完，就被一個聲音給打斷。一開始，聲音極細微，似乎一片樹葉落下就能蓋住它，但等它越接近，聲音就越清楚。

　　滴答，滴答，滴答，滴答。

　　虎克站著發抖，一隻腳提得高高的。

　　他上氣不接下氣地說：「是那隻鱷魚！」他立刻飛奔逃走，水手緊跟在後。

　　是那隻鱷魚沒錯。牠趕過了正在追蹤其他海盜的印第安人，身上淌著水，在虎克身後緊追不捨。

　　孩子們又跑了出來，但夜晚的危機還未結束。忽然間，尼布斯氣喘吁吁地跑了過來，後面跟著一群狼，伸長舌頭，嚎叫聲令人不寒而慄。

　　「救救我！救救我！」尼布斯喊著，跌倒在地上。

　　「我們該怎麼辦？我們該怎麼辦？」

　　這該算是對彼得最大的讚美吧，在這危急時刻，大家全想到了他。

　　「彼得會怎麼做？」他們異口同聲喊道。

　　眾口一聲說：「彼得會從胯下盯著牠們看。」

　　「我們就照彼得的辦法做吧。」他們接著說。

　　要對付狼，這是最有效的辦法了。他們動作一致地彎下腰，從胯下往後看。下一分鐘時間過得很長，不過勝利也旋即到來。男孩們用這可怕的姿勢一逼進狼群，狼就夾著尾巴逃之夭夭了。

這時尼布斯從地上爬了起來，他瞪圓眼睛，其他小孩以為他還在盯著狼，不過他看到的可不是狼。

　　他喊著：「我看見一個更奇怪的東西！」孩子們全急切地圍攏過來。「一隻大白鳥，正往這裡飛過來啦！」

　　「你說那是什麼鳥？」

　　「我哪知道！」尼布斯驚訝地說：「不過牠看起來累呆了，一邊飛，還一邊哼著『可憐的溫蒂呀』。」

　　「可憐的溫蒂？」

　　「我想起來了！」史萊特利立刻說道：「有一種鳥就叫溫蒂。」

　　「看，牠來了！」捲毛指著天空中的溫蒂喊道。

　　這時，溫蒂已經快飛到他們頭頂上。孩子們可以聽到她哀傷的呼叫聲，不過，聽得更清楚的是亭可刺耳的喊叫聲。這個吃醋的小仙女，現在脫下一切友好的偽裝，排山倒海地向溫蒂展開攻擊，她一碰到溫蒂的身體，就狠狠地擰她一把。

　　「喂，亭可！」孩子們驚訝地喊。

　　亭可傳來一聲回答：「彼得要你們射死溫蒂！」

　　彼得下的命令他們向來深信不疑。「那我們就照彼得的吩咐做吧。」這群單純的孩子們嚷道。「快，拿弓箭來！」

　　除了圖圖，男孩們都跳進了樹洞，因為圖圖手上已經拿著弓箭了。亭可一看到他，就搓搓自己的小手。

　　她大聲喊著：「快呀，圖圖，快！彼得會很高興的喔。」

　　圖圖興奮地把箭抵在弓上，高喊：「別擋著，亭可！」接著就把箭射了出去。於是，溫蒂便搖搖晃晃地落到地上，胸口插上了一隻箭。

溫蒂的小屋

Chapter 6

就在其他孩子拿著武器跳出樹洞時，糊塗的圖圖，儼然一副勝利者的姿態站在溫蒂身邊。

他驕傲地喊道：「你們來晚了，我射中溫蒂了，彼得一定會很高興的。」

半空中的亭可大喊了一聲「大笨蛋」，便飛到別處躲藏起來。其他孩子沒聽見她的話，全圍到溫蒂身邊盯著她看。樹林裡寂靜得駭人，要是溫蒂還有心跳，他們一定聽得到的。

史萊特利先開口，聲音帶著驚恐地說道：「這不是鳥，她應該是個小姐。」

「小姐？」圖圖說著，發起抖來。

「而我們殺了她。」尼布斯嗓音沙啞地說道。

大家都脫下了帽子。

捲毛說：「現在我明白了，是彼得帶她來找我們的。」他悔恨地倒在地上。

「好不容易有個小姐可以來照顧我們，卻被你殺了！」其中一個雙胞胎說。

他們為圖圖難過，更為自己難過。所以當圖圖走近他們，他們便轉過身子，不理睬他。

圖圖的臉色涮地慘白，卻也有一分從未有過的莊嚴。

他沉吟著：「是我做的，以前我夢到小姐，就會說：『漂亮媽媽，漂亮媽媽』。現在，她真的來了，卻被我射死了。」

他緩緩走開。

「不要走嘛。」他們同情地說。

他發著抖回答：「我非走不可，我怕死彼得了。」

就在這悲慘的一刻，他們聽到一個聲音，心臟都快跳到喉嚨了，那是彼得的歡呼聲。

他們嚷道：「彼得！」因為彼得每次回來，都會發出這樣的訊號來宣告。

「把她藏起來。」他們低聲說，匆忙用身體圍住溫蒂，而圖圖卻獨自站在一旁。

又一陣歡呼，彼得停落在他們面前。他喊：「哈囉，男孩們！」他們機械地向他行禮後，接著又是一陣沉默。

彼得皺起眉頭。

他很惱火：「我回來了，你們怎麼不歡呼啊？」

他們張開嘴，但歡呼詞卻吐不出來。不過彼得急著要告訴大伙天大的好消息，竟然沒有注意到。

「好消息，孩子們，我終於為大伙兒帶來了一個媽媽了。」他喊。

還是沒有半點聲響，只聽到砰的一聲，是圖圖跪倒在地。

「你們沒有看見她嗎？」彼得問，開始有點不安。「她是往這邊飛的。」

一個聲音說：「唉呀！」另一個聲音說：「喔，真悲慘的一天呀！」

圖圖站起來，冷靜地說：「彼得，我帶你去看她吧。」

別的小孩想把她藏起來，圖圖卻說：「退後，雙胞胎，讓彼得來看。」

於是大家一起往後退，好讓彼得看一看。彼得看了一眼，卻不知手措。

「她死了，」彼得不安地說：「她可能在害怕自己正在死去吧。」

彼得很想用滑稽的步子跳得遠遠的，拋掉她的身影，以後再也不走近這裡。如果他這麼做，男孩們也都會樂意跟著他走。

可是那裡一有支箭，彼得把箭從溫蒂的胸口拔下來，看著他的同伴。

「這是誰的箭？」他嚴厲地問。

「是我的，彼得。」圖圖跪著說。

彼得說：「喔，卑鄙的手啊！」他舉起箭想把它當成短劍用。

圖圖毫不退縮，他袒開胸膛，堅定地說：「刺吧，彼得！刺準一點！」

彼得把箭舉起了兩次，又放下。他驚駭地說：「我辦不到！有什麼在阻止我的手！」

大家驚訝地看著他，除了尼布斯，也還好尼布斯在看著溫蒂。

「是她！是溫蒂小姐，看，她的手臂！」他叫道。

說也奇怪，溫蒂真的舉起手了。尼布斯彎下身，恭敬地聽她說話。「她好像是說『可憐的圖圖』。」他輕聲說道。

「她還活著。」彼得簡短地說。

史萊特利立刻喊道：「溫蒂小姐還活著耶。」

彼得在她身邊跪下，看到了他那顆橡實鈕扣。你應該還記得吧，溫蒂曾把它繫上鏈子，掛在脖子上。

「看！箭射到的是這個，這是我給她的吻救了她一命耶！」他說。

「我記得吻是什麼，」史萊特利趕緊插嘴道：「快給我看看！啊，這是吻沒錯。」

彼得沒聽見他說什麼，他在祈求溫蒂快點復原，好帶她去看美人魚。當然溫蒂還無法回答他，她暈暈迷迷的。而這時，上方傳來一陣悲傷的哭泣聲。

捲毛說：「聽，是亭可！她在哭，因為溫蒂還活著。」

於是他們把亭可的罪行告訴彼得。彼得臉上出現了他們前所未見的嚴厲神情。

他喊道：「喂，亭可！妳再也不是我的朋友了，以後永遠不要在我面前出現！」

亭可飛到彼得肩上求情，卻被他一手撇開，一直到溫蒂又舉起手，彼得才溫和下來說：「好吧，不是永遠，是一整個禮拜。」

你以為亭可會因為溫蒂舉起手臂而感激她嗎？喔，絕不！她反倒更想揍她了。小仙女們真的是奇怪呀，以至於最暸解她們的彼得，常用手掌摑她們。

而溫蒂現在身體這麼虛弱，該如何是好呢？

「我們把她抬到地底家園去吧。」捲毛建議。

「對，是應該這樣對待小姐的。」史萊特利說。

「不，不！你們不能碰她，那太不敬了。」彼得說。

「我也這麼想。」史萊特利說。

「可是如果她再躺在這兒，會死掉的。」圖圖說。

「沒錯，她會死的，」史萊特利承認道：「可是又有什麼辦法呢？」

彼得喊道：「有！有辦法！我們可以圍著她蓋棟小屋。」

　　大家聽了都很高興。彼得命令道：「快，把你們最好的東西都給我拿來，把家裡給掏空吧，動作俐落一點兒。」

　　於是，大伙馬上就像婚禮前夕的裁縫師一樣忙碌了起來。他們東奔西跑，一會兒跑下去取被褥，一會兒又跑上來拿木柴。就在大家忙成一團時，來了兩個人，那不是別人，正是約翰和麥可！他們一步步拖拖拉拉地走過來，腳步一停，就站在那兒打起瞌睡，等清醒了，又往前一步，然後又睡著。

　　「約翰，約翰！」麥可喊道：「醒過來啊！娜娜在哪裡啊？還有媽媽呢？」

　　然後約翰就揉揉眼睛，喃喃說道：「這是真的，我們會飛了。」

　　你可以確定的是，他們一見到彼得就大大鬆了一口氣。

　　「哈囉，彼得。」他們說。

　　「哈囉。」彼得親切地回答，其實他快把他們給忘了。這時他正忙著用腳量溫蒂的身長，看看需要蓋多大的屋子，當然還得留些空位放桌椅。約翰和麥可望著他。

　　「溫蒂睡著了嗎？」他們問。

　　「是啊。」

　　麥可提議說：「約翰，我們把她叫醒，讓她幫我們做晚飯吧。」正說著，只見另外幾個孩子抱著樹枝跑來，準備蓋小屋。「你看他們！」麥可喊。

　　「捲毛，」彼得用他身為隊長最有威嚴的腔調說：「把這兩個孩子帶去幫忙蓋房子。」

　　「是的，是的，老大。」

　　「蓋房子？」約翰叫道。

　　「蓋給溫蒂的。」捲毛說。

「蓋給溫蒂的？」約翰訝異地說道：「為什麼？她是女生耶。」

「就因為這樣，所以我們才都要當她的僕人啊。」捲毛解釋。

「你們？溫蒂的僕人！」

彼得說：「是啊，你們兩個也是，跟他們一塊去吧。」

吃驚不已的兩兄弟被拉去鋸鋸砍砍、搬運木頭。彼得命令：「先做椅子和暖爐架，然後再環繞著它們蓋房子。」

「沒錯，房子就是這樣蓋的，我全記起來了。」史萊特利說。

彼得想得很周到。他命令：「史萊特利，去請醫生來。」

史萊特利立刻回道：「是，是！」然後便搔著頭消失了。他知道彼得的命令是一定要服從的。沒多久，他就戴著約翰的帽子回來了，神情嚴肅。

「這位先生，」彼得走向史萊特利說道：「請問你是醫生嗎？」

彼得和其他男孩不一樣的地方是，雖然他們都知道這是假裝的，但是對彼得來說，假裝的和真的沒什麼兩樣。這一點常讓孩子們感覺為難，比如他們有時就要假裝吃過飯了。

若是他們拆穿了假裝的東西，彼得就會敲他們的關節。

「是啊，小朋友。」史萊特利提心吊膽地回答，因為他的關節都給敲裂了。

「請幫幫忙呀，先生。」彼得解釋：「有位小姐病得很重。」

她就躺在他們腳邊，可是史萊特利假裝沒瞧見。

「嘖，嘖，她躺在哪兒呀？」他說。

「在那邊的空地上。」

　　史萊特利說：「我要把一個玻璃器具放到她嘴裡。」他假裝做著，彼得在一旁等候，看著他把玻璃器具從嘴裡拿出來，真是急死人了。

　　「她怎麼樣了？」彼得問。

　　史萊特利說：「嘖，嘖，這東西治好她了。」

　　「那我真是太高興了。」彼得說。

　　史萊特利說：「今晚我還會再過來，用帶嘴的杯子餵她喝牛肉湯。」他把帽子還給約翰，大大吐了一口氣，那是他躲開麻煩時的一種習慣。

　　這時，樹林裡滿是斧頭砍木材的聲音。蓋一間舒適小屋所需的一切，差不多都已備齊，堆放在溫蒂腳邊。

　　「要是我們知道她喜歡哪一種房子就好了。」有個孩子說。

　　「彼得，」另一個孩子叫道：「她睡著了還在動耶。」

　　「她嘴巴張開了，」第三個孩子喊著，虔敬地盯著她的嘴：「哇，真可愛哇。」

　　「說不定她會在睡夢裡唱歌喔，溫蒂，把妳喜歡的房子唱出來吧。」彼得說。

　　溫蒂雙眼還沒睜開，就立刻唱了起來：

> 希望我有可愛的屋子，
> 小巧到未曾有人見過。
> 它的紅色小牆真稀奇，
> 還有綠如青苔的屋頂。

　　大家聽了高興得咯咯笑，因為他們運氣可真好啊，砍來的木材都流著黏呼呼的紅色樹液，而遍地都布滿了青苔。他們蓋小屋時，也唱了起來：

　　我們蓋了小牆小屋頂，
　　還有一扇可愛的小門。
　　溫蒂媽媽請跟我們說，
　　還有什麼是妳想要的？

　　對於這個問題，溫蒂提出貪心了的要求：

　　喔，接下來我想要的，
　　是四面裝有華麗窗戶，
　　也就是有玫瑰攀進來，
　　還有小嬰兒們往外望。

　　於是他們拳一揮，就裝起窗戶，還用了大片的黃色樹葉做百葉窗，但是，玫瑰花呢……？
　　「玫瑰花啊！」彼得嚴厲地喊。
　　他們立刻假裝沿著牆，種起了最嬌美的玫瑰。
　　那，小嬰兒呢？
　　為了避免彼得要嬰兒，他們趕緊又唱：

　　我們已讓玫瑰攀進來，
　　嬰兒也已來到了門前，
　　因我們以前就是嬰兒
　　所以不能再變造自己。

　　彼得看到這主意不錯，就馬上假裝這是他想出來的。屋子很漂亮，溫蒂待在裡頭一定很舒適，雖然他們當然再也看不到她了啦。儘管屋子看起來像完工了，彼得仍來回踱著步，吩咐大家完成最後的布置，畢竟什麼都逃不過他那雙鷹眼的。

「門上還沒裝門環呢。」彼得說。

他們覺得很難為情，但圖圖倒是把他的鞋底拿來，做成了一個很不錯的門環。

這下可總算完成了吧，他們想。

還差得遠哩。彼得說：「沒有煙囪，我們要有個煙囪。」

「當然要有個煙囪。」約翰煞有其事地說。彼得想到一個點子，他一把抓起約翰頭上的帽子，把帽頂敲掉，扣在屋頂上。小屋子有了這個一流的煙囪，高興極了，像為了表示謝意似的，一陣煙立即從帽裡升起。

這回真的徹底完工了，什麼都不缺，只缺有人來敲門。

「把你們最好的一面表現出來吧，」彼得提醒他們，「第一印象太重要了。」

他倒很慶幸沒人問他什麼是第一印象。大家全都忙著打扮，秀出最好的一面。

彼得有禮地敲了敲門，這時，樹林和孩子們一樣安靜無聲。除了亭可的聲音，再也聽不到任何一丁點聲響。亭可正坐在樹枝上看著他們，大剌剌地譏笑著。

孩子們心想，會不會有人來應門？如果是位小姐，她會長得什麼樣子呢？

門打開了，一位小姐走了出來，正是溫蒂。大家全刷地一聲脫下帽子。

她恰如其分露出驚訝的神情，這正是他們希望看到的。

「我現在在哪兒呀？」她說。

搶先回答的自然是史萊特利了。他急忙說：「溫蒂小姐，我們幫妳蓋了這間小屋喔。」

「啊，說你很喜歡吧！」尼布斯叫道。

溫蒂說：「真是可愛呀，這心愛的屋子。」這也是孩

子們希望她說的話。

「我們是你的小孩。」雙胞胎說。

接著，他們全都跪下，伸出雙臂喊道：「溫蒂小姐，當我們的母親吧。」

溫蒂臉上發出亮光，說道：「我嗎？那一定是很棒的囉，可是你們看，我只是個小女生，沒有當媽媽的經驗耶。」

「那沒有關係的啦。」彼得說道，一副好像他是在場唯一懂的人似的。但其實呢，他是最不懂的那一個。「我們只是需要一個像媽媽一樣好的人。」

「哎呀！你們知道嗎？我覺得我就是那樣的人耶。」溫蒂說。

他們喊道：「對啊，對啊，我們一眼就看出來了。」

「好極了，」溫蒂說：「我會盡力做到的。快進來吧，你們這群頑皮的孩子，我敢說，你們的腳都濕吧，在我送你們上床睡覺前，還有時間講完灰姑娘的故事呢。」

他們走進房子。我不知道小屋裡如何容納這麼多人，不過人們在夢幻島可以緊緊擠在一起。他們和溫蒂度過許多愉快的夜晚，而這只是第一晚。隨後，溫蒂帶他們回去地底，睡在大床上，幫他們蓋好被子，但她自己那晚睡在小屋裡。彼得則拔出刀子在屋外巡邏，海盜還在遠處飲酒作樂，狼群也在四處覓食。黑暗中，小屋顯得舒適安全，百葉窗裡透出亮光，煙囪冒出裊裊輕煙，外面又有彼得在站崗。

過一會兒，彼得也睡著了。那些小仙女們狂歡後正要回家，搖搖晃晃的，只好從他身上爬過去。要是別的小孩在夜晚擋住小仙女的路，她們可是會搗亂的，不過，她們只是擰了擰彼得的鼻子就走過去了。

地底的家園

Chapter 7

隔天，彼得做的第一件事就是幫溫蒂、約翰和麥可量身材，好找適合的空心樹。你應該還記得，虎克曾經嘲笑孩子們每人都有自己的樹洞，其實是他太無知了，因為除非那棵樹很合身材，否則要上上下下是很困難的，而這些孩子的身材都不一樣。一旦樹和身材能配合，只要在樹頂吸一口氣，就能以最適當的速度滑下去；要上來的時候，只要吸氣吐氣不時交替，就能扭動著身體爬上來。當然，等熟悉了這些動作，就能不假思索地爬上爬下，姿態再優美不過了。

不過，身材和樹洞的大小一定得配合才行，所以彼得量身材的時候就像在做一套衣服那麼仔細。唯一的不同點是，衣服是依照你的身材來訂做，但你的身體要配合樹的大小做調整。衣服可以多穿一點或是少穿一點，這通常是很好辦的，但如果你身上某些笨拙的部位凹凸不平，或是唯一能找到的樹長得奇形怪狀，彼得就會在你身上想辦法，那樣你的身材就可以和樹相配了。一旦配得上，就得格外小心保持這個身材，而也正因為如此，溫蒂很高興地發現，全家人都能維持良好的身材。

溫蒂和麥可的樹都是第一次試就很合，但是約翰卻得改好幾次才成功。

練習了幾天以後，他們就像在井裡的水桶一樣，能順利地上上下下了，而他們也都熱烈地愛上了這地底的家，特別是溫蒂。像所有的家庭一樣，它有一間大廳，要是你想釣魚，就可以在大廳的地面挖洞抓蚯蚓，地上還長著色彩迷人的結實蘑菇，可以當凳子坐。有一棵奇幻樹拼命要從房中央長出來，但每天早晨孩子們都會把樹幹給鋸得和地面一樣平。到了下午茶時間，它又長到兩英尺高，孩子們會在樹幹上放一個門板，正好可以拿來當桌子用，等喝完下午茶，再把樹幹鋸掉，屋子裡又有寬敞的地方玩遊戲了。屋裡還有一個巨大的壁爐，幾乎占滿房子的整個角落，你想在哪兒生火都行。溫蒂在爐前繫上許多用植物纖維做的繩子，把洗乾淨的衣服晾在上頭。白天床鋪就靠牆斜立著，到晚上六點半才放下來，床鋪的大小幾乎是屋子的一半，除了麥可之外，其他孩子都睡在這張床上，擠得像罐頭裡的沙丁魚一樣；連翻身都有極嚴格的規定，由一個人發號施令，大家才能一起翻身。麥可本來也該睡在床上，但是溫蒂想要一個嬰兒，而他是年紀最小的，女人是什麼樣子你們是知道的，也因此，麥可睡在了掛起來的搖籃裡。

這個家十分簡陋，就和小熊在同樣條件下在地底建造的家沒什麼兩樣，只是牆上有一個小壁龕，和鳥籠差不多大，那是亭可的獨門公寓，一塊小小的布幔就能和其他地方隔開。亭可是很挑剔的，不論穿衣或是脫衣，都要把布幔拉上，其他女性，包括身材比她高大的，都沒有享受過這樣臥室與起居室結合的精緻閨房。她的臥榻——亭可都是這樣稱呼她的床，是瑪布皇后式的，床腳是三夜草形狀，她會依照當季開的花更換床罩；她的鏡子是長靴貓用的那種款式，在小仙女販賣的貨架上，如今只剩下三面還沒有

打碎；洗臉盆是像派皮一樣，可以翻過來；抽屜不折不扣是產於迷人的六世時代的；地毯是馬傑利和羅賓極盛時代的產品；一盞用亮片裝飾的吊燈，掛在那兒用來擺擺樣子，當然啦，亭可自己發的光就可以照亮整個屋子。而她瞧不起家中其餘的部分，這也是難免的。她的小房間儘管美麗，卻有點太炫耀，看起來就像老是往上翹的鼻子似的。

我想這一切讓溫蒂很著迷，這些吵鬧的孩子讓她忙得團團轉。就真有過好幾個星期，她除了晚上帶些襪子上去補，都沒有上來地面過。就說做飯吧，她的鼻子根本沒離開鍋子，就算鍋裡什麼也沒有，甚至也許根本沒有鍋，她也得一直看著，以防煮沸了。你永遠無法確定，他們到底是真的吃了，還是假裝有吃飯，這都得由彼得來決定。他當然也可以吃飯，如果這是遊戲規則，他會真的吃，可是他不能為了填飽肚皮去吃飯，而這卻是每個孩子最喜歡做的事，而他們其次喜歡的事就是聊吃的。對彼得來說，假裝就是真的，他假裝吃飯的時候，你會看到他真的胖起來了。當然啦，對其他的孩子來說是件苦事，不過，你就是得跟著他做，但如果你能向他證明，你的身材太瘦，和樹洞不合，他就會讓你飽餐一頓。

溫蒂特別喜歡在孩子們上床睡覺後，好好享受縫縫補補的時間。據她的說法，只有在這個時候，她才有喘息的空間，她會利用這時間幫他們做新衣服，在膝蓋補上雙層布料，因為那些地方總是磨損得特別厲害。

每當溫蒂對著一整籃在腳踝處都破了洞的襪子坐下，她就會忍不住舉起雙臂，嘆道：「唉呀，我有時候還真羨慕老姑婆啊。」

她嘆氣歸嘆氣，臉上卻得意洋洋地發著光。

還記得她那隻寵物小狼吧！啊，它很快就發現溫蒂已

經來到島上，還找到了她。他倆一見面就彼此抱在一起，從此以後，牠到哪兒都跟著她。

一天天過去，難道她不想念遠處親愛的父母嗎？這個問題很難回答，因為在夢幻島到底過了多久時間，誰也說不清。時間是用月亮和太陽計算的，但島上的太陽和月亮，比大陸多得多呢。我想溫蒂並不怎麼掛念她的父母，她很確信他們一定會隨時打開窗子，等著她飛回去，這讓她覺得很放心。然而，約翰對父母的記憶卻是模模糊糊的，覺得他們只像他過去認識的人，這讓溫蒂十分不安。至於麥可呢，他倒情願相信，溫蒂就是他的母親。這些事讓她有些害怕，於是她勇敢地負起責任，她幫他們出些考試卷，就像過去她在學校裡考試一樣，想把以往的記憶牢牢釘在他們腦海裡。其他的孩子覺得這實在太有趣了，硬是要參加考試，他們自備了石板，圍著桌子坐，溫蒂用另一塊石板寫下問題，傳給他們，他們看了問題，都努力地去想，認真地去寫，那都是些很普通的問題啦——

　　媽媽的眼睛是什麼顏色？
　　誰比較高，爸爸還是媽媽？
　　媽媽是金髮還是黑髮？
　　盡可能三題都作答。

寫一篇四十字以上的作文，題目是「我如何度過上一次假期」，或「比較父親和母親的性格」，請任選一題作答。或是如以下的問題：

　　一、描述媽媽的笑。
　　二、描述爸爸的笑。

三、描述媽媽的宴會禮服。
四、描述狗屋和屋內的狗。

　　每天出的題目大致上就是這些，要是你不會回答，就畫一個叉叉，就連約翰考卷上的叉叉數量都十分嚇人，而能夠回答所有題目的，自然只有史萊特利。沒有人比史萊特利更想第一個交卷，但他的答案卻都非常可笑，而且實際上他總是最後一個交卷，多可悲呀！

　　彼得不參加考試，一來是除了溫蒂，他根本瞧不起所有的母親；二來，他是島上唯一一個既不會寫字也不會拼字的孩子，連最短的字都不會。他根本是不屑做這些事的。

　　順便提一點，考卷上的問題都是用過去式時態寫的，像是『媽媽的眼睛以前是什麼顏色』等等，你瞧，溫蒂自己都開始忘了。

　　至於冒險嘛，那自然是每天都會發生的，接下來我們就會看到。這一次，彼得在溫蒂的幫忙下，發明了一種新遊戲，玩得簡直入了迷，可後來他突然又不感興趣了，就像我之前告訴你的，他對遊戲向來如此。這個遊戲就是假裝不要冒險，只能做約翰和麥可每天都做的事：坐在凳子上、把球拋到空中、互相推來推去、出去散步、一隻灰熊都不殺就回來了。看彼得無所事事坐在小凳子上的模樣，可真有意思，他總忍不住擺出一本正經的表情坐著不動，這對他來說是在做一件

滑稽有趣的事。他誇口說，為了保持健康，他要出去散步一會兒，這就是他好幾天以來所做過最冒險的事，而約翰和麥可也不得不假裝有趣，否則彼得就會對他們不客氣。

彼得常獨自出門，等他回來後，你也弄不清楚他到底有沒有經歷什麼冒險。或許是他忘得一乾二淨了，所以什麼都沒說，但你一出去，卻又會看到地上有屍體；有時候，他又會大談自己經歷了哪些冒險，卻一具屍體也看不到。有時他回到家，頭上裹著繃帶，溫蒂會過去安慰他，用溫水幫他清洗傷口，他就會講一段精彩的冒險故事，但是你也知道，溫蒂根本不知道故事的真假。她知道有些冒險是真的，因為她自己也參與了，而其他的故事，她知道至少有一部分是真的，因為別的孩子也參與了，都說是千真萬確的。要把這些故事都寫上，大概會有英語拉丁文雙解辭典那麼厚吧，我們頂多能列舉其一，看看在島上的一個小時是怎麼過的。可難就難在該舉哪個例子呢，我們是不是該說說和印第安人在峽谷的那場小衝突呢？這是一場血腥的戰事，有趣的是，它卻表現出彼得的一項特點，那就是在戰鬥進行到一半的時候，他會突然改變陣營，換到敵人那一邊；當他們在山谷裡勝負未定，可能是這一方勝出，下一秒又變成他方會贏時，彼得會大喊：「我今天是印第安人，那你呢，圖圖？」圖圖說：「印第安人，你呢，尼布斯？」尼布斯說：「印第安人，你們是誰，雙胞胎？」就這麼繼續下去，於是他們都成了印第安人。那些真正的印第安人覺得彼得的做法很新鮮，也就同意這一回換成他們來假扮成走失的孩子們，然後重新開戰，打得更加激烈。若非如此，仗也就打不下去了。

這次冒險的結果就是——不過我們還沒決定要講哪一個冒險故事啦，或許另一個更好的故事是印第安人夜襲地底家園，那一回好幾個印第安人鑽進樹洞被卡在裡面，結果不得不像軟木塞似的給拔出來；又或者，我們也可以講講彼得在美人魚的礁湖搭救猛虎莉莉，因而和她結為盟友的故事。

還是我們要說說海盜們做的那個大蛋糕，孩子們只要吃了它就會上天堂，陰險的海盜們一次又一次把它放在絕佳的地點，但每次都被溫蒂從孩子們的手中搶走；漸漸地，蛋糕的水分蒸發，硬得像塊石頭，可以拿來當飛彈用，而虎克就在夜裡讓它給絆了一跤。

要不我們也可以談談彼得的那些鳥朋友，特別是在礁湖邊的樹上逐巢的夢幻鳥，牠們的巢落到了水中，但鳥卻還孵在蛋上，彼得下令不准去打擾牠們。這是個很美的故事，從結局我們可以看到，鳥兒是多麼地感恩圖報，不過，要說這個故事，就不得不講在礁湖上發生的冒險，這樣一來我們就要說兩個故事，而不能只說一個囉。第一個故事比較短，但卻同樣驚險，那就是亭可在一些流浪仙子的幫助下，把熟睡的的溫蒂放在一片大樹葉上，想讓她漂回英國，幸好樹葉沉了下去，溫蒂醒過來，以為那是洗澡時間，就自己游了回來。另外，我們也可以講彼得向獅子挑戰的故事，他用箭在地上繞著自己畫了個圈，想要激獅子們走進圈圈，他等了好幾個鐘頭，別的孩子和溫蒂都屏住呼吸在樹上看，卻沒有一隻獅子敢接受他的挑戰。

我們該從這些冒險故事中選哪一段來講呢？最好的辦法，是擲銅板決定。

我擲過了，礁湖的故事贏了，我們或許會希望，贏的是峽谷，是蛋糕，或是亭可的樹葉。當然我也可以再擲一次，三戰兩勝，不過，最公平的做法還是先講礁湖的故事。

美人魚的礁湖

Chapter 8

如果你運氣夠好，那當你閉上雙眼時，就可能會看到黑暗中懸浮著一池沒有固定形狀的水，水的顏色淡淡的，很好看。然後你瞇瞇眼睛，水池的形狀就會出現，湖水的顏色也會變得鮮艷。若是你把眼睛再瞇得緊一點，池子就會著起火來，而就在著火的前一刻，才能看見礁湖。此時的礁湖和大陸的礁湖長得最像，不過這美好的一刻只發生在一瞬間，要是這瞬間有兩次，說不定你還能看見岸邊的浪花，聽見美人魚唱歌。

　　孩子們常在礁湖上消磨漫長的夏日，他們大多是在游泳啊，在水中漂浮啊，玩玩美人魚遊戲等等的啊，但你可千萬不要以為他們和美人魚們相處融洽。事實正好相反，溫蒂一直遺憾的便是在島上生活的時候，從沒聽美人魚對她說過一句客氣的話。當她偷偷地走近礁湖岸邊，常可以看到成群的美人魚，特別是在「水手岩」上，她們喜歡在那兒曬太陽取暖，慵懶地梳理長髮，讓她看得好不心動。有時她會踮著腳似地偷偷游到離她們很近的地方，但只要她們一發現她，就會紛紛縱身跳入水中，濺了她一身水。而這可不是無心之舉，而是故意的喔。

　　美人魚對待男孩們的方式也是一樣，唯獨對彼得例外。

　彼得會和她們坐在水手岩上促膝長談，在她們嘻皮笑臉，騎
到她們的尾巴上。他還給過溫蒂一把美人魚的梳子。

　　美人魚最好看的時段是在月亮剛升起時，這時她們會
發出奇異的哭聲，而這以後就是礁湖最危險的時刻。在我
們要談的那個夜晚之前，溫蒂還沒見過月光下的礁湖，不
過這倒不是因為她害怕，反正彼得一定會陪著她，而是因
為她對上床時間做了嚴格的規定，只要一到七點，大家都
要上床睡覺。她時常在雨過天晴後來到礁湖畔，那時，會
有一大群美人魚浮到水面上玩水泡。這些五顏六色的水泡
是用彩虹水做成的，她們把水泡當作球，很快樂地用尾巴
拍來拍去。彩虹兩端各有球門，只有守門員才能用手去接

球，有時候礁湖會同時有十幾場比賽在進行，非常壯觀。

　　但只要孩子們想加入，美人魚們就會立刻沉入水中不見了，他們只得自己玩自己的。不過我們有證據顯示，她們也在暗中觀察這群不速之客，而且也會學他們的把戲。比如約翰發明了一種用頭不用手打水泡的新方法，之後的美人魚守門員也採用了這個方法。這是約翰在夢幻島所留下的一個足跡。

　　孩子們在吃過午飯後，會躺在岩石上休息半小時，這個畫面想必也很美。溫蒂堅持他們一定要有半小時的午休時間，就算是午餐是假裝吃的，午休也要來真的。於是他們都在陽光下躺著，身體讓太陽曬得閃閃發亮，溫蒂就坐在他們旁邊，很得意呢。

　　就是在這樣的一個日子裡，他們全都躺在水手岩上。岩石沒比他們的大床大多少，不過大伙都很懂得怎樣節省空間。他們打著盹，至少會閉上眼睛裝裝打盹啦，然後偶爾會趁溫蒂不注意時，互相捏一下。而溫蒂正在忙著呢，在那兒縫縫補補的。

　　就在她正做著針線活時，礁湖起了變化。水面掠過一陣微顫，太陽消失，陰影逐漸籠罩水面，將湖水變冷。溫蒂看不清楚，沒辦法穿針線。當她抬起頭才發現，向來充滿歡笑聲的礁湖，這時看起來卻顯得可怕又冷漠。

　　她知道這不是天要黑了，而是有某種暗如黑夜的東西來到了，不，那種東西比夜晚還要陰暗。它還沒到，就已經從海上捎來一陣顫抖，預告它的到來。它，到底是什麼呢？

　　這讓她想起所有她聽過的那些水手岩的故事。這裡之所以叫水手岩，是因為凶狠的船長會把水手們丟到岩上讓他們淹死。漲潮的時候，當岩石隱沒海中，水手們會被淹死。

她當然應該立刻把孩子們叫醒，這不僅是因為莫名的危險正朝他們襲來，也因為他們睡的大岩石變得愈來愈冰冷，不利於健康。可溫蒂是個年輕的母親，不明白這個道理，她認定了務必要嚴格遵守半小時的午休規定。也因此，就算她感到害怕，很想聽到男生的聲音，也不願把孩子們吵醒。即使她聽到隱約的划槳聲，緊張得心臟都要從嘴裡跳出來，她還是沒叫醒他們。她站在他們身邊，讓他們睡飽，這難道不是勇敢嗎？

　　幸好的是，其中有一個男孩即使睡著了，也能用鼻子嗅出危險。彼得縱身跳了起來，像狗一樣突然地驚醒。他發出一聲警告的呼叫，把大家叫起來。

　　他一動也不動地站著，一隻手放在耳邊仔細聽。

　　「海盜！」彼得大喊。其他人全都緊靠到他身邊，他臉上露出一絲詭異微笑，讓溫蒂看了不禁打了個寒顫。只要他露出這種微笑，就沒有人敢和他說話，只能靜靜站好，等著他下命令。他下命令都是又快又準。

　　「潛進水裡！」

　　只見一陣腳影，礁湖一下子沒了人跡，只剩水手岩孤立無援地立在洶湧的海水中。

　　一艘船慢慢駛近，那是海盜的小艇，艇上有三個人：史密、斯塔奇和一個俘虜。俘虜不是別人，正是猛虎莉莉，她的手腳被捆綁住，她也知道自己接下來的命運。她會被扔到岩上等死，這樣的結局在部落裡的人看來，比被燒死或被折磨而死更可怕，因為部落裡的經書不是明明寫著，一旦到了水裡，就沒有路可以重返幸福的獵場嗎？但是她毫無懼色，她是酋長的女兒，要死也要死得像個酋長之女，這就夠了。

　　猛虎莉莉是在嘴裡叼著刀子攀上海盜船時被抓到的。

It was the pirate dinghy o·o·o·

海盜船其實是沒有人看守的，虎克老是自吹自擂說，憑他的名氣，海盜船的方圓一英里內都嘛是安全的。現在，猛虎莉莉的命運也會成為守護海盜船的助力，又會有一聲哀號聲在今晚被風傳送到四方。

在隨他們而來的一陣陰暗中，兩名海盜看不到水手岩，船就撞上了。

「要逆風行駛啦，你這蠢蛋！」那是史密的愛爾蘭口音，「就是這塊岩石，現在我們只要把這個印第安人抬起來扔到岩石上，讓她淹死在那裡就行了。」

要把這位美麗的女孩丟到岩石上，是很殘酷。而她高傲得甚至不願做任何無謂的掙扎。

在岩石附近視線看不清楚的地方，有兩顆腦袋正在水面一上一下，那是彼得和溫蒂。溫蒂因為第一次目睹慘劇，看得都哭了。這彼得倒是看多了，只是他全忘光光了。他不像溫蒂那樣為猛虎莉莉感到難過，倒是啊，看到兩個人對付一個人，讓他很生氣，所以他決定要救她。最簡單的方法是等海盜離開後再來救她，不過彼得是個不屑輕鬆方法的人。

幾乎沒有什麼事是彼得做不到的，這時他模仿虎克說話的聲音。

他喊道：「唉唷，喂，你們這兩個笨蛋。」聲音維妙維肖。

「船長！」兩個海盜面面相覷地說道。

「他一定是游過來的。」斯塔奇說。他們想找他卻找不著。

「我們正要把印第安人丟到岩石上。」史密大喊。

「放了她！」傳來的回答令人吃驚。

「放了她？」

「對，割斷繩子，放她走。」

「可是，船長……」

「立刻放了她，聽到沒？」彼得喊道：「不照做我就用鐵鉤對付你。」

「可是這很奇怪耶。」史密倒吸一口氣說道。

「最好照船長所說的來做吧。」斯塔奇緊張兮兮地說。

「好吧，好吧。」史密說完，就把莉莉的繩子割斷，莉莉立刻像鰻魚一樣溜過斯塔奇的胯下滑進水裡。

溫蒂看到彼得這麼機靈，當然很得意，可是她知道，彼得自己也一定會得意，甚至歡呼幾聲來讓自己露出馬腳，於是她立刻伸手要去摀住他的嘴，可這時一聲「小艇啊，喂！」讓她打住，湖面上傳來虎克的聲音。而這次，說話的並不是彼得。

彼得本來想歡呼，卻突然撅起嘴吹了一聲驚訝的口哨。

「小艇啊，喂！」又傳來一聲。

現在溫蒂明白了，正牌的虎克也在湖上。

虎克正朝小艇游來，由手下舉著燈籠為他指引路線。不多久他就游到小艇邊，在燈籠的亮光下，溫蒂看到他用鐵鉤勾住船舷，當他全身濕漉漉地爬上小艇時，她看見了他那張凶狠的黑臉，不禁打了個冷顫。她想趕緊游開，可是彼得不肯走，他很亢奮，躊躇滿志。「我不是個天才嗎？啊，我真是個天才！」他小聲地對溫蒂說。雖然溫蒂有同感，不過念及他的名譽，溫蒂很慶幸除了她並沒有其他人聽到他的話。

彼得示意溫蒂聽他們的動靜。

那兩個海盜很好奇是什麼風把船長吹來的，只見虎克用鐵鉤托著下巴坐在那裡，一臉憂愁。

「船長，沒事吧？」他們小心翼翼地問，但虎克只是嘆了悶悶的一口氣。

「他嘆氣了。」史密說。

「他又嘆氣了。」斯塔奇說。

「這是他第三次嘆氣了。」史密說。

「怎麼回事，船長？」

最後他終於激動地開口了。

「計畫失敗了，」他喊道：「那些小男孩找到母親了。」

溫蒂一聽，雖然害怕，卻也感到很驕傲。

「喔，真討厭。」斯塔奇喊道。

「什麼是母親呀？」糊塗的史密問道。

溫蒂震驚得叫了出來：「他竟然不知道！」從此以後，她就覺得，如果要養個海盜當寵物，就應該選史密。

彼得一把將溫蒂拉到水下，因為虎克驚叫了一聲：「什麼聲音？」

「我什麼也沒聽見。」斯塔奇說著舉起燈籠照向水面。海盜們四處張望，卻看到了一個很奇怪的東西，就是我跟你們說過的那個浮在湖面上的鳥巢，而夢幻鳥現在正坐在巢裡頭。

「看！」虎克回答史密的問題說道：「那就是位母親。鳥巢一定是掉到水裡面了，可是母鳥會遺棄她的蛋嗎？不會。真是給我們上了一課呀！」

虎克說講到一半突然停了下來，彷彿是一時回想起純真的時光，可他又鐵鉤一揮，拂開這個軟弱的念頭。

史密很受感動，凝望著那隻鳥，看著鳥巢慢慢漂走。而多疑的斯塔奇卻說：「如果她是母親，那她在這附近漂來漂去，可能是為了掩護彼得。」

虎克抽動著臉部肌肉。「沒錯，」他說：「這就是我所擔心的。」

接著他被史密的聲音從沮喪中給喚醒。

「船長啊，」史密說：「我們何不把孩子們的母親擄來做母親呢？」

「這個詭計太讚了。」虎克喊道，他聰明的腦袋中立刻成形了一個計畫。「把那些孩子捉到船上，讓他們走甲板墜海淹死，溫蒂就變成我們的母親了。」

溫蒂聽得不禁叫了一聲。

「我才不要！」她浮出水面喊道。

「那是什麼聲音？」

但海盜們什麼也看不到，他們想，那一定是風吹落一片樹葉的聲音。「你們同意嗎，夥計們？」虎克問。

「我舉手贊成。」他們兩個說。

「我舉起鐵鉤發誓贊成。」

於是他們都發了誓。他們這時人在水手岩上，虎克忽然想起了猛虎莉莉。

「那個印第安人在哪兒？」他突然問。

虎克有時還很愛開玩笑，他們便以為他現在正鬧著玩。

「都沒問題了，船長。」史密得意地回答：「我們已經把她放了。」

「把她放了？」虎克大叫。

「是你命令的啊。」水手頭結結巴巴地說。

「你在水裡下命令，叫我們把她放了。」斯塔奇說。

「該死啊，」虎克暴跳如雷，「你們在搞什麼鬼呀？」他氣得臉都發黑。等到他發現他們說的是實話，不禁大吃了一驚。「好小子，」他聲音有些顫抖地說：「我沒下過這個命令。」

「那就奇怪了。」史密說。他們全都緊張了起來。虎克拉高嗓子，略帶顫抖。

「今夜在湖上遊蕩的鬼魂，」他喊道：「有沒有聽到我的聲音啊？」

彼得當然是應該保持安靜，不過他當然是不會這樣做的啦。他立刻偽裝成虎克的聲音回答道：

「見你的鬼，我聽到你了啦。」

在這極致的一刻，虎克一點也沒被嚇到，可史密和斯塔奇已經嚇得抱在一塊。

「陌生人，你是誰？說！」虎克問。

「我是詹姆斯‧虎克，」那個聲音回答道：「快樂羅傑號的船長！」

「你才不是，才不是呢。」虎克啞著嗓子喊。

「該死喔，」那聲音回罵道：「你再說一句，我就把錨下到你身上。」

虎克換了較為奉承的態度。「如果你是虎克，」他用恭敬似的語氣說：「那就出來告訴我，我是誰？」

「你是鱈魚，」那聲音回答，「一條鱈魚罷了。」

「鱈魚！」虎克神情茫然地附和。這一刻，他的傲氣被摧毀了。他看到他的手下對著他往後面退縮。

「難道我們一直把鱈魚當成了船長嗎？」他們喃喃地說：「這有損我們的人格。」

他們本來是虎克的狗，現在卻反咬他一口。而虎克雖然成了一個可悲的角色，倒也沒去多注意他們的反應。要反駁這樣一種可怕的指控，他需要的不是他們的信任，而是他自己的自信。他感覺到自我正在溜走。「別丟下我，

惡霸。」他啞著嗓子低聲說。

在他邪惡的本性裡，仍帶有一絲女性的特質，所有偉大的海盜都是如此，而這有時能賦予他一些直覺。突然間，他想玩一玩猜謎遊戲。

「虎克，」他問道：「你還有別的聲音嗎？」

這下子，彼得是一定抗拒不了遊戲的，於是他用自己的聲音快活地答道：「有啊。」

「那你還有別的名字嗎？」

「是啊，有啊。」

「蔬菜嗎？」虎克問。

「不是。」

「礦物？」

「不是。」

「動物？」

「是的。」

「男人！」

「不是！」彼得不屑地大聲答道。

「男孩？」

「答對了。」

「普通的男孩？」

「不是！」

「很厲害的男孩？」

這次的回答是：「是的」。這讓溫蒂很不安。

「你住在英國嗎？」

「不是。」

「你住在這裡嗎？」

「對。」

虎克聽得摸不著邊。「你們兩個，也問他幾個問題吧。」他邊對另外兩個人說，邊擦著汗濕了的前額。

　　史密想了一會兒。「我想不出什麼問題。」他抱歉地說。

　　「猜不到，猜不到，」彼得喊：「你們認輸了吧？」

　　彼得太驕傲，玩遊戲顯然是玩過了頭，讓這幾個惡棍看到機會來了。

　　「是啊，是啊。」他們急忙回答。

　　「那好吧，」他喊道：「我是彼得‧潘！」

　　潘！

　　立刻，虎克又做回了自己，而史密和斯塔奇也再度成了他忠實的手下。

　　「我們逮到他了。」虎克高喊：「史密，潛進水裡！斯塔奇，看著船！不管是死是活，都把他給抓來。」

　　他邊說邊跳下水，這時又傳來彼得快活的聲音。

　　「準備好了嗎？孩子們？」

　　「準備好了！」湖的四面傳來回應聲。

　　「那就向海盜進攻吧！」

　　這一場仗打得簡短俐落。第一個讓敵人流血的是約翰，他英勇地爬上小艇，撲向斯塔奇，經過一陣激烈的搏鬥，海盜手中的短刀掉了下來。斯塔奇掙扎著跳進水中，約翰也跟著跳下去。那艘小艇也就漂走了。

　　湖面上，不時有腦袋冒出來，刀影閃爍，緊接著一聲聲吼叫或嘶喊。在一片混戰中，有時還會攻擊到自己的同黨。史密的開瓶器砍到圖圖的第四根肋骨，但他自己也被捲毛刺傷了。在離水手岩稍遠處，斯塔奇在緊追著史萊特利和雙胞胎。

　　這段時間彼得跑到哪裡了？他想玩更大規模的遊戲。

　　其他的男孩都很勇敢，但他們躲開海盜船長是無可厚非的。虎克的鐵鉤會把周圍變成死亡區，他們像受驚的魚一樣，逃離那片水域。

　　可是有一個人不怕虎克，打算闖入這個區域。

　　奇怪的是，他們並沒有在水中碰頭。虎克爬到水手岩上喘息，就在這時，彼得也從岩石的另一頭爬了上來。岩石像球一樣滑，他們只能匍匐著爬上來，兩人都不知道對方正在爬過來，都想抓住什麼往上爬，沒想到卻碰到了對方的胳膊，驚訝得抬起頭來，差一點兒碰到了對方的臉，兩人就這樣撞見了。

　　有些偉大的英雄承認，他們在交手前，心情都會不免沉重。假如彼得這時也有這種感覺，我一定會直說，畢竟虎克是海盜庫克唯一害怕的人，只不過，彼得可不害怕。他當時只有一種感覺：樂啊！樂得咬起他可愛的小牙齒。他迅雷不及掩耳地拔出虎克皮帶上的刀，正準備狠狠往虎克身上戮過去時，卻發現自己在岩石上的位置比敵人來得高，這樣一來這場仗就打得不公平了。於是，他就伸手拉了虎克一把。

　　就在這時，虎克咬了他一口。

　　彼得嚇了一大跳，不過不是因為疼痛，而是因為這樣是不公平的。他很無力，驚訝得目瞪口呆。每個孩子在第一次遭遇不公平的待遇時，都是這樣的反應的。當他和你真誠相見的時候，他所想到的是自己有權利受到公平待遇。要是你對他不公平，他還是會愛你，只是他將再也不是原來的那個孩子了。沒有人會忘記第一次所受到的不公平待遇，除了彼得。他常遇到這種事，只是他老是忘記。我想這就是他和其他人真正不同的地方吧。

　　所以他現在就像第一次遇到這種事一樣，只能不知所
措地發著呆。而虎克，已經用鐵鉤鉤了他兩次。

　　幾分鐘之後，其他的孩子看見虎克在水裡拼命地游向
小艇，不過他那令人生畏的臉不再得意洋洋，反倒一片慘
白，原來是那隻鱷魚正在他後面緊追不捨。這要是在平時，
孩子們會在一旁游泳、歡呼，可是現在他們卻很不安，因
為彼得和溫蒂都不見了。他們在湖裡到處尋找，叫著他們
的名字。他們找到小艇，搭著小艇回家，沿途不停喊著「彼
得！溫蒂！」可是得不到任何回答，只有美人魚的嘲笑聲。
「他們一定是游回去或是飛回去了吧。」孩子們是這麼認
為的。他們沒有太著急，因為他們是這麼相信彼得。他們
孩子氣地咯咯笑著，因為他們今晚得晚睡了，而這都是溫
蒂媽媽的錯。

　　當他們的聲音消逝後，湖面一片冷寂。隨後，才傳來了一聲微弱的呼叫聲。

　　「救命啊，救命啊！」

　　兩個小小的身影朝著岩石游去，女孩已經昏了過去，靠在男孩的臂上。彼得使出最後的力氣把溫蒂推上岩石，接著就在她身邊倒下。雖然他自己也陷入昏迷，但他知道水正在往上漲，他們很快會被淹死，可是他也無能為力。

　　他們並肩躺著，一條美人魚抓住了溫蒂的腳，想把她悄悄地拖入水中。彼得察覺到溫蒂正在往下滑，立刻驚醒過來，及時把她給拉了回來。不過，他還是得告訴溫蒂實話。

　　「我們在水手岩上，溫蒂，」他說：「可是石面越來越小了，很快就會被水淹沒。」

　　溫蒂一時之間沒聽懂。

　　「我們得離開這兒。」她的反應仍然樂觀。

　　「是啊。」彼得口氣淡淡地回答。

　　「我們是要游泳，還是要用飛的呢，彼得？」

　　彼得不得不告訴她：

　　「溫蒂，要是沒有我的幫忙，妳覺得妳能游泳或是飛到島上去嗎？」

　　溫蒂得承認，她的確是累得沒辦法了。

　　彼得呻吟了一聲。

　　「怎麼啦？」溫蒂問，立刻為彼得擔心起來。

　　「我沒辦法幫妳，溫蒂。虎克打傷了我，我現在不能飛，也不能游泳。」

　　「你的意思是我們兩個會淹死在這兒嗎？」

　　「妳看看水上漲得多快。」

　　他們用手蒙住眼睛不敢看，心想馬上就要完蛋了。當他們這樣坐著的時候，有個什麼像親吻一樣，輕輕地碰了碰彼得，然後停在那裡，就好像是羞怯地在說：「我能幫得上忙嗎？」

原來那是一隻風箏的尾巴。這個風箏是麥可在前幾天做的，後來從麥可的手中掙脫飄走了。

「麥可的風箏。」彼得不感興趣地說，但下一刻，他突然抓住風箏尾端，將它拉了過來。

「它既然能把麥可從地上拉起來，」他喊道：「為什麼不能把妳帶走呢？」

「它可以把我們兩個都帶走！」

「它載不動兩個人的，麥可和捲毛試過了。」

「那我們抽籤吧。」溫蒂勇敢地說。

「不行，你是女生。」這時彼得已經把風箏的尾端繫在她身上。溫蒂抓住他，不肯單獨離開，但彼得說了聲「再見，溫蒂」，就把她推出岩石。沒過多久，她飄走不見了，礁湖上只剩下彼得一個人。

岩面現在變得很小，很快就會被完全淹沒。微弱的光線緩緩籠罩湖面，再一會兒，就能聽到世上最動聽又最淒涼的聲音了：美人魚喚月。

雖然彼得和別的孩子不同，但終究也害怕了。他身上一陣顫慄，就像海面掠過一陣波浪，不過海浪是一波接一波，直到形成無數波濤，但彼得只感覺到一陣顫慄，下一秒，他又挺立了在岩石上，臉上帶著微笑，腦中的鼓咚咚敲著，彷彿在說：「死亡是一次最大的冒險。」

夢幻鳥

Chapter 9

彼得最後聽到的，是美人魚一個個回到海底臥室就寢的聲音，礁湖上只剩下他一個人了，不過因為距離太遠，他聽不到美人魚關門的聲音。在美人魚們居住的珊瑚窟中，每一道門都有一個小鈴鐺，無論開門或關門時都會發出鈴聲（就像英國大陸最體面的房子），彼得聽過那些鈴聲。

海水緩緩上漲，一吋一吋地往彼得的腳淹沒上來。在海水將他吞噬前，為了消磨時間，他就盯著湖面唯一一樣在漂流的東西。彼得想那應該是一張漂浮的紙片，或是那只風箏的一部分，他無聊地猜想著它漂到岸邊需要多少時間。

突然間，他發現這東西有點不尋常，它飄到湖上一定是有目的的，因為它正逆浪而行，有時會戰勝海浪，而每當它戰勝時，一向同情弱者的彼得就會卻忍不住拍起手來。真是勇敢的一張紙片啊！

但事實上，那並不是紙片，而是夢幻鳥。她坐在巢上，努力要往彼得這邊過來。自從她的巢落水後，不知怎的她學會了用翅膀划水，竟也能勉強移動那艘特別的小船（她的巢）。不過，在彼得認出前她之前，她已經精疲力竭了。她是來救彼得的，要把巢讓給彼得，儘管裡面有蛋。我很好奇夢幻鳥的想法，雖然彼得待她不錯，但有時也會作弄她。我只能猜，她大概也像達林太太或其他女性一樣，看到彼得還保有一口乳牙，就動了慈悲心吧。

她大聲地告訴彼得自己過來的原因，彼得也大聲問她在那兒做什麼。不過，他們當然都聽不懂對方的語言啦。在童話故事裡，人可以自由地和鳥兒交談，這一刻我倒真希望在我們的故事裡也是這樣，讓彼得和夢幻鳥可以隨意問答。但最好還是實話實說吧，我只能告訴你實際發生了什麼：他們不但聽不懂對方的話，甚至忘了要保持禮貌。

「我——要——你——進——來——巢——裡，」夢幻鳥喊著，盡可能慢慢地說清楚，「這——樣——你——就——可——以——漂——到——岸——邊，但——是——我——太——累——了，划——不——動——了，所——以——你——得——自——己——游——過——來。」

「你嘰哩呱啦的說些什麼呀？」彼得回答：「為什麼不像平常一樣，讓你的巢隨波逐流？」

「我——要——你……」夢幻鳥重複剛剛的話說道。

接著，彼得也試著慢慢地說清楚一點：

「妳——嘰——哩——呱——啦——的——說——些——什——麼——呀？」他重複說道。

夢幻鳥被惹火了，他們的脾氣都不是很好。

「你這囉哩叭嗦的蠢蛋，」她尖聲叫著：「為什麼不照我說的做？」

彼得發現她在罵自己，也氣沖沖地回了一句：

「妳才是笨蛋呢！」

然後說也奇怪，他們竟彼此罵出同一句話：

「閉嘴！」

「閉嘴！」

然而，夢幻鳥下定決心，只要她做得到就會盡力搭救彼得。於是她再做最後一次努力，使盡全力，終於讓她的巢靠上了岩石邊。隨後她飛離鳥巢，留下了自己的蛋，好讓彼得明白她的意思。

這下彼得終於懂了。他抓住鳥巢，揮手對在空中拍著翅膀的夢幻鳥表達謝意。然而夢幻鳥在空中盤旋，並不是為了要彼得感謝，也不是為了要看他爬進巢裡頭，而是要看看他會如何對待她的蛋。

鳥巢裡頭有兩顆大大的白色鳥蛋，彼得將它們捧起，想著該怎麼辦。夢幻鳥用翅膀摀著臉，不敢看她的蛋會有什麼下場，但還是忍不住從羽毛縫裡偷看。

我忘記有沒有告訴過你們，水手岩上有一根木竿，是很久以前被海盜釘在那裡的，好做為寶藏埋藏地點的記號。那群孩子們早發現了這堆閃閃發光的金銀財寶，有時他們想惡作劇時，就會抓起一把把的金幣、鑽石、珍珠、銀幣等等拋向海鷗，海鷗便會撲過來啄食，等一發現是可惡的惡作劇，就會氣得飛走。那根木竿還在那兒，斯塔奇把他那頂帽緣很高的防水油布帽掛上去。彼得把鳥蛋放進了帽裡，再把帽子放在湖上，帽子漂得很穩呢。

夢幻鳥一看到彼得想出來的辦法，立刻佩服地大叫，而彼得這邊也應聲歡呼。然後他進鳥巢，把木板塊豎起來當旗杆，再將自己的衣服掛上去當風帆，這時，夢幻鳥飛到帽子上，又坐在上面孵起蛋來。牠往這兒漂，彼得往那兒漂，皆大歡喜。

想當然爾，等彼得上岸以後就會把小船（鳥巢）放在夢幻鳥容易找到的地方了。但是那頂帽子實在太好用，夢幻鳥竟然放棄了鳥巢，任它漂來漂去，直到完全散掉。在那之後，斯塔奇每次來到礁湖，總是心疼地看著夢幻鳥坐在他的帽子上。今後，我們不會再見到夢幻鳥了，所以不妨在此一提，那就是現在所有的夢幻鳥都把巢築成帽子的形狀，幼鳥們還可以在帽子的寬邊上散步溜達。

彼得回到地底家園時，受到大家熱烈的歡迎，而隨著風箏東飄西蕩的溫蒂，也在差不多的時間回來了。每個孩子都有一段冒險故事可說，可最偉大的一次冒險，應該算是他們上床的時間已經晚了好幾個小時了。這可讓他們得意得很，為了能更加拖延上床的時間，他們的藉口五花八門，像是要求包紮傷口什麼的。而溫蒂呢，雖然看到每個人都平安歸來讓她覺得很驕傲，但上床時間已經很晚了，她用令人不得不遵從的語氣急喊：「上床睡覺了！上床睡

覺了！」可到了第二天，她又變得無比溫柔，為每個孩子
都包上繃帶，而他們就這麼跛著腳、吊著繃帶，一直玩到
上床睡覺的時間。

快樂家庭

Chapter 10

在礁湖上發生那次小衝突之後，一個重要的結果是，印第安人和孩子們做了朋友。彼得將猛虎莉莉從險惡的命運中救了出來，現在，她和族裡的勇士們願意為彼得做任何事。他們徹夜坐在上方，守衛著地底家園，顯然海盜們的進攻已經近在眼前。即使白天印第安人也都在附近走動，悠閒地抽著菸斗，一副在等著吃美食的模樣。

他們稱彼得為「偉大的白人父親」，在他面前跪拜。彼得很喜歡他們這麼做，但這對他一點兒好處也沒有。

當印第安人俯身在他面前時，他會以極具王者氣勢的口吻對他們說：「偉大的白人父親很高興見到皮卡尼尼族的戰士們幫他保衛他的小屋，抵抗海盜。」

「我猛虎莉莉，」而那可愛的身影會回答，「彼得·潘救了我，我是他的好朋友，我不會讓海盜傷害他。」

莉莉太美麗了，不適合這麼卑躬屈膝地奉承彼得，但彼得卻認為自己受之無愧。他會帶著優越感地說：「那很好，這是彼得·潘說的。」

每當他說「這是彼得·潘說的」這句話時，其實是要他們馬上閉嘴，而他們也只得恭敬從命。不過，對其他的孩子們，印第安人可就沒這麼客氣了。他們認為那些孩子

不過是普普通通的勇士，只會對他們說聲「你好」之類的話。讓其他孩子們生氣的是，彼得竟覺得這是理所當然的。

　　私底下溫蒂頗為同情那些孩子，但她是位非常忠實賢慧的主婦，不願意聽那些抱怨父親的話。無論她個人的意見是什麼，她總是說「父親永遠是對的」。其實她自己的意見就是，印第安人不該叫她「某仔」的。

　　今天，就是他們所稱的「夜中之夜」，因為這天夜裡發生的事情與造成的後果特別重要。白天，一切平靜無事，彷彿在養精蓄銳。此刻，上方的印第安人披著毛毯正在站崗；而在地下，除了彼得，孩子們都正在吃晚飯。而彼得呢，他跑去查詢時間了，在島上要查時間的方法，就是先找到那條鱷魚，然後在他旁邊等肚子裡的鐘敲整點報時。

　　這頓晚飯是一頓假想的茶點。他們圍坐在桌邊，貪心地狼吞虎嚥。他們嘰嘰喳喳、吵吵鬧鬧的聲音，就像溫蒂說的，簡直震耳欲聾。當然，溫蒂並不怎麼在乎這些吵鬧的聲音，但她絕不允許他們搶東西吃，還藉口說是因為圖圖撞了他們的手臂。用餐時有一項嚴格的規定：不准還手。而是應該有禮貌地舉起右手，把爭吵的始末向溫蒂報告：「我要告誰誰誰的狀。」而他們經常不是忘了該這麼做，就是做過頭了。

　　「安靜，」溫蒂喊道。這已經是她第二十次告訴大家不要同時講話了，「你的杯子空了嗎，親愛的史萊特利？」

　　「不怎麼空，媽媽。」史萊特利說，看了一眼想像出來的杯子。

　　「他根本還沒開始喝牛奶呢。」尼布斯插嘴。

　　他這是在告狀，史萊特利逮住了機會。

　　「我要告尼布斯的狀。」他立刻喊。

不過，約翰先舉起了手。

「什麼事，約翰？」

「我可不可以坐彼得的椅子？反正他不在。」

「約翰要坐父親的椅子！當然不行！」溫蒂認為這簡直不成體統。

「他又不是我們真正的父親，」約翰回答：「他根本不知道父親要做些什麼，那還是我教他的呢。」

他發著牢騷。「我們要告約翰的狀！」雙胞胎喊道。

圖圖也把手舉了起來，他是孩子們當中最謙遜的，說實在也是唯一的一個，所以溫蒂對他特別溫柔。

「我想，」圖圖沮喪地說：「我是不能當父親的。」

「當然不行囉，圖圖。」

圖圖很少開口，可是一開口就會傻傻地說個沒完。

「既然我當不成父親，」他心情沉重地說：「麥可，我想你也不肯讓我當小嬰兒吧？」

「不，我不要。」麥可厲聲回答。這時他鑽進了搖籃。

「既然我不能當小嬰兒，」圖圖心情越來越沉重地說道：「你們覺得我可以當雙胞胎嗎？」

「不，不行，雙胞胎是超級難的。」雙胞胎回答。

「既然我什麼重要角色也做不成，」圖圖說：「那你們有誰願意看我耍一套小把戲？」

「不要。」大家齊聲回答。

這下，他終於住口了。「我沒指望了。」他說。

但讓人厭煩的告狀又開始了。

「史萊特利在飯桌上咳嗽。」

「雙胞胎先吃馬米蘋果耶。」

「捲毛又吃塔帕卷又吃甜薯。」

「尼布斯嘴裡還含著食物就說話。」

「我要控訴雙胞胎。」

「我要告捲毛的狀。」

「我要控告尼布斯。」

「天哪，天哪，」溫蒂喊道：「我有時候真覺得小孩子帶來的麻煩比快樂還要多。」

她叫他們解散，然後自己坐下來做針線活兒。照例，籃子裡堆滿了長襪子，每隻襪子的膝蓋部位都破了洞。

「溫蒂，我長得太大了，不能睡搖籃了。」麥可抗議。

「一定要有一個人睡搖籃，」溫蒂近乎刻薄地說：「你是最小的了，搖籃是屋子裡最有家的味道的擺設了。」

她在縫縫補補時，孩子們在一旁玩耍，那麼多張快樂的臉龐和活蹦亂跳的雙手雙腳，被浪漫的爐火照得紅亮。這是地底家園常見的畫面，不過這將成為最後的絕響了。

上面有腳步聲，當然，溫蒂是第一個聽到的。

「孩子們，我聽見你們父親的腳步聲了，他喜歡你們到門口去迎接他。」

而在地面上，印第安人向彼得鞠躬致意。

「勇士們啊，好好守著，這是我說的。」

然後，就像往常一樣，歡天喜地的孩子們將他從樹洞拖了下來。這事過去常發生，但以後再也不會有了。

他為孩子們帶回了核果，也替溫蒂帶來準確的時間。

「彼得，知道嗎？你慣壞他們了。」溫蒂呵呵地笑道。

「是啊，老婆大人。」彼得說著把他的槍掛起來。

「是我跟彼得說，他們都叫媽媽為老婆大人的。」麥可悄悄對捲毛說。

「我要告麥可的狀。」捲毛馬上說。

雙胞胎的大哥走到彼得跟前說：「爸爸，我們想跳舞。」

「那就跳吧，我的小紳士。」現在興致很好的彼得說。

「可是我們要你也跳。」

彼得其實是他們當中最會跳舞的一個，但他故作驚訝道：「我？我這把老骨頭可是會咯咯作響。」

「媽媽也來跳吧。」

「什麼？都是一大群孩子的媽了，還跳舞！」溫蒂喊道。

「今天可是星期六晚上耶！」史萊特利意有所指地說。

其實那並不是星期六夜晚，不過也可能是啦，畢竟他們早就忘了算日期了。但如果他們想做些特別的事，總會說那是星期六晚上，然後就順理成章地做了。

「當然啦，今天是星期六的晚上，彼得。」溫蒂口氣緩和了地說道。

「溫蒂，像我們這樣的人家……」

「這裡就只有我們和孩子嘛。」

「也對，也對。」

於是他們告訴孩子們可以跳舞，不過得先換上睡衣。

「可不是嗎，老婆大人，」彼得在一旁對溫蒂說。他在火爐邊取暖，低頭看著溫蒂坐在那兒補襪子。「在一天的勞累之後，我們坐在火爐前，還有那群小傢伙圍在身邊，沒有什麼比這樣的夜晚更讓人愉快了。」

「這很甜蜜吧，彼得，你說是不是？」溫蒂心滿意足地說道：「彼得，我覺得捲毛的鼻子長得很像你。」

「麥可長得也很像妳。」

溫蒂走到彼得面前，把雙手搭在他肩膀上。

「親愛的彼得，要照顧這麼一個大家子，我的的青春都消耗在這兒了，你不會想把我扔下換一個吧？」溫蒂說。

「不會的啦，溫蒂。」

他當然是不想換囉，可是他卻不安地望著溫蒂。他眨了眨眼，像是剛睡醒或是愛睏的樣子。

「彼得，怎麼回事啊？」

「我只是想，」他有點害怕地說：「我只是在假扮成他們的父親吧？」

「是啊。」溫蒂嚴肅地說。

「你瞧，」彼得帶著歉意接著說，「要是做他們真正的父親，我就顯得太老了。」

「可是他們是我們的孩子，彼得，是你和我的。」

「但溫蒂，這不是真的吧？」彼得焦急地問。

「要是你不願意，那就不是真的。」她回答道，清楚地聽到了彼得鬆了一口氣。「彼得，」她極力讓口氣鎮定地問：「你對我到底是什麼感覺？」

「就像孝子對母親的感覺一樣，溫蒂。」

「我就知道。」她說著，走到屋裡最遠的角落，獨自坐下。

「妳真是奇怪，猛虎莉莉也是這樣，她想要做我的什麼人，但又說不要當我的母親。」彼得一臉困惑地說道。

「是啊，她的確是不能當的。」溫蒂刻意加重語氣。

現在我們知道她為什麼對印第安人有偏見了吧。

「那她想當什麼？」

「那可不是淑女該回答的。」

「喔，好啊，反正亭可會告訴我。」彼得有點火大地說。「當然囉，亭可會告訴你嘛。」溫蒂不屑地回了一句道：「她那個放蕩的小東西。」

這時，亭可正在自己的閨房裡偷聽，尖聲嚷出了一句無禮的話。

「她說她以放蕩自豪。」彼得翻譯道。

彼得忽然想道：「說不定亭可願意當我的母親？」

「你這大笨蛋！」亭可氣憤地大喊。

這句話亭可已經說過太多次了，溫蒂根本不需要翻譯就懂了。

「我和她有同感。」溫蒂冷不防地說到。真想不到溫蒂居然也會這麼說！可見她是受夠了。但她也沒料到晚上會有事發生，要是她早知道就不會這樣說了。

他們誰也沒料到會有事情發生，不過什麼都不知道可能反而是最好的，可以讓他們多享受一小時的歡樂時光。這將是他們在夢幻島上的最後一個小時，就讓我們一齊慶祝這快樂的六十分鐘吧！他們穿著睡衣唱唱跳跳，這首歌曲悅耳卻令人不寒而慄，在歌曲裡，他們歌假裝自己害怕自己的影子，完全不知道很快就會有陰影籠罩下來，讓他們陷入真實的恐懼之中。他們吵吵鬧鬧好不愉快地跳著舞，在床上你一拳我一拳的，與其說是跳舞，更像是在打枕頭戰。架打完之後，那些枕頭還想再繼續較量下去，就像在互相訣別的夥伴一樣。在溫蒂講床邊故事以前，他們自己已經說了多少故事啊！就連史萊特利也想說個故事，只是故事一開頭就悶得不得了，連他自己也不想聽，於是他沮喪地說：「是啊，這個開頭真是無趣，我說啊，就把它當作結局吧。」

最後，大家爬上床聽溫蒂說故事。這是他們最愛聽而彼得最不愛聽的故事，平時，只要溫蒂一開始講這個故事，彼得就會走出小屋，或是用手摀住耳朵。要是他這一次也這麼做，那他們現在或許還繼續留在島上。可是今晚，彼得卻還坐在他的小凳子上，而我們將目睹發生的一切。

溫蒂的故事

Chapter 11

「好，聽著，」溫蒂邊說，邊坐好準備講她的故事。麥可坐在她的腳邊，另外七個孩子坐在床上。「從前，有一位先生……」

「我倒希望是一位女士。」捲毛說。

「我希望他是一隻白老鼠。」尼布斯說。

「安靜，」媽媽下命令說：「還有一位女士，而……」

「啊，媽媽，」雙胞胎大哥說：「你是說還有一位女士，是不是？她還活著，對不對？」

「是啊。」

「我真高興她還活著，」圖圖說：「你高興嗎，約翰？」

「我當然高興。」

「那你高興嗎，尼布斯？」

「很高興。」

「你們高興嗎，雙胞胎？」

「我們非常高興。」

「喔，天哪。」溫蒂嘆氣。

「你們小聲一點！」彼得喊。他認為應該公平一點，讓溫蒂把故事說完，雖然他很討厭這個故事。

「那位先生，」溫蒂接著說：「叫達林先生，而那位

女士呢，叫達林太太。」

「我認識他們。」約翰說道，想惹惱其他的孩子。

「我想我也認識他們。」麥可有些懷疑地說。

「他們結婚了，知道吧，」溫蒂解釋，「你們覺得他們會有什麼？」

「白老鼠。」尼布斯突然想到。

「不是。」

「這可真是超級難猜呀。」圖圖說，儘管他已經把這個故事給背下來了。

「安靜，圖圖。他們有三個後代。」

「什麼是後代呀？」

「你就是一個後代啊，雙胞胎小孩。」

「你聽見了嗎，約翰？我就是一個後代。」

「後代就是孩子。」約翰說。

「唉，天哪！」溫蒂嘆氣道：「好，這三個孩子有個非常忠心的褓母，叫做娜娜，可是達林先生生了她的氣，把她拴在後院，結果三個孩子就飛走了。」

「這故事實在棒透了。」尼布斯說。

「他們飛呀飛，」溫蒂繼續說著，「飛到了夢幻島，那些走失的孩子們也住在那裡。」

「我就知道他們住在那兒，」捲毛興奮地插嘴道：「不知道為什麼，我就是覺得他們住在那兒的。」

「啊，溫蒂，」圖圖喊道：「在那些走失的孩子裡，是不是有一個叫圖圖的？」

「是的。」

「我在故事裡耶，唷呼，我在故事裡啦，尼布斯。」

「噓！現在，我要你們想一想，那對不幸的父母在孩子們飛走之後，會有怎樣的心情呢？」

「唉！」他們全都哀聲嘆氣了起來，雖然他們並沒有真的想過那對不幸的父母會有怎樣的心情。

「想想那些沒人睡的空床！」

「唉！」

「那真叫人傷心啊。」雙胞胎大哥開心地說。

「我看這故事的結局一定不好。」雙胞胎弟弟說：「你認為呢，尼布斯？」

「我很擔心。」

「如果你們知道母親的愛有多偉大，」溫蒂得意地告訴他們，「那你們就不會覺得害怕了。」接下來她的故事就要進行到彼得最討厭的部分了。

「我真喜歡母親的愛了。」圖圖一邊說著，一邊拿枕頭丟尼布斯，「你喜歡母親的愛嗎？尼布斯？」

「我可喜歡了。」尼布斯說，再把枕頭丟回去。

「你瞧，」溫蒂滿意地說道：「故事裡的女主角知道，母親會一直把窗子打開，讓她的孩子們飛回來，所以孩子們就在外面待了好多年，玩個痛快。」

「他們有沒有回去過？」

「現在，」溫蒂鼓足勇氣說：「讓我們來偷偷看一看故事未來的發展吧。」隨後大家都扭了扭身體想看得更清楚。「很多年過去了，那個看不出年齡、在倫敦車站下車的高雅淑女是誰呢？」

「啊，溫蒂，她是誰？」尼布斯喊，興奮不已，好像他真不知道似的。

「會不會是──是──不是──沒錯──就是美麗的溫蒂！」

「哇！」

「那在她身邊儀表堂堂的兩位男子漢又是誰？會不會是約翰和麥可？沒錯！」

「啊！」

「『看啊，親愛的弟弟，』溫蒂邊指著上方說道：『窗戶還是開著的，那是因為我們對母親的愛有崇高的信心，所以有這個獎賞。』說著，他們就飛回到媽媽和爸爸的身邊，那快樂的場景，是筆墨無法描寫的，我們就在這裡落幕吧。」

這個故事就是這樣，聽者和說者一樣高興。你看，每件事都合情合理，有時我們就像這樣沒心肝地說走就走，孩子們就是這樣，但也討人喜愛。離開後我們會自私地玩個痛快，需要關心時再回來，而且還很有把握的是，回來之後，從母親那兒得到的會是擁抱，而不是一巴掌。

他們深信母親的愛就是這麼偉大，所以總覺得還可以在外面多逗留一些時間。

可是，有個人比他們懂得更多。溫蒂說完故事以後，那人發出了一聲沉重的呻吟。

「怎麼啦，彼得？」溫蒂喊著，跑到他身邊，以為他生病了，很關心地摸著他的胸口。「哪兒疼啊，彼得？」

「不是那種疼。」彼得陰沉地回答。

「那是什麼樣的疼？」

「溫蒂，你對母親的想法是錯的。」

他們全都不安地圍到他身邊，對彼得的激動感到驚慌。隨後，彼得坦承了他一直深藏在內心裡的話。

彼得說：「很久以前，我跟你們一樣，覺得媽媽會永遠把窗戶打開等我回去，所以，我在外面待了一個月又一個月。然而，等我回去時，窗戶卻被鎖起來了。媽媽已經

完全把我忘了，而且我的床上還睡了別的小男孩。」

我不確定這件事的真假，但彼得認為是真的，這嚇壞了孩子們。

「你確定母親都是這樣子的嗎？」

「是啊。」

原來母親都是這樣子的，真是卑鄙！

不過還是小心些好，只有小孩能最快知道什麼時候該放棄一些東西。「溫蒂，我們回家吧。」約翰和麥可同時喊道。

「好。」溫蒂說著抓起他們。

「不會是今晚吧？」走失的孩子們困惑地問。他們心裡知道，即使沒有母親，日子也能過得很好。只有母親才會認為，孩子沒有她們就會過得不好。

「馬上就走。」溫蒂果斷地回答，因為她有了一個可怕的想法，「說不定此刻媽媽已經在哀悼他們了。」

這種恐懼使她忘記了彼得的心情，她突然對彼得說：「彼得，可以請你幫我們安排嗎？」

「如果妳想的話。」他回答道，口氣很冷淡，好像溫蒂只是請他遞給她核果似的。

他們兩個人連一句道別的話也沒說！要是溫蒂不在乎分離的話，那他也要讓她知道，他彼得也是不會在乎的。

然而，他當然是非常在乎的。他對大人有滿肚子的怨恨，大人老是什麼事都搞砸，所以他鑽進樹洞時，就會故意呼吸得又急又淺，一秒鐘呼吸個五次左右。而他之所以這麼做，是因為在夢幻島有個傳說：你每呼吸一次，就有一個大人會死，所以彼得想要報復，讓他們死得愈多愈好。

他先對印第安人下了一些命令之後，又回到地底家園。而在他不在的那段時間裡，家裡發生的事可真不像話。孩子們因為擔心會失去溫蒂，竟威脅起她來。

「事情會比她來以前更糟。」他們嚷道。

「我們不要讓她走。」

「我們把她關起來吧。」

「好，把她鎖起來。」

在絕望中，溫蒂靈機一動，想到應該向誰求助。

「圖圖，」她喊道：「我想請你幫忙。」

這不是很奇怪嗎？她竟找圖圖來幫忙，圖圖是裡頭最笨的小孩。

可圖圖回答得很具架勢。因為在那一刻，他甩開了愚笨，說話變得很有威嚴。

「我只不過是圖圖，沒人在乎我，但要是有人對溫蒂不禮貌、不像個紳士，那我就會狠狠地刺他幾刀。」他說。

他拔出刀，表現出高昂的氣勢，使其他孩子們不安地往後退。這時彼得回來了，他們立刻就看出來彼得是不會幫助他們的，因為他不會去強迫女生留在夢幻島。

他在房子裡踱來踱去，說道：「溫蒂，我已經交代印第安人帶你們走出樹林，因為飛行會把你們給累垮的。」

「謝謝你，彼得。」

「還有，」他繼續用頤指氣使的急促聲音說道：「亭可會帶你們越過大海。尼布斯，叫醒她。」

尼布斯敲了兩次門，才得到回答。但其實亭可早就坐在床上，偷聽一段時間了。

「你是誰啊？大膽！快走開。」她嚷道。

「妳該起床啦，亭可，要帶溫蒂出遠門。」尼布斯喊道。

亭可聽說溫蒂要走當然非常高興，可是她已經下定決心，絕對不幫溫蒂帶路。於是她用更不客氣的話表明心意

後，又假裝睡覺了。

「她說她不要。」尼布斯大聲說，很吃驚她竟然這樣公然違抗命令。於是，彼得態度堅定地走向亭可的房間。

「亭可！如果妳不馬上起床換衣服，我就把窗簾打開，那樣我們就都會看見妳穿睡袍的樣子了。」他大喊道。

她一下子就跳到地上，喊道：「誰說我不起床？」

在這同一時間，孩子們愁雲慘霧地望著溫蒂，她和約翰及麥可都已經收拾好旅途要用的東西。孩子們沮喪不已，不只是因為他們即將失去溫蒂，也是因為他們覺得好像有什麼好康在等著她，而他們卻沒有參與的份。新奇的事物對他們一向都很有吸引力的。

但溫蒂以為他們有什麼更深刻的感觸，不由得心軟了。

「親愛的孩子們，」她說：「要是你們和我一起回去，我幾乎可以確定，我可以說服爸爸媽媽收養你們的。」

這個邀請原本是特地要對彼得說的，但每個孩子都以為指的是自己，立刻高興得跳了起來。

「可是他們不會嫌我們麻煩嗎？」尼布斯邊跳邊問。

「啊，不會的，」溫蒂很快就想出辦法說道：「只要在客廳多加幾張床就行了，每個月的第一個星期四，可以把床藏在屏風後面。」

「彼得，我們可以去嗎？」孩子們全都大聲懇求。他們想，只要大家都去，彼得理所當然也會一起去。不過呢，他們其實並不怎麼在乎彼得去不去，孩子們就是這樣，只要有新鮮事來叩門，他們就會扔下最親愛的人。

「好吧。」彼得苦笑著回答，孩子們立刻衝去收拾自己的東西。

「現在，彼得，」溫蒂心想一切都準備妥當了，「在

走之前，我要先餵你們吃藥。」她喜歡餵他們吃藥，而且還老是給了太多劑量。不過那當然只是清水而已啦，水是裝在瓶子裡的，她總會先搖一搖瓶子，數數看幾滴，這就讓清水有了療效。然而她這一回沒有餵藥給彼得吃，因為就在她準備餵他時，彼得臉上的表情讓她心情很沉重。

「收拾你的東西吧，彼得。」溫蒂顫抖地喊道。

「不要！我不要和你們去，溫蒂。」他裝作毫不在意。

「好啦，彼得。」

「不要。」

為了要表現出他對溫蒂的離開無動於衷，彼得在房裡晃來晃去，愉快地吹奏，發出無情的笛聲。溫蒂只得跟在他後面，雖然這樣有點丟臉。

「去找你的母親嘛。」溫蒂勸他說。

現在，就算彼得真的有母親，他也不再想念她了；而就算沒有母親，他也能過得很好。他早就把有關母親的一切都給想通了，他現在記得的只有她們的缺點。

「不要！不要！」彼得斬釘截鐵地告訴溫蒂說：「她可能會說我已經長大了，可是我只想做個小男孩，能一直玩。」

「可是，彼得……」

「我就不要！」

把這件事告訴其他孩子們吧。

「彼得不會一起走的。」

彼得不會一起走的！孩子們茫然望著他，每個人肩上都扛著根棍子，棍子的一頭掛著包袱。他們第一個想到的是，要是彼得不去，他可能會改變主意，也不讓他們去了。

不過彼得的自尊心那麼強，他是不會這麼做的。「要是你們找到了媽媽，我希望你們會喜歡她們。」他陰沉地說。

　　這句話講得酸溜溜的，讓孩子們感到很不自在，大多數人看起來都變得有些遲疑。他們臉上的表情似乎在說，到頭來是不是只有傻瓜才會去呢？

　　「好啦，」彼得喊道：「別緊張，也別哭喪著臉，再見，溫蒂。」他很快活地伸出手，彷彿他們現在就得走了，因為他還有要事要辦。

　　溫蒂只好去握他的手，因為彼得並沒有表示他想要個「頂針」。

　　「記得要換上你的法蘭絨衣服，彼得！」溫蒂邊說，邊不捨地頻頻回頭。她對他們的法蘭絨衣裳一直非常在意。

　　「好。」

　　「要記得吃藥喔。」

　　「好。」

　　該說的似乎都已經說完了，跟著是一陣彆扭的沉默。可彼得是那種不會在人前表現軟弱一面的人。「妳準備好了嗎，亭可？」他大喊一聲。

　　「好了，好了。」

　　「那就帶路吧。」

　　亭可飛上最近的一棵樹，卻沒人跟著她，因為就在此時，海盜對印第安人展開了猛烈的攻擊。地面上原本是一片平靜，現在卻被嘶喊聲和兵器的敲擊聲給劃破。地面下，一片死寂。每個人都驚訝得張大嘴巴閉不起來。溫蒂跪了下來，雙手往彼得伸去。每個人都像是被風刮向同一個方向一般，同時把手伸向了彼得。他們向彼得發出無聲的請求，求他不要拋下他們。而彼得緊握住他的劍，就是那把他以為自己曾用來殺死巴比克的劍。他的眼神裡，閃耀著渴望戰鬥的光芒。

孩子們被抓走了

Chapter 12

海盜這次的攻擊完全是出其不意的，而這也透露出了虎克領導不當，因為以白人的智慧來說，是無法成功突襲印第安人的。

依照野蠻民族的不成文規定，率先發動攻擊的都是印第安人。憑著族人的機智，他們會進行日出前的攻擊，因為他們深知這是白人士氣最低落的時間。白人在那片高低起伏的山頭築起了一道簡陋的柵欄，山腳下有一條潺潺小溪，因為要是離水太遠就無法生存了。他們就在柵欄旁等著印第安人的偷襲。沒有經驗的菜鳥會握緊手槍，踩在枯枝上逡巡，老手們則會安穩地睡著，天要亮時再起床。

在漫長漆黑的夜裡，印第安哨兵在草叢裡匍匐潛行，靈活得像條蛇，被撥開的草叢在他們經過後自動密合，安靜的就像鼬鼠潛入沙中。他們一點聲響也聽不到，除了偶爾學一下狼嚎，發出一聲淒涼的嗥叫。其他勇士會跟著呼應，有些人的狼嗥，甚至會比那些不擅嗥叫的土狼叫得更好。寒夜就這麼慢慢過去，長時間的擔驚受怕對那些初次體驗的白人來說，真是特別難熬。而這對有經驗的老手來說，那些嚇人的嗥叫聲，以及更嚇人的寂靜無聲，只不過是黑夜行進的腳步罷了。

　　這些情況，虎克是知道得一清二楚的，如果他疏忽了，就絕不能以無知為藉口而原諒他。

　　至於皮卡尼尼族人，他們相信虎克是知道這個原則的，因此他們整個的黑夜行動和虎克是截然不同的。他們一件不漏地照辦了那些讓他們部落成就美名的行動。他們所擁有的靈敏感應能力，讓文明人既羨慕又害怕，只要有一個海盜踩到了一根樹枝，他們立刻就會知道海盜們已經來到了島上，然後眨眼間就會響起土狼的嗥叫聲。

　　從海盜登陸的海岸，到位於地底下的家園，當中的每一吋土地都被穿著鹿皮軟鞋的印第安勇士暗地裡偵察過了。他們發現那裡只有一座小土丘，土丘下有一條小河，因此虎克別無選擇，只能暫時停在那兒，等候黎明的到來。印第安人憑著他們的機智狡猾，將一切布置妥當，主力戰士就圍著毯子，以他們族人認為最有男子氣概的鎮定態度，守在孩子們家園的地面上，等待決戰時刻的來臨，去面對黑暗的死亡。

　　他們坐在這裡做著白日夢，想著天亮時要好好地折磨虎克，但這些心思單純的印第安人卻被奸詐的虎克給逮著了。根據一位後來從大屠殺中逃出來的哨兵說，虎克並沒有在小土丘多作停留，儘管在灰濛濛的夜光中，想必他一定有看到那座小土丘。他那難以捉摸的心裡，自始至終就沒打算等著印第安人來攻打，他甚至連等黑夜過去都等不及。他唯一會想到的策略，就是立刻攻擊。在發出土狼的哀號聲，致命地暴露了自己的位置之後，那些徬徨的印第安哨兵，又能做些什麼呢？他們原是精通各種戰術的，而這一次，他們只得無可奈何地跟在虎克後面。

　　在勇敢的猛虎莉莉身邊，圍繞著十二名最驍勇善戰的戰士。突然，他們發現那群詭計多端的海盜正向他們襲擊過來，那些勝利的白日夢霎時破滅。現在等著他們的不是去拷問虎克，而是戰魂即將前往的幸福獵場。這一點他們心裡明白，但是身為印第安人的子孫，他們要表現得不辱身分。如果他們迅速地圍在一起，排成方陣，敵方就很難攻破，但印第安的傳統禁止這樣做。他們明文規定，高貴的印第安人不能在白人面前表現得驚慌失措。海盜的突襲，難免嚇到他們，但他們當下依然不動如山，肌肉連個抽動都沒有，就好像敵人是應邀來做客似的。他們英勇地堅守傳統，握緊武器，發出撼天動地的嘶喊聲。只是，一切都太晚了。

與其說這是一場戰鬥，不如說是一場屠殺，而我們就不去描述了。皮卡尼尼許多優秀的戰士，就這樣喪失了性命，但他們也並非是白白犧牲，因為海盜瘦狼倒下了，阿爾夫・梅森也送了命，西班牙海岸從此平靜。還有喬治・斯庫利、查斯・托利、屬於亞爾薩斯人的佛格帝，也一命嗚呼。托利死在黑豹的斧頭下，黑豹和莉莉以及少數存活下來的族人，最後殺出一條血路逃了出來。

在這次戰鬥中，虎克的戰略與功過，就讓歷史學家去決定吧。若是他選擇待在土丘上等待正當的時刻，說不定他和手下早就被幹光了。這一點，歷史學家當然也得考慮進去。或許他應該做的是，預先通知敵人他有新的計畫，不過他如果這麼做，就無法攻其不備，那計謀自然也就會落空。因此，這個問題是很難下結論的。不過，他能想出這樣一個大膽的計畫，利用他狠毒的天才去實現，我們多少也不得不由衷地佩服。

在勝利的時刻，虎克又是如何想的呢？他的走狗們是很想知道的。他們氣喘吁吁，擦著刀，遠遠躲開那只鐵鉤，用貂一樣的眼睛斜瞄著這個怪人。現在虎克心裡想必是洋洋自滿，不過這從他臉上是看不出來的。他個性陰沉孤僻，無論是在精神或身體上，總是和手下保持距離。

這一晚還不算功德圓滿。虎克這次出擊並不是為了殲滅印第安人，印第安人只不過是用煙薰出來的蜜蜂，而他要的是蜂蜜。他要的是彼得‧潘，還有溫蒂和那一群孩子，但最主要的目標還是潘。

彼得這麼一個小男孩，為什麼虎克那麼恨他，實在叫人想不透。沒錯，他是曾經把虎克的一條手臂扔給鱷魚，鍥而不捨的鱷魚也讓虎克的生命受到威脅，但這還是不足以解釋虎克為何這樣恨他入骨。事實是，彼得身上的某種特質，讓這個海盜船長非常的抓狂。那種特質不是勇氣，不是他那逗人喜愛的外表，不是……也用不著拐彎抹角了，我們都很清楚那是什麼，也不得不招認：那就是彼得囂張的態度。

這正是虎克看不順眼的地方，讓他恨得鐵鉤直打顫，在夜裡，這又像煩人的蟲子讓他不能安睡。只要彼得還活著，飽受折磨的虎克就覺得自己是被關在籠裡的獅子，而彼得就是飛來飛去擾他安寧的麻雀。

他們現在的問題是，要如何鑽進樹洞呢？或是說，要如何讓他的走狗們鑽進樹洞？他抬起貪婪的雙眼環視四週，想找出最瘦小的人。海盜們不安地扭著身子，因為他們知道，虎克會不惜用棍子把他們捅下樹洞的。

此時，孩子們這邊又是如何呢？我們看到，在剛開始戰鬥時，他們像石頭一般動也不動，張大著嘴，伸出手臂向彼得求助。現在，他們已經把嘴巴閉上，收回了手臂。

地面上的混戰一下子停止了，一如它來得那般突然，如同一陣狂風吹過。但他們知道，風暴過後，他們的命運已經決定了。

哪一方勝利了呢？

海盜們在樹洞口屏息偷聽，聽到了孩子們提出的問題，不妙的是，他們也聽到了彼得的回答。

「如果印第安人勝利了，」彼得說：「他們會敲戰鼓，那是他們勝利的訊號。」

史密找到了那只戰鼓，因為他此刻正坐在鼓上呢。「你們再也聽不到鼓聲了。」史密喃喃道，聲音小得誰也聽不見，因為虎克嚴令不許出聲。然而讓史密很驚訝的是，虎克竟對他打了個暗號，要他擊鼓。史密慢慢地才領悟到，這個命令是多麼陰險！頭腦簡單的史密，這下是對虎克佩服到底了。

史密擊了兩次鼓，然後歡欣地停下來豎起耳朵聆聽。

「是鼓聲，」這些壞蛋聽見彼得喊說：「印第安人勝利了！」

劫數已到的孩子們一陣歡呼，聽在上面那些黑心肝的人耳裡，簡直是美妙的樂音。緊接著，又聽到孩子們在向彼得說再見，這讓海盜們不解。不過，海盜們現在一心快活，因為敵人就要從樹洞爬出來了。他們相視奸笑，搓著掌心。虎克立刻悄悄下達命令：一人守一棵樹，其他人相隔兩碼，排成一行！

你相信仙子嗎？

Chapter 13

這段恐怖的故事，越快說完越好。第一個跑出樹洞的是捲毛，他一出來，立刻就落在契科手裡。契科把他扔給史密，史密把他扔給斯塔奇，斯塔奇把他扔給比爾·鳩克斯，比爾又把他扔給努得勒。他就這樣被他們一個接一個扔過去，直到最後被扔到了黑臉虎克的腳邊。每個孩子從樹洞出來後，都是這樣無情地被拋來拋去，有幾個孩子還被拋到半空中，像傳一包包的貨物一樣。

最後出樹洞的是溫蒂，她受到了不同的待遇。虎克嘲弄地裝出彬彬有禮的樣子，對她舉起帽子，還用手臂挽著她，護送她到囚禁其他孩子的地方。虎克的動作和神態是如此高貴，溫蒂像著迷似的，竟然沒有哭出來。她只是個小女孩呀！

要說虎克這一刻真的迷惑了溫蒂，似乎是在搬弄是非，但我們會提到這件事，是因為溫蒂此刻的疏忽造成了意想不到的後果。要是她高傲地放開虎克的手（我們當然希望情形是如此），她就會像其他的孩子一樣被扔到空中。如果是這樣，那虎克就不會看到孩子們被綁起來的情形；假如他當時沒看到孩子們被綁，那他就不會發現史萊特利的祕密；要是他沒有發現那個祕密，那他也就不會卑鄙地想要彼得的命。

為了防止孩子們逃跑，海盜把他們綁了起來，將膝蓋貼著耳朵捆成一團。為了捆綁他們，黑臉虎克把一根繩子剪成等長的九段。所有孩子都順利地被綁好，直到輪到捆史萊特利，捆了幾圈，他們發現繩子的長度不夠打結，這就好像繩子在打包包裹時不夠長那樣，讓他們很生氣。海盜們氣得踢了他幾下，就像在踢包裹一樣（說句公道話，被踢的應該是繩子）。但說也奇怪，叫他們住手的竟是虎克。虎克撅著唇，一副陰險又得意的樣子。

　　他的手下在捆綁這個可憐的小男孩時，只要綁住他身體的這一邊，另一邊就會像吹氣一般地膨脹起來，所以怎麼綁都只會累得海盜們汗水直流。精明的虎克識破了史萊特利的把戲，看出了內情。他洋洋得意的表情，透露出他知道了內幕。史萊特利臉色發白，他知道虎克發現了他的祕密。一個脹大了的小孩能鑽進去的樹洞，會是一個普通的大人不用棍子捅也進得去的。可憐的史萊特利，現在是孩子裡最不幸的一個了，因為他為彼得感到很擔心，深深懊悔自己做過的事。原來，有一次他覺得熱，就拼命喝水，把肚子脹得像現在這麼大，結果他沒有減肥去遷就樹洞，而是偷偷地把樹洞削大來配合他現在的身材。

　　這就夠了，虎克相信彼得終究是逃不出他的手心。他用那顆邪惡腦袋所想出來的計謀，半個字也沒洩露，他只是打了個手勢，命令手下把這些俘虜們押到船上，他要獨自留下。

　　要怎麼把孩子們運到船上呢？他們被繩子綁成一團，可以像水桶一樣滾下山坡，但是整趟路程當中大部分是沼澤地。虎克的天才又再度克服了這個困難，他指示手下把小木屋用來當作運輸工具。孩子們被扔進小屋，四名強壯的海盜把它扛在肩上，其餘的海盜跟在後面。這支怪異的隊伍在樹林間行進，又唱起那首討厭的海盜歌。我不知道孩子們有沒有人在哭，要是有，那哭聲大概也被歌聲給淹沒了。當小屋逐漸消失在樹林裡時，小屋的煙囪卻升起了一縷細微又勇敢的青煙，彷彿是在挑戰虎克似的。

　　虎克看到了這縷煙，這對彼得很不利，因為這憤怒的海盜即使原本還有一絲惻隱之心，此刻也都消失殆盡了。

　　黑夜迅速降臨，虎克所做的第一件事，就是躡手躡腳走到史萊特利的那棵樹前，確定自己能從那裡鑽進去。他沉思好長一段時間，把他那頂不祥的帽子放在草地上，讓風輕撫頭髮。他的心雖然很黑暗，湛藍的眼睛卻像春花一般柔和。他專注聽著地底下的動靜，可是地下地上一樣寂靜無聲，地底家園彷彿是比空屋更寂靜。那男孩到底是睡著了，還是正站在史萊特利的樹下，手裡握著刀子等著他？

　　除了下去，別無他法可以得知。虎克把外套輕輕放到地上，咬著雙唇，直到流出骯髒的血，接著踏進了樹洞。他是個勇敢的人，這時卻不得不停下來擦拭額頭，他額上的汗水像蠟燭油一樣淌著。然後，他悄悄地進到那個他一無所知的地方。

　　他平安地來到樹洞底下，靜靜地站住，直到他不再喘氣。等他逐漸習慣了地底家園昏暗的光線，才看清楚屋裡的每一樣東西。不過他貪婪的目光只找一樣東西。找了好一陣子，他終於看到了那張大床，床上躺的是熟睡的彼得。

　　彼得完全不知道地面上發生的慘劇，孩子們離開沒多久，他又繼續開心地吹著笛子：他無疑是故意這麼做的，好證明他一點也不在乎。然後，他還決定不吃藥，想讓溫蒂傷心。接著，他躺在床上不蓋被子，好讓溫蒂更煩惱，因為溫蒂總是會幫孩子們把被子蓋好，怕半夜會著涼。想

著想著，彼得幾乎要哭出來，但他忽然想到，要是他不哭反笑，溫蒂會多麼的生氣。於是，他就得意地大笑，可還沒笑完就睡著了。

　　彼得偶爾會做一下夢，而他的夢比其他的孩子都更痛苦。他常會在夢裡哭泣，好幾個小時都擺脫不了惡夢的糾纏。我想，這應該是和他來歷不明的身世有關。在這種時候，溫蒂通常會把他從床上扶起來，讓他坐在自己腿上，用她自己的方法安慰他。等他稍微平靜一點，趁他還沒清醒時，又把他放回床上，這樣就可以不讓他知道自己被安慰，而有損尊嚴。但是今天，彼得完全沒有作夢，一隻手臂垂在床邊，一條腿彎成弓形，笑到一半的大笑還掛在嘴上。他張著嘴，露出珍珠般的牙齒。

　　彼得就這樣毫無防備地被找到了。虎克靜靜站在樹腳下，隔著房間望著他的敵人。他那陰暗的心裡，難道沒有一絲同情嗎？這個人並不是極端邪惡：他愛花（我聽說的），愛美妙的音樂（他彈豎琴彈得不錯）。我們得坦承，眼前這幅純真的畫面深深地感動了他。要是他善良的一面占了上風，他也許會勉強地走回樹上。不過，他留下來了，只為了一件事。

　　讓虎克留下來的是彼得那副傲慢的睡姿：嘴巴張得大大，垂下著手臂，膝蓋弓得彎彎的，這些姿勢湊在一起，簡直就是十足驕傲自大的化身。在虎克那雙敏感的眼睛看來，再也沒有比這更惱人的了，這讓虎克又硬起心腸。要是這怒火讓他氣得爆炸，他會裂成幾百塊碎片，然後每一塊碎片都會不顧一切地飛向正在熟睡的那個孩子。

　　儘管有一盞燈光微弱地照著床，但虎克站在暗處裡。他才鬼鬼祟祟地向前邁出一步，就碰到了一個障礙，那是

史萊特利樹洞下的門。這個門和樹洞的大小並不完全吻合，虎克仔細檢查，想伸手去找把手，卻很生氣地發現把手太低，他搆不著。現在，在他那混亂的腦袋裡，彼得的那張臉和姿態顯得益發可惡了。他使勁搖晃著門，用身子去撞門。他的敵人究竟能不能逃出他的毒手呢？

那是什麼？虎克漲紅的雙眼瞧見彼得的藥就擺在他伸手可及的架子上，他立刻明白那是什麼，知道這個熟睡的孩子已經逃不出他的手掌心了。

為了避免被敵人活捉，虎克總是隨身攜帶一瓶致命的毒藥，那是他用各種毒草親自調配而成的。他將這些毒草熬成黃色的汁，連科學家都沒見識過這種東西。這大概是目前世上最毒的毒藥了。

他在彼得的杯子裡滴了五滴毒藥，雙手一直抖個不停，但這不是因為羞恥，而是因為喜悅；他在下毒時，眼睛也盡量不去看彼得，不是因為怕自己會心生憐憫，而是怕自己會因為太興奮把藥給灑了出來。他幸災樂禍地盯著他的受害者好長一段時間，然後才轉過身，在樹洞裡蠕動著身子辛苦往地面上爬去。虎克從樹上鑽出來時，看起來就像是真的惡魔出了魔窟。他斜戴著帽子，看起來流裡流氣，身上披著披風，一邊拉著衣角遮住身體，想讓自己隱沒在夜色中。其實，他才是黑夜裡最黑暗的存在。他怪里怪氣地喃喃自語，穿過樹林溜走了。

彼得還在睡，燈光閃了一下後熄滅，整個屋子陷入一片黑暗，可他還繼續睡著。在彼得不知道被什麼驚醒，忽然從床上坐起來的時候，鱷魚肚裡的鐘一定超過十點了。他的樹上傳來了又輕又謹慎的敲門聲。

雖然敲門聲又輕又謹慎，但在這樣安靜的夜裡也是有危險的。彼得伸手握住刀子，然後問道：

「是誰？」

許久都沒有回應，然後又是一陣敲門聲。

「你是誰？」

還是沒有回應。

彼得一陣毛骨悚然，這正是他最喜歡的。他跨了兩步，走到門前。這個門和史萊特利的門不同，是被遮起來的，所以他看不到外面，敲門的人也看不到他。

「你不出聲，我就不開門。」彼得喊道。

最後，對方總算開口了，發出了可愛的鈴噹聲。

「讓我進來，彼得。」

那是亭可，彼得立刻打開門閂讓她進來。她興奮地飛進來，臉紅通通的，衣服上沾滿了一點一點的泥巴。

「怎麼回事？」

「啊，你絕對猜不到。」她嚷著，還讓彼得猜了三次。「妳快點說！」彼得大喊。於是，亭可用一句不合文法的長句子，長得像從魔術師嘴裡抽出來的絲帶一樣，告訴彼得溫蒂和孩子們被海盜抓住的經過。

彼得聽著，心臟噗通噗通地跳。溫蒂被抓上了海盜船。她熱愛世界上的一切，卻落得如此下場！

「我要去救她。」彼得喊著跳起來抓起武器。在他跳起來的時候，他想到了一件可以讓溫蒂高興的事：他可以把他的藥吃了。

他伸手要去拿致命的藥水。

「不要喝！」亭可尖叫。她在虎克匆匆忙忙穿過樹林時，聽到他嘟囔著自己幹了什麼好事。

「為什麼？」

「藥裡面有毒。」

「有毒？誰會下毒？」

「虎克。」

「別傻了。虎克怎麼可能下來這裡？」

哎呀！亭可沒辦法解釋，因為她並不知道史萊特利樹洞的祕密。但是虎克的話是毋庸置疑的，藥水裡頭的確是下了毒。

「況且，」彼得極有自信地說：「我根本就沒睡著。」

他拿起杯子。用說的來不及了，直接行動吧，亭可像閃電一樣，迅速地鑽到彼得的嘴和杯子之間，一口氣把藥喝光。

「妳在做什麼，亭可？竟敢喝我的藥？」

亭可沒有回答，只是搖搖晃晃地在空中打轉。

「妳怎麼了？」彼得喊起來，突然感到害怕。

「藥裡有毒，彼得，」亭可小小聲說：「我馬上就要死了。」

「啊，亭可，你喝毒藥是為了救我嗎？」

「是的。」

「但是為什麼呢，亭可？」

她的翅膀已經無法支撐她的重量了，但為了回答問題，她落到彼得的肩上，在他鼻子上親暱地咬了一口，並在他耳邊悄悄地說：「你這大笨蛋。」接著，她搖搖欲墜回到她的房間，倒在床上。

彼得悲傷地跪在她的床邊，他的頭幾乎佔滿了整間斗室。亭可的亮光越來越暗淡，彼得知道，一旦亮光完全熄滅了，那麼亭可也就不在了。亭可喜歡彼得的眼淚，她伸出美麗的手指，讓眼淚滑過指間。

一開始，她的聲音很微弱，彼得根本聽不到她說什麼，後來他聽懂了，原來亭可說著：只要小孩子相信有仙子，仙子就會好起來的。

彼得伸出了雙臂。他們身邊沒有小孩子，而且現在已經那麼晚了。不過，他對所有正夢到夢幻島的孩子們說話，穿著睡衣的男孩和女孩，還有光著身子、睡在樹上搖籃裡的印第安小娃娃。其實這些小孩子都離彼得很近，沒有你所想的那麼遠。

「你們相信有仙子嗎？」他大聲喊道。

亭可立刻從床上坐起來，聆聽她的命運。

她隱隱約約聽到了肯定的回答，但又不那麼確定。

「你覺得他們說什麼？」她問彼得。

「要是你們相信，」彼得對孩子們大喊：「就拍拍手，不要讓亭可死。」

很多孩子都拍了手。

有些孩子沒拍手。

有幾個沒心肝的小畜牲發出噓聲。

拍手聲忽地停止了，聽起來好像有數不清的母親衝進育兒室，看看到底發生了什麼事。不過，亭可已經得救了。她先是聲音變大聲，接著她像一陣風似地跳下床，在屋裡飛來飛去，飛得比過去來得還要快活，還要傲慢。她才沒有想到要去感謝那些拍手的孩子，只一心想著要去對付那些發出噓聲的孩子。

「現在該去救溫蒂了。」

彼得鑽出樹洞時，月亮正在雲裡穿行。他配帶上武器和其他一點東西，準備出發冒險。但如果能選擇，他才不會挑今晚來冒險。他本來想要低空飛行，靠近地面，這樣一來，所有不尋常的事都逃不過他的眼睛。但是，今晚月光若隱若現，他如果低空飛行，影子會投射在樹上，不但會驚動鳥兒，也會讓敵人發現他的行動。

　　現在彼得很後悔為島上的鳥兒取了一些奇奇怪怪的名字，使牠們變得野性難馴，不易接近。

　　現在也沒別的辦法了，只能學印第安人，貼著地面爬行，也幸好這他很在行。只是，該往哪個方向去呢？他還不能斷定孩子們是不是被帶到了船上。地面上留下的腳印，被剛下的一點雪給掩埋掉了。島上籠罩著一片死寂，看起來像是大自然被剛才那一場屠殺給嚇到似的。彼得曾經教過孩子們一些森林的知識，而這是他從莉莉和亭可那兒學到的。他相信，縱使遇到緊急狀況，他們也不會忘記的。舉例來說吧，史萊特利要是有機會，會在樹上刻上標記，捲毛會在地上撒下種子，溫蒂會在重要的地方扔下手帕。但是，要找到這些記號得等到天亮，可他不能再等了。上面的世界在召喚他，卻不給他一點指引。

　　鱷魚從他身邊爬過，除此之外，再沒有其他活著的生物會沒有一點聲響和動靜。彼得心裡明白，死亡或許就在前面一棵樹那裡等著他，或正從他身後撲過來。

　　他發了這樣一個毒誓：「不是我死，就是虎克亡。」

　　彼得如蛇一般往前爬行，突然，他站直身體，飛快跑過一片月光照亮的空地，一手按著嘴唇，一手握著短刀做好準備，興奮得不得了。

海盜船

Chapter 14

　　一盞綠色的桅燈，斜睨著海盜河口附近的吉德灣，表明那艘雙桅橫帆船「快樂羅傑號」就停在那兒。它的船身彷彿是一隻張牙舞爪的大鷹，每一根羽毛都傷痕累累，顯露凶狠的肅殺之氣。它是海上的食人番，即使沒有那盞如炬的桅燈，只憑它昭彰的惡名，也能在海上暢行無阻。

　　船身被夜幕籠罩著，一點聲響都無法傳到岸上，不過船上本來也就沒什麼聲音，除了正在使用的那架縫紉機所發出的聲響，而使用縫紉機的人正是擁有平常人那種勤勉有禮的特質的可憐史密。我不知道他為什麼都這樣可憐，也許就因為他不覺得自己可憐吧。即使是最堅強的男子漢，也不忍多看他一眼。在夏日的夜晚裡，他竟不止一次觸動了虎克眼淚的泉源，使他淚流不止。對於這件事，史密一如往常，亦渾然不覺。

　　有幾個海盜靠在船邊深深地吸著夜霧，其他人趴在水桶邊擲骰子、玩紙牌。那四個負責抬小屋的海盜，精疲力竭地倒在甲板上；即使在睡夢中，他們也能靈活地滾來滾去，翻身避開虎克，免得在他經過他們身邊時，習慣性地用爪子抓一下。

　　虎克在甲板上踱步沉思，他可真是個高深莫測的人

啊！現在是他勝利的時刻，彼得已經被除掉，再也不能擋他的路了。其他孩子也全被捉到船上，等著走跳板。這是繼他解決巴比克之後，最輝煌的一次戰績。我們知道人性是多麼的虛榮，所以就算他現在在甲板上搖搖擺擺地踱著步，因勝利而趾高氣揚，也不足為奇。

　　但是，他的步伐毫不得意，反而與他悶悶不樂的心情齊頭並進。虎克的心情極為沮喪。

　　每當夜深人靜，他總是在船上暗自思忖。這是因為，他感到極度的孤單。這個人總是讓人猜不透，每當身邊圍著那群手下，他卻更感孤獨。手下們的社會地位遠不及他。

　　虎克不是他的真實姓名。要是透露他的真名，即使在今天，也照樣轟動全英國。不過，細心看書的人一定早就猜到，虎克曾經唸過一所著名的學校。至今，那所學校的傳統仍像衣服一樣緊跟著他。不過說實在的，學校的傳統大多也和衣服有關。所以，時至今日，如果他身上穿的還是佔領這艘船時所穿的衣服，他一定會感到厭惡。他走路的姿勢還保持著在學時那種高雅不凡的慵懶神態，但最重要的是，他仍保有良好的行為風範。

　　良好的行為風範！無論他再怎麼墮落，也知道這才是最重要的。

　　他聽到發自內心深處的一陣嘎嘎聲，就像打開一扇生銹鐵門時所發出的聲音；門外傳來莊嚴的噠噠聲，那是夜裡無法入睡時會聽到的錘擊聲。「你今天保持良好的行為風範了嗎？」在他內心裡永不間斷地詢問著。

　　「名聲，名聲，那閃閃發光的小東西，是屬於我的。」他喊道。

　　「做任何事都出人頭地，就算是良好的行為風範嗎？」

從學校發出的噠噠聲反問著他。

「我是巴比克唯一害怕的人，」他連忙說：「弗林特都對巴比克怕得不得了呢。」

「巴比克，弗林特，他們是什麼家庭出身的？」那聲音嚴厲地反駁。

但最讓人憂慮的是，一心想要保持良好的行為舉止，難道就是好風範嗎？

這個問題搞得虎克五臟六腑翻攪不已，就像他心上的一隻鐵鉤，比手上的鐵鉤還更銳利，狠狠地撕裂著他。一滴滴汗珠從他的油臉上淌下來，在衣服上留下一道道汗漬，他頻頻用袖子擦拭臉頰，可是止不住淌下的汗水。

唉，不用羨慕虎克。

虎克有預感自己會死得早，好像彼得發的那個毒誓已經降臨了這條船。虎克憂鬱地想發表臨終遺言，不然恐怕等一下就來不及說了。

他喊道：「對虎克而言，要是他沒那麼大野心就好了。」他只有在最低潮的時候，才會用第三人稱稱呼自己。

「沒有小孩愛我。」

奇怪的是他居然會想到這一點，這問題過去從沒有困擾過他，說不定是那架縫紉機害他這麼想的。他自言自語好一會兒，盯著那個正在靜靜縫衣邊、自以為所有的孩子都怕他的史密。

怕他？怕史密？事實上，就在那一夜，所有被帶到船上的孩子都喜歡上他了。那時史密講恐怖故事給他們聽，還用手掌打他們（因為他不能用拳頭打），可孩子們卻更纏著他，麥可還想要戴他的眼鏡呢。

虎克恨不得能告訴可悲的史密，說孩子們覺得他很和

藹，但這實在太殘酷了，虎克決定把這個祕密藏在心裡。為什麼孩子們會覺得史密和藹？虎克像警犬一樣對這個問題窮追不捨：如果史密是個可親的人，是什麼讓他受孩子們的歡迎呢？一個驚人的答案忽然浮現：「良好的行為風範！」

史密這名水手，對自己所散發出的良好風範渾然不自覺？這一點，不正是風範的絕佳表現嗎？

虎克想起來了，你得先證明不知道自己具備良好的行為風範，才有資格成為波普俱樂部的一員。

虎克憤怒地一吼，對史密舉起了鐵鉤，可他並沒有下手，忽然的一個念頭讓他打住：

「因為別人有良好的行為風範，就對他下手，這又算什麼呢？」

「惡劣的風範！」

傷心的虎克，一下子變得有氣無力，像被折斷的花朵一樣垂頭喪氣。

手下們以為虎克不再嫌他們礙手礙腳，立刻就鬆懈下來，跳起喝醉時才跳的舞蹈。這讓虎克像被潑了一桶冷水似的，頓時振作了起來，所有人性的軟弱一掃而空。

「安靜，你們這些渾蛋！」他嚷道：「再吵我就使出鐵鉤！」一時之間立刻安靜了下來。「孩子們都綁好了沒有？別讓他們給跑了。」

「好啦，好啦。」

「那就把他們帶上來。」

除了溫蒂，那群命運悲慘的的俘虜全都給拖出來，排成一列，站在虎克面前。起初，虎克對他們視而不見，他慵懶地坐著，哼著幾句粗野小調，手拿著紙牌耍弄，嘴裡叼著雪茄，雪茄微弱的火光映出他臉上的顏色。

「好吧，臭小子們，今晚你們有六個人得走跳板，另外兩個可以留下來打雜，該留下哪兩個呢？」虎克乾脆地說。

「除非萬不得已，不要惹他發火。」溫蒂在貨艙裡曾經這樣告訴過他們，所以圖圖有禮貌地往前走了幾步。他才不想做這人的手下，直覺告訴他，他可以把責任推給一個不在場的人。他是有點笨啦，但還是知道只有母親是願意代孩子受苦的。每個孩子都知道這一點，因此看不起母親，卻又時常利用母親這個弱點。

所以啦，圖圖謹慎地解釋說：「你知道，先生，我想我母親是不會希望我成為海盜的。你母親會希望你當海盜嗎，史萊特利？」

他對史萊特利擠擠眉眼，史萊特利悲傷地說：「我想她不會。」一副言不由衷的樣子。「你們的母親會願意讓你們當海盜嗎，雙胞胎？」

「我可不這麼認為。」老大說，他也跟其他孩子一樣機靈。「尼布斯，你……？」

「少廢話。」虎克吼道，把說話的孩子給拉了回去。「小子，就是你，」虎克指著約翰說：「你看起來比較勇敢，你有沒有想過要當海盜啊，我的乖乖？」

約翰在做數學習題的時候，曾經有過這樣的想法，但虎克突然把他叫出來問這個問題，倒讓他感到有點詫異。

「我有想過把自己取名叫『血腥手傑克』。」約翰不是很有自信地說。

「好名字，要是你入夥，我們就這樣叫你。」

「麥可，你覺得呢？」約翰問。

「要是我加入，你們要叫我什麼？」麥可問。

「黑鬍子喬。」

麥可自然是很感興趣。「你覺得呢，約翰？」他想找約翰幫他做決定，約翰也想找他幫忙做決定。

　　「我們要是加入，還能是在英國女王統治下當受人尊敬的國民嗎？」約翰問。

　　虎克從牙縫裡擠出這幾個字：「你們要發誓，『打倒國王』。」

　　或許約翰之前的表現不怎麼好，不過現在可別小看他。

　　「那我拒絕。」他捶著虎克面前的水桶喊道。

　　「我也拒絕。」麥可喊。

　　「大英帝國萬歲！」捲毛高呼。

　　被激怒的海盜們出手打了他們的嘴。虎克大吼道：「你們完蛋了。把他們的媽媽帶上來，把跳板準備好。」

　　他們只是小男孩，看到鳩克斯和契科抬來那塊要命的跳板，臉都嚇白了。可是當溫蒂被帶過來時，他們努力裝出勇敢的樣子。

　　沒有任何字眼能說明溫蒂有多麼鄙視這些海盜，男孩們至少覺得海盜這個職業多少有點吸引人，但溫蒂只看到，這艘船有很多年都沒有好好打掃了。沒有一扇窗戶的玻璃是乾淨的，髒得都能用手指在上面寫「骯髒的豬」這幾個字了，而溫蒂已經在好幾個窗上寫下了。不過，當男孩們圍在她身邊時，她一心只想著如何救出他們。

　　「現在，我的小美人，」虎克像是嘴巴沾了蜜糖地說：「你就要看著你的孩子們走跳板啦。」

　　雖然虎克是一名紳士，可是他吃東西吃得過急，弄髒了領口。突然間，他發現溫蒂正盯著他的衣領，他連忙想遮蓋起來，可是已經來不及了。

　　「他們會死嗎？」溫蒂問，表情極度的輕蔑，虎克幾

乎氣暈了。

「對！」他吼著。「大家都安靜下來！」他幸災樂禍地大喊：「讓母親和她的孩子們話別吧。」

這一刻，溫蒂顯得十分莊嚴偉大。「我親愛的孩子們，這是我最後要對你們說的話，」她神情堅定地說：「我覺得，你們真正的母親有話要我對你們說，那就是：『我希望我的兒子能死得像個英國紳士。』」

連海盜們聽了這句話，也深表敬畏。圖圖發瘋似地大叫：「我要照我母親希望的去做。你呢，尼布斯？」

「我也要照我母親希望的去做。你們會怎麼做，雙胞胎？」

「我們也要照母親希望的去做。約翰，你……」

這時虎克又說話了。

「把她綁起來！」他大叫著。

把溫蒂綁在桅杆上的是史密。「聽著，小乖乖，」史密悄悄地說：「如果妳答應當我的母親，我就救妳。」

但就算是史密，溫蒂也不願答應。「我寧可一個孩子也沒有。」她不屑地說。

說起來也真悲哀，史密把溫蒂綁在桅杆上的時候，沒有一個孩子望著她，他們的眼睛全都盯著跳板：那是他們最後要走的幾步路程。男孩們已經不敢指望自己能昂首闊步地走過去，他們早就失去思考能力，只能呆呆地望著跳板直發抖。

虎克咬牙切齒卻面帶微笑地朝溫蒂走去，他想要把她的臉轉過來，讓她親眼目睹孩子一個一個走上跳板。然而，虎克沒能走到她面前，也沒能聽到他想要逼她發出的痛苦叫聲，因為他聽到了另一個聲音。

那隻鱷魚肚子裡可怕的滴答聲。

　　他們全都聽見了：海盜們、孩子們，還有溫蒂。每個人的頭都立刻朝同一個方向轉去：不是朝著發出聲音的水裡，而是朝著虎克。大家都知道，即將發生的事情，只會與他有關。他們本來是演戲的，現在忽然都變成看戲的了。

　　而發生在虎克身上的轉變才真讓人震驚：他就像全身的關節都被針刺到一樣，整個人癱成一團。

　　滴答聲緩緩靠近，鱷魚還沒到，駭人的念頭就先跑到虎克的腦袋裡了：「鱷魚就要爬上船了。」

　　虎克的鐵鉤也毫無生氣地垂下，好像它也知道自己不是敵人想得到的那副身軀的一部分。要是別人遇到這種情況，早就倒在地上、閉上眼睛等死了，可是，虎克那巨大頑強的頭腦還在活動。他在頭腦的指揮下，雙膝著地，跪在甲板上往前爬，能逃離滴答聲越遠越好。海盜們恭敬地為他讓出一條路，他一直爬到船舷才開口說話。

　　「把我藏起來。」他嘶啞地喊著。

　　海盜團團把他圍住，眼睛一刻不離地等著看那個即將爬上船的生物。他們沒想過要和牠對抗，這是命運的安排。

　　虎克躲起來以後，只有孩子們出於好奇，又活動了起來。他們一窩蜂擁到船邊，看著那隻鱷魚爬到船上。而這時，他們發現今晚最驚人的一個祕密：原來正要來救他們的，不是鱷魚，而是彼得。

　　彼得打了個手勢，示意他們不要發出驚喜的叫喊，免得引起海盜懷疑，然後繼續發出他滴答滴答的聲音。

和虎克拼個
你死我活

Chapter 15

每個人一生中，都會遇到一些奇怪的事，但是在事發當下卻毫無所覺。舉例來說，當我們突然發現一隻耳朵聾了，卻不知道到底聾了多久，就會說，大概聾了半個鐘頭吧。那天晚上，彼得也遇到這種情況。上次我們見到他時，他正悄悄地穿越夢幻島，一手摀著嘴，一手握住刀。他看見鱷魚從身邊爬過，沒發覺有什麼異樣，過了好一會兒突然發現，鱷魚沒有發出滴答聲！一開始，他覺得很怪，不過，他很快就明白，時鐘已經沒有電了。

彼得完全沒想到，突然失去了親密夥伴的鱷魚，會有多傷心；但他倒是立刻想到，要怎麼利用這件事幫助他行動。他決定自己發出鱷魚肚裡的滴答聲，那些野獸聽到，會以為他是鱷魚，而不敢傷害他。他模仿滴答聲維妙維肖，沒料到招致了意想不到的結果：鱷魚也聽到了滴答聲，便一直跟著他。到底鱷魚是想找回牠失去的東西，還是以為牠的夥伴又開始滴答響了，我們永遠不會知道。鱷魚是一種很蠢的動物，就像奴隸一樣，總是死守著某個念頭，不肯改變。

彼得平安到達岸邊後，繼續往前直走，腿碰到了水也毫不覺得異樣，有一些動物從陸地上走進水中也是這樣的，但我沒見過有人類會這樣。當他游泳時，心中只有一個想法：「不是我死，就是虎克亡。」他發出滴答滴答的聲音實在太久，渾然不覺自己一直在發出這個聲音。發出滴答聲登上海盜船固然是一條妙計，但彼得可從沒有過這樣的念頭，如果他知道自己還正在發出鬧鐘的滴答聲，早就會停下來了。

　　和事實正好相反，彼得以為自己像老鼠一樣無聲無息地爬上了船邊。因此，當他看到海盜們畏畏縮縮想要避開他，虎克緊張地躲在他們中間，一副像是看到鱷魚似的神情，便讓他驚訝不已。

　　鱷魚！彼得才想起鱷魚，就聽到了滴答滴答的聲音。一開始，他以為那是鱷魚發出的滴答聲，便立刻回頭一看，而這才發現，聲音是從自己身上發出來的。轉瞬間，他才明白了是什麼狀況。「我真是太聰明了！」彼得腦中霎時浮現這個想法，還示意孩子們不要拍手歡呼。

　　這時，舵手愛德・坦特從艙裡走到甲板上。現在，請你看著錶，計算事情發生的時間。彼得往他身上一砍，又準又深；約翰搗住這名倒楣海盜的嘴，搗住垂死的呻吟聲；愛德往前倒下，四個孩子上前抓住他，以免他砰地一聲倒在地上。彼得一打暗號，他們就把他拋到海裡去了，先是水花四濺，接著就是一片寂靜，總共多久時間？

　　「一個！」（史萊特利已經開始計算。）

　　沒過多久，彼得踮著腳，一溜煙消失在船艙裡。有幾個海盜鼓起勇氣往四處張望，他們已經能夠聽到其他人發出的驚恐喘息聲，可見更嚇人的滴答聲已經走遠了。

　　「牠已經走了，船長，」史密擦了擦眼鏡說道：「又恢復平靜了。」

慢慢地，虎克把頭從衣領伸出來，仔細聽著是否還有滴答滴答的餘音。一點聲音沒有，他這才直挺挺地站了起來。

「好，走跳板的時間到了。」虎克厚著臉皮喊道。現在他更痛恨那群孩子了，竟讓他們見到他的狼狽相。突然，他唱起那首邪惡的小調：

> 唷呵，唷呵，躍動的跳板，
> 沿著跳板往前走
> 連人帶板往下掉，
> 到海底去見大衛·瓊斯嘍！

為了再嚇嚇他的這群俘虜，虎克不顧尊嚴，假裝沿著跳板跳舞，一邊唱一邊對他們做鬼臉，唱完還對孩子們說：「要不要在走跳板前先嚐嚐九尾鞭的滋味啊？」

孩子們害怕地跪下。「不，不要。」他們喊得那麼可憐，讓那群海盜忍不住笑出來。

「鳩克斯，把船艙裡的鞭子拿過來。」虎克說。

船艙！彼得就在船艙裡！孩子們你看我、我看你的。

「好，好。」鳩克斯樂不可支，大步走進船艙。孩子們的視線緊緊跟著他，根本沒注意虎克又唱起歌。這一次，他的走狗也一起加入：

> 唷喝，唷喝，抓人的貓，
> 它的尾巴有九條，
> 要是落到你背上……

歌詞的最後一句是什麼，我們永遠不會知道，因為船艙裡突然傳來一聲恐懼的尖叫聲，響徹全船。尖叫聲接著慢慢變弱、消失，然後傳來的是一聲孩子們再熟悉不過的歡呼聲，可是這在海盜們聽來，卻比尖叫還要令人毛骨悚然。

「那是什麼？」虎克喊。

「兩個！」史萊特利正經地數著。

義大利人契科猶豫了一會兒，大搖大擺地走下船艙，之後卻跌跌撞撞地退了出來，嚇得臉都綠了。

「比爾‧鳩克斯到底怎麼了，你這狗東西？」虎克從牙縫擠出這幾個字，惡狠狠地盯著他。

「出事了，他死了，被砍死了。」契科壓低嗓門地回答。

「比爾‧鳩克斯死了！」海盜們驚叫道。

「船艙裡暗得像墓穴一樣，」契科語無倫次地說：「但有個嚇人的東西在裡面，就是發出歡呼聲的那個東西。」

孩子們興高采烈，海盜們垂頭喪氣，虎克都注意到了。

「契科，」虎克用最硬的語調說道：「去把那咯咯叫的東西給我帶過來。」

契科，海盜中的勇者，在他的船長面前忍不住發抖地喊道：「不，不！」但是，虎克咆哮著舉起了鐵鉤。

「你說你要去吧，契科？」

契科絕望地聳聳肩走下去，海盜們不再唱歌，只是靜靜聽著。接著，又是一聲垂死的慘叫，然後又一陣歡呼。

「三個。」只有史萊特利開口說道。

虎克打了個手勢，把手下集合起來。他暴跳如雷地說：「混帳，豈有此理，誰去把那咯咯叫的東西給我抓來？」

「等契科上來再說吧。」斯塔奇喃喃道，其他海盜紛紛附和。

「我好像聽到你說要自願去看看喔，斯塔奇。」虎克說道，又發出咆哮聲。

「沒有，老天爺，我沒有說！」斯塔奇大喊。

「我的鐵鉤覺得你說了，」虎克邊向他逼進邊說道：「聰明的話，最好照著鐵鉤的意思去做，斯塔奇。」

「我寧願被吊死也不過去。」斯塔奇固執地回答，又得到其他船員的支持。

「你們要造反是吧？」虎克顯得格外愉快地說：「由斯塔奇策畫？」

「船長，饒了我吧。」斯塔奇嗚咽著，渾身發抖。

「握個手吧，斯塔奇。」虎克邊說邊伸出鐵鉤。

斯塔奇環顧四周想尋求支援，但是所有人都背棄了他。他往後退一步，虎克就往前逼近一步，眼中冒出嗜血的紅光。斯塔奇絕望地叫了一聲，就跳上長湯姆，往海裡跳下去。

「四個。」史萊特利叫著。

「現在，」虎克有禮地問：「還有哪位先生要造反？」他抓起一把燈籠，威嚇地舉起鐵鉤，「我會親自去把那小鬼抓上來。」說罷，就很快走進了船艙。

「五個。」史萊特利很想這麼說。他舔了舔唇準備好，但虎克搖搖晃晃退了出來，手裡的燈籠已經不見。

「有個東西吹熄了我的燈籠。」他不安地說。

「有個東西？」穆林斯重複道。

「契科怎麼了？」努得勒問。

「他死了，和鳩克斯一樣。」虎克簡短地說。

虎克不願回到船艙的舉動，對船員們產生極大的影響，造反的聲浪又起來。海盜們可都是很迷信的，庫克森嚷著：「人家說船上如果有不乾淨的東西，船就一定會出事的。」

「我還聽說，」穆林斯嘟嚷著說：「不乾淨的東西都是最後一個上船的，它有尾巴嗎，船長？」

「人家說，」另一個海盜不懷好意地盯著虎克說：「那東西來的時候，外表就和船上最邪惡的人差不多。」

「他也有鐵鉤嗎，船長？」庫克森無禮地問。海盜們也一個接一個地附和：「這艘船被詛咒了。」這一刻孩子們忍不住歡呼起來，虎克差點把這些俘虜給忘了。他一轉頭看到他們，臉上就亮了起來。

「夥計們，」虎克對他的船員喊著：「我有個辦法，打開艙門，把他們推下去，就讓他們去跟那個東西拼命吧。如果他們殺了那東西，那就太好了；要是那東西把他們殺了，對我們也沒壞處。」

這是海盜們最後一次對虎克感到佩服了。他們忠實地執行他的命令，那群男孩子們假裝掙扎，被海盜推進船艙，然後門就被帶上。

「現在，聽好！」虎克喊，大家都靜靜聽著，但卻沒有人敢面對著那扇門。不！有一個人敢，溫蒂！她一直被綁在桅杆上。她等的不是尖叫聲，也不是歡呼聲，她在等的是彼得重新露面。

彼得沒讓她等太久。他在船艙找到他想要的東西：打開孩子們手銬的鑰匙。現在，他們偷偷地溜到各處，佩戴好找到的武器。彼得先打暗號叫他們藏起來，然後溜出來幫溫蒂割斷繩索。現在，他們要一起飛走是再輕易不過的事了，但有一件事阻止了他，那就是他的那句誓言，「不是我死就是虎克亡」。他解開溫蒂的繩子後，悄悄告訴她，要她和其他孩子一起躲起來。他站在溫蒂被綁的桅杆前，披上她的大衣，深深吸進一口氣，然後大聲叫喊。

海盜們聽到這聲喊叫，以為船艙裡所有孩子全都給殺光了，嚇得魂不附體。虎克想激勵他們，但他們已經被他訓練得像狗一樣，他們現在對他齜牙咧嘴。他心裡明白，

要是不緊緊盯著他們，他們準會撲上來咬他。

「夥計們，」虎克說，準備騙騙他們，必要的話就對他們動手，但絕不在他們面前退縮，「我想起來了，這船上有一個約拿。」

「沒錯，」水手們咆哮，「一個手上有鐵鉤的人。」

「不，夥計們，是女孩，只要有女人登上海盜船，就會倒楣，只要她走，船上就太平了。」

有些人想到弗林特有說過這話。「試試看也無妨。」他們半信半疑地說。

「把那女孩扔到海裡。」虎克喊道，海盜們立刻朝披著大衣的人衝過去。

「現在沒人救得了妳啦，丫頭。」穆林斯發出怪聲嘲笑說。

「有個人可以。」那個人兒回答。

「是誰？」

「復仇者彼得・潘！」一句可怕的回答！彼得說著，拋去大衣，這下他們明白了是誰在艙裡作怪。虎克兩次想說話，卻怎麼也說不出來。在這可怕的一刻，我想他殘暴的心都碎了。

最後他喊了出來：「把他給劈開！」但他的聲音已經沒多大自信了。

「出來吧，孩子們，衝向他們。」彼得的聲音響徹雲霄，下一秒，船上就響起一片武器撞擊聲。如果海盜們在打鬥時緊靠在一起，勝利會是他們的，但是他們一遇到襲擊就東奔西竄，揮刀亂砍一通，每個人都以為自己是唯一的倖存者。如果這是場一對一的決鬥，他們會表現得更好，但他們現在只能防守，這讓孩子們不但能夠以眾擊寡，還可以隨意選擇對手。有些海盜跳下海，有些躲在角落，但都被史萊特利給找到。史萊特利沒有下去打，他只是提著燈跑來跑去，用燈照海盜們的臉，讓他們什麼也看不見，只能成為其他孩子刀下的犧牲品。船上大都只聽得到兵器的鏗鏘聲，偶爾一聲慘叫，或落水聲，還有史萊特利沒什麼新意的算數，五個、六個、七個、八個、九個、十個、十一個。

我想，當那群粗魯的孩子把虎克團團圍住時，其他的海盜都已經被幹掉了。虎克身上彷彿有魔法，周圍就像有個火圈，讓孩子們無法接近他。他的手下都已經被解決，但他一個人就能對付所有的孩子。他們一次又一次地逼近他，他也一次又一次地殺出重圍。他用鐵鉤勾起一個孩子，拿他當作盾牌，這時，有另一個孩子，剛用劍刺穿了穆林斯的身體，也跳過來加入戰鬥。

「把武器收起來，孩子們，」新加入的孩子喊道：「這個人是我的。」

突然間，虎克發現和他面對面的是彼得。其他的孩子都往後退，在他們身邊圍了一圈。

誓不兩立的仇人對看了好長一段時間，虎克微微顫抖，彼得臉上掛著奇異的微笑。

「所以，潘，」虎克終於說：「這些都是你幹的。」

「沒錯，詹姆斯·虎克，」他正經地答道：「那都是我幹的。」

「傲慢無禮的年輕人，迎接你悲慘的命運吧！」虎克說。

「凶狠邪惡的大壞蛋，」彼得回答：「準備領死吧！」

話不多說，兩人就打了起來，有一段時間雙方不分勝負，彼得劍法超群，閃躲也快，讓人眼花撩亂。他不時虛晃一招，趁對方不備時猛刺一劍，只是他的手不夠長，無法命中目標。而虎克呢，他的劍法也毫不遜色，只是手腕的活動不如彼得靈活，想靠突襲猛攻佔優勢。他想用巴比克在里奧地區教過他的刺法，馬上結束敵人的性命，但卻驚訝於自己屢刺不中。虎克往前逼近，想用他的鐵鉤給彼得致命的一擊，因此在空中不斷揮舞。彼得低頭躲開，往虎克狠狠一刺，便刺進了他的肋骨。虎克看到自己的血，你們還記得吧？那詭異的顏色，是他最害怕的。劍從他手上滑落到地上，他敗在了彼得的手裡。

「就是現在！」孩子們大喝一聲。然而，彼得卻擺了個極高貴的姿勢，要敵人拿起他的劍。虎克立刻拿起劍，心裡卻一陣悲哀，因為彼得展現了良好的風範。

一直以來，虎克都覺得和他對抗的是個惡魔，可是現在他深深地懷疑著。

「潘，你是誰？你到底是什麼？」虎克粗聲喊道。

「我是年輕人，我是喜悅，」彼得隨口答道：「我是剛從殼裡鑽出來的小鳥。」

當然，這是胡說八道，但在不幸的虎克看來，這卻證明彼得完全不明白自己是誰、是什麼東西，而這正是良好風範的最高表現。

「再來吧。」虎克絕望地喊。

他像個人形錘鍊般揮來揮去，無論是大人或小孩，只要一碰到這駭人的劍，都會被揮成兩段。但彼得卻能在他周圍閃避得宜，就彷彿那劍煽出的風將他吹出了危險地帶。他一次又一次往前突擊、猛刺一陣。

虎克現在已不抱任何勝利的希望，他那顆殘暴的心，也不再乞求活命，只希望得到唯一的恩賜：在屍體冰冷前看到彼得失去風範。

虎克放棄打鬥，衝進彈藥庫，點燃引線。

「不到兩分鐘，這艘船就會被炸得粉碎了。」他喊道。

現在，就是現在，虎克想，會見到各人的真面目。

可是彼得從彈藥庫裡跑出來，手拿著炮彈，不慌不忙地把它扔到海裡。

虎克表現出的又是怎樣的風範呢？他雖然誤入歧途，我們對他不抱同情，但我們還是很高興看到他最後能謹守傳統。其他孩子們圍在他身邊飛著，譏笑他，嘲弄他，他踉蹌地走上甲板，虛弱無力地還擊。他的心思已經不在他們身上，而是飛回很多年以前，那時他在運動場上，在揚帆遠航，或是在觀看一場精彩的壁球比賽，當時他的鞋子、背心、領結、襪子，都整整齊齊地穿戴好。

好歹也是一條好漢的詹姆斯・虎克，永別了。

因為他的終點站已經到了。

看到彼得舉著劍緩緩向他逼近，虎克跳上了船舷，一躍投入海中。他不知道鱷魚正等著他，我們故意讓鐘停下來，不讓他知道，也算是最後對他所表示的一點敬意吧。

虎克最後還是得到了一場小小的勝利，我們也不妨一提：當他站在船舷上，回頭看著彼得向他俯衝過來，他做了個手勢，示意彼得用腳踢。彼得果然沒拿劍刺，而是用腳踢了他。

終於，虎克得到他渴望的恩賜。

「沒風範！」他譏笑地喊道，心滿意足地投入鱷魚的懷抱。

詹姆斯·虎克就這樣消失了。

「十七個。」史萊特利大聲唱了出來。但他算得不太準確，當晚只有十五名海盜為他們犯的罪付出代價，另外有兩個逃到岸邊，斯塔奇被印第安人捕獲俘虜，逼他當嬰兒的褓母，對於一個海盜而言，這樣的下場算是悲慘的；而史密呢，戴著他的眼鏡從此到處漂泊，逢人便說，詹士·虎克只怕他一個人，藉以維持有一頓沒一頓的生活。

當然，溫蒂沒有參加戰鬥，只是兩眼發光地一直注視著彼得。現在既然仗已經打完了，她又變得重要起來。她一視同仁地稱讚他們，當麥可指給她看殺海盜的地點時，她高興得發抖。之後，她把孩子們都帶到虎克的船艙裡，指著掛在釘子上的錶，時間指著「一點半」。

已經這麼晚了，這可是最重要的一件事，於是溫蒂很快安頓他們在海盜的床舖睡下，除了彼得。彼得在甲板上來回踱步，最後終於倒在長湯姆大砲旁邊睡著了。那一晚他做了一場大夢，在夢中哭了很久，溫蒂緊緊摟著他。

踏上歸途

Chapter 16

第二天清晨鐘才響三聲，他們就全都跑來跑去地忙了起來，因為海面上的風浪越來越大。圖圖是孩子們的水手長，他手中握著纜繩的一端，嘴裡還嚼著煙草。孩子們都穿上海盜服，把海盜服膝蓋以下的部分剪掉，好配合他們的身材。他們的臉刮得乾乾淨淨的，像真正的水手一樣，提著褲管，匆匆忙忙地在船上跑來跑去。

誰是船長，自然不必再說了。尼布斯和約翰是船上的大副和二副，船上有一位女性，剩下的都是住在前艙的普通水手。彼得掌穩舵後，將手下全都召集起來，做簡短的精神訓話，希望大家能夠付出心力，盡忠職守，不過他也知道他們都是出身李奧和黃金海岸的粗人，要是誰敢對他不敬，他就把誰撕裂。彼得這些虛張聲勢的粗話，他們都聽得懂，還對他發出一陣強有力的歡呼聲。接著船長下了幾道嚴苛的命令，他們就將船掉頭，往大陸地區航行。

潘船長看了航海圖之後推算，要是天氣持續不變，他們大概會在六月二十一日到達亞速爾群島，從那兒開始飛就能省下一些時間。

有些孩子希望這船規規矩矩地航行，有些則希望把它當成海盜船來開，不過船長把他們當成狗一樣看待，讓他

們不敢發表任何意見，連匿名陳情也不敢，只有立刻服從命令才是保障自身安全的唯一辦法。有一回，史萊特利奉命測量水深，臉上卻露出茫然的表情，就被打了十二大板。大夥兒認為，彼得為了化解溫蒂的懷疑，故作老實；但等到新衣裳做好之後，態度就會改變。那件衣服是用虎克最邪惡的一件海盜服做成的，溫蒂本來是不願意做的。等做好之後，大家都在竊竊私語，說彼得穿上這件衣服的第一晚，在船艙裡坐了很久，嘴上還叼著虎克抽雪茄的煙斗，一隻手握著拳，食指彎成鐵勾的形狀，擺出恐嚇的姿態。

　　先別提那艘船，回過頭看看那個寂寞的家庭吧。那三個無情的孩子就這麼飛走，已經有很長一段時間了。說來慚愧，我們也有很長一段時間沒再提起十四號這一家了，但我敢說達林太太一定不會怪我們的。要是我們早一點回來，帶著深深的同情地看著她，她或許會喊：「別傻了，我會有什麼事？快回去好好看著孩子們吧。」只要母親一直抱持這樣的態度，孩子們就會利用這個弱點佔便宜，遲遲不肯回家。

　　即使我們現在進入那間熟悉的育兒室，也是因為它合法的主人已經在歸途中，我們只不過早他們一步，看看他們的床單是不是都曬過了，確定達林夫婦那天晚上不會出門。我們的身分不過是僕人罷了。但孩子們當時走得那樣匆忙、那樣不知感恩，又何必為他們曬床單呢？要是他們回家，發現父母到鄉間渡假去了，不也是他們應得的報應嗎？這是從我們認識這些孩子以來，他們應得的教訓。不過如果事情真是這樣發展，達林太太是決不會原諒我們的。

　　有一件事我真想馬上就做，就是像其他作者一樣，直接告訴達林太太，孩子們要回來了，就在下禮拜四。這樣一來，溫蒂、約翰和麥可原本準備讓大家驚喜的計畫便落空了。在船上的時候他們已經計畫好：媽媽會狂喜，爸爸會歡呼，娜娜會最先跳起來擁抱他們，而他們所要準備的，就是絕口不提歸期。如果我們先把這消息洩露出來，破壞他們的計畫，會有多痛快！當他們神氣地走進家門，達林太太或許根本不會去親吻溫蒂，達林先生會不耐煩地大喊：「真是的，那些臭小子又回來了。」不過，這麼做可得不到任何感激，現在我們已經越來越瞭解達林太太了，可以肯定的是，她一定會責怪我們不該剝奪孩子們這一點小小的樂趣。

「可是，親愛的夫人，到下禮拜四還有十天，先把事情告訴妳，我們就可以為妳省下十天傷心的日子。」

「沒錯，但代價多大呀！剝奪孩子們十分鐘的快樂。」

「唉，如果你是這樣看這件事的話……」

「還能怎麼看呢？」

你看看吧，這位女士的情緒不太好，我本來想幫她說說好話的，不過我現在瞧不起她，也不想再提其他人了。其實，根本不用對達林太太說孩子們要回來，請她把東西準備妥當，因為一切早已都安排好了：床單都已經曬過了，達林太太從不出門，再看看吧，窗戶也是開著的，看來我們留下來也沒什麼幫助，還不如回到船上去。不過既然已經來了，不妨留下來觀察一下，反正我們本來就是旁觀者嘛，沒有人真正需要我們！我們不妨就在一旁看著，說幾句刺耳的話，好叫誰聽了不痛快。

育兒室裡唯一的變化，是從晚上九點到早上六點，裡面不再放狗屋。自從孩子們飛走以後，達林先生就打心底怪自己把娜娜給綁了起來，事實證明由始至終娜娜都比他聰明。當然，我們已經知道，達林先生是個單純的人，要是沒有禿頭，說不定他還會被別人當作小男孩；另一方面，

他也有高貴的正義感，只要他認為是對的事，他都會鼓起勇氣去做。孩子們飛走後，他苦苦思量一段時間，便俯身爬進娜娜的狗屋。達林太太安撫著勸他出來，但他只哀傷而堅定地回答：

「不，親愛的，這才是我應該待的地方。」

在沉痛的自責下，他發下誓言，只要孩子們不回來，他就不離開狗屋。當然這事讓人傷心，但達林先生做事總是這麼極端，若非如此，他很快就會放棄不做。如今的喬治‧達林謙遜無比，再也不像過去那般自負了，他會坐在狗屋和太太談到孩子們和他們可愛的小模樣兒。

他對娜娜的尊敬可真叫人感動，他不讓娜娜進狗屋，但在其他的事情上，他都毫不猶豫地聽從娜娜的意見。

每天早上達林先生會待在狗屋，讓人搬上計程車，拉到辦公室，下午六點，再用同樣的方式回家。我們知道這人有多麼在乎鄰居的看法，因此可以看出他的性格是如此堅強，因為現在他的一舉一動都吸引人們詫異的關注。在他內心一定忍受著極大的折磨，但是當年輕人批評他的狗屋時，他外表依然保持鎮靜，還會禮貌地對往裡面望的女士脫帽致意。

這看起來似乎帶點唐吉訶德的味道，卻也十分高貴。沒多久這件事情的原委傳開了，深深感動人們的心。人群跟在計程車後面，為他高聲歡呼；迷人的女性爬上車，跟他要親筆簽名；他的訪問登上了出名的新聞報刊；上流社會的家庭邀請他去做客，還加上一句：「請坐在狗屋出席。」

在那個禮拜四即將到來的星期，達林太太待在育兒室等喬治回家，眼神十分憂傷。現在，我們仔細端詳她，想到她只是因為失去了孩子，過去的快樂都已不再。我發現自己實在不忍心說她的壞話了，她實在太愛孩子們，連她自己也無法控制。她現在就坐在椅子上，睡著了。她總是會首先被注意到的嘴角，現在已經漸漸憔悴，她的手托著胸口不放，彷彿那兒隱隱作痛。有些人最喜歡彼得，有些人最喜歡溫蒂，可是我最喜歡達林太太，為了讓她高興，我們可以趁她熟睡時，在她耳邊悄悄地說，那幾個搗蛋鬼就要回來了。他們現在離窗戶只有兩英里了，正努力地飛著呢！但我們還是小小聲說，他們已經在回家的路上了。就讓我們這樣說吧。

我們這麼做真是太糟糕了，因為達林太太忽然跳起來，喊著孩子們的名字，但屋裡除了娜娜，沒有其他人。

「喔，娜娜，我夢到我的寶貝們回來了。」

娜娜還睡眼惺忪呢，她所能做的只有把手掌輕輕地放在女主人腿上安慰著，他們就這樣坐在一起，直到狗屋回來。當達林先生把頭伸出來親吻妻子時，我們看到他的臉比以往憔悴得多，但神情也溫和多了。

他把帽子交給莉莎，她不屑地接過去，因為莉莎沒有想像力，也無法了解這男人的行為。屋外，跟著計程車來的一群人還在為他歡呼，達林先生自然十分感動。

「聽聽他們，」他說：「真是令人安慰。」

「一群小毛頭。」莉莎嘲諷。

「今天有好幾個大人。」他有些臉紅地對莉莎保證，但她輕蔑地把頭轉過去，達林先生也沒有責備她半句。受到廣大歡迎並沒有使他得意忘形，反倒使他變得更加體貼。有時候他坐會在狗屋，一半身體在外和達林太太談著他在社交上的成功，當達林太太說希望他不會被這沖昏頭時，他會緊緊握著她的手，請她放心。

「幸好我不是個軟弱的人。」達林先生說：「天啊，如果我是個軟弱的人就好了。」

達林太太有些擔心地說：「喬治，你還在自責，是嗎？」

「自責得不得了，親愛的，看我怎麼懲罰自己：住在狗屋裡！」

「你的確是在懲罰自己嗎，喬治？你確定不享受住在裡面的生活？」

「什麼話嘛，親愛的？」

當然，達林太太請他原諒，接著達林先生覺得睏了，便蜷縮在狗屋裡睡下了。

「妳能不能到遊戲房，」他請求，「彈鋼琴為我催眠？」當達林太太經過孩子們白天的遊戲房，他漫不經心地說：「把窗戶關上，我覺得有一陣風。」

「啊，喬治，永遠別叫我把窗戶關上，窗戶一定要一直為他們開著，永遠，永遠。」

這次輪到達林先生請她原諒了；她走到遊戲房彈起鋼琴，很快地達林先生就睡著了。就在他睡著當下，溫蒂，約翰，麥可飛進了房間。

不對，其實事情不是這樣的，我會這麼寫，是因為在我們離開海盜船之前，他們原本是這樣安排好的，不過在我們離開之後，一定是有什麼事情發生了，因為飛進來的不是他們三個，而是彼得和亭可。

彼得的話道出了一切。

「快啊，亭可，」彼得悄悄地說：「把窗戶關上，鎖起來，沒錯。我們現在得從門口飛出去，等溫蒂回來，會以為她媽媽把她關在外面，那樣她就得和我一起回去了。」

現在，我終於明白了一直在我腦中盤旋不去的疑問：為什麼在解決海盜以後彼得不回夢幻島，讓亭可護送孩子們回家就好？原來這個計畫他已經想了很久了。

彼得非但不覺得這樣的行為有何不妥，反而開心地跳起舞來。接著他往遊戲房裡偷看，看是誰在彈鋼琴。他輕輕地對亭可說：「那是溫蒂的媽媽，她是漂亮的太太，但沒有我媽媽漂亮。她嘴上掛滿頂針，但也沒有我媽媽嘴角上的多。」

　　當然，彼得對自己的母親根本一無所知，但有時候他會誇耀地談到她。

　　彼得沒聽過那首曲子，那是《可愛的家》，不過他知道那首曲在唱著「回來吧，溫蒂，溫蒂，溫蒂」。他得意得喊：「妳再也見不到溫蒂啦，太太，因為窗戶已經被鎖上了。」

　　他又往屋裡偷看琴聲為什麼停了，只見達林太太把頭靠在琴箱上，眼睛含著兩滴眼淚。

　　「她想要我打開窗戶，我才不要呢，決不。」彼得心想。

　　彼得又往裡面偷看，還是有兩滴眼淚，不過已經換成另外兩顆。

　　「她真的很喜歡溫蒂。」彼得對自己說。他現在很氣達林太太，她怎麼就不明白為什麼她不能再得到溫蒂呢。

　　原因很簡單：「因為我也很喜歡溫蒂，我們兩個人不能同時擁有溫蒂呀。」

　　可是這位太太卻不肯放手，對這一點彼得很不滿意。他不再看她，但即使如此她也不放過他。彼得在房間裡蹦蹦跳跳、做鬼臉，可是只要他一停下來，就彷彿達林太太在他心裡不住地敲著。

　　「啊，好吧。」終於，他打開了窗戶，喊道：「來吧，亭可，」他對這大自然的法則狠狠瞪了一眼，「我們才不要這種傻母親呢！」接著他就飛走了。

　　也因此，當溫蒂、約翰和麥可回來時，窗戶總算是開的，雖然他們根本不配得到這樣的待遇。他們降落到地板上，完

全不覺得慚愧，最小的那個甚至已經忘記他的家了。

他疑惑地向四周張望，說道：「約翰，我覺得我好像來過這裡。」

「當然來過，你這傻瓜，那就是你的床啊！」

「是啊。」麥可說，聲音沒多大自信。

「你看，」約翰喊：「是狗屋！」他衝過去往裡面看。

「說不定娜娜就在裡面。」溫蒂說。

但是約翰吹了聲口哨，說：「哈囉，裡面有個男人。」

「是爸爸！」溫蒂驚叫。

「讓我看爸爸。」麥可急切地請求，他仔細地看了一眼。「他還沒有我殺的海盜來得大呢。」他的口氣帶著那麼明顯的失望。我真慶幸達林先生睡著了，要是他聽見他的小麥可最先說的竟是這樣一句話，會有多傷心啊。

看見父親睡在狗屋，溫蒂和約翰也大吃一驚。

「說真的，」約翰說，彷彿對自己的記憶力失去信心，「他不會是一直都是睡在狗屋裡吧？」

「約翰，」溫蒂也遲疑了，「說不定我們對過去的記憶，根本沒有那麼多。」

他們覺得身上一陣顫慄，這是他們應得的報應。

「媽媽實在太粗心了，」約翰這個小壞蛋說：「竟然沒有在這兒等我們回來。」

就在這時，達林太太又開始彈琴了。

「是媽媽！」溫蒂一邊喊著，一邊偷看。

「可不是嘛！」約翰說。

「那妳真的不是我們的母親囉，溫蒂？」麥可問，他一定很睏了。

「噢，天啊！」溫蒂驚嘆，第一次真正感到後悔，「我

們的確是該回來了。」

「我們偷偷溜進去，用手蒙住她的眼睛。」約翰提議。

可是溫蒂有更好的辦法，她認為應該用更溫和的方式宣布這個好消息。

「我們都鑽回床上，等媽媽進來的時候，我們全都在床上躺著，就好像我們從來沒有離開一樣。」

因此，當達林太太回到房間，看達林先生是不是睡著的時候，所有的床都被躺滿著孩子。孩子們等著聽她歡呼，卻一直沒有等到。她是看到他們了，但不相信他們真的在那兒。你瞧，她太常夢到孩子們躺在床上，這一次也以為是在做夢。

她在壁爐邊的椅子上坐下，她過去總是坐在這兒照顧孩子們。

他們不明白這是怎麼回事，三個孩子都覺得渾身發冷。

「媽媽！」溫蒂喊道。

「那是溫蒂。」她說，但她還是很確定自己在做夢。

「媽媽！」

「那是約翰！」她說。

「媽媽！」麥可喊，他現在認得媽媽了。

「那是麥可。」她伸出雙臂，去抱那三個自私的孩子，她本以為再也沒辦法擁抱的三個孩子。但她抱到了，她摟住了溫蒂、約翰和麥可，他們全都溜下了床，跑到了她的身邊。

「喬治，喬治！」達林太太喊，她終於說得出話了。達林先生醒來分享她的喜悅，娜娜也衝進來，再也沒有比這更美妙的景象了，但目睹到這一幕的只有一個陌生的小男孩，他正從窗外向裡面望著。他經歷過無數快樂的事，那都是每個孩子從不知道的快樂，但唯有這一次，他隔著窗子看到的快樂，是他被阻隔在外、永遠得不到的。

溫蒂長大了

Chapter 17

我希望你們都想知道其他的孩子怎麼樣了，他們其實都在樓下等溫蒂解釋他們的來歷。當他們數到五百的時候，就上樓來了。他們是走樓梯上來的，這樣可以給人一個好印象。他們脫下帽子在達林太太面前站成一列，心裡但願自己身上穿的不是海盜的衣服。他們什麼也沒說，眼神卻在懇求達林太太收留他們。本來他們也應該望著達林先生，可是他們卻完全忘了有這個人。

當然，達林太太立刻就表示願意收留他們，但達林先生卻異常的憂鬱，他們看得出來，他認為六個太多了。

「我要說啊，」他對溫蒂說：「做事不可以只做一半。」這句話中的不情願，雙胞胎覺得是衝著他們來的。

老大自尊心比較強，他紅著臉對達林先生說：「先生，你覺得我們人太多了嗎？如果是這樣，我們可以走。」

「爸爸！」溫蒂喊，震驚不已，但達林先生還是滿面陰霾，他知道這麼做很卑劣，可他又能有什麼辦法？

「我們幾個可以擠在一起。」尼布斯說。

「喬治！」達林太太驚呼，看到她親愛的丈夫表現得如此不受人讚賞，心裡很難過。

達林先生突然迸出眼淚，這才真相大白，他也和達林太太一樣很高興收養這群孩子。他只是希望孩子們除了達林太太以外，也能徵求他的意見，不要把他當成家裡的隱形人。

「我不覺得他是家裡的隱形人。」圖圖立刻大聲說：「你覺得呢，捲毛？」

「我也不覺得，你覺得呢，史萊特利？」

「當然不是，雙胞胎，你們覺得呢？」

結果沒有一個孩子認為達林先生是家裡的隱形人，奇怪的是他竟感激不已，還說要是合適的話，可以把他們全部安置在客廳裡。

「絕對合適，先生。」孩子們保證。

「那就跟著隊長我做。」他興奮地說：「聽我說，我不確定我們有沒有客廳，不過我們可以假裝有，反正都一樣嘛。啊哈！」

接著他在屋裡跳起舞來，孩子們也全都高喊「啊哈」，跟在他後面跳舞，尋找客廳。我不記得他們到底找到沒有，但無論如何，他們找到一些角落，適合他們住下。

至於彼得，他離開前來看了溫蒂一次，他沒有特地飛到窗前，只在經過時輕輕碰到窗戶，如果溫蒂願意，她可以打開窗子呼喚他，溫蒂也這樣做了。

「嗨，溫蒂，再見。」他說。

「啊，親愛的，你要走了嗎？」

「是啊。」

「彼得，」溫蒂有些遲疑，「你不想和我父母談談那件很棒的事嗎？」

「不要。」

「關於我的事，彼得？」

「不。」

　　達林太太走到窗前，她現在一直密切注意著溫蒂。她告訴彼得，她已經收養了那些男孩，也很願意收養他。

　　「妳會送我去上學？」彼得警覺地問。

　　「會呀。」

　　「接著去上班？」

　　「應該是吧。」

　　「很快我就會變成大人？」

　　「非常快。」

　　「我不想上學去學那些正經八百的東西，」他激動地對她說，「我不想變成大人。溫蒂媽媽，要是我一覺醒來，摸到自己有鬍子，那真是太可怕了！」

　　「彼得！」溫蒂安慰他說：「就算你有鬍子，我還是會愛你的。」達林太太對他伸出雙臂，但彼得將她推開。

　　「太太，妳退後，沒有人可以抓住我把我變成大人。」

　　「可是你以後要住哪兒？」

　　「和亭可一起住在我們幫溫蒂蓋的小屋裡。仙子會把它抬到樹枝上，她們晚上就睡在那裡。」

　　「真好啊！」溫蒂羨慕地喊，達林太太卻把她抓得更緊了。

　　「我以為所有的仙子都已經死了。」達林太太說。

　　「會一直有年輕的仙子出現。」溫蒂解釋，她現在可是專家了。「因為妳知道嗎，每個嬰兒第一次發出笑聲的時候，就有一個仙子誕生。只要一直有新生的寶寶，就會有新生的仙子。他們住在樹上的巢裡，淡紫色是男的，白色的是女的，藍色的是小傻瓜，不知道自己是男是女。」

　　「我會過得很快樂。」彼得說，用一隻眼睛看著溫蒂。

　　「晚上我坐在火爐邊時會很寂寞。」溫蒂說。

「我有亭可作伴。」

「亭可很多事都做不到。」她有點尖酸地提醒他。

「搬弄是非的奸詐小人！」亭可不知從哪個角落突然冒出一句。

「那沒關係。」彼得說。

「彼得，你知道那有關係的。」溫蒂說。

「那好，和我一起回小屋吧。」

「我可以去嗎，媽媽？」

「當然不行，妳好不容易回家了，我不會讓妳再離開。」

「可是他很需要母親啊。」

「妳也是啊，我的小乖。」

「啊，那就算了。」彼得說。好像他只是出於禮貌才邀請溫蒂，但達林太太看到彼得微微扭曲的嘴角時，她提出一個大方的建議：每年春天讓溫蒂去住一個禮拜，幫他做春季大掃除。溫蒂希望去的時間能更長一點，而且她覺得春天還很久，但這個承諾讓彼得歡歡喜喜地走了。他沒有什麼時間觀念，有那麼多冒險等著他，這對他只是微不足道的一小段時間。我想溫蒂深知這一點，所以她最後憂傷地對他說了這樣一句：

「在春季大掃除以前，你不會忘記我吧，彼得？」

當然不會，彼得保證，然後他便飛走了，還帶走了達林太太的吻。那個誰也得不到的吻，彼得卻輕而易舉獲得，真有趣，但達林太太看上去也十分滿足。

沒錯，所有孩子都上學去了，大部分是上三年級，只有史萊特利先上四年級，後來又改上五年級，但一年級是最高的年級。他們上學還不到一個禮拜，就後悔離開夢幻島那美好的生活，可是太遲了。他們也很快地安頓下來，像你、像我、像小詹金斯一樣過著平凡的日子。說來真讓人傷心，他們漸漸失去飛行的本領，剛開始娜娜把他們的腳綁在床柱上，以防他們半夜飛走，白天他們就會在那兒玩一種假裝從公車上掉下來的遊戲。可是他們慢慢發現，如果不抓住那根綁腳繩，從公車掉下來時就會摔傷。再後來他們甚至抓不住被風吹走的帽子，這都是因為缺乏練習，不過這只是他們的講法。其實，這句話背後的含義是，他們已經不再相信這一切了。

麥可比其他男孩相信了更長的一段時間，雖然他們老是譏笑他。所以當彼得在第一年的年底來找溫蒂時，他還是和溫蒂一起去。溫蒂和彼得一起飛走時，身上穿著她在夢幻島用樹葉和莓果編成的裙子，她擔心彼得會發現裙子變短了，可是彼得根本沒注意到，他自己有太多事要說了。

溫蒂本想和他談談那些冒險的往事，可是他腦中的新冒險早就把那些往事給擠掉了。

「誰是虎克船長？」當溫蒂提到這個敵人時，彼得十分感興趣地問。

「你不記得了嗎？」溫蒂驚訝地問：「你是怎麼除掉他，救了我們大家的命？」

「我除掉了他們以後，就把他們忘記了。」他漫不經心地回答。

當溫蒂表示，她不認為亭可看到她會高興時，彼得問：「亭可是誰？」

「啊，彼得。」溫蒂很詫異。即使她向他解釋，彼得還是想不起來。

「她們數量太多了，我想她大概已經不在了。」他說。

我想彼得是對的，仙子的壽命不長，但因為她們很小，

很短的時間對她們來說就很長了。

　　還有一點讓溫蒂感到難過的是，過去這一年，對彼得而言就像昨天一樣過去了，但對她來說卻是長時間的等待。不過，彼得還是像過去一樣討人喜歡，他們在樹上的小屋裡，進行了一次愉快的春季大掃除。

　　第二年彼得沒有來接她。她穿上新裙等著他，舊的那一件已經穿不下了。可是彼得沒有來。

　　「說不定他生病了。」麥可說。

　　「你知道他從不生病的。」

　　麥可湊到溫蒂面前，打了個冷顫說：「也許根本沒有這個人，溫蒂！」要不是麥可哭了，溫蒂也會哭的。

　　第三年彼得來接溫蒂了。奇怪的是，他竟不知道他漏掉了一年。

　　這是小女孩時期的溫蒂最後一次見到彼得。有一段時間，她為了彼得努力不讓自己感覺痛苦，當她在通識課得獎時，她覺得是自己背叛了彼得。但是，一年一年過去了，這位粗心大意的孩子再也沒有出現。等他們再見面時，溫蒂已經是一位已婚婦人，彼得對她而言，已成為玩具箱上的一點灰塵。溫蒂已經是成人了，你不必為她感到遺憾。她是屬於喜歡長大的那一種人，甚至希望比別的女孩長得更快一點。

　　男孩子們這時也都長大了，沒必要再多談他們的事，某一天你可能會看到雙胞胎、尼布斯和捲毛正在往辦公室的途中，手上還提著公事包和雨傘。麥可是火車司機；史萊特利娶了一位貴族女子，而他自己也有了頭銜。你有沒有看見一位戴假髮的法官從鐵門裡走出來？他以前叫作圖圖。還有那個留著鬍子，從不為孩子講故事的男人，曾經叫作約翰。

溫蒂結婚時穿著白色婚紗，上面裝飾著粉紅色的絲帶。想來奇怪，彼得竟沒有飛進教堂，反對這場婚禮。

一年年就這麼飛逝，溫蒂有了一個女兒，這件事不該用墨水而是應該用金粉寫下來大肆宣傳。

女兒叫珍，總帶著一副發問的表情，彷彿她一來到世上，就有許多問題要問。等她大到可以問問題了，多半是問和彼得有關的問題。她喜歡聽彼得的故事，溫蒂把她所能記得的事全講給女兒聽，而她說故事的地點，正是那間他們曾經飛行的育兒室。現在這裡是珍的育兒室，珍的父親以百分之三的價錢向達林先生買下這棟房子。達林先生現在已經不喜歡爬樓梯，而達林太太已經去世，被遺忘了。

現在育兒室裡只剩兩張床，珍的床和她褓母的床。那裡不再有狗屋，因為娜娜也死了。她是壽終正寢，最後的那幾年，她的脾氣很壞，很難相處，自認為除了她，沒有人懂得怎麼照顧孩子。

珍的褓母每個星期會休一天假，這時就由溫蒂照顧她，陪她上床睡覺，那是床邊故事時間。珍發明一種遊戲，把床單蒙在媽媽和自己的頭上，假裝那是一頂帳篷，兩人在黑暗中說著悄悄話：

「我們現在看到什麼？」

「今晚我什麼也沒看見。」溫蒂說。她心想，如果娜娜還在，一定不會讓她們談下去。

「妳看得見，妳還是小女孩的時候就看見了。」珍說。

「那是很久很久以前的事，我的寶貝，」溫蒂說：「唉，時間飛逝！」

「時間也會飛嗎？」這個機靈的孩子問：「就像妳小時候那樣飛嗎？」

「像我那樣飛！妳知道嗎，珍，我有時候不確定那時是不是真的會飛。」

「是的，妳飛過。」

「我會飛，那真是美好的時光。」

「為什麼妳現在不能飛，媽媽？」

「因為我長大了，小乖。人一長大，就忘了怎麼飛了。」

「為什麼會忘了怎麼飛？」

「因為他們不再快樂、不再天真、不再沒心沒肺了。只有快樂、天真、沒心沒肺才能飛。」

「什麼叫快樂、天真、沒心沒肺？我真希望我也是快樂、天真、沒心沒肺的。」

這時溫蒂承認她真的想到了點什麼。「我想，這都是因為這間育兒室的緣故。」她說。

「我想也是，」珍說：「繼續說啊。」

於是她們開始談到了去冒險的那一夜，先是彼得飛進來找他的影子。

「那個傻孩子，他想用肥皂把影子黏起來，黏不上他就哭，他的哭聲把我吵醒了，我就用針線幫他縫上。」溫蒂說。

「你漏掉了一點。」珍插嘴說，她現在比母親知道的還清楚，「你看見他坐在地板上哭的時候，你說了什麼？」

「我坐起來問他：『小男孩，你為什麼哭？』。」

「沒錯，就是這樣。」珍說，吐了一大口氣。

「後來，他帶我飛到夢幻島，那裡還有仙子，有海盜，有印第安人，有人魚的礁湖，有地底家園，還有那間小屋。」

「對了！妳最喜歡什麼？」

「我想我最喜歡地底家園。」

「我也是。彼得最後對你說的話是什麼？」

「他最後對我說的話是：『只要妳一直等我，妳有一天晚上就會聽到我的叫聲。』」

「沒錯。」

「可是，唉！他已經完全把我給忘了。」溫蒂微笑著說。她已經長得那麼大了。

「彼得的叫聲是什麼樣的？」珍有一晚問。

「是這樣的。」溫蒂說，試著學彼得的叫聲。

「不對，不是這樣，」珍認真地說，「是這樣的。」她學得比母親還像。

溫蒂有點吃驚：「寶貝，你怎麼知道的？」

「我睡著的時候常常聽到。」珍說。

「是啊，很多女孩都是在睡著的時候聽過，只有我是在醒著的時候聽過。」

「妳真幸運。」珍說。

之後某一個夜晚，悲劇發生了。就在那一年的春天，珍聽完床邊故事，躺在床上睡覺，溫蒂坐在非常靠近壁爐的地板上縫衣服，育兒室裡除了火爐沒別的亮光。就在補衣服的當兒，她聽到一聲快樂的喊叫，窗戶像過去一樣被吹開了，彼得跳到地板上。

他還是和從前一模一樣，完全沒改變，溫蒂立刻注意到他還保有著乳牙。

他還是個小男孩，但她卻已經長大成人了。她在爐邊縮成一團，動也不敢動，既無助又難堪，這麼一個大女人。

「哈囉，溫蒂。」彼得說。他完全沒注意到有什麼不同，因為他總是只想到自己，而在昏暗的火光中，溫蒂穿的白裙的確很像他們第一次見面時所穿的睡衣。

「你好，彼得。」她有氣無力地回答，想努力把自己

440

縮得越小越好，她體內有個聲音在呼喚：「女人啊女人，放我走吧。」

「喂，約翰在哪兒？」他問，突然發現少了第三張床。

「約翰現在不在這兒。」溫蒂憋著氣說。

「麥可睡著了嗎？」他問，隨意瞥了珍一眼。

「是的。」溫蒂回答。她現在覺得自己對彼得和珍都不誠實。

「那不是麥可。」她連忙改口，以免遭報應。

彼得看了半晌：「咦，這是新的孩子嗎？」

「嗯。」

「男孩還是女孩？」

「女孩。」

現在彼得總該懂了吧。但是他一點也不懂。

「彼得，」她問，顫抖著嗓音，「你想要我跟你一起飛走嗎？」

「當然啦，我就是為這個來的。」他帶點嚴肅地補充：「你忘了現在是春季大掃除的時間嗎？」

溫蒂知道，即使告訴他已經漏了好多年的春季大掃除也是沒用的。

「我不能去，」她抱歉地說：「我忘記怎麼飛了。」

「我可以馬上再教妳。」

「啊，彼得，別在我身上浪費仙塵了。」

她站起來，彼得這才感到恐懼。「怎麼回事？」他喊著，一邊往後退縮。

「我把燈打開，」溫蒂說，「你自己看就明白了。」

就我所知，這是彼得有生以來第一次覺得害怕。「不要開燈。」他喊。

溫蒂伸手撫摸這可憐孩子的頭髮，她已經不再是為他傷心的小女孩，而是一位成年婦人。她微笑地看待這一切，但卻是帶淚的微笑。

　　溫蒂把燈打開，彼得看到了她，他痛苦地大叫一聲，當這位高大美麗的婦人要彎下身去抱他時，他疾速往後退。

　　「怎麼回事？」他又問。

　　溫蒂不得不告訴他。

　　「我老了，彼得，我二十好幾了，早就長大成人了。」

　　「妳答應過不會長大的！」

　　「我沒辦法控制……我現在是已婚婦人了，彼得。」

　　「不，妳不是。」

　　「是的，躺在床上的小女孩就是我的孩子。」

　　「不，她不是。」

　　他猜想這孩子應該真的是溫蒂的女兒。他往熟睡的孩子面前走去，把短劍高舉起來。當然他沒有刺向她，反而坐在地板上哭泣。溫蒂不知道該怎麼安慰他，雖然過去這對她而言是那麼輕而易舉，現在，她只是一個女人了，於是她走出房間，思考該如何是好。

　　彼得還在哭，很快地，珍就被吵醒了。她坐起來，對彼得有莫大的興趣。

　　「小男孩，」她說：「你為什麼哭？」

　　彼得站起來對她欠了個身，她也在床上彎腰示意。

　　「妳好。」彼得說。

　　「你好。」珍說。

　　「我叫彼得‧潘。」他告訴她。

　　「是，我知道。」

　　「我回來找我母親，帶她去夢幻島。」彼得解釋說。

「我知道，」珍說：「我一直在等你。」

溫蒂不安地走回房間，看到彼得坐在床柱上高興得大喊大叫，而珍呢，穿著睡衣快樂地在房裡飛來飛去。

「她是我母親。」彼得解釋。珍停下來，站在彼得旁邊，她臉上那副女性們注視彼得的神情，是彼得最喜歡看到的。

「他是多麼需要一個母親啊。」珍說。

「是呀，我知道，」溫蒂有些難過地承認，「沒有人比我更明白了。」

「再見了。」彼得說，他飛到了空中，不懂害羞的珍也跟著他飛起來，這已經是她最習慣的活動方式了。

溫蒂衝到窗前。

「不，不要。」她大喊。

「只是去春季大掃除而已，」珍說：「他要我每年都去幫他做春季大掃除。」

「我要是能跟你們一起去就好了。」溫蒂嘆了口氣。

「但妳不能飛呀。」珍說。

溫蒂終究還是讓他們一起飛走了。這是我們最後一次見到溫蒂，她站在窗前，望著他們向天邊遠遠飛去，直到他們的身影變得和星星一樣小。

當你再見到溫蒂時，會看到她頭髮變白，身體變得更小，因為這些都是很久以前發生的事。珍現在是一個普通的成年人了，她的女兒叫瑪格麗特。每到春季大掃除的時間，除非彼得忘記了，他總是來帶瑪格麗特去夢幻島，她會給他講彼得自己過去的故事，他聽得很認真。等瑪格麗特長大以後，也會有個女兒，再成為彼得的母親，只要孩子們一直是這麼快樂、天真、沒心沒肺的，那麼夢幻島的故事就會一直繼續下去。

彼得潘 Peter Pan

作者 _ J. M. Barrie
插圖 _ Gwynedd Hudson, Alice B. Woodward, Flora White,
　　　Roy Best, Mabel Lucie Attwell, Charles A. Buchel
譯者 _ 羅竹君
校對 _ 代雲芳
編輯 _ 安卡斯
封面設計 _ 林書玉
製程管理 _ 洪巧玲
發行人 _ 周均亮
出版者 _ 寂天文化事業股份有限公司
電話 _ +886-2-2365-9739
傳真 _ +886-2-2365-9835
網址 _ www.icosmos.com.tw
讀者服務 _ onlineservice@icosmos.com.tw
出版日期 _ 2018年6月 初版一刷（250101）
郵撥帳號 _ 1998620-0 寂天文化事業股份有限公司

國家圖書館出版品預行編目資料

彼得潘（原著雙語彩圖本）/ J. M. Barrie 著；
羅竹君 譯. 一初版. 一[臺北市]：寂天文化,
2018.6 面；公分. 中英對照; 譯自：Peter Pan

ISBN　978-986-318-662-5 (25K平裝)

873.59　　　　　　　　　107002107